Eagle Station

Eagle Station

A Novel

Dale Brown

HARPER LARGE PRINT

An Imprint of HarperCollins*Publishers*

EAGLE STATION. Copyright © 2020 by Creative Arts and Sciences LLC. All rights reserved. Printed in the United States of America. No part of this book may be used or reproduced in any manner whatsoever without written permission except in the case of brief quotations embodied in critical articles and reviews. For information, address HarperCollins Publishers, 195 Broadway, New York, NY 10007.

HarperCollins books may be purchased for educational, business, or sales promotional use. For information, please e-mail the Special Markets Department at SPsales@harpercollins.com.

FIRST HARPER LARGE PRINT EDITION

ISBN: 978-0-06-284309-8

Library of Congress Cataloging-in-Publication Data is available upon request.

20 21 22 23 24   LSC   10 9 8 7 6 5 4 3 2 1

"Beautiful, beautiful. Magnificent desolation."

—BUZZ ALDRIN, APOLLO 11 ASTRONAUT,
STEPPING ONTO THE MOON

". . . for countries that can never win a war with the United States by using the method of tanks and planes, attacking the U.S. space system may be an irresistible and most tempting choice."

—WANG HUCHENG, CHINESE MILITARY ANALYST
(QUOTED IN *CSIS SPACE THREAT 2018:
CHINA ASSESSMENT*)

Acknowledgments

Falcon 9, Falcon Heavy, and Dragon are products of SpaceX. The Blue Moon lunar lander is a product of Blue Origin. Bigelow inflatable habitat modules are a product of Bigelow Aerospace. The Delta IV Heavy is a product of United Launch Alliance. The Xeus lunar lander is a concept pioneered by Masten Space Systems and United Launch Alliance.

As always, thanks to Patrick Larkin for his skill and hard work.

Cast of Characters

AMERICANS

JOHN DALTON FARRELL, president of the United States of America

ANDREW TALIAFERRO, secretary of state

DR. LAWRENCE DAWSON, Ph.D., White House science adviser

ELIZABETH HILDEBRAND, CIA director

SCOTT FIRESTONE, admiral, U.S. Navy, chairman of the Joint Chiefs of Staff

COMMANDER AMANDA DVORSKY, U.S. Navy, captain of USS *McCampbell* (DDG-85)

U.S. SPACE FORCE

COLONEL KEITH "MAL" REYNOLDS, commander, Eagle Orbital Station

CAPTAIN ALLISON STEWART, sensor officer, Eagle Orbital Station

MAJOR IKE OZAWA, Thunderbolt plasma rail gun officer, Eagle Orbital Station

CAPTAIN WILLIAM CARRANZA, laser weapons officer, Eagle Orbital Station

COLONEL SCOTT "DUSTY" MILLER, S-29B Shadow armed spaceplane pilot

MAJOR HANNAH "ROCKY" CRAIG, S-29B Shadow armed spaceplane copilot

LIEUTENANT GENERAL DANIEL MULVANEY, commander, U.S. Space Force Missile and Space Launch Warning Center

MAJOR GENERAL PETE HERNANDEZ, U.S. Space Force Missile and Space Launch Warning Center

COLONEL KATHLEEN LOCKE, director, Morrell Operations Center, Space Launch Complex 37B, Cape Canaveral Space Force Station

GENERAL RICHARD KELLEHER, chief of staff, U.S. Space Force

BRIGADIER GENERAL JILL ROSENTHAL, senior watch officer, U.S. Space Force Operations Center, Peterson Air Force Base

JOINT SKY MASTERS AEROSPACE INC.– SCION SPACEPLANE PROGRAM

HUNTER "BOOMER" NOBLE, Ph.D., chief of aerospace engineering, Sky Masters Aerospace, Inc., lead trainer for U.S. Space Force spaceplane pilots

BRAD MCLANAHAN, spaceplane pilot trainer and Cybernetic Lunar Activity Device (CLAD) pilot

MAJOR NADIA ROZEK, spaceplane pilot trainer and CLAD pilot

PETER CHARLES "CONSTABLE" VASEY, former pilot in the Royal Navy's Fleet Air Arm, spaceplane pilot

JASON RICHTER, colonel, U.S. Army (ret.), Ph.D., chief executive officer of Sky Masters Aerospace, creator of the Cybernetic Lunar Activity Device

SCION

KEVIN MARTINDALE, president of Scion, former president of the United States of America

PATRICK MCLANAHAN, technology and intelligence expert, former lieutenant general, U.S. Air Force (ret.)

IAN SCHOFIELD, Scion deep-penetration expert, former captain in Canada's Special Operations Regiment

SAMANTHA KERR, operative, Scion Intelligence

MARCUS CARTWRIGHT, operative, Scion Intelligence

DAVID JONES, operative, Scion Intelligence

ZACH ORLOV, computer operations specialist, Scion Intelligence

LIZ GALLAGHER, lieutenant colonel, U.S. Air Force (ret.), copilot, S-29B Shadow spaceplane

PAUL JACOBS, defensive systems officer, S-29B Shadow spaceplane

RUSSIANS

MARSHAL MIKHAIL IVANOVICH LEONOV, minister of defense, and de facto ruler of the Russian Federation

VIKTOR KAZYANOV, minister of state security

DARIA TITENEVA, foreign minister

MAJOR GENERAL ARKADY KOSHKIN, chief of the Federal Security Service's Q Directorate

COLONEL GENERAL SEMYON TIKHOMIROV, commander of the Aerospace Forces

MAJOR STEPAN GRIGORYEV, MiG-31 pilot

CAPTAIN ALEXEY BALANDIN, MiG-31 weapons system officer

CAPTAIN OLEG PANOV, Mi-8MTV-5 helicopter pilot

MAJOR YURI DRACHEV, Ka-52 Alligator gunship pilot

LIEUTENANT GENERAL NIKOLAI VARSHAVSKY, commander, Central Military District

COLONEL KIRILL LAVRENTYEV, Space Forces cosmonaut, co-commander, Korolev Base

CAPTAIN DIMITRY YANIN, Space Forces cosmonaut, Korolev Base weapons officer

MAJOR GENERAL OLEG PANARIN, senior staff officer for Marshal Leonov

MAJOR ANDREI BEZRUKOV, Space Forces cosmonaut, Korolev Base, expert KLVM pilot

CHINESE

LI JUN, president of the People's Republic of China

GENERAL CHEN HAIFENG, commander of the Strategic Support Force

ADMIRAL CAO, commander, People's Liberation Army Navy

LIEUTENANT GENERAL TAO SHIDID, commander, People's Liberation Army Rocket Force

CAPTAIN YANG ZHI, People's Liberation Army Navy, commander, Yŏngxīng Dǎo island garrison

PENG XIA, foreign minister

COLONEL TIAN FAN, military taikonaut, co-commander, Korolev Base

MAJOR LIU ZHEN, military taikonaut, senior sensor officer, Korolev Base

CAPTAIN SHAN JINAI, military taikonaut, junior watch officer, Korolev Base

Real-World News Excerpts

HELIUM-3 MINING ON THE LUNAR SUR-FACE, European Space Agency, 2007—. . . Unlike Earth, which is protected by its magnetic field, the Moon has been bombarded with large quantities of Helium-3 by the solar wind. It is thought that this isotope could provide safer nuclear energy in a fusion reactor, since it is not radioactive and would not produce dangerous waste products. . . .

CHINA THREATENS TO FURTHER FORTIFY ITS MAN-MADE ISLANDS IN DISPUTED REGION AS TENSIONS WITH US ESCALATE—*The Independent,* 9 January 2019—China may seek to further build up its man-made islands in the South China Sea if it feels the outposts are under threat, one of the country's senior naval officers has said.

The country reserved the right to do as it pleased on the islands it has created in the strategically vital waterway, which it claims virtually in its entirety, according to Senior Captain Zhang Junshe, a naval academy researcher.

"If our on-island personnel and installations come under threat in future, then we necessarily will take measures to boost our defensive capabilities," he said during a briefing with journalists. . . .

UNITED STATES SPACE FORCE—Military. com, 2018—On June 18, 2018, President Donald Trump directed the Pentagon to begin planning for Space Force: a 6th independent military service branch to undertake missions and operations in the rapidly evolving space domain. The U.S. Space Force would be the first new military service in more than 70 years, following the establishment of the U.S. Air Force in 1947.

Vice President Mike Pence and the Department of Defense released more details about the planned space force on August 9, 2018, citing plans to create a separate combatant command, U.S. Space Command, in addition to an independent service overseen by a civilian secretary. . . .

Eagle Station

PROLOGUE

TAURUS-LITTROW VALLEY, THE MOON
DECEMBER 14, 1972

For more than three and a half billion years after lava flows and fire fountains marked its birth, the Taurus-Littrow Valley, surrounded by gray hills and massifs, slumbered in airless silence. But over the course of seventy-five hectic hours, two men from Earth, Apollo 17 astronauts Gene Cernan and Harrison "Jack" Schmitt, broke in on its age-old isolation. On foot and aboard a four-wheeled rover, they explored the mountain valley's slopes, impact craters, and boulder fields, carrying out experiments and collecting more than two hundred and fifty pounds of priceless geological samples.

A remotely programmed television camera mounted

aboard the abandoned rover vehicle showed their four-legged Lunar Module, *Challenger,* starkly outlined against the smooth, rounded peaks rising along the western edge of the Taurus-Littrow. For long minutes, radio channels to Earth and to the Command-and-Service Module, *America,* high overhead in orbit, were full of chatter as the two NASA astronauts ran through their final pre-liftoff checklists. Then, abruptly, it was time to go.

"Ten seconds."

"Abort Stage pushed. Engine arm is Ascent."

"Okay, I'm going to get the Pro . . . 99. Proceeded. 3 . . . 2 . . . 1—"

Bright blue, red, and green sparks cascaded away from the midsection of the spacecraft as four explosive bolts detonated, separating its upper ascent stage from the four-legged lower half. Almost simultaneously, its Bell Aerospace rocket engine lit in a flash of searing orange flame. "Ignition."

Propelled by thirty-five hundred pounds of thrust, *Challenger*'s ascent stage leapt into the black, star-filled sky. For the next twenty-six seconds, the camera followed the small spacecraft as it climbed rapidly toward its planned orbital rendezvous and docking with *America* and its pilot, Ron Evans.

And with that, an era came to an end.

In the course of forty months, six separate Apollo missions had successfully landed a total of twelve American astronauts on the desolate surface of the moon. All twelve men returned safely home to Earth. A scattering of footprints, rover tracks, emplaced scientific instruments, and jettisoned gear remained— offering silent testimony to a time when humans had, however briefly, lived and worked on another world.

For more than half a century, there would be no manned presence on the lunar surface.

But that was about to change . . .

ONE

USS *MCCAMPBELL* (DDG-85), SOUTH OF WOODY ISLAND (YŎNGXĪNG DĂO), AMONG THE PARACEL ISLANDS IN THE SOUTH CHINA SEA
  SPRING 2022

Sunlight glittered on the azure waters ahead of USS *McCampbell*'s wide, flaring bow. Except for a patch of low-lying clouds on the distant northern horizon, the sky was clear in all directions. About two thousand yards to the southwest, a flash of white and gray showed where a small, twin-boomed, propeller-driven UAV, a drone, slowly orbited at low altitude—silently tracking the American destroyer as it drew closer to the heart of the Chinese-occupied island group.

"We're coming up to Point Bravo, Captain," the quartermaster of the watch announced. The young

Navy petty officer kept his eyes resolutely fixed on the glowing integrated navigation display at his station. With the ship's captain on the bridge acting as officer of the deck, this was no time to slack off. "Steady on course three-four-five. Speed twelve knots."

"Very well," Commander Amanda Dvorsky said calmly, keeping a tight rein on her own expression. Point Bravo was a purely notional spot in the sea. But it marked a moment of decision for the two ships under her command today—her own *McCampbell* and another *Arleigh Burke*–class destroyer, USS *Mustin,* trailing along a thousand yards behind. Turning back to the west or southwest would keep them out of waters illegally claimed by the People's Republic of China, the PRC. Turning north would take a well-deserved poke at Beijing's puffed-up territorial pretensions. Doing so, however, was sure to set off a diplomatic firestorm . . . or worse, if the communist nation's notoriously touchy military overreacted.

Inwardly, she shrugged. Her orders to conduct a FONOP, a Freedom of Navigation Operation, were clear. She turned to her conning officer, Lieutenant Philip Scanlan. "All right. Let's go trail our coat, Phil. Bring her to course zero-zero-zero."

He swallowed once and nodded. "Aye, Captain." He raised his voice slightly. "Helm, come right, steer course zero-zero-zero." Aboard a U.S. Navy ship, only steering orders issued by its conning officer could be obeyed.

The helmsman, a wiry sailor barely old enough to be out of high school, reacted instantly, spinning *McCampbell*'s small steering wheel with practiced ease. "Come right to course zero-zero-zero, aye, sir," he repeated loudly. "My rudder is left three degrees, coming to course zero-zero-zero."

Dvorsky felt the deck under her feet heel only slightly as her destroyer swung north. The wide-beamed *Arleigh Burke*s were incredibly stable ships, especially when moving so slowly. One corner of her mouth twitched upward in a fleeting smile. *McCampbell* ordinarily cruised at twenty knots. Steaming straight through the middle of the Chinese-claimed Paracel Islands at just twelve knots was the naval equivalent of moseying onto a rival street gang's turf with your hands buried deep in your pockets and a smart-ass grin on your face.

Part of her enjoyed imagining the heartburn and indignation this exercise was going to cause her Chinese counterparts and their superiors. But what she didn't like was going into this situation without better intelligence. Reports claimed that the PRC had significantly beefed up its military forces in this region recently, especially on Woody Island, or Yǒngxīng Dǎo as the Chinese called it, the largest of the Paracels. Unfortunately, those same reports contained almost no detail on the new Chinese sensors, combat aircraft, and missiles her ships might face. Equally unfortunately, those fragmentary estimates were the best the U.S. intelligence community could currently provide.

Up to a few months ago, information gathered by America's network of radar, spectral imaging, and signals intelligence (SIGINT) reconnaissance satellites could have painted a clear picture of the PRC's current force structure in the Paracel Islands. Now those satellites were gone—systematically destroyed by an armed space station, Mars One, that the Russians had rapidly and secretly deployed into orbit. Although a daring and desperate spaceborne commando attack had succeeded in capturing Mars One, it had come far too late to save any of the U.S., allied, and commercial surveillance satellites in low Earth orbit.

Dvorsky knew replacements were being lofted into space, but that was a slow and extremely expensive process. Spy satellites were essentially handcrafted, painstakingly assembled by specialists with intricate precision. So it would be years before America and her allies regained full global situational awareness. Until then, they were forced to rely almost entirely on whatever imagery could be collected by astronaut crews aboard the captured Russian space platform, now designated Eagle Station. The trouble was Eagle's orbital track allowed only occasional observation of limited swaths of the world as it swung overhead . . . and its movements were predictable. Hostile powers like Russia and China could easily conceal or camouflage anything they wanted to keep secret before the space station came into view.

Which left old-fashioned reconnaissance by aircraft and ships as the fastest and most efficient means of intelligence-gathering left to the United States. Hence her orders to carry out a "freedom of navigation" operation right past this heavily fortified Chinese island base. Of course, pushing in up-close-and-personal like this could be dangerous, especially against adversaries with itchy trigger fingers. Back during the Cold War, before the advent of satellites, nearly forty U.S. aircraft on intelligence-gathering missions were shot down by Russian and Chinese fighters and antiaircraft weapons. And no one in the U.S. Navy could forget the fate of the USS *Liberty*, accidentally bombed and strafed by Israeli jets during 1967's Six-Day War, or the USS *Pueblo*, attacked and captured by North Korea in 1968.

Well, Dvorsky thought, she sure as hell had no intention of being caught off guard by any level of Chinese reaction to this unannounced intrusion into what they considered their own territory. She turned to the boatswain's mate standing next to the controls for the ship's 1MC public address system. "Sound general quarters."

Shrill warning horns sounded throughout *McCampbell*. Her crew, briefed thoroughly during the run-up to this operation, rapidly and efficiently donned their protective gear and then headed for their battle stations.

On the bridge, Commander Dvorsky finished putting on her own anti-flash hood and gloves. With a nod of thanks, she took the Kevlar helmet a young sailor offered. "Okay, everyone stay sharp," she said firmly. "Now let's go see what our pals from the PRC are up to out here."

PEOPLE'S LIBERATION ARMY NAVY GARRISON COMMAND POST, YŎNGXĪNG DǍO (ETERNAL PROSPERITY ISLAND)
THAT SAME TIME

Navy Captain Yang Zhi studied the televised pictures of the two American warships as they turned north toward the island under his command. The images came from a small *Yinying* or Silver Eagle drone flying less than two kilometers from the lead ship, USS *McCamp-*

bell. It had been shadowing the enemy vessels for more than an hour, ever since the Americans steamed past a floating surveillance platform anchored at Bombay Reef, on the outer edge of the Paracel Islands Defense Perimeter.

His jaw tightened. This sudden northward turn plainly signaled the U.S. Navy's intention to violate China's territorial waters. These so-called freedom of navigation operations were a constant irritant—proof that the arrogant Americans did not see the People's Republic as an equal. In the past, the PLA Navy's own warships would have harassed them, crossing their bows at high speed and maneuvering close alongside to force the intruders to alter course . . . or risk collision. But for some unfathomable reason, his superiors in the South Sea Fleet had recently recalled the pair of Type 052 *Luyang II*–class guided missile destroyers that normally patrolled these islands. By now those ships were rocking uselessly at anchor at Zhanjiang Naval Base, more than five hundred and fifty kilometers to the north. And before the *Luyang*s could return, the Americans would be long gone.

Yang tapped a control on his console, zooming in on the aft section of the leading enemy destroyer. A large, unmarked shipping container was tied down on her helicopter pad. Thick bundles of what looked like power and fiber-optic cables ran across the deck between the container and the ship's hangar. That was strange. This improvised installation made flight operations by *McCampbell*'s embarked SH-60 Sea Hawk helicopters impossible. He turned to his chief of staff. "Your evaluation?"

The other man leaned in closer. "I suspect that container is crammed full of intelligence-gathering equipment, Comrade Captain. New devices to spy on us. And the Americans have adopted a crude but effective means of concealing this equipment from our view."

Yang nodded. That was his own guess as well. Besides humiliating China by steaming unmolested through its territory, the enemy also intended to collect vital information on Yǒngxīng Dǎo's defenses. He frowned. They were probably hoping to taunt him into turning on his surface-to-surface missile tracking and fire control radars or sortieing the Shenyang J-15 fighter-bombers concealed in hardened shelters adjacent to the island's 2,700-meter-long runway.

If so, that was a game he would not play. At least not without direct orders from those higher up in his chain of command. "Has there been any response from Vice Admiral Zheng?"

"Not yet, sir," his chief of staff said. He shrugged. "Our data is being relayed in real time to Zhanjiang, though, so the fleet commander must be aware of this situation."

Aware and quite probably sitting on his immaculately manicured hands, too afraid to make any decision that Beijing might disavow later, Yang thought bitterly. Like too many in the PLA Navy's upper reaches, Vice Admiral Zheng was more a political animal than a naval strategist or tactician. Having foolishly stripped away the patrolling Chinese warships that were his subordinate's best hope of dealing with this latest American provocation, Zheng probably saw no benefit in involving himself directly now.

To Yang's surprise, the command post's secure phone buzzed sharply.

His chief of staff picked it up. "Yǒngxīng Dǎo Command Post, Commander Liu speaking." He stiffened to attention. "Yes, Admiral! At once." Eyes wide, he turned to Yang and held out the receiver. "It's Beijing. Admiral Cao himself is on the line."

Yang whistled softly. Admiral Cao Jiang was the commander of the whole PLA Navy. What the devil was going on here? Why was naval headquarters in the capital bypassing not only the South Sea Fleet, but also the whole Southern Theater Command? He grabbed the phone. "Captain Commandant Yang Zhi here."

"Listen carefully, Captain," Cao said in short, clipped

tones. "The orders I am about to give you come from the highest possible authority, from the president himself. You will immediately contact the senior officer aboard those U.S. Navy ships. Once in communication, you will—"

Yang listened to his instructions in mounting astonishment and exultation. Far from catching his country's leaders off guard, it was clear that this high-handed American incursion into Chinese territory had instead set in motion a carefully prepared and long-planned response.

ABOARD USS *MCCAMPBELL*
MINUTES LATER

"Attention, McCampbell, this is Captain Commandant Yang Zhi of the People's Liberation Army Navy. Your ships have illegally entered territorial waters of the People's Republic of China. Accordingly, you are ordered to withdraw immediately, at your best possible speed. Acknowledge the receipt of my transmission and your intention to comply without delay. Over."

Commander Amanda Dvorsky listened coolly to the strident voice coming over the bridge loudspeakers. The Chinese officer's English was excellent. Too bad his language skills weren't matched by a grasp of diplomacy or tact. She keyed her mike. "Captain Commandant Yang, this is USS *McCampbell*. Your transmission has been received. However, we will *not*, repeat *not*, comply with your demands. Under international law, your country has no valid claim to these waters. Nor do you have any right to interfere with our freedom of navigation on the high seas. We are proceeding on course as planned. *McCampbell*, out."

Dvorsky ignored the nods and pleased looks from the rest of her bridge crew. Yang's demand and her refusal were only the opening moves in this confrontation—like the ritual advance of pawns in a chess game . . . or the first tentative attack and parry in a fencing match. Now they would see what else, if anything, the Chinese had up their sleeves.

The radio crackled again. *"Yang to McCampbell. This is your final warning. Your ships are now inside a special defense test zone. You are in imminent danger. Unless you obey my previous directive without further delay, the People's Liberation Army Navy cannot guarantee the safety of your vessels. Yang, out."*

"Well . . . that's interesting," Dvorsky muttered, more to herself than to any of her officers or crew. It looked as if all those highly classified briefings she'd received before *McCampbell* departed her home port in Japan were about to come into play. She swung back toward the boatswain's mate at the 1MC system. "Patch me through to our passengers on the helicopter pad. I think they're about to earn their keep."

SCION SPECIAL ACTION UNIT
THAT SAME TIME

Blue-tinged overhead lights glowed softly inside the converted shipping container tied down on the destroyer's aft section. Like the subdued lighting used in warship combat information centers, this made it easier for its occupants to read the array of computer-driven multifunction displays and other electronic hardware crammed into virtually every square foot of space.

"Your analysis matches ours, Captain," Brad McLanahan said into his headset mike. "We'll stand by."

The tall, broad-shouldered young man tapped an icon on one of his large displays, temporarily muting his connection to *McCampbell*'s bridge. He swiveled slightly in his seat so that he could see his two companions. "Standing by is one thing," he said with a quick, edgy grin. "But I sure wish I didn't feel so much like a sitting duck in this crate."

"Too bloody right," Peter Charles "Constable" Vasey murmured from his station. Like the others, the Englishman was an experienced aviator, ex–Fleet Air Arm in his case. Working for Scion, a private military and defense intelligence company, had accustomed them all to flying high-tech aircraft and single-stage-to-orbit spaceplanes that could get into, and just as important, *out* of trouble at supersonic and hypersonic speeds. Compared to that, heading into possible action aboard even this sleek, thirty-knot-plus destroyer felt like they were strapped into a lumbering bus.

Perched between the two bigger men, dark-haired Nadia Rozek only shrugged. In one action after another against the Russians with Scion's Iron Wolf Squadron, the former Polish Special Forces officer had proved herself tough-minded, focused, and fearless. "This is why they pay us so well, correct?"

Brad raised an eyebrow. "We're getting paid?"

"Well, I *am*, at least," she said, thumping him gently in the ribs. The diamond engagement ring on her left hand glittered briefly in the dim blue light. "Did you forget to sign your contract again?"

Vasey laughed. "Come now, you two. You can't fight in here. This is a war room, remember? Save that for later, when you're married and it's all aboveboard and legal."

Abruptly, the sophisticated electronic detection system mounted in their container broke in. *"Warning, warning. Multiple I-band and S-band surface and air search and tracking radars detected. Bearing zero-zero-two and one-seven-five degrees. Sources evaluated as land-based Type 366 naval-grade radars, JY-9 mobile radars, and unknown-type associated with Bombay Reef Ocean-E anchored surveillance platform. Signal strength indicates positive identification and probable target lock-on."*

"Well, that ups the ante," Brad said quietly. He swung back to his displays and unmuted his connection to *McCampbell*'s bridge. "Special Action Unit, here, Captain. Our Chinese friends are lighting up everything they've got."

"So I hear from my CIC team," Commander Dvorsky replied curtly. "Recommendations?"

"That we carry on as planned. I'm contacting RANGE BOSS now."

"Very well," the ship's captain said. "Keep me in the loop."

"Yes, ma'am." Brad punched another icon, this one activating a secure satellite video link to a location nearly seventy-five hundred nautical miles and twelve hours' time difference away. A window opened immediately, showing a man with a square, firm jaw and a heavily lined face. Automatically, he straightened up in his seat. "Sir."

"Y'all ready to proceed, Major McLanahan?" the

other man asked quietly. "Because from the data we're getting on this end, I'd say this thing is just about ready to kick off."

"Yes, sir," Brad confirmed. "We're ready."

"Well, all right, then," John Dalton Farrell, president of the United States, told him. "You have the green light. I figure it's time to send the powers that be in Beijing the kind of message those sons of bitches will understand."

TWO

COMMAND CENTER, CENTRAL MILITARY COMMISSION OF THE PEOPLE'S REPUBLIC OF CHINA, AUGUST 1ST BUILDING, BEIJING THAT SAME TIME

A brisk northerly wind had temporarily freed Beijing from its near-perpetual blanket of thick, choking smog, and the August 1st Building's tall white walls and columns gleamed in the spring sunshine. The whole enormous edifice, with its faintly pagoda-style roofs, loomed over its neighbors in the capital city's western reaches as a reminder of the state's power and authority. Named for the Nanchang uprising of August 1, 1927—a bloody clash between Communist and Nationalist forces later celebrated as the founding of the People's Liberation Army—it was the headquarters of the Chinese Communist Party's Central Military Commission.

In a command center buried deep below the surface, the commission's seven permanent members and an array of other senior PLA officers had gathered to control the events unfolding thousands of kilometers away in the South China Sea. In both law and current practice, the Central Military Commission exercised complete authority over China's armed forces. Its chairman was always the Party's general secretary, the man who also served as president of the People's Republic. And now, more than ever, the ruling communist elite was determined to keep the levers of military power firmly in its own hands.

Several years before, the machinations of an ambitious chief of the general staff, Colonel General Zu Kai, had threatened the Party's absolute authority over the nation. Once his coup was quietly quashed, China's shaken civilian autocrats had tightened their control over the armed forces. Purges disguised as anti-corruption campaigns had systematically eliminated a whole generation of senior officers tainted by what was labeled "inappropriate interest in politics."

The younger generals and admirals who survived were only too aware that their careers, and even their very lives, now rested entirely in the hands of China's new leader—President Li Jun. He was younger, better educated, and far more ruthless than his aging and ill predecessor, Zhou Qiang. Zhou's hold on the Party had weakened steadily in the wake of the attempted military coup and his abject kowtowing to Russia's now-dead leader, Gennadiy Gryzlov, during yet another confrontation with the United States. Last year's orbital battles between Russia's Mars One space station and America's revolutionary spaceplanes had struck the final blow. Confronted by the shattering realization that *both* Russia and America had leapfrogged China in critical areas of military space technology, a cadre of Party leaders organized by Li had shunted Zhou aside—sending him into retirement in permanent, guarded seclusion.

A skilled political infighter with a thorough grounding in the technologies of the future, Li Jun kept himself fit and trim. He moved with the athletic grace of a man in peak physical condition and perfect health, ostentatiously refraining from the "Western vices" of alcohol and tobacco. Part of this was from personal conviction. More of it was the result of pure, cold-blooded political calculation. Zhou's growing illness had been the catalyst for his ouster, eventually persuading the Party's top echelons that the old man was too feeble to threaten them. Li Jun had no intention of sending any similar signals of weakness. In the fiercely competitive and sometimes deadly sphere of China's internal politics, it was essential that he remain the apex predator.

With that in mind, Li studied the others seated around the long rectangular table. Most of them were relatively new to their posts, handpicked by him for their loyalty, competence, and eagerness to pursue innovative weapons, strategies, and tactics. One by one they met his gaze and nodded. If any of them had doubts about what he planned, those doubts were well hidden.

Satisfied, Li turned to Admiral Cao. "The Americans have ignored our repeated warnings?"

"Yes, Comrade President," the stocky naval officer said. "Their ships are still continuing on course into our territorial waters."

Li shook his head in mock dismay. "Most unfortunate."

He turned to a middle-aged army officer farther down the table. General Chen Haifeng headed the Strategic Support Force—an organization that combined the PLA's military space, cyberwar, electronic warfare, and psychological warfare capabilities in one unified command. "Are your satellites in position, General?"

"They are, Comrade President," Chen said calmly. He activated a control on the table in front of him. Immediately, high-definition screens around the room lit up, showing the sunlit surface of the South China Sea as seen from orbit. At the touch of another control, the view zoomed in—focusing tightly on the two U.S. Navy destroyers as they steamed northward. "This is a live feed from one of our Jian Bing 9 optical naval reconnaissance satellites. We are also receiving good data from a synthetic aperture radar satellite in the JB-7 constellation. And three of our JB-8 electronic intelligence satellites have successfully triangulated the radio signals and radar emissions emanating from those enemy warships."

Li nodded in satisfaction. Between the tracking data streaming down from China's space-based sensors and that acquired by ground- and sea-based radars in the Paracel Islands, his forces now knew, to within a meter or so, precisely where those American ships were at any given moment. They were like flies trapped in an invisible electromagnetic web. "What is the current position of the armed American space station?"

"Eagle Station is currently crossing over South America on its way toward Europe," Chen answered. "For the next fifty minutes, it will be beyond our visual and radar horizon—unable to intervene with its plasma rail gun."

"What excellent timing . . . for us," Li commented dryly.

There were answering smiles from almost everyone else in the room. Only the high-ranking foreigner the president had specially invited to witness today's "weapons test" looked unamused. In fact, the man's broad Slavic face appeared frozen, almost as though it were carved out of ice. Hardly surprising, Li thought.

Marshal Mikhail Ivanovich Leonov had been the mastermind behind the creation of the Mars One space station, its powerful satellite- and spacecraft-killing Thunder plasma weapon, and the breakthrough small fusion generator that powered both of them. Their capture by the Americans had been a disaster for Russia— a disaster magnified when a missile fired from Mars One, either accidentally or deliberately, obliterated the center of the Kremlin . . . killing Russia's charismatic, though increasingly unhinged, leader, Gennadiy Gryzlov. Although Leonov himself had emerged unscathed from the political chaos that followed, the reminder that his prized weapons were in enemy hands could not be pleasant.

Li dismissed the new Russian defense minister's irritation from his mind. For too long, Moscow had taken China for granted, despite the fact that its economy was four times larger and its population almost ten times bigger. If nothing else, what was about to take place in the South China Sea should prove that Beijing was still a power to be reckoned with—whether as an ally . . . or an enemy.

He turned to the chief of the PLA's Rocket Force. "Are you ready to carry out our planned missile readiness exercise and flight test?"

Lieutenant General Tao Shidi nodded. For the first time in decades, some of the advanced weapons he had spent his career developing were about to see action in earnest. "Yes, Comrade President," he confirmed. His raspy voice betrayed the faintest hint of excitement. "My launch crews are prepared. They have received the updated targeting data supplied by General Chen's satellites."

"Very well," Li said flatly. "You have my authorization to fire."

THREE

Brad McLanahan stiffened as his central display lit up with a series of red-boxed alerts and then a digital map of China and the South China Sea overlaid with projected missile tracks. "Well, shit. We were right," he muttered. He turned his head toward Nadia and Vasey. "We've got a flash launch warning from Space Command at Cheyenne Mountain."

"Through SBIRS?" Nadia asked.

He nodded. SBIRS, the Space-Based Infrared System, was a network of five missile launch and tracking satellites positioned more than twenty-two thousand miles above the earth in geosynchronous orbit. From the Mars One space station in low Earth orbit, Russia's plasma rail gun hadn't had the range to hit them, so they were some of the few surviving U.S. military spy satellites. That was fortunate since the SBIRS network was a key component in the U.S. early warning system—with sensors able to detect significant heat signatures like rocket launches, large explosions, major wildfires, and even plane crashes anywhere around the globe.

Without waiting any longer, Brad opened his connection to the destroyer's bridge. "Captain, this is McLanahan. Space Command confirms four separate PRC launches. Missiles are evaluated as DF-26s and they're heading our way. Estimated time to impact is five minutes, thirty seconds."

"Very well," Dvorsky said. Her voice sounded tight. China's intermediate-range DF-26 ballistic missiles were ship killers, capable of carrying nuclear or conventional warheads with enormous striking power. Intelligence reports she'd read claimed they couldn't score hits against warships smaller than aircraft carriers. But those claims were a lot less comforting with real missiles racing toward her two destroyers at fifteen thousand miles per hour. "Should we take evasive action?"

"No, ma'am," Brad replied. "Recommend you hold

this course and speed. We've got this." He muted the connection again and crossed his fingers below his console. "At least I hope so."

Nadia smiled at him. "Have a little faith. Everything is proceeding as we have foreseen." She pushed a com icon on her own central display. "Shadow Two-Nine Bravo, this is Bait Eight-Five. Four DF-26 IRBMs inbound to this location. You are up and at bat."

SHADOW TWO-NINE BRAVO, OVER THE SOUTH CHINA SEA THAT SAME TIME

Two hundred nautical miles southeast of the Paracel Islands, a large, black blended-wing aircraft rolled into a slow turn toward the northwest. To a layman's eye, it looked a lot like a bigger version of the SR-71 Blackbird, only with four huge engines mounted below its highly swept delta wing instead of two, and a fifth engine atop its aft fuselage. In order to avoid detection by China's air search radars, the Scion-operated S-29B Shadow spaceplane had been flying a fuel-conserving racetrack pattern at low altitude, a little more than five hundred feet above the sea.

". . . You are up and at bat."

"Copy that, Bait Eight-Five. We're heading out

now," Hunter "Boomer" Noble promised. He glanced quickly across the cockpit at his copilot. "Good grief. Now Brad's got Nadia—Nadia 'I can break you in half with my little finger' Rozek!—using baseball jargon?"

Liz Gallagher, a former U.S. Air Force lieutenant colonel and B-2 bomber pilot, smiled back at him. "Fair's fair, Boomer. McLanahan's picked up a bunch of Polish swearwords from her, right?"

"Well, yeah," Boomer allowed absently, refocusing his attention on his head-up display. As the steering cue provided by their navigation system slid right and then stabilized, his gloved left hand tweaked a sidestick controller a scooch, bringing the big spaceplane out of its slow right bank. His right hand settled on a bank of engine throttles set in the center console between the S-29B's two forward seats. "Are we configured for supersonic flight?"

"All checklists are complete," Gallagher said, watching her displays closely. The spaceplane's advanced computers had just finished running through their automated programs. A slew of graphic indicators flashed green and stayed lit. "All engines and other systems are go."

"Roger that," Boomer said. He keyed the intercom to the aft cabin, where the S-29's three other crewmen—a data-link specialist, offensive systems officer, and defensive systems officer—sat at their stations. "Buckle up, boys and girls. And stand by on all weapons and sensors. This mission just went hot."

As terse acknowledgments flooded through his headset, he advanced all five throttles. Instantly, the growling roar of the S-29's LPDRS (Laser Pulse Detonation Rocket System) triple-hybrid engines deepened. These remarkable "leopard" engines could transform from air-breathing supersonic turbofans to hypersonic scramjets to reusable rockets, and they were powerful enough to send the Shadow into Earth orbit.

Pressed into his seat by rapid acceleration, Hunter Noble gently pulled back on his stick. Climbing higher, the big black spaceplane streaked northwest at ever-increasing speed.

ABOARD USS *MCCAMPBELL*
A SHORT TIME LATER

"Bridge, Combat, new tracking data received from SBIRS. All four warheads have separated from their boost vehicles. Speed now Mach twenty. Estimated time to impact one hundred twenty seconds."

"Combat, Bridge. Very well." Commander Amanda Dvorsky stood motionless, fighting down the useless urge to rush out onto the bridge wing and stare up into the clear blue sky. Those incoming DF-26 warheads were still close to five hundred nautical miles downrange and well above the atmosphere. And for all the good the surface-to-air missiles nestled in *McCampbell* and *Mustin*'s vertical launch tubes could do right now, those Chinese warheads might as well have been on the moon. Her two destroyers were armed with shorter-ranged and slower SM-2 Standard Missiles, not the upgraded, antiballistic missile-capable SM-3s deployed aboard newer *Arleigh Burke* destroyers and *Ticonderoga*-class cruisers.

Another call from the Combat Information Center blared over the speakers. "Bridge, Combat! Friendly air contact bearing one-six-five degrees at angels three. Speed is Mach three and increasing. Positive IFF. Range sixty-four nautical miles and closing."

Dvorsky nodded. That must be the mystery aircraft the Scion special action unit had said was on its way. Whatever it was, it was moving like a bat out of hell for a manned aircraft . . . but even Mach three, nearly two thousand knots, was still as slow as an arthritic tortoise compared to the speed of those incoming missiles. "Combat, Bridge, understood. Weapons tight, acknowledge."

"Bridge, Combat, weapons tight, aye," the CIC repeated. The apprehension in his voice was real and apparent to everyone on the circuit.

"Get me *Mustin*," she told the boatswain's mate, took the handset he offered, and issued the same order. With that Scion aircraft moving into their engagement zone, she didn't want to risk a "blue-on-blue" friendly fire incident.

"*McCampbell*, this is *Mustin*, weapons tight, aye," she heard Mike Hayward, her fellow destroyer captain, confirm.

One side of Dvorsky's mouth twitched upward for just a fraction of a second. She could almost swear that she had heard Hayward's teeth grinding together over the VHF circuit. After their top secret briefing for this mission, *Mustin*'s commanding officer hadn't bothered hiding his deep-seated reluctance to entrust the safety of his ship to "a bunch of fucking private-enterprise spooks and their crackerjack high-tech gizmos."

To be honest, it was a feeling she shared—only partially alleviated by the willingness of those same Scion operatives to put their own lives on the line. Mentally, she crossed her fingers. Right now, the lives of everyone aboard her two destroyers, more than 760 officers and enlisted sailors, depended entirely on a handful of civilians, some of whom weren't even American citizens. That was not a situation guaranteed to make any serving U.S. military officer comfortable.

"Bridge, Combat, we've got those inbound warheads on our own radar!" she heard her operations officer report urgently from the CIC. "Bearing three-five-four degrees. Altitude fifty-nine miles. Range is three-four-zero nautical miles. Inbounds are slowing a bit as they reenter the atmosphere. Time to impact now one hundred ten seconds." There was a moment of appalled silence. And then, "Ma'am, those warheads are inside the upper atmosphere and maneuvering at hypersonic speeds! They're zeroing in on our track."

Dvorsky felt her pulse kick into even higher gear as adrenaline flooded her system. She swallowed hard against the sudden taste of bile. All along, this was what she had feared most. Images of DF-26 IRBMs had shown four finlike control surfaces around their nose sections. Now it was clear those weren't just for show. Coupled with inertial guidance systems, their own onboard radars, and data links to China's reconnaissance satellites, the four enemy warheads headed her way were far more accurate than earlier U.S. intelligence analysis had suggested. Instead of a CEP, circular error probable, measured in hundreds of feet—making a miss against a smaller moving target like a destroyer far more likely than a hit—the DF-26s were true precision weapons.

Which meant that she and everyone else aboard the USS *McCampbell* and USS *Mustin* were probably well and truly screwed . . . unless the Scion team's equipment worked as advertised. Those warheads were coming in much too fast for her SM-2 missiles to successfully engage. Nor was last-second, evasive maneuvering likely to save her ships. With the kinetic energy imparted by such high speeds and a blast effect of up to four thousand pounds of high explosive, four times the amount carried by a Tomahawk cruise missile, even a near-miss could easily rip one of her destroyers in half.

SCION SPECIAL ACTION UNIT
THAT SAME TIME

"Warning. Warning. Time to impact is forty seconds," the threat analysis computer reported without emotion.

Brad McLanahan forced himself to ignore its persistent alerts. Right now, his task was to make sure his sensors captured every possible piece of data on those incoming DF-26 warheads for later analysis by Scion and Sky Masters technical experts. Since this was the first time China's most advanced ship-killing ballistic missiles had been fired in earnest, his team was being handed a golden opportunity to ferret out their real operational characteristics under combat conditions.

Yeah, it's all good right up to the point we screw up, his subconscious nagged. "Not going to let that happen," he muttered to himself.

"Thirty seconds. Two warheads targeted on Mc-Campbell. Two aimed at Mustin," the computer said. *"Closing speed now Mach ten. Range fifty-five nautical miles. Altitude one hundred thousand feet."*

Four windows blinked open on his right-hand multifunction display. The long-range automated cameras they'd mounted at various points on the destroyer's superstructure had zoomed in on the enemy warheads as they slashed through the sky. At this distance and altitude, they were only visible as wavering orange blobs superheated by friction as they ripped deeper into the atmosphere. Streamers of ionized gas curled behind them.

Brad whistled under his breath. "Jesus, those things must be pulling twenty-plus G's when they maneuver."

"Excellent engineering," Nadia agreed coolly from beside him. From her tone, she could have been commenting on the weather. But then he felt her warm hand slide into his. "I am crossing my fingers now, too, Brad."

"Trzymam kciuki," he echoed, using the Polish

equivalent of the English idiom for good luck. Smooth move, McLanahan, he told himself. Find the woman of your dreams, persuade her to marry you, and then haul her into deadly danger. Even knowing that she would never have stood for being left out of this operation didn't make that seem any smarter.

Their threat computer broke in again. *"Ten seconds to impact. Range eighteen nautical miles."*

Okay, Boomer, *now* would be a *really* good time to show up, Brad thought, feeling his stomach muscles tighten. This was suddenly a binary equation. Either their plan worked perfectly . . . or they were dead.

SHADOW TWO-NINE BRAVO
THAT SAME TIME

Through the spaceplane's forward cockpit canopy, Hunter Noble saw the two U.S. Navy destroyers, haze gray against the brilliant blue sea, transform from distant, indistinct blurred shapes to close-up, razor-sharp silhouettes bristling with weapons and antennas. And then they were gone, vanishing far astern as the S-29B flashed overhead at more than three thousand miles per hour.

High above them, he spotted four glowing specks of light ripping south across the sky with incredible speed.

"Emitters locked on!" Paul Jacobs, the Shadow's defensive systems officer, shouted over the intercom. "Firing!"

Weirdly, there was no sound over the roar of their engines. No added vibration. No evidence aboard the spaceplane that anything had just happened.

But instantly all four DF-26 warheads veered off course, corkscrewing wildly across the sky in widening spirals until they slammed headlong into the sea miles away from the American warships. Huge geysers of churning foam and superheated steam erupted from the center of each impact point, rising hundreds of feet into the air before plunging harmlessly back down into the roiled waters.

"Nailed 'em!" Boomer heard Jacobs crow.

The Chinese weapons had just been zapped by the S-29B's four retractable microwave emitter pods—two set near its wing tips, one atop the forward fuselage, and one mounted under the aft fuselage. Operating autonomously, in an engagement that lasted only milliseconds, the Shadow's defensive systems had sent directed bursts of high-energy microwaves sleeting through the DF-26 warheads, frying their electronics and flight controls, and sending them tumbling out of control.

"Good kills, Paul!" Boomer confirmed. Smiling

now, he keyed his mike. "Bait Eight-Five, this is Shadow Two-Nine Bravo. Splash four. Repeat, splash four."

"Copy that, Shadow," Nadia Rozek replied. Her voice sounded only slightly strained. *"Well done."*

Boomer's smile widened. "All part of the service package, Eight-Five. Need anything else today?"

"Negative, Shadow," she said. *"We will take it from here."*

"Roger, Eight-Five," Boomer acknowledged. "See you back home in a few days." He tugged his stick slightly to the right, rolling the big spaceplane into a shallow, curving turn around to the east. Then, climbing steeply, the S-29B streaked away—heading for the upper reaches of the stratosphere, where its engines could transition to scramjet mode and kick it to full hypersonic speed.

FOUR

PLA NAVY COMMAND POST, YǑNGXĪNG DǍO (ETERNAL PROSPERITY ISLAND)
THAT SAME TIME

Navy Captain Commandant Yang Zhi glared at the pictures transmitted by his Silver Eagle drone. The two American warships steamed on unscathed, still heading north as though nothing had happened. The waves emanating from each DF-26 warhead's distant impact point rippled past those ships without doing more than rocking them a few degrees from side to side.

His secure phone buzzed. "Yang here." He straightened up to his full height as he listened to the staccato orders barked out from Beijing. When the furious voice fell silent, he nodded rapidly. "Yes, Comrade Admiral. It will be done!"

Yang hung up and turned to his chief of staff. "That was Admiral Cao. This American interference with our missile test was a hostile act. We are authorized to engage and sink those destroyers without further warning." He eyed the other man. "Your recommendation?"

Liu's brow furrowed in thought, but only for a moment. "I recommend that we attack using our YJ-62 anti-ship cruise missiles, Comrade Captain," he said confidently. "The Americans are only twenty kilometers offshore. That is practically point-blank range for our weapons. By the time the enemy detects our missiles in flight, their close-in defenses, jammers, and decoys will have little or no time to react."

Yang nodded. Liu's thoughts matched his own. His island garrison had two full batteries of YJ-62 missiles—each equipped with four launch vehicles carrying three missiles. Attacking each enemy destroyer with a full salvo of twelve sea-skimming missiles should guarantee at least three or four hits, and probably more. And each of those cruise missiles carried a 210-kilogram, semi-armor-piercing warhead. Even a single hit could send an *Arleigh Burke*–class vessel straight to the bottom . . . or leave it a burning cripple that could easily be finished off later.

His teeth flashed in a quick predatory smile. "Let it be so, Commander. Order both coastal defense batteries to open fire at once. We'll hit the Americans before they finish congratulating themselves on avoiding our last attack."

SCION SPECIAL ACTION UNIT,
ABOARD USS *MCCAMPBELL*
THAT SAME TIME

"*Warning. Emissions from the enemy's land-based Type 366 radars indicate transition to fire control mode,*" Brad McLanahan's threat analysis computer announced.

He frowned. "These bastards aren't giving up."

"Would you?" Nadia Rozek asked.

"Probably not," he admitted. "Okay, it's showtime. Cue SPEAR."

Nadia's fingers danced across her touch-screen displays as she brought their ALQ-293 Self-Protection Electronically Agile Reaction system online. Like most of their advanced equipment, including the S-29 Shadow spaceplane, SPEAR was the product of Sky Masters Aerospace—easily the world's most innovative aviation, electronics, and weapons design company. When it was active, SPEAR transmitted precisely tailored signals on the same frequencies used by enemy radars. Altering the timing of the pulses sent back to those radars enabled the system to trick them into believing their targets were somewhere else entirely. And for this mission, Sky Masters technicians had integrated SPEAR with *McCampbell*'s incredibly powerful AN/SPY-1 phased-array radar—massively increasing both its speed and accuracy and the range of frequencies it could cover.

Her eyes widened in delight as she realized the full range of capabilities now at her fingertips. Operating the basic SPEAR system was like being a highly gifted musical soloist as she single-handedly fought for the attention of an audience. But this merger with the destroyer's enormous radar was like conducting an entire symphony orchestra made up of the world's finest musicians—effortlessly wrapping thousands of listeners in an intricate cocoon of sound and rhythm.

Within seconds, Nadia effectively controlled every military-grade Chinese radar on Woody Island. None of their surface search or fire control radars showed an accurate position for the two American ships. And not one of the garrison's air search radars could offer a clear picture of the airspace anywhere within a hundred nautical miles. They were all dazzled by hundreds of false contacts moving along random courses on dozens of different bearings.

She turned toward Brad with an exultant expression.

"SPEAR is active. The enemy radars are completely blind. They cannot provide correct targeting data to any of their missile launchers or antiaircraft batteries."

"Nice work!" Brad felt his own eagerness for battle rising. He'd hated just sitting helpless while those damned Chinese ballistic missiles plunged down out of space toward their slow-moving ship. Now it was their turn to hit back. He looked at Vasey. "All right, it's your turn, Constable. Go ahead and slip the leash on our Ghost Wolves."

The Englishman nodded, with his own fingers already blurring across his interactive displays. "Attack parameters laid in. Flight systems are nominal." He tapped a final icon with deep satisfaction. "Autonomous programs engaged. The Wolves are on the hunt."

GHOST WOLF FORCE,
OVER THE SOUTH CHINA SEA
THAT SAME TIME

Twenty miles south of the two U.S. Navy destroyers, a group of six black flying-wing aircraft orbited in a tight circle barely one hundred feet above the surface of the ocean. Abruptly, one by one, they broke out of the circle and darted north toward Woody Island at more than five hundred knots—accompanied by the shrill howl of wing-buried turbofan engines going to full military power.

All six aircraft were covered in a special radar-absorbent coating that sucked up most of the electromagnetic energy from radar waves and shunted it off as heat. No windows or cockpit canopies broke their smooth lines. On radar, the entire group would have shown up as nothing more than a small flock of seagulls.

These were Sky Masters–designed MQ-77 Ghost Wolf combat drones, unmanned aircraft flown entirely by remote control or under the guidance of their own sophisticated onboard computers. They were a larger and more expensive evolutionary variant of an earlier Sky Masters model—the MQ-55 Coyote—which had proved itself many times over in combat service with the Iron Wolf Squadron against the Russians. Significantly harder to detect, faster, more maneuverable, and with a larger weapons payload than their predecessors, the MQ-77 Ghost Wolves were designed to fly and fight on their own, or in tandem with manned modern jet fighters like the F/A-18 Hornet, F-22 Raptor, and F-35 Lightning II.

Just four minutes after receiving their attack orders from Peter Vasey, the first Ghost Wolf drones screamed in low toward the tiny island. Aboard each batwing-shaped aircraft, bay doors whined open. Dozens of small, tear-shaped bombs rippled out and fell toward the earth along precisely calculated arcs.

One by one these tiny, twenty-five-pound bombs detonated within a few yards of every PLA Navy radar, missile launcher, barracks, headquarters building, and hardened aircraft shelter on the island. But rather than exploding in a fiery cloud of lethal fragments, each device went off in a large and relatively harmless puff of white smoke. Instead of wartime munitions, each Ghost Wolf had just dropped a full load of BDU-33 practice bombs.

Engines howling, the six combat drones banked away and flew back out to sea—vanishing as quickly as they had come.

Watching through their long-range cameras from twelve miles out, Brad grinned appreciatively at the sight of dozens of smoke clouds rising above Woody Island's tree-lined shores. "Man, I bet there are a ton of guys over there who just pissed their pants."

Nadia nodded more seriously. "And, I imagine, there are a great many more red faces, both on the island and elsewhere in the PRC."

To the Chinese military garrison and its masters in Beijing, the message conveyed by those drifting puffs of white smoke was unmistakable: if this had been a real air strike, the island's defenses would have been obliterated by a single, unstoppable attack. And when it mattered most, every one of the advanced weapons and sensors the People's Republic had spent so much time and money developing had proved absolutely useless.

With the Stars and Stripes streaming proudly from their radar masts, USS *McCampbell* and USS *Mustin* paraded slowly past Woody Island.

FIVE

COMMAND CENTER, CENTRAL MILITARY COMMISSION OF THE PEOPLE'S REPUBLIC OF CHINA, BEIJING
THAT SAME TIME

For a long, painful moment, a shocked and dangerous silence pervaded the underground command center. No one had expected the two U.S. Navy destroyers—which were not even the most advanced of their type—to so easily swat away China's "accidental" ballistic missile attack. No one had foreseen the sudden intervention by the enemy's hypersonic-capable spaceplane as it struck like a lightning bolt sizzling down out of a clear, cloudless sky. Nor had anyone anticipated the overwhelming counterstroke launched against the island's defenses by a previously undetected group of stealth attack aircraft.

At every turn, the Americans had defeated them with contemptuous ease.

As the silence lengthened, none of the assembled PLA officers and high-ranking Party officials dared look at their nation's new president. Li Jun's loss of face was staggering, especially since this catastrophe had occurred under the cold gaze of his invited foreign guest, Marshal of the Russian Federation Mikhail Ivanovich Leonov.

At last, Li made a single, curt gesture. "Get out. All of you. *Now.*"

His subordinates obeyed, quickly and quietly filing out of the room. But as Leonov started to push his own chair back from the table, China's president held up a hand. "A moment, if you please, Comrade Marshal."

With a polite nod, the Russian sat back down.

When they were alone, Li sighed and took off his wire-frame glasses. Closing his eyes, he pinched the bridge of his nose hard, and then put his glasses back on. Wearily, he looked at Leonov. "I suppose I should have listened to your earlier warnings about the effectiveness of these new American weapons—their space-planes, manned combat robots, remote-piloted attack drones, and all the rest."

Leonov shrugged. "In your place, I would have done the same, Comrade President. Secondhand reports are never particularly persuasive. Seeing these war machines in action, however, is . . ." He let his voice trail off suggestively.

"Remarkably unnerving," Li agreed sourly.

Leonov only nodded. He knew how important it was not to rub the other man's face in this failure. After all, Russia had suffered its own embarrassing defeats in recent confrontations with the United States and its Polish ally—defeats made even more painful because they had been primarily inflicted by a private military company, Scion, and its Iron Wolf Squadron. Now it was China's turn to suffer humiliation at the hands of these technologically advanced mercenaries.

It was a matter of bitter irony for both men that English was the only language they had in common. Like that of most middle-aged and younger Chinese technocrats, Li Jun's education had focused on America, rather than on the crumbling Soviet Union and its successor state, the Russian Federation. For similar reasons, his Russian counterpart's early training as a fighter pilot and cosmonaut had encouraged him to learn the language of his nation's most dangerous adversary.

"It is not pleasant to see an enemy grow so strong," Li Jun said finally.

"No, it is not." Leonov nodded toward the display screens around the room, which still showed satellite images of the two U.S. warships steaming on unmo-lested across a now-empty sea. "If nothing else, this unfortunate incident demonstrates that America, par-ticularly under its current political leadership, pos-sesses a significant military edge. One that would make it difficult for either your country or mine to prevail in any purely *earthbound* conventional conflict."

"A situation that Russia's own meddling helped cre-ate," Li reminded him tartly.

"True," Leonov admitted. "Former president Gry-zlov was not always the wisest of men."

Now *there* was an understatement, he thought grimly. Nearly two years before, Gennadiy Gryzlov had struck against the United States with his own mercenary force. Using Russia's own war robots, reverse-engineered from captured enemy equipment, these troops had smashed American military bases, aircraft factories, and research facilities. The then-American president, Stacy Anne Barbeau, had dithered in the face of this crisis, unwilling to admit her country might be under attack by a hostile power, rather than by stateless ter-rorists. But then Gryzlov had gone too far. Hoping to spark a political crisis that would consume the United States for years to come, he'd ordered his war robots to assassinate Barbeau's opponent in the upcoming presi-dential election, Texas governor John Dalton Farrell.

They had failed. Gryzlov's mercenaries had been defeated in a bloody battle by a small covert force sent by Poland and Scion's Iron Wolf Squadron. With Russia's guilt laid bare before a furious American public, the ensuing political firestorm had cost Barbeau the election and carried Farrell into the White House.

Since then, the new American president had strengthened the alliances Barbeau's ineptitude and isolationism had weakened. Worse, from Leonov's perspective, he had insisted that the U.S. military embrace the revolutionary new weapons technologies and tactics pioneered by Scion and Sky Masters. Slowly at first, and then faster, America's defense establishment had begun to shake off the torpor and stale thinking of recent years.

Faced with this mess of his own making, Gennadiy Gryzlov had rolled the dice again—ordering Russia's top secret Mars One armed space station rushed into orbit to destroy America's military satellites and seize control of the high ground—outer space itself—before the United States could react. In Leonov's judgment, this action had been woefully premature. He had been proved right when Scion-flown spaceplanes and combat machines successfully stormed and captured Mars One, along with all its highly advanced weapons and fusion power system.

Only Gryzlov's death in the ruins of the Kremlin—shattered by a Russian-made Rapira ground attack missile fired from Mars One as it orbited over Europe—had saved Leonov himself from being arrested and summarily executed as a scapegoat for this latest fiasco. The attack had made Russia's unstable leader a martyr, yet another victim of America's brutal Scion mercenaries.

Leonov hid a thin smile. Only a handful of others in Russia knew that he was the one who'd actually launched the Rapira, using secret fail-safe protocols built into the space station at his insistence. Years of watching Gryzlov use and then brutally discard competent officers he blamed for his own errors had taught Leonov the importance of striking first. On the outside, like most of his countrymen, he mourned the loss of Russia's charismatic president. On the inside, he reveled in his newfound freedom to restore his country's fortunes and military greatness.

This secret visit to the People's Republic of China was a vital step toward achieving those ends. Events had shown that Russia, by itself, could not defeat the United States. So a renewed and strengthened alliance with Beijing was imperative.

Coolly, Leonov looked across the table at the Chinese president. "No matter what may have sparked the Americans' current quest for absolute military supremacy, neither of our two great nations can allow them to succeed."

"Indeed not." Li Jun's fingers drummed lightly on the table. "But if the Americans have an overwhelming advantage in conventional weaponry, what other avenues lie open to us?" His mouth tightened. "A coordinated, preemptive nuclear strike . . . using both our strategic arsenals—"

"Would be unthinkable," Leonov countered bluntly. He gestured toward the display screens, where the waters of the South China Sea glimmered with reflected sunlight. "No matter how much damage we inflicted on America's already-weakened ICBM and bomber forces, its ballistic missile submarines would survive, lurking deep beneath the earth's oceans—ready to strike back with devastating force." He shook his head. "Neither of us would profit from ruling over a handful of savages roaming across a radioactive wasteland."

The other man frowned. "Then what do you suggest?"

"That we combine our technological and military resources—and our most advanced research programs—to open a new battlefield, a new arena of conflict," Leonov said. "One where the Americans will have fewer advantages."

"And where is this new arena of yours?" Li demanded.

"In space."

One of the Chinese president's eyebrows rose. "In space? Are you serious?" he asked skeptically.

Leonov nodded. "Space technology is an area where our two nations are much closer to parity with the United States. And in some areas, I believe we are ahead. The fact that the Americans were forced to capture my country's new plasma weapon and fusion power system merely to match our own achievements proves this."

Li looked thoughtful at that. Russia's breakthroughs in directed-energy weapons and fusion power were undeniably impressive. And the implied promise to share those amazing advances with an ally certainly made the proposal more tempting.

"But even if that was not so, it would be a terrible mistake for us to surrender the exploitation and control of space to the Americans," Leonov continued forcefully. "It would be a blunder which history would not forgive. After all, whoever controls outer space will inevitably dominate the world . . . both economically and militarily."

Slowly, Li nodded. The Russian defense minister's

belief was shared by China's communist theoreticians, military strategists, and scientists. Watching him, Leonov knew he'd made his point. After a few more moments of silence, Li looked up. "I concur, Marshal Leonov. Such an alliance would undoubtedly be in the best interests of the People's Republic."

"Thank you, Comrade President," Leonov said sincerely.

"But for the moment, I consider it essential that the details of any new military and scientific pact between our two countries remain a closely guarded secret."

"Absolutely," Leonov agreed. He smiled coldly. "After all, what the Americans do not know, *will* hurt them."

SIX

MCLANAHAN INDUSTRIAL AIRPORT, BATTLE MOUNTAIN, NEVADA
A WEEK LATER

It was midmorning when the solid black executive jet came in low over the rugged slopes of Antler Peak and down across the Copper Basin. Even this late in the spring, snow still clung to the higher elevations. Twin turbofan engines rumbling, the jet crossed south of the city of Battle Mountain and then made a sharp turn back to the northwest.

Inside the Gulfstream G600's luxurious passenger cabin, the pilot's crisp voice came crystal clear over the speakers. "McLanahan Tower, Scion Six-Zero-Zero, six thousand descending, fifteen miles southeast, full stop."

"Scion Six-Zero-Zero, McLanahan Tower, winds light and variable, runway three-zero, cleared to land," the control tower replied immediately.

Immediately, the jet slid lower. Hydraulics whined and thumped softly under as its underwing landing gear and nosewheel came down and locked in position.

Nadia Rozek glanced across the aisle at Brad McLanahan. The tall, blond-haired young man sat straight up, intently peering out through the Gulfstream's large oval windows at the harsh Nevada landscape. Despite the aircraft's astonishingly comfortable furnishings, he looked on edge.

She understood that. Like a great many skilled pilots, Brad was definitely not happy being flown by someone else. She doubted he'd slept much during their ten-hour flight home from Japan. His attitude wasn't really a lack of trust in other professionals. It was just that he preferred being the master of his own fate whenever possible.

Nadia smiled privately. He was definitely not one of nature's placid passengers, content to drift on life's currents wherever they carried him. Then again, she admitted to herself, neither was she. They were well matched in that respect, despite their differences of nationality and upbringing.

With a very slight jolt, the Scion executive jet touched down. It rolled along the runway, braking smoothly as its turbofans spooled down. Outside the windows, the Sky Masters Aerospace complex slid past in a sprawling maze of huge aircraft hangars, office buildings, machine shops, labs, and warehouses.

Nadia reached across the aisle and touched Brad's arm. "Welcome home," she murmured.

"You, too," he said, smiling now himself. "At least to one of them, anyway." He nodded out the window at the snow-dusted brown heights towering a couple of thousand feet above the high desert plain. "It's not exactly Kraków, though."

"Not exactly, no," she said with a quick, amused snort. "But we will be there soon enough."

Brad nodded seriously. The date they'd picked out for their wedding was now just a few months away. What had once seemed like a far-off, fairy-tale dream took on more substance with every day that passed.

They'd first met almost five years before, at a time of grave crisis for Poland and its people. With the Russian Army massing on the border for a threatened invasion, the Poles had turned for help to Scion and its fledgling Iron Wolf Squadron. Nadia had been assigned as Polish president Piotr Wilk's military liaison to the multinational unit. Later, she'd joined the squadron as a combat officer in her own right, serving at Brad's side on several risky covert missions deep into Russian territory and later even into the United States itself. And what he'd thought might just be a short, fun fling—a "beautiful local girl takes pity on a lonely foreigner" kind of deal— had very quickly blossomed into a much deeper, lasting, and far more passionate romance.

The Scion jet taxied off the runway, swung through a wide turn, and came to a full stop not far from the airport operations center. Ground crewmen bundled up against the unseasonal chill were already rolling a mobile boarding ramp toward the Gulfstream's forward cabin door.

Seeing it coming, Nadia unbuckled her seat belt and stood up—balancing gracefully on the twin tips of her black carbon-fiber running blades. Nearly two years before, she'd been severely wounded in a battle against Russian assassins sent to murder the man who was now America's president. To save her life, trauma surgeons had been forced to amputate both legs below the knee. Months of painful rehabilitation and exhausting physical training had taught her to master these agile, incredibly flexible running blades, along with other, more conventional prosthetic limbs. But in the end, despite all her hard work, it had become clear that she would never be able to stay on active duty in Poland's Special Forces. So, at Brad's urging, she'd transferred to a joint Scion–Sky Masters private space enterprise based here in Nevada. Learning to fly the incredible S-series spaceplanes and work in outer space had been like a dream come true. In zero-G, her missing legs were no handicap at all . . . a fact she had proved beyond a doubt during Scion's desperate assault on Russia's Mars One orbital platform.

Brad offered her his arm as they waited for the aircraft's lone steward to unlatch and open the door. Nadia took it gladly, not because she needed any physical support, but simply because she delighted in his touch and presence. Her first fears that a lingering sense of guilt about the injuries she'd suffered would drive him away had long since disappeared.

The door swung open in a blast of cold air, revealing Hunter "Boomer" Noble already ambling up the ramp to greet them. Wearing a huge, welcoming grin, he shook Brad's hand and gave Nadia a quick hug. "Welcome back to the ass end of nowhere," he declaimed. "Otherwise known as Battle Mountain—home of the sweetest flying machines known to mankind . . . and not much else."

That was a typically Boomer-grade wild exaggeration, Brad thought with amusement. Since Sky Masters Aerospace moved its operations from Las Vegas, both the company and the surrounding area had blossomed—high-tech companies from all over the world moving here had turned the sleepy little mining town into a bustling, modern city.

When he wasn't flying special missions for Scion, the tall, lanky Boomer Noble—so nicknamed because his early engine designs had a bad habit of unexpectedly and spectacularly exploding—was the chief of aerospace engineering for Sky Masters. He also ran the company's advanced aircraft and spaceplane training programs. Not many other people could have managed what were essentially three-plus full-time jobs. But "work hard, play hard" had been Boomer's motto for most of his life.

"Nice to see you, too," Brad said, matching his friend's grin.

"Say, where's Vasey?" Boomer asked, peering inside the jet's empty passenger cabin curiously. "You guys get tired of that hoity-toity British accent of his and dump him out somewhere over the Pacific?"

Brad laughed. "Nope." He donned an innocent look. "And there's no way you can prove anything, even if we did."

"Constable decided to take some long-overdue R&R," Nadia explained patiently. "He said something about visiting relatives in Australia and New Zealand."

"Relatives," Boomer snorted cynically. "I bet. More likely that Brit has a cunning plan involving a couple of curvy female flight attendants and a few cases of champagne."

Smiling, Nadia shook her head in mock dismay. "Oh, Boomer, you really should not assume everyone shares your devious and debauched nature."

"*Moi?* Debauched? Perish the thought," the other man said, dramatically putting his hand over his heart. "I'm a reformed character these days. Drinking, dames, and dice are strictly a faint echo of my long-vanished past."

Brad and Nadia exchanged a quick, meaningful look. They'd heard the gossip about Boomer and his copilot, Liz Gallagher. The two of them were supposed to be seeing a lot of each other outside of working hours. A lot. Maybe the rumors were accurate for once. If so, the petite redhead would certainly be a huge step up from the ditzy casino cocktail waitresses he usually chased. In fact, she was just the kind of levelheaded, highly intelligent woman who might finally be able to successfully corral the hard-driving, hard-living Hunter Noble.

"Speaking of R&R, though," Boomer continued. "What do you guys have planned for yourselves? A couple of weeks in the Caribbean? A jaunt to Paris or

Rome? Tell me all, so I can grit my teeth and bitch and moan about my hard luck being stuck here with a couple of hundred wannabe space cadets to train."

"Well, we might—" Brad started to say.

Shaking her head sadly, Nadia cut him off. "Alas, we are not going anywhere. We have too much work to do."

"We do?"

She nodded firmly. "Yes, we most certainly do, Brad McLanahan. As you should remember." She started ticking items off on her fingertips. "There are guest lists to finalize. Invitations to write out and send. Thank-you notes for engagement presents to compose. Bridesmaid and groomsmen's gifts to select—"

Brad turned pale. "Ack." He looked at Boomer and mouthed, "Help."

"Not me, brother," the other man said with heartfelt sincerity. If anything, his smile grew even wider. "I'm not dumb enough to get between Major Rozek here and anything she's got her mind firmly set on."

"Thank you, Boomer," Nadia said, matching his tone perfectly. "I always knew you were a wise man."

"Gee, thanks."

But now her own smile carried a hint of wicked glee. "No matter what everyone else has always said."

SEVEN

President John Dalton Farrell looked up at the sharp rap on his open door. "Yes?"

A short, pert woman with shoulder-length, silver-blond hair poked her head inside the Oval Office. "Well, J.D., those fellas you've been waitin' on finally drifted in," she said brusquely, with more than a hint of a West Texas twang. "That old hipster fart and the spaceman, I mean. You want to see 'em now?"

Farrell hid a grin. In her own words, Maisie Harrigan had been his "personal go-fer, bottle washer, and all-around ass-kicker" for decades—going back to a time when his entire oil and gas business consisted of one leased drilling rig and a couple of broken-down pickup trucks. Now, as executive assistant to the president, she ran Oval Office operations with an iron fist. It was also no secret that she saw one of her main jobs as making sure her boss and those around him didn't get too big for their britches. "Sure thing, Maisie. Show them in, please."

He worked even harder to keep the smile off his face when she ushered his two visitors in, lectured them not to "waste too much of J.D.'s time, you hear?," and then departed with an audible sniff.

Kevin Martindale looked after her with a hint of awe. "My God, but that woman scares me, Mr. President," he said, shaking his head. "I've got ex–Navy SEAL bodyguards I wouldn't bet a dime on if they went up against her."

"She *is* a force of nature," Farrell agreed.

Martindale's long gray hair, neatly trimmed beard, and fondness for very expensive, open-necked suits *did* make him look a bit like some aging and dissolute playboy, Farrell decided. But that was only if you ignored his shrewd, penetrating gaze . . . and didn't know that he'd occupied this same office as president of the United States.

Since leaving the White House, the other man had thrown his energies into Scion, the private military and intelligence company he'd created. For the past several years, Martindale had recruited, organized, and equipped the ultra high-tech air and ground units and covert operatives who had helped defend Poland and its smaller Eastern European allies against Russian aggression. Now, working mostly behind the scenes, Scion was coaching America's regular armed forces in the advanced equipment and new war-fighting techniques it had so successfully pioneered.

Farrell's other visitor, retired Air Force Lieutenant General Patrick McLanahan, had played his own vital part in Scion's successes—both on and off the battlefield. Unfortunately, the terrible price he had paid for those victories was immediately apparent. Years ago, he'd been critically injured on a mission over the People's Republic of China. He was alive now only thanks to a remarkably advanced piece of medical hardware, the LEAF, or Life Enhancing Assistive Facility. Without its carbon-fiber-and-metal exoskeleton, life-support backpack, and clear, spacesuit-like helmet, he would die within hours—killed by wounds that were far beyond the ability of modern medicine to heal.

"Maybe we'd better move on expeditiously through our business today, Mr. President," Patrick suggested, with a crooked smile visible through his helmet. "Yon dragon lady out there is right about the value of your time . . . and I'd sure hate to piss her off. For one thing, there's no way I can outrun her in this Mechanical Man rig." Servo motors whined softly when he shrugged his shoulders.

Farrell laughed. "It does make you wonder who's running this outfit, doesn't it? Me or Maisie?"

"Well, 'you've gotta dance with those that brung ya,'" Martindale quoted Ronald Reagan with a thin smile of his own.

Farrell nodded. Of course, the classic reminder to stay loyal to your supporters applied just as much to the two men seated before him as it did to Maisie Harrigan. Together with the general's son Brad, Nadia Rozek, and a handful of others, they'd risked their lives to save his miserable hide. Now they were among his most trusted national security and intelligence policy advisers—a fact that he knew irritated many in Washington, D.C.'s status-conscious establishment. The fact that neither man held an official position in his administration made their obvious preeminence even more galling to some in the Pentagon and at the CIA's Langley, Virginia, headquarters.

Which said more about their critics than anything else, he decided. Washington was full of "experts" who'd failed upward, attaining higher and higher government positions despite repeated mistakes and blunders. To people like that, Kevin Martindale and

Patrick McLanahan—and Farrell himself, he knew—
were a threat, because they cared more about results
than prestige.

He waved the two men into chairs and then leaned
back against the corner of his desk. "Okay, shoot.
What's first on the agenda?"

"The Paracel Island freedom-of-navigation exercise,"
Martindale told him.

Farrell snorted. "More like the Paracel Island tur-
key shoot, at least from what I've read."

"Not the most diplomatic way of putting it," Patrick
said with a quick laugh. "But accurate nonetheless. We
pulled in a treasure trove of intel on some of the PRC's
most advanced ballistic missiles—"

"And gave Comrade Li Jun a well-deserved black
eye," Martindale finished, with intense satisfaction.
"With luck, our little show of nonlethal force should
discourage Beijing from further escalating tensions in
the South China Sea for some time to come."

Farrell nodded somberly. "Amen to that." China's
expansionist and aggressive moves among the reefs and
islands that dotted the South China Sea had already
sparked a number of international crises and even open
naval and air clashes with its neighbors and the United
States. Puncturing Beijing's confidence that its armed
forces could take on America's military and win had

been one of the primary objectives of last week's combined Navy and Scion operation.

And the very fact that it *had* been a successful combined operation should achieve another of his objectives—demonstrating the value of using Sky Masters and Scion weapons, aircraft, and electronic warfare systems as a force multiplier for America's regular armed forces. Like most bureaucracies, the Defense Department had a serious case of "not invented here" syndrome. For too many generals and admirals, weapons, equipment, and software that didn't emerge from the Pentagon's labyrinthine procurement processes were automatically suspect. But after they studied the awestruck after-action reports from *McCampbell's* captain and her officers, Farrell was willing to bet that a lot of folks in both the Navy and the Air Force would be desperate to get their hands on ALQ-293 SPEAR systems of their own and the Sky Masters–designed MQ-77 Ghost Wolf unmanned attack aircraft.

The same thing went for the S-29B Shadow . . . but he'd already allocated control over all armed space-planes to the newly formed U.S. Space Force. After last year's battles with the Russians in low Earth orbit, his push to create a sixth branch of the U.S. armed forces had sailed through Congress. Fully uniting the separate space-related programs and commands previously split between the Air Force, Navy, and even the Army was a long-overdue reform.

Right now, standing up the Space Force as a fully functioning outfit was still very much a work in progress. The other services weren't happy about losing big chunks of budgetary authority and seeing many of their best young space-minded officers and enlisted personnel reassigned . . . and they were dragging their feet wherever possible. Fortunately for Farrell, Martindale and Patrick McLanahan were both old hands at circumventing bureaucratic resistance to new ideas. Their advice made it easy for him to distinguish between reasonable objections to his directives and purely parochial, empire-building bullshit.

"We're not quite where we need to be yet," Patrick told him bluntly when Farrell asked how things were going. "At least when it comes to getting the Space Force full control over its own procurement and logistics. That's where the dead-enders in the various services are putting up a real bitch of a fight."

Farrell nodded. Although procurement and supply functions weren't seen as especially glamorous, they always absorbed a huge fraction of the budget in any big organization. They also tended to attract men and women who were very good at operating within clearly defined limits . . . but who were often leery of the whole idea of change. "What about the operations side of the Space Force?"

"That's running considerably more smoothly," Martindale replied. "For example, Eagle Station is now fully crewed by active-duty Space Force personnel. I just got the word from orbit on the way over here. Our Scion team finished its formal handover of all systems about half an hour ago."

"Now that is some seriously good news," Farrell said enthusiastically. They'd needed Scion technicians and mission specialists to run Eagle Station's sensors, weapons, and fusion power generator after its capture from the Russians. But there was no denying that the company's continued control over the space station had been a huge public relations headache. Typically over-the-top Russian propaganda blamed Scion's "homicidal space pirates" for the deaths of Gryzlov and hundreds of others when the center of the Kremlin got blown to smithereens. Nobody who counted bought that line of bull, although it had been judged expedient to disarm the remaining Rapira missiles aboard the station as part of the ensuing cease-fire agreement with Moscow. What mattered more were those in Congress and in the media who hadn't been happy about a for-profit private corporation running a strategic military asset like the armed orbital station. He made a mental note to have his press secretary make an announcement, preferably with a live television feed from Colonel Reynolds, Eagle's new commander.

"The first active-duty spaceplane squadron is working up pretty fast, too," Patrick reported. "We've been running likely candidates through intensive training out at Battle Mountain, using the simulators there. As you'd expect, the washout rate is pretty high, but Hunter Noble and his instructor team have already certified a full crew as flight-ready. In fact, they're taking the new S-29B Sky Masters just delivered into orbit tomorrow for its final test flight and systems checks."

"One rookie crew and one spaceplane fresh off the factory floor doesn't exactly add up to much of a squadron," Martindale commented dryly.

"Maybe not yet," Patrick allowed. "But there are two more Shadows nearing completion. By the time Sky Masters rolls them out, we'll have enough trained pilots and crew specialists to fly and fight them."

Farrell considered that. While the S-29B was only an armed version of the original S-29 spaceplane, intended to carry passengers and cargo into orbit, it was still a remarkably complex and expensive machine. Plus, the design had already proved itself in action, both inside the atmosphere and in orbit. So watching the United States put three fully operational Shadows out on the flight line in less than a year should definitely send a chill up certain spines in Moscow and Beijing—and firmly signal America's resolve to maintain its current edge in space combat capability. He looked at both men. "Basically, cutting to the chase, it sounds like y'all agree that we're in pretty good shape militarily."

Martindale glanced quickly at Patrick and then back at the president. "In general, I guess that's a fair assessment," he said. "The lack of real-time satellite intelligence is still a problem, but that should diminish as we launch new recon birds into Earth orbit. Plus, as we move additional S-29s to operational status, we can use them for directed space reconnaissance against high-value targets."

Farrell eyed him closely. "Seems to me I'm hearing a mighty big unspoken 'yes, but' hanging out there, Kevin."

"True," Martindale said with a rueful smile. "Based on what we know, our current strategic situation seems mostly satisfactory." He hesitated. "It's what we *don't* know that I find worrying."

Farrell frowned. "Anything in particular?"

Patrick leaned forward. "What neither Kevin nor I can forget is how completely the Russians blindsided us last year." Through his clear helmet, his lined face now looked grim. "We never expected Moscow to beat us to the punch with the world's first long-range energy weapon *and* with its first honest-to-God compact nuclear fusion generator."

"Both of which were based on original research they stole from American labs," Farrell reminded him.

"Sure, but what matters is that the Russians took concepts our government stuck in a drawer and forgot about—or never adequately funded—and *they* made them damn well work," the other man said stubbornly. "Plus, those bastards did it without letting us get so much as a whiff of what they were planning until it was almost too late."

Farrell pondered that for a moment and then shrugged his own big shoulders. "Fair enough. On the other hand, that rabid son of a bitch Gryzlov is dead and gone."

"And currently burning in hell, I earnestly trust and hope," Martindale agreed. He frowned. "Unfortunately, Marshal Mikhail Ivanovich Leonov is still very much alive. And much as I regret to say it, I suspect he may be an even more dangerous opponent than the late and utterly unlamented Gennadiy Gryzlov."

Patrick nodded. "Leonov is certainly cagier. Nominally, he's just Russia's defense minister, one of a cabinet full of equals. But considering how powerful the military is in the political system over there, it's a pretty safe bet that he's calling the shots when it counts."

"You think this Leonov character may be planning a new move against us?" Farrell asked bluntly.

"We do," Martindale said. "Russia's a declining geopolitical power at the moment, especially with its economy under serious pressure from our rapidly increasing oil and gas production. Add in the fact that its political stability took a serious hit with Gryzlov's assassination—"

"Assassination?" Farrell interrupted sharply.

Martindale nodded. "Somebody deliberately aimed and fired that missile from orbit," he pointed out. "And it sure as hell wasn't us." He sighed. "Not that we can prove anything now."

"More's the pity," Farrell agreed. He motioned for the other man to go on.

"My point is that the Russians—especially their ruling elites—have every incentive to take risks just now. Unless they can somehow tilt the global balance of forces back into their favor, they're ultimately screwed. And while a few of the current government's ministers might hope they can ride things down to a soft landing as a second-rate power, most of them probably know that's not a safe bet."

"Especially not someone like Leonov," Patrick added. "I've studied his record. The man's certainly brutal and ruthless. But he's also a Russian patriot. He won't settle for watching his country slide peacefully into oblivion."

Farrell frowned. "So what are you suggesting we do? Preemptively strike Moscow . . . just in case?" His tone made clear how little he thought of that option.

Martindale shook his head. "Even setting aside the probability of unwinnable nuclear escalation, that isn't really an option." He smiled thinly. "After all, we *are* the good guys."

"Well, I'd argue for a targeted hit on Leonov himself," Patrick said, not mincing words. "If I saw a way we could pull it off." His exoskeleton whirred quietly again as he sat up straighter. "Killing an enemy commander might not seem very sporting, but it can be extremely effective. It sure worked out pretty well when our P-38 fighters shot down Japan's Admiral Yamamoto during World War Two."

"During a *declared* war," Martindale noted.

Patrick shrugged again. "War's war, declared or not."

Farrell shook his head. "I take your point, General." His face tightened. He'd only narrowly escaped the Russian effort to murder him. Nevertheless, he wasn't going to get sucked into a game of tit-for-tat with human lives on the line. That was the kind of game you lost simply by playing. "But we are not going down that road on my watch. *Comprende?*"

"Completely, Mr. President."

"So, setting aside the thought of going to all-out war or operating my own little version of Murder Inc., what are my choices here?"

"First, we keep our eyes wide open," Martindale said flatly. "My intelligence operatives inside Russia already have instructions to poke into every nook, cranny, and corner they can find."

Farrell nodded his approval. Over the past several years, Scion's espionage operations had proven far more effective than any of those run by the CIA or other official U.S. intelligence agencies, which had been too caught up in political correctness and partisanship to focus on their primary mission. "And second?"

"That we keep pushing hard—both in space itself and by rapidly exploiting the incredible technological breakthroughs we captured aboard Mars One," Patrick said.

"Like that ten-megawatt fusion power generator the Russians built?"

"Yes, sir."

Farrell shook his head. "Y'all are forgetting I'm an old hand in the energy business," he said bluntly. "And

I've read the Department of Energy's report on that reactor. There's no doubt the damned thing's a technological and engineering marvel, but it ain't a game changer . . . not in domestic energy production nor for our defense programs."

Martindale sighed. "Because of the fuel mixture it uses."

"Bingo," Farrell said. "That Russian fusion generator relies on a deuterium-helium-3 mix to operate. To produce those ten megawatts it needs a supply of two and a half kilograms of helium-3. On the face of things, that doesn't sound like much . . . feed in less than six pounds of this helium isotope and hey, presto, you get enough electricity to run ten thousand American homes for five whole years."

"The catch being that helium-3 is an incredibly rare substance, sir," Patrick said wryly.

"*Rare* is one serious piece of understatement, General." Farrell shook his head. "You can't just go mine this stuff anywhere on Earth. It doesn't exist. Most of what we do produce comes from refurbishing deteriorating H-bombs. The Energy Department points out that even at the height of the Cold War, our total national production of helium-3 came to only about eight kilograms per year. And after all our weapons cuts, we're down to under a kilogram."

He held up a hand with a slight smile. "Now before y'all start pushing, I am *not* going to order a huge expansion of the U.S. nuclear weapons arsenal as a means of boosting domestic helium-3 generation."

"I suppose that might send the wrong diplomatic signal to the rest of the world," Martindale agreed with an equally humorless smile.

"So there you go," Farrell went on. "Our existing stockpiles and production can keep Eagle Station's own fusion generator fueled up, but that's about the limit. Breakthrough or not, the technology's basically a dead end."

Patrick shook his head. "You're overlooking other possibilities, Mr. President." He leaned forward in his chair again, wholly intent on making his point. "You're right that there aren't any significant natural deposits of helium-3 on Earth. But there's a lot out there elsewhere in the rest of the solar system, just waiting for the taking. Heck, the gas giants of the outer system— Jupiter, Saturn, Uranus, and Neptune—are practically awash in the stuff."

"All of which are a hellaciously long way from here." Farrell folded his arms. "I mean, NASA hasn't even built a rocket that can put astronauts back on the moon yet . . . and that's practically spitting distance compared to going to Jupiter and beyond." He chuckled. "I know people expect folks from Texas to think mighty big, but there's a pretty bright line between being naturally ambitious and just plain loco. And I'd just as soon stay on the right side of that divide."

"The company the Russians stole the original fusion reactor tech from had plans for direct fusion drives," Patrick pointed out. "Build one of those drives and put it on a spacecraft and you can get out farther a *lot* faster."

"How much faster?" Farrell asked, intrigued in spite of himself.

"Some of our robotic probes took more than six years to reach Jupiter," Patrick told him. "A fusion-powered spaceship could cover the same distance in less than a year."

Farrell reined himself back in. "That'd be something, all right," he agreed slowly. "But we're going round in circles here, like trying to figure out which came first: the chicken or the egg. The way I see it, we need more helium-3 to seriously exploit this fusion power breakthrough. But we can't round up enough helium-3 without developing these fusion drives you're talking about . . . and we can't build those drives without the helium-3 resources we don't have." He shook his head regretfully. "Like I said before, it's a dead end."

"Not quite," Martindale said quietly. "There are large reserves of this isotope much closer than the outer planets."

Farrell raised an eyebrow. "Oh?"

"The solar wind's been bombarding the moon with helium-3 for billions of years," Martindale explained. "And since the moon doesn't have a magnetic field like Earth, there's nothing to deflect it away. Soil studies of material collected by the Apollo missions and other probes have found significant amounts of the isotope trapped in the lunar regolith."

"How significant?" Farrell prodded.

"Concentrations as high as twenty parts per billion."

Farrell snorted again. Those were the kinds of numbers he had a lot of experience wrestling with. "For crying out loud, Kevin . . . that's almost as bad as saying we could strain the gold out of seawater and all get rich. You're talking about processing upwards of fifty thousand *tons* of this lunar regolith just to extract one lousy kilogram of helium-3. There's no way that'll ever be a paying proposition."

"If we were talking about a conventional earthbound mining operation, that would be true," Martindale responded calmly. "But automation is the solution to this problem. The European Space Agency and a number of universities and corporations have already worked through what it would take to extract the helium-3 and the other valuable materials—nitrogen, hydrogen, and carbon, for example—trapped in the moon's surface soils. They've drawn up plans for systems of robotic bulldozers, automated conveyer belts, and solar-powered furnaces. My people have vetted their numbers, and we estimate a carefully designed automated lunar mining operation could produce up to fifty kilograms of helium-3 per year."

"Which would be more than enough to power a vast array of advanced space systems and fusion drive development programs," Patrick added. He looked in dead earnest. "We're talking about the key that could eventually unlock the whole solar system, Mr. President. Conventional chemical rockets like those we use now can only take us so far. Mastering fusion, both for power generation and as a means of propulsion, could put the United States and our allies in a position of overwhelming economic and military advantage for decades to come."

Slowly, the president nodded. "I take your point, General." But then his face clouded over. "Which is too damned bad, because right now the NASA slugocracy isn't able to put so much as one doggone pound down on the lunar surface."

"Probably not," Patrick said. "But I bet there are private space companies who can—Sky Masters, SpaceX, Blue Origin, and a bunch of others."

Martindale nodded. "Offer to buy helium-3 at the right price and I guarantee you the private sector will find ways to meet the demand."

"Maybe so," Farrell agreed judiciously. When it came to solving problems, there was almost no one better than a sharp-eyed businessman backed by a solid engineering team—so long as there was a real potential for a serious profit. There was certainly no doubt that the reusable rockets pioneered by a number of companies were already cutting per-pound launch costs far below what they'd been in the Apollo era. What would once have been unaffordable, at least at any cost U.S. taxpayers would swallow, might now be within reach.

He let his breath out. "Hell's bells, but it sure would be nice to give this country of ours something big to shoot for—something that could really change the world for the better. We've been playing small ball for too long, piddling around with penny ante projects like electric cars and windmills."

"Yes, sir," Patrick agreed. Somberly, he looked across the desk at the president. "And if we don't do it and do it soon, I'm pretty sure others will."

"Meaning what?" Farrell asked.

"The Russians and the Chinese aren't blind to the

potential of mining the moon," Patrick told him quietly. "In fact, a Chinese geologist was one of the first scientists to seriously push the idea of extracting helium-3 and other valuable resources from the lunar surface."

"So?"

"That man is now the chief scientist for China's lunar exploration program," Patrick said. "If we really are in a race for the moon again, we might be starting out behind."

EIGHT

ABOARD EAGLE STATION, IN ORBIT
THE NEXT DAY

Eagle Station slid silently through space high above the North Atlantic, heading toward Africa's western coast at close to seventeen thousand miles per hour. Behind it, a curving line of darkness, the solar terminator, obscured South America. Patches of bright yellowish light dotted the blackened landmass, each marking the presence of a major city still waiting for the oncoming dawn.

The large space station was made up of four, linked 115-foot-long cylinders. Three—two dedicated weapons and sensor modules with a command node connecting them—formed a vertical shape that looked very much like a capital *I* turned on its side. Like their Russian predecessors, its U.S. Space Force crew often compared this basic silhouette to that of a TIE fighter from *Star Wars*. The fourth section, containing the station's fusion power generator, extended horizontally off the central command module.

Antennas of various sizes and shapes studded Eagle's radar-absorbent outer skin. Two long clear tubes—Sky Masters–designed combat-grade lasers replacing lower-powered Russian systems destroyed when the station was captured—were fixed in swivel mounts at the bottom of the two weapons modules. The mount for the orbital platform's primary armament, its Thunderbolt plasma rail gun, rose above the command node. It was an odd-looking device, with a stubby rod at its center surrounded by an array of electronic components in a six-armed starfish pattern.

Inside the cylindrical command node, Colonel Keith "Mal" Reynolds glided down a narrow, dimly lit corridor lined with storage cabinets and conduits and on though an open hatch. He came out into a somewhat larger compartment crammed full of computer consoles and high-resolution displays. Moving with practiced ease, he grabbed a handhold and arrested his momentum. One more gentle fingertip push off the nearest wall sent him floating over to the nearest console. He hooked his feet beneath it to hold himself in place and plugged his headset into the panel.

The Space Force officer on sensor watch, Captain Allison Stewart, glanced away from her displays. "Good morning, sir."

"Morning, Allie," Reynolds said. It was one of those rare moments when station time coincided—however briefly—with the visual cue of the sun rising above the curve of the earth ahead of them. At this altitude, four hundred miles above the planet, they experienced fourteen or fifteen dawns and sunsets during any given twenty-four-hour period. "Anything to report?"

"No, sir. It's been pretty quiet so far this shift."

"*Alert. SBIRS sensors have picked up a major heat bloom over the Aegean Sea,*" Eagle's threat-warning computer suddenly intoned calmly.

"**Is that** a missile?" Reynolds snapped.

"No, sir," Stewart told him. "This looks like a non-ballistic trajectory. My computer evaluates it as a spacecraft headed into orbit."

Reynolds frowned. There were a couple of private U.S. space companies with air-launched rockets in their inventory. But why light one off just south of Greece?

"New data, sir," Stewart said rapidly. "I evaluate

that thermal signature as an S-29B Shadow spaceplane. SBIRS detected the Shadow when its engines transitioned to rocket mode and initiated an orbital burn." She passed her revised data to his screen. "The S-29 is currently at an altitude of two hundred miles. It's in a retrograde orbit inclined at 128.4 degrees."

"So it's headed our way," Reynolds said. Eagle Station's orbit took it from west to east around the world, with an inclination or tilt of 51.6 degrees. That Shadow was circling the earth from east to west along the opposite track.

She nodded. "Yes, sir. And fast. On its current orbital track, that spaceplane will cross two hundred miles directly below us—with a combined closing speed of more than thirty-four thousand miles per hour."

The colonel raised an eyebrow. He was starting to get an itchy feeling on the back of his neck. It looked a whole lot like the Space Force's new senior officers were running a snap readiness exercise to test Eagle Station's commander and crew. He tapped an icon on his own console. Instantly, alarms blared in every compartment in all four connected modules. "Action stations," he announced over the intercom. "All personnel report to their action stations. This is a drill. Repeat, this *is* a drill."

Reynolds heard voices echoing through other open

hatches as those crewmen who'd been off duty scrambled out of tiny sleeping cabins and skimmed through corridors to their assigned places.

One by one, readiness reports flowed through his headset. The station's fusion power plant, environmental controls, and life-support systems were all functioning within their expected parameters.

"Lasers are fully charged. Firing status is green. Simulated controls operational. Primary control systems are temporarily locked down," he heard from the forward weapons module. Good, he thought. Nobody wanted real weapons firing accidentally during a training exercise.

From the aft weapons module, Major Ike Ozawa, the officer in charge of Eagle's Thunderbolt plasma rail gun, announced, "Thunderbolt's supercapacitors are charged. I'm ready to fire. Awaiting handoff of radar tracking data."

Reynolds glanced toward Stewart. The young captain was busy with her equipment.

"Our X-band radar is online," she told him a moment later. She looked back over her shoulder with a hint of barely suppressed amusement. "Oh, how I love the smell of burnt plasma in the morning. It smells like—"

"An easy kill." The colonel nodded. The plasma rail

gun was Eagle Station's main weapons system. Using energy stored in its starfish-shaped supercapacitor array, Thunderbolt created a ring of extremely dense plasma, essentially a form of ball lightning, and then accelerated it with a powerful magnetic pulse. Those glowing, meter-wide toroids of plasma flew through outer space at more than six thousand miles per second—destroying targets by a combination of kinetic impact, heat, powerful electromagnetic pulse effects, and high-energy X-rays.

"New radar contact," the station computer announced abruptly. *"Bearing zero-five-one degrees. Altitude two hundred miles. Range three thousand, five hundred miles. Closing velocity nine point five miles per second. Contact is friendly. Repeat, friendly. Positive IFF."* The S-29 had just crossed their radar horizon.

And then a familiar-sounding voice crackled over through Reynolds's headset. *"Eagle Station, this is Shadow Bravo One. Do you copy?"*

A grin creased his face. "Five by five, Bravo One. Welcome to outer space, Dusty," he radioed.

"Thank you kindly, Eagle," Colonel Scott "Dusty" Miller replied. He was the Space Force's first S-29B-qualified command pilot. *"Say, Mal, are your boys and girls ready to dance?"*

"We may be a little out of your league, Bravo One,"

Reynolds said, still smiling to himself. "That pea-shooter two-megawatt laser you're carrying won't be in range for a while yet . . . and our rail gun can zap you the moment you cross our visual horizon." He glanced down at his display. "Which is in just about fifteen seconds from now."

Miller's reply sounded equally amused. *"Well, that's mighty bold talk for a man strapped into a fat, floating tin can, Mal. Fight's on!"*

"Roger that, Bravo One. Fight's on," Reynolds acknowledged. He cued the intercom again. "All personnel, stand by to engage that S-29 spaceplane in simulated combat." He looked across the compartment toward Allison Stewart. "Anytime you're ready, Captain."

She nodded. "The target is in visual line of sight. Our radar is locked on. Handing off tracking data to—" She broke off and muttered, "Well, crap."

"Clarify that!" Reynolds demanded.

"Sorry, sir," Stewart said, turning faintly red with embarrassment. "The radar can't develop an acceptable fire control solution. The S-29 is maneuvering erratically, using its thrusters—not its main engines."

Reynolds stared down at his own display in surprise. The icon representing Dusty Miller's spaceplane jittered wildly, yawing, rolling, and pitching through all three dimensions as its thrusters fired in short pulses. And try as it might, Eagle Station's powerful X-band fire control radar was having real trouble figuring out exactly *where* the S-29B would be when the Thunderbolt rail gun's plasma shot arrived.

"Damn, that's clever," he muttered.

Once it was fired, the weapon's plasma toroids could not turn or change course. They streaked along a straight, undeviating path until they lost coherence roughly one second, and six thousand miles, later. If the target wasn't where the computer said it would be along that path, the shot would miss. As the range dropped and the time of flight for the plasma projectiles diminished, the job of making that calculation should get easier. If nothing else, once flight times dropped to just fractions of a second, the S-29's thrusters might not be able to move the spacecraft out of the way in time.

He looked back at Stewart. "How long before that spaceplane gets within striking range of this station?"

"A little under five minutes, Colonel."

He nodded. "Okay. Can you run a pattern analysis on the S-29's observed evasive maneuvers? See if you can crack whatever program they're running, so our computer can predict its next moves?"

She chewed her lower lip, deep in thought. "I can try, sir."

Left unspoken was the probability that whatever automated maneuver program Dusty Miller and his Shadow crew had running was using randomly generated numbers to select which particular thrusters fired and for how long. If it was using the more typical pseudo-random number generators common to many computer programs, the algorithm and seed used might be discoverable . . . in time. If it was using a so-called true random number generator and extracting randomness from physical phenomena—radioactive source decay, for example—there was probably no way to crack it.

Thinking it through, Reynolds was willing to bet there were hard limits coded into the S-29's evasion program. You couldn't leave *everything* to pure random chance—not on a working spacecraft with set reserves of hydrazine thruster fuel. There were also definite limits to the amount of torque and tumbling you could inflict on a spaceplane without harming the crew or risking its structural integrity.

He opened a circuit to Major Ozawa in the aft weapons module. "Ike, I want you to take every possible shot at these guys, understand? Even if you can't get a solid fire control solution, *take* the shot."

Ozawa whistled softly. "Pretty long odds against scoring a hit that way, Colonel. Not at anything over a few hundred miles, anyway."

"Maybe so," Reynolds agreed. "But long odds are better than no odds."

"Yes, sir," Ozawa said.

Reynolds closed out that circuit and opened a new one, this time to the laser weapons officer in Eagle Station's forward module. "This may get to close quarters, Bill. If it does, I'm counting on you to nail that S-29 fast. Once they're within range of your lasers, you're only going to have a minute to finish this fight. Right?"

"Yes, sir," Captain William Carranza acknowledged. "One thing to consider, Colonel. If we can't hit them, they may have trouble holding their own laser on target long enough to inflict serious damage on us."

Reynolds nodded. "Yeah, which could make this a mutually assured destruction scenario. If possible, that's not a game I want to play. This station is worth a lot more than one spaceplane."

"Understood," Carranza said.

Reynolds frowned deeply. Was there anything else he could do? There were just minutes before Eagle Station and Dusty Miller's spaceplane passed each other within two hundred miles. Weird as it seemed, that was practically knife-fighting range for weapons that hit at light speed and considerable fractions of light speed. Then he shrugged. When all was said and done, this simulated space battle was going to come down to a completely unpredictable interaction between the laws of physics, probability, and Lady Luck.

SHADOW BRAVO ONE,
OVER THE NORTH ATLANTIC OCEAN
TEN MINUTES LATER

"Eagle Station is below our visual horizon. No other immediate threat detected," a calm, female voice announced.

"Copy that. Discontinue evasion program," Colonel Scott "Dusty" Miller ordered through gritted teeth as another sharp jolt, this time from the spaceplane's aft thrusters, shoved him hard against his seat straps.

"Order confirmed. Evasive flight program discontinued," the S-29's flight control computer said.

The difference was immediately apparent. Instead of bucking around like a wild-eyed bronco on LSD, their winged spacecraft glided smoothly along its prescribed orbital track. They were still pitched nose down, which offered a spectacular view of the cloud-laced Atlantic through the forward cockpit canopy.

"Well, that was one hell of a ride," Miller muttered,

fighting down a wave of nausea. Short and stocky, and built like a wrestler, the command pilot had years of experience flying B-2 Spirit stealth bombers before transitioning to the U.S. Space Force. But not even the worst air turbulence really compared to what he'd just endured—ten solid minutes of wholly unpredictable motion, where his body and, more important, his inner ear hadn't known from one fraction of a second to the next in which direction their spacecraft was going to pitch, veer, roll, or yaw.

Breathing out slowly, he glanced across the cockpit at his copilot. "You okay, Major?"

Major Hannah "Rocky" Craig had been a test pilot for the F-35 fighter program before qualifying as a NASA astronaut and then transferring to the newly formed Space Force. Despite her years of intensive acrobatic flight training, even she still looked faintly green around the gills. She forced a sickly grin. "I'm fine, Dusty." She winced. "Jeez. That was like Mr. Toad's Wild Ride dialed up to eleven."

He nodded carefully and then keyed the intercom to the S-29's aft cabin. "Everyone still breathing back there?"

There was a long pause and then a pinched, oddly nasal voice answered. "Mostly."

"Mostly?"

"Well, Jensen puked about halfway through . . . so we're kind of being careful about the whole breathing thing," the voice, which he now recognized as belonging to the spaceplane's data-link specialist, replied.

Miller winced. Part of their Sky Masters training for space operations had involved multiple flights in an aircraft aptly nicknamed the Vomit Comet. Repeated high-angle parabolic maneuvers created short periods of weightlessness . . . and all too often induced airsickness. So he didn't need an overly active imagination to visualize what it was like being trapped in a tight compartment with globules of vomit floating everywhere.

Beside him, he heard Hannah Craig stifle a laugh. He shook his head. "Show a little sympathy, Major."

His dark-haired copilot donned an appropriately contrite look. "Sorry, Dusty." Then her natural mirth bubbled up again. "It's just that I'm really glad we're riding at the front of this bus . . . and not in back with Jensen and his miraculously reincarnated breakfast, lunch, and dinner."

Miller snorted, fighting hard against his own urge to burst out laughing. "Amen to that, I guess." His gaze sharpened. "So, how does the all-seeing, all-knowing computer say we did?"

Her fingers rattled across the largest of her multifunction displays, interrogating the S-29's attack and threat-warning computers. In response, text boxes and schematics flashed across her screen—graphically illustrating the results of their simulated battle against Eagle Station. Her mouth turned down slightly at the corners. "It's kind of a coin toss."

"As in?" he asked.

"The computer figures we got nailed at least twice. Both times when we were within just a couple of hundred miles of the station."

He nodded. No real surprise there. The Thunderbolt rail gun's plasma projectiles flashed across that distance in just over three one-hundredths of a second. Barring luck, that was much too short an interval for any random thruster pulse to kick their S-29 safely out of harm's way. "And on the plus side?"

Craig gave him a thumbs-up. "We scored at least three solid hits on Eagle before we got killed. So, if this had been a real fight, Colonel Reynolds and his crew would have been learning how to breathe space dust right about now."

"Not bad for a first whack at this whole space combat deal, I guess," Miller decided.

She shrugged against her harness. "I guess not."

"But?"

"Ties don't count for shit," Craig said simply. "It's

not really a win unless you zoom off in one piece, leaving the other guy drifting downwind under his parachute and wondering what just happened."

Miller nodded seriously. "Yeah. I see your point." He checked his own displays. "But since that one pass just burned over seventy percent of our hydrazine, we're done for today. Let's get this crate configured for powered reentry on the next orbit. Then we'll head back to base, rethink our tactics, and try again tomorrow."

"Sounds like a plan," she said. Her smile returned. "You know, Colonel Reynolds is really going to get tired of seeing us pop up on his radar."

Miller shrugged. "Probably so. Still, Mal shouldn't gripe too much about sharpening up his team in mock battles against us—not when the alternative is tangling with the Russians or the Chinese for real."

Craig looked seriously at him. "You think that's likely?"

"Oh hell, yes," he said. "Those guys aren't going to sit dirtside forever. Sooner or later, they'll come boiling back up out of the atmosphere, spoiling for a fight. And when they do, that'll be a *very* interesting day, Major."

NINE

The enormous neoclassical General Staff building curved around the vast expanse of Palace Square. Two wings, one on the west and one on the east, were joined by a huge triumphal arch commemorating Imperial Russia's victory over Napoleon. The Winter Palace, once home to the tsars, loomed directly across the square in regal splendor.

Until last year, one wing of the building had been occupied by the headquarters of Russia's Western Military District. Now, with much of the Kremlin reduced to blackened rubble, its offices were filled by a number of senior government officials and their staffs. What was supposed to have been a temporary emergency relocation to the old imperial capital showed signs of becoming permanent—at least for the ministers and their closest aides. They found the grandeur and luxury of St. Petersburg's palaces far more appealing than Moscow's official government buildings, many of them uncomfortable concrete relics of the Stalinist era.

Marshal Mikhail Leonov was an exception to this new rule. By staying in Moscow, he had become the de facto face of authority for the hundreds of thousands of bureaucrats, military officers, and intelligence officials who carried out the real work of government. That was not an accident. Because the other ministers were reluctant to subject themselves to another all-powerful autocrat like Gennadiy Gryzlov, they'd delayed elections for a new president yet again. But what they seemed not to understand, Leonov thought coldly, was that the Russian people instinctively craved strong leadership. And the eyes of the people were already turning toward him.

But even he found it useful to conduct certain meetings—those with his new Chinese allies, in particular—amid St. Petersburg's imperial pomp and magnificence. The abandoned Kremlin, with its surviving damaged buildings covered in scaffolding, was a stark reminder of weakness and defeat. It was better by far, Leonov knew, to give President Li Jun's representatives an impression of strength and stability.

With that in mind, he had chosen to hold this conference in an ornate chamber that dwarfed the small number of participants—Leonov himself, his aides, and a handful of senior Chinese generals and staff officers. The room's high ceilings and walls were covered by elaborate molding and gold leaf. Intricate geometric designs were repeated across its parquet flooring. Nineteenth-century murals depicted Russian military triumphs against the French, the Turks, and savage Asiatic tribesmen. A round conference table and chairs occupied the middle of the enormous room—with a portable, flat-panel LED screen as the sole concession to modernity.

Right now, selected footage from several different U.S. and European news programs flickered across the screen. The American president's recent declaration that his nation planned to establish a permanent mining colony on the moon within five years had generated a firestorm of commentary. Roughly half of the commentary condemned the idea as lunacy, a sordid bid to funnel tax dollars to favored private contractors. The other half hailed it as a long-overdue bid to rekindle

America's pioneering spirit, a bold move that could lead to the formation of a true space-faring civilization.

When the clips ended and the lights came up, Leonov turned toward General Chen Haifeng, the commander of China's Strategic Support Force. Early on during his previous visit to Beijing, he'd realized that the balding, middle-aged military officer was one of Li Jun's most trusted and forward-looking subordinates. The other members of the Chinese delegation were essentially window dressing. Chen was the man he needed to convince. His control over China's military space, cyberwar, electronic warfare, and psy ops units would put him front and center in any future conflict with the United States or its allies.

"Comments, Comrade General?" Leonov asked politely.

Chen shrugged his shoulders. "As always, I am amused by the ability of so many Western journalists and politicians to speak for so long and so vehemently, while saying so little of any real value." He smiled thinly. "In my country, we conduct our public business with more decorum."

Left unspoken was the fact that Chinese reporters who failed to toe the approved Party line tended to disappear or turn up dead. The same went for any government officials foolish enough to disagree with policies approved by their superiors.

"There is certainly strong American political opposition to Farrell's plans," Leonov noted carefully. It was important to draw this other man out, to learn his honest opinions. Chinese negotiators had a well-deserved reputation for masking their true intentions behind a façade of meaningless politeness. They were masters at the diplomatic art of delay. But the American president's sudden decision to radically accelerate his nation's space efforts meant neither Russia nor China could afford the luxury of watching events unfold.

He had Li Jun's promise of an alliance with Russia. Now it was time to find out how much that alliance really meant to the People's Republic.

Chen waved a dismissive hand at the now-dark LED screen. "Mere noise, signifying nothing." He shrugged again. "Our political analysts are sure that President Farrell controls more than enough votes in the U.S. Congress to win approval for his lunar mining enterprise."

Leonov nodded. "My experts say the same." Farrell had cleverly structured his proposal so that his government's initial outlays would be relatively minor. Larger costs would come only if the Americans actually succeeded in establishing a working mine on the moon's surface. It was a far cry from earlier grandiose plans submitted by NASA for various manned missions to the moon and Mars, all with price tags in the hundreds of billions of dollars.

"What really matters," Chen continued, "is whether or not the proposed American program is technically and economically feasible."

"And?" Leonov prompted.

Chen looked pained. "Unfortunately, our analysis suggests that it is. Certainly, there are serious scientific and engineering challenges involved. But none of those challenges are insurmountable." His mouth tightened. "In fact, my country's space scientists and engineers have been working very hard on plans for similar lunar mining operations."

"As has Roscosmos," Leonov acknowledged, referring to the government megacorporation that ran Russia's civilian space program. "But we will not be in a position to build such an enterprise, at a cost we can bear, for many years to come, perhaps not until the mid-2030s."

Frowning, Chen nodded his understanding. At the moment, Russia and the People's Republic could almost match the United States in the automated mining technology needed for a lunar helium-3 mine. But America's current lead in reusable rocket technology put it years ahead in achieving affordable access to space.

The Energia-5VR heavy-lift rockets Russia had built to put its Mars One space station into orbit were remarkably powerful, able to carry close to one hundred tons of payload. But they were expendable rockets, which made every Energia launch incredibly expensive. Just getting into space consumed roughly 96 percent of every rocket's mass. True, with a crash engineering and rocket production program, Marshal Leonov's country might be able to land robotic mining equipment on the moon within several years—but only at an enormous cost that could easily bankrupt Russia's already strained economy.

If anything, the People's Republic of China was even further behind. While many components of its planned robotic and manned lunar missions were well along in development, putting the necessary heavy payloads into orbit affordably was a major stumbling block. Beijing's aerospace engineers were working on a reusable rocket of their own, the Long March 8. They were also designing a massive, Saturn V–class launcher, the Long March 9. But neither rocket could possibly be ready to fly much before 2030.

Boiled down to the essentials, neither Moscow nor Beijing could possibly match President Farrell's ambitious timeline. Much as it galled Chen to admit it, this new civilian space race was probably already lost.

"Your conclusions are irrefutable," Leonov said, after listening to the Chinese general work through his reasoning.

If anything, Chen's expression grew even more dour. "Then our two nations face a most serious threat."

"Agreed," Leonov said. "Allowing the Americans to forge an insurmountable edge in space and fusion power–related technologies would be an enormous strategic error."

Chen scowled. "But if this race is already lost?"

"Then we must change the terms of the contest," Leonov said coolly. "If we cannot yet match the Americans in the civilian space arena, then we must deny them any chance of exploiting the moon's valuable resources."

Chen raised an eyebrow. "And how do you propose to achieve such an end?"

"As I told your president," Leonov answered him patiently. "By combining our resources. And by being willing to take risks the Americans would never dare dream of." He glanced toward one of his aides and nodded slightly.

The younger officer tapped a control on his laptop. Instantly the large LED display lit up, revealing the first page of a document headed *Operatsiya Nebesnyy Grom,* or Operation Heaven's Thunder.

Speaking carefully, Leonov walked through the framework of his intricate, highly complex plan. Computer-generated graphics accompanied each stage of every proposed mission—illustrating how he believed Russian and Chinese space and weapons technologies could be fused into a greater whole.

When he finished, Chen bowed his head slightly in admiration. "A brilliant concept, Comrade Marshal." His fingers drummed quietly on the table for a few moments, while he considered what he had just been shown. At last he nodded decisively. "I will recommend its approval to President Li Jun."

Leonov smiled. "Thank you, Comrade General."

"But absolute secrecy remains essential," Chen warned. "With surprise, what you propose is possible. But if the Americans discover what we are doing too soon, the consequences for both our nations could be severe." He shrugged. "I hope you will forgive me for pointing out that a great many of your most precious secrets seem to have leaked to the West in recent years."

"True enough," Leonov agreed coldly. Thorough study of Gennadiy Gryzlov's past failures had turned up significant evidence that American spies—probably working for Scion—had repeatedly penetrated even the tightest Russian security. "Which is why I plan a series of special measures designed to distract our enemies while we prepare."

He nodded again to his aide.

New images appeared on the large flat-panel screen. Drawn from radar and visual observations made by ground- and space-based Russian telescopes and surveillance satellites over the past several weeks, they showed some of the new U.S. Space Force S-29 spaceplanes making repeated passes—at varying altitudes and orbital inclinations—against Eagle Station.

Chen watched them in silence. When the screen went black again, he looked back at the Russian. "So? We've captured much of the same data with our own satellites."

"And what is your evaluation of this activity?" Leonov asked.

Chen shrugged. "It seems obvious. What we see are war games. The American space station is practicing its defense against attacks by hostile spacecraft."

"Exactly," Leonov said with a thin smile. "And in doing so, the Americans reveal to us what they fear most."

For a brief moment, Chen could not hide his confusion. "So?"

Leonov's smile widened as he explained. "Remember what your own great countryman, the formidable strategist Sun Tzu, wrote: 'Engage people with what they expect; it is what they are able to discern and confirms their projections. It settles them into predictable patterns of response, occupying their minds while you wait for the extraordinary moment—that which they cannot anticipate.'" His gaze grew colder. "We will let the Americans chase after a chimera, while we, in turn, will hunt them."

TEN

ST. MARY'S BASILICA, KRAKÓW, POLAND
SUMMER 2022

Brad McLanahan only came out of his daze when the lilting, joyful strains of Handel's "Arrival of the Queen of Sheba" filled the vast interior of the ancient Gothic church. He looked down into Nadia Rozek's beautiful, blue-gray eyes. "What the heck just happened?" he whispered.

She smiled up at him. "We are married. And *you* just kissed me."

"Wow." Brad felt as though he were waking up after a months-long slumber. He remembered standing nervously in front of the high altar, looking down the center aisle past pews filled with expectant faces—waiting for Nadia to make her entrance. He'd felt his pulse pounding harder than it ever had before, even under the stress of combat.

And then she'd appeared, clad in a dazzling floor-length, white silk wedding dress, silhouetted against sunlight streaming through the basilica's open doors. From that moment on, his memories were a blur, more a swelling cascade of emotion than of conscious thought. The whole elaborate wedding ceremony itself, with its ancient rites and responses, had slid past in what seemed like only seconds, submerged beneath an overwhelming tide of pure happiness.

"Now what?" he asked quietly.

Nadia laughed and lovingly took his hand in hers. "Now we endure a few minutes more of pomp and circumstance . . . and then we begin our life together."

Brad grinned. Pomp and circumstance was the perfect phrase, he thought. Their first plans for a quiet, private wedding in Nadia's home village had been overruled by Poland's president, Piotr Wilk. Instead, he'd insisted on a lavish, state-funded public ceremony to honor them. Wilk, who'd led Poland through the dark years of struggle against renewed Russian aggression, had long wanted to give them the recognition he thought they deserved.

"Your marriage is more than just a union of two hearts and two lives," Wilk had explained seriously, when they'd protested his decision. "It should also be a celebration of the alliance which saved Poland—and a celebration of the victory earned by your courage and devotion and sacrifice." In the end, Brad and Nadia, faced with enthusiastic support for Wilk's idea from her parents, his father, Kevin Martindale, and President Farrell, had reluctantly yielded.

Some good, at least, had come out of the Polish president's determination to make this partly a political show, Brad thought. Instead of a tuxedo, Wilk had encouraged him to wear his Iron Wolf Squadron dress uniform. And there was no doubt that he felt more comfortable in this familiar dark, rifle-green uniform jacket, white collared shirt, and black tie. The squadron patch on his right shoulder, a metal-gray robotic wolf's head with glowing red eyes on a bright green background, was almost the only splash of bright color besides the flowers entwined in Nadia's dark hair and her bridal bouquet.

Together, Brad and Nadia turned and started down the basilica's long central aisle—passing through a sea of delighted onlookers. Apart from a handful of close friends and family, most of those in the church were military and political dignitaries from Poland, the United States, and half a dozen Eastern European allies.

For one brief moment, Brad's elation faltered. That so many of these faces were those of relative strangers was a reminder of the grim price paid on the way to this joy-filled day. Too many of their fellow pilots and soldiers had been killed in action against the Russians in the past few years. Now their names and faces crowded in on his memory. It was almost as though they were calling out to him . . . begging not to be forgotten.

But then, as if she'd sensed his darkening mood, Nadia gently squeezed his hand. "Our comrades are never truly gone. Not while we remember them," she told him softly.

He nodded, grateful all over again for the undeserved good fortune that had brought this amazing woman into his life. "*Kocham cię*," he murmured into her ear. "I love you."

"I am very pleased to hear that," she said, with a quick grin. "Because otherwise, this marriage would be off to a somewhat rocky start."

Brad was still struggling not to laugh out loud when they passed through the basilica's entrance and came out onto Kraków's Main Market Square. The moment they appeared, spontaneous cheers rang out from the large crowd of ordinary men, women, and children gathered outside the church. Ranks of Polish and allied soldiers and airmen in full dress uniform snapped to attention, presenting arms with long-practiced precision. Bayonet-tipped rifles and swords flashed bright in the sun.

Suddenly acutely aware that they were the sole focus of several thousand pairs of eyes, Brad felt his face redden slightly. In contrast, Nadia looked radiant, even regal, in the long, flowing dress that concealed her prosthetic blades. Beaming, she raised her floral bouquet above her head in a salute, acknowledging the greeting. They cheered even louder in response.

He started to relax a bit.

Movement near the edge of the square caught his eye. Flanked by motorcycle police escorts with flashing lights, a long black limousine nosed slowly through the throng. Small red, blue, and white flags fluttered from its hood.

"What the hell?" Brad muttered. Those were Russian flags.

Nadia followed his gaze. Though she kept smiling, her eyes darkened with anger. "*Skurwysyn.* Son of a bitch," she said through gritted teeth. "So someone from Moscow decides to interfere with our wedding day?"

The limousine rolled to a stop a few yards away. A smartly uniformed Russian army colonel emerged. He carried a silver-wrapped gift box under one arm. Followed closely by a pair of dour-looking Polish plainclothes security officers, he advanced toward them.

"Diplomacy, remember?" Brad whispered with a slight smile of his own—aware that Nadia's first instinctive impulse would be to kick the Russian officer in the groin.

"I will be good," she promised. "For now."

The Russian stopped a few feet away and tossed off a quick, formal salute. "Major McLanahan. Major Rozek. My name is Colonel Vasily Artamonov. I am my country's military attaché to Poland."

"Colonel," Brad said, not bothering to return the salute. There were limits to his own capacity for diplomacy. "What can we do for you?"

Artamonov smiled politely, ignoring the slight. "On behalf of Marshal Mikhail Ivanovich Leonov, I offer this small personal token, as a gift on your marriage." He held out the wrapped box.

Nadia raised an eyebrow and then nodded at one of the Polish security officers. He took the box for her. "Tell Marshal Leonov that we accept his present in the same spirit in which it is given," she said coldly.

"Of that, you can be sure, Major," the Russian said in reply. His own tone was equally unemotional. He saluted again and strode back to his waiting car.

Brad waved a hand toward the gift box. "Aren't you at all curious to see what's inside?"

Nadia shook her head dismissively. "Not in the slightest." She shrugged. "Let the experts wrestle with Marshal Leonov's odd psychological games." Smiling more genuinely now, she slipped her hand through his arm. "After all, we have a wedding reception to attend, do we not?" Her voice turned husky. "With a long and very private honeymoon to follow, I understand?"

"Oh, yes, ma'am," Brad said fervently.

IRON WOLF SQUADRON HEADQUARTERS,
33RD AIR BASE, NEAR POWIDZ, POLAND
THE NEXT DAY

Patrick McLanahan looked up with a frown when Kevin Martindale entered the secure conference room. "What have you got for me, General?" Martindale asked.

"Nothing clear," Patrick admitted.

Martindale crossed the room and stared down at the collection of small wooden figurines scattered across the table. "That's what was in this wedding gift from Leonov?"

Patrick nodded. "It's a Matryoshka set. You know, one with small and smaller dolls nesting inside each other." He picked out two of the larger figurines for the other man to see. "And obviously handcrafted."

Martindale stared down at the two dolls, one painted to resemble a young man in a dark green military uniform, and the other a young woman in a white dress. He arched an eyebrow. "All of the dolls are supposed to be either Brad or Nadia?"

"All of them, except for this," Patrick said grimly, fishing out a very tiny piece. He handed it to Martindale, along with a magnifying glass. "This was nesting inside the smallest figurine."

The other man studied the miniature carefully. His lips pursed. This was definitely *not* a doll. Instead, he decided, it was shaped like some kind of futuristic-looking aircraft. He frowned. Or possibly it was supposed to be a spaceplane, like the one flown by Brad, Nadia, and Peter Vasey when they'd captured Russia's Mars One station last year. This one, however, had a roundel on one wing—showing a dark blue chevron rising across a stylized globe striped in the red, blue, and white bands of the Russian flag.

Martindale's frown deepened. That was the emblem of Russia's Space Forces. He looked up. "Was there anything else in that damned gift box?"

"Just this," Patrick said. He slid a small, handwritten note across. "It was attached to the doll set before we took it apart."

Martindale stared down at the note. Written in the Cyrillic alphabet it read: В будущем. Slowly, he puzzled through the unfamiliar characters, switching them out for their Latin alphabet equivalents. "To the future?" he translated.

"That's what it says," Patrick agreed.

"And there was nothing else?"

"Nope," Patrick said. "No hidden listening devices. No lethal toxins. Nada." He scowled. "Which leaves us with one big question—"

"What sort of message is Leonov trying to send?" Martindale finished for him.

Patrick nodded. "Admittedly, we don't know much about his psychology. But nothing suggests he shares Gennadiy Gryzlov's psychotic craving for personal revenge. If anything, Leonov's supposed to be one cold-hearted bastard—never making a move unless he's analyzed it six ways from Sunday."

"Which makes him more dangerous," Martindale commented sourly. "He's not as easy to predict . . .

or to manipulate . . . as the late and very unlamented Gennadiy."

"Too true."

Martindale tapped the tiny spaceplane miniature with the tip of one finger. "Then the simplest explanation may also be the most likely." He looked up. "By now the Russians must realize how valuable our single-stage-to-orbit spaceplanes are, both for military and civilian space operations."

Patrick nodded again. The Russians had their own Elektron spaceplanes, but they were primitive compared to the hypersonic S-series ships built by Sky Masters. The S-29 Shadow and its counterparts could take off and land on runways built for ordinary commercial airliners. In contrast, the Russians could only launch their comparatively tiny, single-pilot spacecraft atop expendable rockets. And even when they reached orbit, they were easily outgunned and outmaneuvered by their larger, more capable American rivals. "So?"

"Well, this little exercise could just be Leonov putting us on notice that he plans to build his own versions of the S-29 Shadow and our other spaceplanes," Martindale mused.

"Why give us any warning at all?" Patrick asked, not hiding his skepticism.

Martindale shrugged. "Leonov might be playing a weak hand to the best of his ability. After all, there's no way in hell he could hope to hide a full-scale space-plane development and flight test program. Not for very long, anyhow."

"He hid the Energia heavy-lift rocket program from us for years," Patrick pointed out quietly.

Martindale looked pained. "That's not a mistake my Scion intelligence teams will make again." He went on. "Anyway, maybe he just wants to make us sweat a little, while his engineers and scientists work on reverse-engineering Sky Masters technology, just like he did with our CID combat robots."

Patrick winced. Learning that the Russians had successfully built their own robotic war machines, their *Kiberneticheskiye Voyennyye Mashiny*, had come at a terrible price—one that included thousands of dead American civilians, airmen, and sailors . . . and both of his beautiful new daughter-in-law's legs. "Is there any evidence at all that Moscow has a serious spaceplane R&D program under way?"

Reluctantly, Martindale nodded. "For the past couple of months, my people inside Russia have been picking up rumors of something called *Proyekt Zhar-Ptitsa,* the Firebird Project."

"Firebird," Patrick said heavily.

"That is dismayingly suggestive," Martindale agreed.

"So why is this the first time I'm hearing about it?" Patrick asked.

Martindale sighed. "Mostly because all I had were a few unsubstantiated bits of information, more random gossip than hard intelligence. Not anything worth sounding the alarm about, especially with Brad and Nadia's wedding coming up."

"And that's changed recently?"

Martindale nodded. "My operatives have learned that, whatever this Firebird Project is, it involves some of the top aerospace engineers and designers from Sukhoi, Tupolev, and Mikoyan." Those were the top Russian military aircraft manufacturers.

"Then we'd better make damned sure Sky Masters tightens up its security," Patrick growled. "Because those LPDRS triple-hybrid engines it produces are the key component for any real spaceplane program."

Martindale nodded his understanding. All the other elements needed to build a working single-stage-to-orbit spaceplane—hypersonic airframe designs, composite materials, advanced computer flight controls, and the like—were already readily available. So if the Russians ever got their hands on Sky Masters' revolutionary engine technology, all bets were off. Moscow could have its own fleet of hypersonic aircraft and spacecraft flying within one or two years—completely upsetting the favorable balance of power the United States had so recently achieved.

ELEVEN

AEROSPACE CITY, BEIJING,
PEOPLE'S REPUBLIC OF CHINA
SEVERAL WEEKS LATER

From the outside, activity at Beijing's Aerospace City—the center of China's national space program—appeared normal. Civilian engineers, scientists, and other workers arriving at the main gate for their shifts were still only subject to the usual, routine identity checks. Nothing else immediately suggested anything out of the ordinary, though a keen observer might have wondered why so many lights were on all night in various office buildings, labs, and spacecraft production facilities scattered across the 577-acre complex.

Once beyond the main gate, however, it was clear that significantly tighter security measures were in effect. Type 08 eight-wheeled infantry fighting vehicles armed with 30mm autocannons were parked near key intersections. Soldiers in camouflaged battle dress and body armor manned checkpoints outside several buildings. Civilians entering these facilities were subject to a much higher level of scrutiny.

Even more troops were currently deployed around Production Building Number Five. Three full platoons formed a protective cordon around the three Harbin Z-20 medium-lift helicopters that had recently touched down in a nearby parking lot. No one was taking any chances with the safety of the three VIPs those helicopters had ferried to Aerospace City.

Inside Building Five's cavernous main hall, Marshal Mikhail Leonov, President Li Jun, and General Chen Haifeng walked together along a raised platform. A gaggle of aides and security guards trailed them at a respectful distance. From time to time, the three men paused at large, clear windows, intently examining several of the spacecraft under construction in separate clean rooms.

Leonov stopped longer at one of the observation windows. Gowned and masked technicians were carefully fitting a docking collar to the top of a four-legged space vehicle sheathed in layers of what appeared to be gold foil. Others were at work at various points around the upper half of the ungainly-looking craft—inspecting thrusters and a number of dish and wire antennas.

"That is one of our Chang'e landers," Chen said with pride.

Leonov nodded. He'd studied schematics and photographs, but seeing the actual spacecraft up close like this was far more impressive. "It bears a striking resemblance to the American Apollo vehicle," he commented.

Li Jun shrugged. "That is so. After all, form follows function." He smiled. "But the Chang'e benefits from all the technological advances of the past fifty years. Its flight controls, electronics, and other systems are orders of magnitude beyond anything the Americans possessed in 1969."

"Will your lander be able to dock successfully with our Federation orbiter?" Leonov asked. The Federation was Russia's next-generation manned spacecraft, replacing the antiquated Soyuz. Similar in shape and size to NASA's Orion and SpaceX's Dragon, each Federation could carry up to six crewmen into space. Its robust life-support systems and substantial stores of food, water, and oxygen allowed missions of up to thirty days in duration.

"Without a doubt," Chen confirmed. "Fortunately, our docking mechanisms are completely compatible. A team of top aerospace engineers from our two nations has already run hundreds of simulations—working through every detail of the necessary approach and docking procedures. Other groups are busy refining the plans for our first series of joint space missions."

"And crews of your military cosmonauts and our taikonauts are training together now in some of our facilities," Li Jun added. "My advisers tell me they are making good progress."

"That is excellent news," Leonov said, and he meant it. Necessity had forced him to delegate preparations for many of the first, crucial elements of Operation Heaven's Thunder to his Chinese allies. After all, their space program had the required expertise and it was providing essential hardware. Of almost equal importance, China was much harder for Western intelligence organizations to penetrate. Decades of repression and propaganda had created a population wary of anyone who might be a spy. This atmosphere of government-stoked paranoia, combined with an enormous and highly efficient internal security apparatus, made it almost impossible for foreigners to operate unnoticed.

He moved on to the next observation window. The spacecraft being assembled in this clean room was even bigger. Like the Chang'e, it had four retractable landing struts, but it was dominated by a large spherical fuel tank mounted below an open deck studded with attachment points and what appeared to be a small cargo crane.

Leonov glanced toward Li Jun and Chen. "And this machine?"

"That is the first prototype of our new Mǎ Luó automated cargo lander," Chen explained. "Its payload capacity is close to ten metric tons."

Leonov whistled softly, impressed. Translated, *Mǎ Luó* meant "mule." It seemed an apt name for a spacecraft able to carry far more payload to the lunar surface than anything ever built before. But, like its Chang'e counterpart, there was something hauntingly familiar about this design. He looked closer, studying its key features. Then he saw it. With a wry smile, he turned back to his hosts. "That's an enlarged version of the American-designed Blue Moon lander, isn't it?"

Chen nodded, matching his amused expression. "We were able to acquire the technical specifications and design blueprints from its creator, the private space company Blue Origin."

"Without their knowledge, I suspect?" Leonov said dryly.

"Naturally," Chen replied.

Leonov felt a moment's envy. Over the past several decades, China's Ministry of State Security had painstakingly planted deep-cover intelligence officers and agents-of-influence in many of America's government departments, private corporations, and universities. As a result, its ability to pry secrets loose far surpassed that of Russia's Foreign Intelligence Service, the SVR, or the GRU, the armed forces' Main Intelligence Directorate. While that was a clear advantage now, it was also an unwelcome reminder of just how dependent Russia was on its larger and richer Asian ally.

But then he looked down again at the prototype cargo spacecraft. It was much too heavy for any existing Chinese launch vehicle to carry into Earth orbit— let alone send to the moon. Only Russia's powerful Energia-5VR rocket could do the job. He let his momentary irritation subside, soothed by this realization. So long as Beijing remembered that Moscow brought its own strengths to this combined enterprise, all would be well.

TWELVE

KANSK-DALNIY MILITARY AIR BASE,
EAST OF KRASNOYARSK, RUSSIA
SOME WEEKS LATER

Kansk-Dalniy's 2,500-meter-long runway stretched across a flat countryside of fields and scattered patches of woodland. Revetments for the regiment of MiG-31BM Foxhound long-range interceptors stationed at the airfield were clustered near both ends of the strip. Hangars, maintenance shops, weapons bunkers, and barracks for the pilots and ground crews lined the runway's northwest edge.

Located more than two thousand miles east of Moscow, this relatively isolated rural base was the last place one would ordinarily expect to find a large crowd of Russian military and government officials, along with

representatives from the country's top aircraft companies and design bureaus. And yet, here they were—
waiting with growing anticipation to witness what was
described as a key test flight in Russia's top secret Firebird high-speed experimental aircraft program.

Many of the spectators occupied bleacher seating set
up along the runway. Others milled around near a large
temporary aircraft shelter erected next to the airfield's
wide concrete apron. Enlisted personnel circulated
through the crowd, offering drinks and *zakuski,* hors
d'oeuvres of cold cuts, fish, and vegetables.

One of the guests, a trim, efficient-looking lieutenant
colonel with short blond hair and icy blue eyes, took a
glass of sparkling wine. She nodded curt thanks to the
airman who'd served her and then motioned him away.
"Quite a festive atmosphere," she murmured to the big,
beefy man in civilian clothes standing next to her.

He snorted. "All but the weather, Colonel."

Lieutenant Colonel Katya Volkova glanced up at
the sky and nodded. Thick gray clouds stretched from
horizon to horizon. Her mouth twisted slightly. "Not
exactly ideal conditions for a test flight," she said.

"Do you think it'll be postponed?"

"God, I hope not," Volkova said with a short laugh.
"Another day spent hanging around this provincial
dump? No, thank you."

Many of those within earshot nodded their own agreement. Moscow was enjoying its best weather of the year right now—a far cry from the gloomy overcast currently covering most of this part of Siberia. Stadium-sized video monitors tuned to cameras broadcasting from Novosibirsk and Omsk showed the same dreary gray skies. And security concerns or not, it seemed absurd to stage this Firebird demonstration flight so far from the capital. Even Krasnoyarsk, the nearest decently sized city, was almost 125 miles away.

As it was, there were only limited windows of opportunity to conduct this test without fear of enemy observation. Careful timing was essential to ensure that America's Eagle Station and its handful of newly launched reconnaissance satellites were in the wrong orbits to see anything over this sparsely populated portion of the Motherland.

Suddenly, a harsh alert tone blared through loudspeakers around the air base. "*Vnimaniye!* Attention! The test flight will now commence. Stand clear of the aircraft shelter. Repeat, stand clear of the aircraft shelter."

More airmen moved across the tarmac in a line, ushering the crowd away from the shelter. Slowly, the giant shelter's clamshell doors swung open—revealing a very large, swept-wing aircraft with four enormous engines mounted beneath its wings. Those engines were already spooling up, splitting the air with a deafening, shrill howl.

Through narrowed eyes, Volkova studied the huge jet as it rolled slowly out into the open air and turned onto the taxiway. It looked very much like a modified Tu-160 supersonic bomber, she decided, though those engine nacelles were a different shape and significantly larger. That made some sense, since the Tu-160's airframe was already designed to handle supersonic flight. On the other hand, she doubted strongly that it was suitable for operations outside the atmosphere. If so, this aircraft must be intended primarily as a test bed for those massive new engines.

As soon as it reached the far end of the runway, the modified Tu-160 swung into position and started its takeoff roll—thundering past the crowd at an ever-increasing speed. Three-quarters of the way down the runway, it rotated and soared skyward, trailing plumes of faintly yellowish exhaust. Within moments, it vanished among the low-hanging, thick gray clouds.

Only seconds later, the sharp *crack* of a sonic boom rattled windows and teeth across the air base. This evidence of incredibly swift acceleration created a stir of excitement among the waiting crowd. Nothing short of a high-performance modern jet fighter should be able to reach supersonic speeds so rapidly.

Eight minutes after that, the big-screen video monitor tuned to Novosibirsk, five hundred miles to the west, registered a second loud sonic boom. Another exultant murmur rippled through the onlookers.

"Does that mean what I think it means?" the big man said, keeping his voice low.

Samantha Kerr, currently masquerading as Lieutenant Colonel Volkova of the Russian Aerospace Forces, nodded tightly to her colleague, Marcus Cartwright, another Scion field operative. "If I've done my mental math right, what we just heard was an aircraft moving at Mach Five, right at the edge of hypersonic speeds . . . and a hell of a lot faster than anything else in the Russian inventory."

The loudspeakers blared again, relaying information that was unnecessary for anyone who'd been paying the slightest attention. "The Firebird has just passed over Novosibirsk at high altitude. Now it is flying on toward Omsk."

Cartwright lowered his voice even further. "Well, now we know why our Russian friends made it so hard to wangle invitations to their party."

Sam nodded again. Several weeks ago, Scion's intelligence operation inside Russia had picked up rumors about this upcoming Firebird flight demonstration. Careful poking around inside several different Defense Ministry classified databases had shown that technical information about the Firebird Project itself was hidden behind a series of impenetrable computer security firewalls. Fortunately, the official list of several hundred military officers, government officials, and aviation industry bigwigs cleared to witness the Kansk-Dalniy test was guarded by slightly less imposing barriers. But even then, it had taken Scion's best hackers days of painstaking effort to covertly breach those protocols and add their carefully forged credentials—as Lieutenant Colonel Volkova and Sergei Kondakov from the Ministry of Industry and Trade—to the approved list.

As it was, Sam knew that only Moscow's seemingly odd decision to unveil its top secret Firebird program to so many people at one time made this dangerous covert operation even remotely possible. Posing as a Russian bird colonel and a mid-ranking bureaucrat, even with top-notch fake documents, would have been far too dangerous at a smaller, more intimate, gathering of real experts.

But now that she'd seen this prototype hypersonic aircraft in action, she understood why Marshal Leonov was willing to risk someone spilling the beans. If the

Russians already had a manned aircraft that could reach speeds of Mach Five or higher in controlled flight, they were very close to being able to build true single-stage-to-orbit spaceplanes. And the moment a brand-new, experimental spaceplane started flying to the upper reaches of the atmosphere and beyond, the whole world would know exactly what Moscow was doing.

"I guess it's a good thing I don't mind being the bearer of bad tidings," Sam said softly to Cartwright. "Because this news is definitely *not* going to make Mr. Martindale's day."

PHANTOM THREE,
AT HIGH ALTITUDE OVER OMSK
MINUTES LATER

Ten thousand meters above the Siberian industrial city of Omsk, a large, gray twin-tailed fighter rolled out of the slow, racetrack holding pattern it had been following for several minutes. The railroads and waterways that gave the city its importance as a transportation hub were invisible, obscured by a solid layer of thick clouds.

Inside the MiG-31's forward cockpit, Major Stepan Grigoryev kept a careful eye on the digital timer counting down along the edge of his head-up display. "Stand by, Alexey," he announced over the intercom. "Twenty seconds."

"Standing by," Captain Balandin, his weapon systems officer, acknowledged from the fighter's rear cockpit. "Cloud cover remains at one hundred percent. There are no air contacts on my radar."

"Understood," Grigoryev said. That was good news. All civilian and military air traffic had been diverted away from this region for the duration of the "Firebird flight test." After all, there was no point in staging this little magic act if anyone on the ground or in the air could see what was happening. Abruptly, the timer on his HUD flashed to zero.

"Going supersonic," he snapped. His left hand shoved the MiG's throttles all the way forward and then slightly to the left—going to full military power, past the detent, and into afterburner. Raw fuel poured into the exhaust stream of both huge Soloviev D-30F6 engines and ignited. Immediately, he felt himself shoved back against his seat as the fighter accelerated with astonishing rapidity.

Seconds later, the *boom* created by its sudden transition beyond the sound barrier rippled across Omsk and its suburbs. For those watching the monitors back at Kansk-Dalniy, it would seem as if the mythical Firebird test aircraft had just slashed through the sky high above the city at more than six thousand kilometers per hour.

Beneath his oxygen mask, Grigoryev bared his teeth in a wolfish smile. Not a bad piece of sleight of hand, he thought. First, send a Tu-160 bomber—fitted out with fake engine nacelles—up through the clouds and well away from the airfield, out of sight and out of hearing. And then, at precisely calculated intervals, have each of the three MiG-31 fighters stationed over Kansk-Dalniy, Novosibirsk, and Omsk suddenly accelerate beyond the speed of sound . . . creating the perfect illusion of a hypersonic-capable aircraft streaking across central Russia at incredibly high speed.

Q DIRECTORATE, FEDERAL SECURITY SERVICE (FSB) HEADQUARTERS, THE LUBYANKA, MOSCOW THAT SAME TIME

For more than one hundred years, the Lubyanka had been the center of state terror in Russia. From its maze of identical corridors and cryptically numbered offices, the secret police, whether called the Cheka, OGPU, NKVD, KGB, or FSB, waged a never-ending clandestine war against foreign spies and anyone else unlucky enough to be declared an enemy of the state. It was a brutal conflict fought without pity or remorse. Those dragged inside the Lubyanka for questioning rarely left its dank, bloodstained cellars alive.

In recent years, however, the old ways of extracting information desired by the Lubyanka's masters—physical torture, truth drugs, and sleep deprivation—had been supplemented by more subtle means. Q Directorate's skilled programmers and supercomputers were among the most important of these new weapons. Originally organized to conduct offensive cyberwar and computer-hacking operations, the directorate was now also expected to defend Russia's critical industries and computer systems against foreign espionage and sabotage.

It carried out this vital work from a highly secure facility built into the very heart of the Lubyanka. Thick walls, floors, and ceilings with interwoven layers of metal paneling, wire mesh, acoustic fill, and gypsum wallboard protected its offices from electronic eavesdropping. The rooms themselves were utterly plain, devoid of anything but desks, chairs, and masses of ultramodern computer equipment. There were no windows. And the only way in or out was barred both by armed guards and rigorous biometric screening procedures.

The Spartan décor of Major General Arkady Koshkin's private office matched those of his subordinates, with only a small sideboard and silver samovar for making tea as obvious luxuries. At first glance, Koshkin's physical appearance was equally unimposing. He was a short, slight man with a high, wrinkled forehead and thick spectacles. Anyone passing him on the street would have mistaken him for a minor functionary in some unimportant ministry.

All in all, the head of Q Directorate was a textbook example of how first impressions could be deceiving, Marshal Leonov thought approvingly. Only Koshkin's eyes, gleaming with ambition and intelligence, gave him away.

In an odd sense, the man sitting beside Leonov in front of Koshkin's desk was an illustration of the same principle. Though tall and powerfully built, Minister of State Security Viktor Kazyanov was a physical and moral coward, fit only to be a toady and yes-man for those who were stronger and more ruthless. Gennadiy Gryzlov had kept him on as head of Russia's intelligence services for precisely those reasons. Now Kazyanov's weaknesses served Leonov's own purposes. Through Kazyanov, he could exercise effective control over the nation's secret police and foreign intelligence operations without unduly alarming the other government ministers who unwisely imagined they were still his equals.

The sleek computer on Koshkin's desk chimed once. "Well?" Leonov demanded.

"We have a match for one of our two suspects," Koshkin said evenly. He turned his flat-panel display so that the others could see the image it displayed. The broad-featured face of a very large man filled the screen. "According to his identity papers, this is Sergei Kondakov—a mid-ranked official in the Ministry of Industry and Trade." His thin smile never reached his eyes. "And if we were relying only on the personnel records of that ministry, we would believe him to be exactly who he says he is."

"Because those records have been hacked," Leonov said dryly. Koshkin nodded. "So who is he really?"

"Probably an American. And almost certainly an agent for Scion." Koshkin touched a key, bringing up a new picture. This one showed the same man, only this time wearing a far more stylish business suit. "But for the past several years, we have believed him to be a German national named Klaus Wernicke, a senior executive for Tekhwerk, GmbH."

Leonov's eyes narrowed. "How . . . *interesting*," he ground out.

"Indeed," Koshkin said flatly. Tekhwerk, GmbH was supposedly a jointly owned German and Russian import-export company specializing in advanced industrial equipment. Since its operations helped Russia evade Western sanctions, Moscow's law enforcement and regulatory agencies tended to allow it wide latitude, often turning a blind eye to its occasionally irregular business activities. If, as now seemed likely, the company was actually a front for Scion's spies operating on Russian soil, that had been an unforgivable error.

The computer chimed again. Two new images appeared—the first showing the attractive, blond-haired woman the Defense Ministry's digitized personnel files identified as Lieutenant Colonel Katya Volkova of the Aerospace Forces. The second showed what was unmistakably the same woman, only in this photo she wore elegant civilian business clothes and her hair was a dark red color.

"And this one?" Leonov asked grimly.

"She is also supposedly a German national."

Leonov snorted. "Who is also employed by Tekhwerk?" he guessed.

"Yes," Koshkin said. "According to her passport, her name is Erika Roth. Nominally, she's a corporate accounts executive—though based in Berlin, rather than here in Moscow." He sat back, looking pleased with himself. "It appears that the glittering lure of the Firebird's magical feathers has worked just as we hoped."

Leonov nodded. Besides helping create the illusion of a serious Russian program to develop its own version of America's spaceplanes, the Firebird test was also a trap. Q Directorate specialists had created two initially identical lists of those authorized to witness the Kansk-Dalniy demonstration flight—one protected by a tough, but hackable, security firewall, and the other, the real one, sheltered behind impenetrable barriers. A cross-check of both lists several hours ago had immediately revealed evidence of tampering . . . and the false identities being used by the two imposters.

Armed with that information and using concealed cameras rigged at various points around the airfield, Koshkin's experts had easily obtained a number of high-resolution photographs of "Lieutenant Colonel Valkova" and "Sergei Kondakov." These pictures were then fed into one of Q Directorate's supercomputers. Sophisticated facial recognition software first developed by a leading American high-tech company for the People's Republic of China made it possible to cross-check them against a large number of government and industry databases in near real time . . . yielding these more accurate identifications of the two Scion agents.

Leonov discounted the possibility that Wernicke and Roth were operatives for the CIA or one of the other Western intelligence services. The boldness and skill with which these two spies had infiltrated what was supposedly a top secret flight demonstration had all the hallmarks of a Scion operation. Government-run espionage organizations were far more cautious, hobbled by bureaucratic and political restrictions that inevitably reduced their effectiveness.

More information scrolled across Koshkin's screen. "Both agents arrived at Krasnoyark's Yemelyanovo International Airport this morning on a flight from Moscow," he reported. He smiled wryly. "Like everyone else genuinely invited to Kansk-Dalniy, they have tickets on a return flight to Sheremetyevo leaving this evening."

Leonov snorted his own amused understanding. Apparently, no one from Moscow would willingly spend an hour longer in a Siberian rural backwater than was absolutely necessary. Not even a couple of enemy agents.

For the first time, Viktor Kazyanov spoke up. "I can have an FSB team ready to arrest these spies at Sheremetyevo when they land," he suggested hesitantly.

"Absolutely not! Don't be an idiot!" Leonov snapped. He saw the other man's face turn gray with anxiety and sighed. Useful though Kazyanov's timidity was to him, watching him act more like a mouse than a man could still be extremely irritating.

"Look, Viktor, there's no point in spooking the Americans now," he explained patiently. "Remember, we want Wernicke and Roth to pass on the false information we've just fed them." He shook his head decisively. "No, we'll give these Scion agents plenty of room for the moment."

"While we dig deeply into Tekhwerk and *all* of its operations?" Koshkin suggested.

"That's exactly right, Arkady," Leonov agreed. He looked at both Koshkin and Kazyanov. "Understand this: I want a very thorough, but also extremely careful, investigation, gentlemen. Q Directorate will handle the cyber end of things, while the FSB does the physical legwork. But before you move in to make any arrests, make sure you've learned just how far this Scion front company has burrowed into our military and defense industry infrastructure."

He stabbed a finger at Koshkin's computer screen, which now showed new live pictures of the two foreign spies. They were standing side by side, looking up at the sky as the modified Tu-160 made its final approach back to the airfield. "Of themselves, those two are nothing. But if we play our cards right, they'll lead us right where we want to go. And when the time comes, I want Scion's whole Russia-based espionage network in the bag. *Here.* In the Lubyanka's basement cells . . . singing like birds while your interrogators work them over. Is that clear?"

"Perfectly clear, Marshal," Kazyanov said quickly. Koshkin merely nodded.

"Good." Leonov stood up. His jaw tightened. "Because it's high time we cut this damnable cancer out of the Motherland. Now get to it."

THIRTEEN

**EVOLUTION TOWER,
INTERNATIONAL BUSINESS CENTER, MOSCOW
A COUPLE OF HOURS LATER**

The weirdly twisting Evolution Tower soared more than eight hundred feet above the right bank of the Moskva River. Its odd, DNA-like double spiral was created by a slight, three-degree offset of each floor from the one below it. High up on one of the eastward-facing spirals, the large suite of offices leased by Tekhwerk, GmbH occupied a substantial share of the building's forty-second floor. From here the company's senior managers had sweeping views of Moscow's crowded city center. The shattered ruins of the Kremlin were plainly visible, as was the roof of the Lubyanka, just three and a half miles away.

Only a tiny handful of those working out of these offices understood the irony of the views they enjoyed. The vast majority of Tekhwerk's staff believed they were employed by a legitimate export-import company. And, in fact, well over 90 percent of its day-to-day operations were perfectly legal, or at least winked at by the ruling authorities. A byzantine web of holding companies and investment firms completely concealed Scion's ownership of the enterprise. As far as Kevin Martindale was concerned, it was icing on the cake that Tekhwerk's profits—largely derived from Russian government contracts—funded so many of Scion's covert-action and intelligence-gathering operations.

Zach Orlov was one of the few in on the secret. Supposedly a native Russian Tekhwerk information technology specialist, he had actually been born in the United States and he was one of Scion's top computer hackers. From his émigré parents, one a brilliant mathematician and the other an accomplished musician, he'd picked up perfect fluency in Russian. Gifted with high intelligence and focus, he'd been so bored in regular school that he'd spent most of his teenage years systematically and illegally breaking into every computer network he could access. If Martindale hadn't recruited him into Scion, it was probably a coin toss whether he'd have ended up behind bars—or working for the U.S. government's National Security Agency.

Unlike most of those on the forty-second floor, his office had no windows at all. Secure behind a keypad-controlled electronic lock, the room looked much smaller than it was—largely because almost all the available space was taken up by floor-to-ceiling racks of computer hardware. There was just enough room for a desk, chair, and a very large wastebasket usually full of crumpled paper coffee cups and takeout containers. Whenever Orlov was immersed in a complicated task, he rarely took any time off to sleep or eat . . . or even to change his clothes.

Right now, wearing a wrinkled polo shirt and dirty jeans, he sat hunched over a keyboard. While Sam Kerr and Marcus Cartwright were out in the field at Kansk-Dalniy, he'd been following a lead gained from hacking emails exchanged between a high-ranking Russian Space Forces officer and a production manager at Voronezh's KB Khimavtomatika (KBKhA), the Chemical Automatics Design Bureau.

KBKhA was one of Russia's leading high-tech companies. Its factories turned out everything from liquid-propellant rocket engines to nuclear space reactors to high-power lasers. That strongly suggested the company was somehow involved in Leonov's spaceplane program—most probably in advanced engine development. And several of its senior engineers and executives had been specially invited to the Firebird demonstration, which only made the connection seem more certain.

But what had really caught Orlov's attention was a cryptic reference in one of the emails to something called *Nebesnyy Grom,* Heaven's Thunder. He was willing to bet that was a code name for the high-powered hybrid turbofan-scramjet-rocket engines any real single-stage-to-orbit spaceplane needed. Once their engines entered production, Russians usually slapped on dull-as-dishwater numbers, like the RD-0150 . . . but nothing stopped them from indulging in a little romance while a project was still classified.

Since then, he'd been chasing down every possible reference to Heaven's Thunder. Most of them had dead-ended, but a few had led him to a top secret Russian Defense Ministry database. He was pretty sure it contained critical files pertaining to the Firebird Project. And for hours and hours, he'd been digitally prowling around its outskirts, looking for a way inside.

Unfortunately, this was as close as Orlov dared get. Whoever had designed its security firewall had done one hell of a job. From what he could tell, this database was essentially guarded by the computer equivalent of motion sensors, IR detection gear, radar, land mines, barbed wire, machine guns, flamethrowers, and heavy artillery—with a side order of nuclear weapons thrown in for good measure.

"Fucking Q-boys," he growled under his breath, taking his hands off the keyboard. He was pretty sure Q Directorate's specialists were the ones who'd sheathed this database in so many layers of digital death. Their coding work wasn't exactly discreet. It was more like they'd slapped on a bunch of garish neon signs blazing, "Abandon All Hope Ye Who Hack Here." Then again, he admitted to himself, their computer security work didn't have to be discreet, just effective.

Orlov shook his head in dismay. Short of Sam Kerr using her feminine wiles to charm the necessary passwords out of some lust-stricken Russian officer, there was no way in hell anyone from Scion was going to get a peek at those classified files. Not even an all-out, brute force hacking attack would break through those defenses.

Yawning, he sat back and rubbed at his tired eyes. They felt raw, like someone had been scraping them with sandpaper. No surprise, there, he thought blearily. The clock readout in the lower right corner of his monitor showed that he'd been working this angle for nearly twenty hours without a real break. Maybe it was time to punch out, grab some sleep, and come back at the problem fresh another day.

Still yawning, Orlov started to push back his chair . . . but then he froze in place, staring at his screen.

A red-outlined box had just flashed into existence: WARNING. INTRUSION ATTEMPTS DETECTED. INTRUSION ATTEMPTS ARE ONGOING.

He felt cold. Someone out there was trying to hack into Tekhwerk's own computer network. And whoever it was had just tripped hidden warning subroutines he'd buried very deeply in what would otherwise look like an ordinary corporate security firewall. Shit. Shit. Shit. Had his own reconnaissance of that special Defense Ministry database set off alarms he'd missed?

Then Orlov shook his head. That wasn't very likely. He'd been operating at arm's length through a linked series of zombie computers—machines he'd infiltrated months ago and now secretly controlled. Even if he'd triggered an alarm, there should be no way anyone could have traced him back here through all those cutouts. Not this fast, anyway.

Another series of alerts popped up. Now digital tripwires he'd planted in government and financial industry databases in both Russia and Germany were sending up flares. He swallowed hard. The people probing Tekhwerk's business activities were casting a very wide net.

For people, read Q Directorate, Orlov thought edgily. The hairs on the back of his neck rose . . . and he had to fight down a sudden urge to get up and run. In the shadowy internet world of binary 1s and 0s, he was used to being the hunter . . . not the hunted.

Acting on a sudden hunch, he opened a back door he'd planted in the Aeroflot computer reservations system and pulled up the Russian airline's ticketing and reservation information for Sam Kerr in her Lieutenant Colonel Katya Volkova persona. Sure enough, the hidden access counter he'd installed glowed bright red.

"Okay, this is bad. This is *really* bad," Orlov muttered to himself. Someone besides him had secretly reviewed those files within the past hour. And this wasn't just a routine Aeroflot query about passengers on its evening flight out from Krasnoyarsk's Yemelyanovo International Airport. Anyone using an official Aeroflot log-in wouldn't have triggered his counter. Which meant Sam's cover was blown.

A quick check of Marcus Cartwright's ticketing information showed the same thing.

Any hope Orlov had that Scion's Moscow-based intelligence team could just hunker down, play innocent, and ride out this sudden Q Directorate probe disappeared. Russia's security services weren't just mildly curious about Tekhwerk and its activities. They were actively prosecuting a full-on espionage investigation, and somehow they'd already tied both Sam and Marcus to the company . . . despite their carefully created cover stories and perfectly forged identity papers.

For what seemed like an hour, but couldn't really have been more than a minute or two, he sat motionless—mentally running through his options. Then he shrugged helplessly. In the end, there weren't many. This was basically an intelligence operative's nightmare. His priority right now was to try to minimize the damage. And then to get his ass safely out of Russia if at all possible. Like all Scion field agents, he had an escape and evasion kit, complete with new false papers and credit cards, and enough cash to bribe his way across the border if that proved necessary.

Orlov pulled out his smartphone. First, he needed to clue in Scion's upper echelons back in the United States. Quickly he connected to a special number and texted a two-word emergency code phrase: RED DAWN.

There was a short pause before the reply came back: CONFIRM RED DAWN.

Rapidly, he tapped in a reply, using the special alphanumerical code that confirmed he was acting on his own volition and not under enemy control: BRAVO ZULU

SIX. RED DAWN CONFIRMED. Any other combination of letters and numbers would have signaled that he was acting under duress.

This time the reply came faster: CLEARANCE LEVEL POSSIBLE?

Orlov contemplated that. Understandably, Martindale wanted to know how thoroughly he could "sanitize" the Moscow offices—destroying or removing any information that might compromise Scion operations and sources. A lot depended on how much time he had before Q Directorate gave up on breaking into his computer network and sent in the FSB goon squads. He shrugged. There was no easy answer for that question. Which, he decided, meant it was far better to be safe now, rather than sorry later inside a Lubyanka torture chamber. In answer, he typed in LEVEL TWO ONLY.

His office equipment included an industrial-grade shredder, so he could destroy his computers' solid-state hard drives as fast as he could strip them out of the machines. But there was no way he could completely sterilize the whole office complex, wiping away fingerprints and potentially incriminating DNA fragments. Not on his own. Doing a thorough job would have required the services of a whole specialist cleaning crew and at least a full day.

LEVEL TWO CLEARANCE APPROVED, Martindale

texted back. GOOD LUCK. THIS CONTACT NUMBER TER-
MINATES NOW.

You could practically see the man metaphorically
washing his hands, Orlov thought sardonically, just
like Pontius Pilate. He supposed it went with the territory. Spymasters who saw their agents more as people
than as pieces on a chessboard probably didn't stay sane
long.

Without wasting any more time, he moved on to
his next task. He dialed another number on his smartphone.

"Yes?" a lilting Welsh voice answered immediately.

"Davey, it's Zach. Listen carefully. Both Kerr and
Cartwright are blown. So is the office here. I don't
know how, exactly. But I'm bailing out ASAP, per orders. I suggest you do the same. Because as far as I can
tell, you're still in the clear."

Scion field agent David Jones, currently stationed in
Krasnoyarsk as the backup man for the Kansk-Dalniy
operation, was silent for a moment. "Are Sam and Marcus in enemy hands?"

Orlov shrugged his shoulders. "I don't know. But if
they aren't already in custody, it's gotta be because the
Russians have them on a string, waiting to see where
they go and who they contact."

"Right then," he heard the other man say slowly.

"Well, you'd best be off, Zach. I'll follow along after I do a bit of checking up on this end. With luck, I'll see you back in the States soon enough."

Orlov sighed, hearing the ironclad determination in Jones's voice. "You're not going to ditch them, are you? Even though getting out fast and on your own is the smart play?"

He heard the short, slender Welshman laugh softly. "Look, boyo, no one ever said I was terribly bright. See, Sam and Marcus and I have been in many a tight spot together over the years. So I owe it to them not to just cut and run. Not until I'm sure there's no hope at all of shaking them loose."

"You be careful, then," Orlov said quietly.

"As ever I can be," Jones agreed.

Sadly, Orlov tapped his phone, ending the call. He had a bad feeling that he would never hear from David Jones again.

FOURTEEN

ON THE AVTODOROGA BAYKAL (BAYKAL ROAD), SEVERAL KILOMETERS OUTSIDE KRASNOYARSK, RUSSIA
A SHORT TIME LATER

Sam Kerr tapped the brakes gently as soon as she saw the battered pale blue UAZ delivery van parked off on the shoulder of the tree-lined, two-lane highway. Their rented Mercedes sedan slowed in response—giving her time to read the crude, hand-lettered cardboard sign held up by the short, skinny young man standing beside the van. It read, NEED 520 RUBLES FOR PETROL. PLEASE HELP ME.

Five hundred rubles came to only about eight U.S. dollars, so that wasn't an extravagant request for money—if it had been genuine.

Her eyes automatically noted the sedan's current odometer reading as she sped back up and drove on past.

"We've got trouble," Marcus Cartwright said tersely.

Sam nodded. Seeing David Jones waiting for them with an emergency signal meant something, somewhere had gone very badly wrong. The 520 rubles on his sign indicated they were approximately 5.2 kilometers from the place he'd picked out for a covert rendezvous. A quick glance at her rearview mirror showed the Welshman climbing back into his van.

Five kilometers down the highway, they passed a gas station on the left. The next turnoff was a dirt road roughly two hundred meters farther on.

Sam took it, driving slowly uphill past a truckers' café and a run-down motel. There, not far ahead, was an apparently abandoned garage. Graffiti daubed its pitted concrete-block walls. A section of its rusted metal roof had fallen in at one corner, and there were no windows or doors left—just black openings into an unlighted interior strewn with moldering piles of junk and debris.

Not exactly a garden spot, she thought, but just the place for some quiet, unobserved conversation. She turned in next to the dilapidated building, following a winding, bumpy driveway choked with tall weeds.

Around the back, there were a couple of wrecked Ladas that had been stripped and left to rust out in the open a long time ago. She pulled the Mercedes in close beside them and turned off the ignition.

Two minutes later, Jones parked his blue delivery van behind the black rental sedan and clambered out from behind the wheel. Sam and Cartwright went over to meet him.

"How bad is it?" she asked.

"About as bad as bad can be," Jones told her bluntly. "The whole outfit's blown sky-high. You, Marcus there, and the Moscow office entirely."

They listened closely while he briefed them on Orlov's frantic call. "The only good thing I can see in this is that you're not being actively tailed right now," he finished.

"That's because the Russians know exactly where we're headed," Cartwright pointed out grimly.

Sam nodded. Since the FSB's counterintelligence officers knew they were both booked out on a flight to Moscow in a couple of hours, why risk alarming their quarry prematurely? As far as they knew, she and Marcus were still blissfully ignorant of the danger they were in . . . and would trot along to Krasnoyarsk's airport like good little lambs on their way to slaughter.

Which meant that was the last thing they should do,

she decided. Even if the Russians didn't plan to arrest them immediately, or as soon as they touched down at Moscow, it was still too risky to play along with the FSB's game. Once they were under close surveillance, shaking loose and evading capture would become almost impossible. Anyway, as soon as Q Directorate's hackers realized they weren't going to get anything useful out of the Tekhwerk computer network, the Russians were bound to come down on them fast and hard.

Cartwright agreed with her reasoning. "So what's your plan?" he asked.

"Step one is we ditch the Mercedes here," Sam said firmly. One corner of her mouth quirked upward in a short-lived, wry smile. "From the look of this dump, nobody's likely to stumble across it for a while. And I bet anyone who does is just as likely to strip the car for salable parts as they are to report it to the police."

Both men nodded. Cash was king in poverty-stricken, rural Russia . . . and certainly worth a lot more than a meaningless pat on the head from local law enforcement. Especially since poorly paid regional police officers might be equally tempted to consider the abandoned rental sedan as a treasure trove for themselves.

"And step two?" Cartwright wondered. "Because

all hell's going to break loose as soon as we miss our plane."

"There *are* going to be a number of seriously pissed-off FSB agents wondering where we've disappeared to," Sam agreed.

"Not to mention their bosses in Moscow," Cartwright said dryly.

"Them, too. Which is why the three of us need to be at least a couple of hundred kilometers away before that particular balloon goes up." She turned to Jones. "Does that piece of Russian-built crap you're driving still have its little hidey-hole?"

"It does," he said, with a nod of understanding. The UAZ delivery van had been used for a number of other Scion covert missions. And among its special features was a small passenger compartment hidden in the cargo space—concealed behind what looked like a floor-to-ceiling mass of shipping crates, boxes, and parcels.

"I'm not exactly built for this," Cartwright said, with a pained glance at the van.

Sam patted him on the shoulder. "File it under 'the sacrifices we make not to get caught,'" she said soothingly. Even for her, riding around inside that hidden compartment would be a tight squeeze. It would be far more painfully cramped for the big man. But they didn't have any other options, not if they wanted to keep out of sight while still putting distance between themselves and Krasnoyarsk . . . which would be ground zero for the inevitable FSB manhunt.

"We need to be far, far away, to be sure," Jones said. "But in which direction?"

"There's the rub," Sam said flatly. "As I see it, heading west or east is totally out."

The others nodded their agreement. Only one major east-west highway crossed this relatively sparsely populated region. Before trying to use it as an escape route, they might as well just drive straight up to the local FSB headquarters and surrender—because the end result would be the same.

Driving south was also a nonstarter, she decided. The road net in that direction was equally limited. Plus, going south would ultimately bring them squarely up against Russia's heavily guarded borders with the People's Republic of China and Mongolia . . . neither of which would offer sanctuary to Western intelligence agents with a price on their heads.

"We move north," Sam told them. "At least if we head that way, we can pick and choose among a few more local roads."

Cartwright frowned. "Roads to nowhere," he argued. "For Christ's sake, Sam, there's nothing north of here but Siberian forest, forest, and even more forest. Plus a few small and midsize towns, where any strangers—like us, for example—will be an instant sensation."

"I'm not saying it's ideal," she said with a slight sigh. "But north is still our best option. If nothing else, there are a number of logging and hunting cabins scattered through those woods that should be empty at this time of year. So we find one and hole up—at least for a day or two."

"And then what?" Jones asked seriously.

Sam sighed. "Then we hope like hell that Mr. Martindale can figure out some slick way to pull us out of Russia before the FSB's snatch teams figure out where we've gone to ground."

SCION SECURE VIDEOCONFERENCE
AN HOUR LATER

"Your secure audiovisual link is live," a Scion communications technician announced over the speakers. "We have a solid signal."

Brad McLanahan and Nadia Rozek-McLanahan saw the big LED screen on the wall of the Sky Masters conference room light up. Kevin Martindale and his father looked back at them from the passenger cabin of one of Scion's executive jets, currently somewhere high over the United States between here in Nevada and Washington, D.C. The image was slightly grainy, an inevitable consequence of the complicated process of bouncing encrypted signals between several different communications satellites.

"I'm glad to see you two," Martindale said without preamble. Despite the polite words, his face was grim. "Though I certainly wish the circumstances were happier."

Brad nodded somberly. He and Nadia had returned from their long and thoroughly enjoyable honeymoon— spent traveling across Europe and then various Caribbean islands—some weeks before. But then they'd plunged immediately into the day-to-day grind of helping Hunter Noble train U.S. Space Force crews for duty aboard new S-29 Shadow spaceplanes as they rolled out of Sky Masters production facilities and onto the flight line. They'd both been far too busy to keep an eye on the bigger picture . . . right up to the moment when emergency signals started blazing across Scion's secure com links with its operatives inside Russia.

"Where do we stand?" he asked.

"In a world of hurt, with no U.S. cavalry on tap to ride over the hill," his father said bluntly. Through his

LEAF's clear visor, Patrick's expression was equally bleak.

Martindale nodded his agreement. "Put simply, our intelligence operation inside Russia is royally screwed." He spread his hands. "At this point, it's pretty much just a matter of counting our losses."

Nadia leaned forward. "How so?" She raised an eyebrow. "My understanding was that Ms. Kerr and her team have evaded capture so far."

Though her voice would have sounded perfectly calm and in control to a stranger, Brad heard an undercurrent of narrowly suppressed anger. *Oh, boy,* he thought. Even at the best of times, Nadia had never particularly admired Martindale's seeming ability to detach himself emotionally from those who risked their lives at his orders.

"That's true, Major," Martindale said. He shrugged his shoulders. "For the moment, anyway."

"Meaning?" Nadia demanded.

Martindale's mouth tightened. "Meaning that their luck is bound to run out—and probably sooner, rather than later." He shook his head. "Look, I wish it wasn't so, but we have to face the cold, hard facts. Before too long, every counterintelligence and police officer between Vladivostok and Moscow will be hunting them.

And right now, Ms. Kerr and the others have almost nowhere left to run and very few places to hide."

"Then we must get them out as quickly as possible," Nadia said matter-of-factly. Brad nodded.

Martindale shook his head again. "Unfortunately, there's simply no feasible way to extract Sam's team." He opened a map file that mirrored in the corner of their screen. A red dot pulsed slowly just outside Krasnoyarsk, showing the Scion team's last reported position. "They're more than two thousand miles from the nearest friendly territory. Even if we could get a rescue aircraft that deep into Russia, past all the radars, SAM sites, and roving fighter patrols, the odds against anyone making it back out in one piece are astronomical. A four-thousand-mile round-trip flight through hostile airspace? That's a suicide mission."

"It'd be tough, sure. But not impossible," Brad argued. "It's been done before. Twice, in fact."

"True," Nadia said quietly. Three years ago, she and Brad had flown a covert ops team deep into the Ural Mountains, to carry out a raid against a heavily fortified Russian base. And although the assault team itself had suffered terrible losses, they'd returned safely to Poland, if only by a very narrow margin. Then, just last year, she and Peter Vasey had succeed in rescuing Brad himself from Russia's tightly guarded Pacific coast, after his spacecraft had been shot down while on a reconnaissance mission against the Mars One orbital station.

Martindale frowned. "It was one thing to risk lives and valuable equipment going after a vital strategic target, or even to retrieve someone whose head happened to be stuffed full of crucial information about our spaceplane technology. But the equation's significantly different in this situation, where most of the damage has already been done. Whatever happens to Sam Kerr and her team, the Russians are already in a position to roll up most of our intelligence network inside their country."

"The *equation?*" Now Nadia didn't bother hiding her disdain. "Is that how you see this? As a bloodless mathematical game where you assign values to human lives . . . and discard them if the numbers don't balance?"

"I call it like I see it, Major," Martindale said dispassionately. "Sam and the others are professionals. They knew the risks going in." His eyes were cold. "Let me be clear: I will not authorize some wild-eyed rescue mission that would only throw away more lives and more equipment. Our task now is to figure out how to save what we *realistically* can—and then to start thinking about how to rebuild our Russian operations once the heat dies down."

Quickly, before she could erupt, Brad laid a restraining hand on Nadia's arm. Surprised, she glanced at him. "Let me take this," he said. She nodded tightly.

"This question is not open for further discussion, Major McLanahan," Martindale warned.

"I don't plan to *discuss* anything," Brad continued quietly. "Whether you authorize it or not, Nadia and I are going to start prepping a mission to extract Sam and her team. And if it's at all doable, we're going." He noticed a quick look of approval cross his father's lined face.

Martindale's eyes narrowed. "That sounds a lot like mutiny."

Brad shrugged. "Call it what you like." He looked right into the camera. "Neither Nadia nor I are bean counters. We're soldiers." He smiled crookedly. "Though admittedly a little on the irregular side. And as soldiers, our code says you do *not* throw your people to the wolves just because the fucking cost-benefit ratio doesn't look favorable."

"If I fire you for insubordination, you won't have access to Scion-owned aircraft, weapons, or equipment," Martindale pointed out carefully.

"Yep, that's so," Brad said in agreement, without dropping his smile. "Then again, I bet we can talk Hunter Noble into letting us 'borrow' a few toys from the Sky Masters inventory if we have to." He looked the other man straight in the eye. "So it's your decision, Mr. Martindale: You can back us on this now, despite the risks. Or you can sit back and watch a pretty fair-sized fraction of your stateside operations team jump ship at the same time the shit's hitting the fan in Russia."

For a long, uncomfortable moment, Martindale sat quiet, glaring back at him out of the screen. Brad held his breath, wondering if he'd gone too far. He felt Nadia press her warm palm against his back, offering reassurance.

Then his father spoke up. "My son's right, Kevin. This isn't a fight you can win. For that matter, this isn't really a fight you should *want* to win. Sam Kerr and the others have obtained priceless intelligence for us in the past . . . and risked their lives in the process. We owe them a chance now, however small it may seem."

"*Et tu,* Patrick?" Martindale retorted.

With a whir of tiny exoskeleton motors, Patrick McLanahan held up an open hand. His face creased in a slight smile. "No dagger, see? Just the truth, as I see it."

Martindale grimaced. "Very well, then." His eyes were still cold. "Much as I dislike yielding to pure emotional blackmail, I'll make an exception in this case. This *one* case," he stressed. He turned back to

Nadia and Brad. "All right. You can prep your rescue mission."

"Thank you, sir," Brad said. "I appreciate this."

"Don't thank me too quickly, Major McLanahan," Martindale snapped. "You may have just bought yourself—and Nadia—a one-way ticket. If things go wrong out there, that's it. I will not risk any more lives on some damned fool crusade. Is that understood?"

"Yes, sir," Brad said evenly. "We'll do our best."

Martindale's angry expression softened slightly. "Oh, I don't doubt that." He sighed. "But I'm afraid that even your best isn't likely to be good enough. Not this time."

FIFTEEN

FEDERAL SECURITY SERVICE (FSB) HEADQUARTERS, THE LUBYANKA, MOSCOW
A COUPLE OF HOURS LATER

Frowning deeply, Viktor Kazyanov leaned over his desk, studying the priority report he'd just been sent. He flipped from one page to the next, hoping to find some buried nugget of good news that he could pass on to Russia's minister of defense. On paper, he and Leonov held equivalent cabinet ranks, but he was shrewd enough to see the way the wind was blowing. Where it counted, in military, space, and intelligence affairs, the other man was already effectively president in all but formal title—and that was probably only a matter of time and inclination.

He looked up, irritated, when one of his aides burst in without knocking. "What is it, Ivanov?"

"Minister, it's Marshal—"

Leonov himself barreled in right on Ivanov's heels. He jerked a thumb toward the exit. "Get out. And close that door behind you." Flustered, Ivanov obeyed.

Kazyanov took a short, quick breath. "It's good to see you, Mikhail Ivanovich—"

"Spare me the usual, meaningless pleasantries," Leonov said bluntly. "My health is good. Your grandchildren are blossoming. And the weather outside is pleasant. All true?"

Quickly, Kazyanov nodded. "Yes."

"Fine. Then let's get to work." Leonov took one of the seats in front of Kazyanov's desk and nodded pointedly at the minister's own chair. "Sit down, Viktor. Stop bouncing around like your shoes are on fire." With a sigh, Kazyanov obeyed. "Well," Leonov demanded. "What's the situation?"

For a moment, Kazyanov wrestled with the temptation to shade the truth, to give it some patina of optimism—however thin. He pushed the idea aside. Like Gennadiy Gryzlov before him, Leonov was not a man it was safe to mislead. In many ways, the defense minister's carefully controlled, cold-eyed anger was even more frightening than his predecessor's wild, raging tantrums. Kazyanov indicated the report from his team in Krasnoyarsk. "In all honesty, the situation is not good."

"Go on."

"Wernicke and Roth, or whoever they really are, did not turn up for their scheduled flight forty-five minutes ago," Kazyanov admitted reluctantly. "My people have just finished going through all the security camera footage from Yemelyanovo. There's no sign of them."

Leonov grunted. "They had a rental car, correct?"

"A black Mercedes sedan," Kazyanov confirmed, paging through the report. "Hired by the Roth woman in her pose as this fictional Lieutenant Colonel Volkova." He looked up. "The car has not yet been returned to the agency."

Leonov nodded heavily. "Of course not." His fingers drummed briefly on the other man's desk. "And Koshkin's *komp'yutershchiks*? Have they been able to break into Tekhwerk's computer networks?"

"Not yet," Kazyanov admitted. "Arkady says his tech geeks are being extremely cautious. Apparently, the security software guarding those networks is effective. Remarkably effective."

"It would be," Leonov said dryly. He frowned.

"What about your teams surveilling the company's Moscow office? Are they, too, being careful?"

"Very careful," Kazyanov assured him hurriedly. His face clouded over. "But it's an extraordinarily difficult task, Mikhail Ivanovich. The Evolution Tower complex is enormous. Thousands of people work there. And there are multiple exits, including several directly to the Vystavochnaya metro station and the Bagration Bridge." He shrugged. "If I could deploy my surveillance teams inside the building itself—?"

"They would probably be spotted in minutes," Leonov pointed out. Gloomily, Kazyanov nodded.

"Not that it matters much," Leonov said grimly. "All of this clever tiptoeing around . . . at Krasnoyarsk, on the internet, and here in Moscow . . . it's all been a complete waste of time and effort."

"You think the American agents know their cover is blown?" Kazyanov asked.

Leonov nodded. "Why else would they miss their flight back to Moscow?" He shook his head. "No, Viktor. Somehow, in some way, they've been tipped off. Maybe Arkady's tech geeks tripped some computer alarm. Or maybe they spotted some of your people watching the airport and got cold feet." He shrugged. "How we fucked up isn't really important. Not now."

"But these Scion agents can't possibly escape," Kazyanov said, desperately hoping he was right. "Where can they go from Krasnoyarsk?"

Leonov snorted. "Krasnoyarsk isn't a black hole, Viktor. There are roads and railroads and rivers into and out of the city. So the Americans certainly *will* escape, if we don't pull our fingers out of our asses and get to work hunting them down." He checked his watch. "Assuming the worst, that they learned we were onto them as soon as Koskhin's people tried probing their computers, they've already been on the run for at least three or four hours."

"*Mater' Bozh'ya,*" Kazyanov muttered. "Mother of God." He pulled up a map of the region on his computer. "They could easily be a couple of hundred kilometers away by now. Or more."

"Exactly." Leonov nodded. "Which is why we need to cast our nets as widely as possible."

Studying the map, Kazyanov whistled softly. "That's going to take an enormous amount of manpower."

"No question about that," Leonov agreed. "We'll need to mobilize every police officer in the region, units from the National Guard, and more troops from the regular armed forces." He stood up. "Your FSB teams will coordinate the search inside Krasnoyarsk itself, in case the Americans have gone to ground at a safe house inside the city."

Kazyanov nodded quickly. "Yes, Marshal."

"Start distributing the photographs of Wernicke and Roth, in both of their identified personas," Leonov ordered. "Along with a description of their rental car." He showed his teeth in a tight, humorless grin. "If, as I suspect, Scion is already reeling in its espionage networks, capturing them alive is probably our best remaining hope of learning how many of our precious secrets the Americans already know."

Again, Kazyanov nodded obsequiously. "We'll find them," he vowed.

Leonov's answering laugh was harsh. "You shouldn't give so many hostages to fortune, Viktor," he said icily. "Whoever these Scion spies really are, they're the first team. So they aren't going to be easy to run to ground."

JUST OUTSIDE LESOSIBIRSK,
ALONG THE YENISEI RIVER, RUSSIA
AN HOUR LATER

Looking ahead along the beams of his van's headlights, David Jones saw the pair of white-and-blue police patrol cars parked sideways across each shoulder of the narrow two-lane highway. Two officers in yellow reflective vests stood in the center of this hurriedly improvised checkpoint, waving flashlights as they signaled him to stop.

A thin screen of birch trees lined both sides of the road, their narrow trunks glowing a pale, ghostly white in the light of the slowly rising full moon. Not a bad spot to set up a roadblock, he thought coolly. Short of trying a wild bootlegger's reverse and peeling back out the way he'd just come, he didn't have any option but to obey.

Playing it safe, Jones braked smoothly and rolled to a complete stop only a few feet away from the waiting police officers. Raising his voice slightly, so that only his concealed passengers could hear him, he said, "We're at a checkpoint. Stay cool. I've got this."

He unrolled his window as the officers approached, splitting up to cover both sides of the UAZ van. The policeman coming around the passenger side kept his hand on the butt of his holstered 9mm pistol. The other had an open notebook and a pencil. He was already jotting down the vehicle's license number and appearance.

"Hey there," Jones called out, in flawless Russian. "What's up?"

"Nothing much. Just a routine matter," the officer with the notebook said calmingly. He held out a hand. "May I see your license?"

Routine, my ass, Jones thought cynically, fishing out his driver's license. This cop wasn't a very good liar.

He kept quiet while the policeman recorded his information. Talking too much was the fastest way to trip yourself up when dealing with the Russian authorities.

With a nod of thanks, the officer handed his license back. "So, where are you headed?"

Jones shrugged. "Lesosibirsk. I've got a bunch of deliveries to make."

The Russian policeman frowned. "A little late, isn't it? Most places will be closed by now."

"Yeah," Jones agreed, smiling ruefully. "I got fucked by heavy traffic coming into Krasnoyarsk. I'll have to lay over tonight and drop the packages off tomorrow morning."

"Are you staying in a hotel? Or a guesthouse?"

Jones laughed sourly. "Does this piece-of-shit van look like my boss would spring for a hotel room?" He sighed. "Nah, I'll probably just park off the road somewhere in town and try to catch some sleep on the seat here." He donned a worried look. "I mean, if that's not going to be a problem for you guys?"

The policeman shook his head. "Not as long as you don't block traffic." He flipped to a new page of his notebook. "Now, just for our records, where exactly are you making those deliveries tomorrow?"

Thankful for the internet and Sam's insistence that he build a halfway decent cover story, Jones handed over a clipboard with several local businesses listed—a restaurant, a couple of retail shops, and one of the big wood-processing plants that were the town's economic mainstay. But it was still disturbing to see the police officer writing them down in his notebook. On the other hand, Russia's bureaucrats, like those of every country, thrived on compiling useless statistics . . . so with luck, those names would end up moldering away in some dusty file folder in the local government archives.

With a disinterested nod, the officer gave the clipboard back.

"Is that it?" Jones asked.

"Just one more thing," the policeman said, with obviously feigned nonchalance. He pulled a sheaf of glossy color printer pages out of the back of his notebook and handed them over. "Have you seen either of those two people recently? In Krasnoyarsk? Or on the way here?"

Jones stared down at the color photographs of both Sam Kerr and Marcus Cartwright for a moment, fighting to keep his first startled reaction from showing. *Jesus*, he thought, the Russians had a whole bloody fashion portfolio on the two Scion agents. No wonder Tekhwerk's cover was blown to smithereens. But then he shook his head as he gave them back. "No, I haven't." He donned a small leer. "And I'd definitely have noticed a sexy-looking woman like that blonde. Is she some kind of high-class hooker?"

"No, a suspected drug smuggler," the policeman said tersely. He stuck the photos back in his notebook. "How about a black Mercedes four-door sedan? Registration plate K 387OC 124?"

"Back in Krasnoyarsk? Maybe, but I wouldn't swear to it," Jones said slowly, as if thinking deeply. "But heading this way?" He shrugged. "It seems like all I've seen for the last hundred kilometers are logging trucks."

The officer nodded. The timber industry was this isolated region's lifeblood. He scribbled a mobile phone number on a torn sheet from his pad. "If you do see either of those people . . . or their Mercedes . . . call that number immediately. Got it?" He smiled. "There's a big fat reward involved."

With a grateful smile, Jones tucked the phone number in his shirt pocket. "Will do."

"All right, then," the officer said, stepping back and waving him on. "You can go. Drive safe now."

Nodding cheerfully, Jones put his van in gear and drove on through the checkpoint. But his smile vanished as soon as he drove around a bend. Discovering that the Russians were already searching for Sam and Marcus this far north of Krasnoyarsk—nearly two hundred miles—was seriously alarming. Any search spread that widely had to involve hundreds, perhaps even thousands, of police and internal security troops. Which meant the men in Moscow wanted them very badly indeed.

With a cold shiver, the Welshman had the sudden, eerie impression that the moonlit forest around him was stirring, coming magically to life in the silvery half-light. It was as if the witches of Russian myth were summoning the trees themselves out of their age-old slumber to join in the hunt for them.

"Oh, stop scaring yourself, Davey," he muttered crossly. "You're not in one of your old grannie's ghost stories." Scowling, he hunched over the steering wheel, forcing his attention back onto the narrow highway unrolling in his high beams. This was no time to indulge in wild fantasies. Not when he still had several more hours of hard driving left to reach the cabin Sam had picked out as a possible safe house . . . with the last bit certain to be the hardest of all, feeling his way along a maze of rutted dirt logging trails in the pitch dark.

But out there in the darkness beyond the van's wavering headlights, at the very edge of his vision, he couldn't help sensing a lurking malevolence—as though the whole countryside and every man's hand were now turned against them.

SIXTEEN

Until last year, Major Ian Schofield had led the Iron Wolf Squadron's commando teams, training them in the dark arts of ambush, long-range reconnaissance, and sabotage carried out deep inside enemy territory. Now the lean, wiry Canadian did much the same thing for Scion itself.

He'd been leading his most recent group of Scion recruits, all of them already veterans from half a dozen of the free world's best special forces units, through an intensive wilderness survival course when the emergency call from Battle Mountain came in. Ferried by

helicopter to this remote city only a few hundred kilometers south of the Arctic Circle, he'd barely had time
to wash up and change before hustling back to the edge
of the flight line.

NORAD's Forward Operating Location Yellowknife was a secure military hangar complex sited
immediately adjacent to the civilian airport. One of
four similar small facilities built across Canada's far
northern frontier, it was intended to strengthen the
sparsely populated region's air defenses. Currently,
two Canadian CF-18 Hornet fighters were on standby
here, forward-deployed to deter long-range Russian
reconnaissance flights over the polar region.

"That aircraft you're waiting for is on final approach,
Major," the Royal Canadian Air Force warrant officer
assigned as his escort said helpfully. "It's coming in low
over the Great Slave Lake."

Obediently, Schofield swung his binoculars to the
southeast. Even this late, past ten at night, there was still
plenty of light. Sharp-edged shadows slanted past him
across the tarmac. The sun, a fiery orange ball, was at
his back—hanging just above the northwest horizon.
This close to the Arctic Circle, late summer days were
long and the nights were very short.

He squinted, fiddling with the focus, while he
zoomed in on a black batwing-configured aircraft

descending rapidly toward Yellowknife's Runway 28. Four large engines were buried in the wing's upper surface, and he caught just a quick flash of gold-tinged sunlight reflecting off a cockpit canopy.

"I don't recognize the type," the Canadian airman beside him commented.

Schofield's teeth gleamed white in a face weathered by years spent outdoors in all climates and seasons. "You wouldn't," he said cheerfully. "It's quite literally the only one of its kind."

"And if you told me more—"

"I'd have to kill you," Schofield said, sounding even more cheerful. "Though of course with the greatest regret."

As the approaching aircraft crossed the lake's rocky shoreline and flew low over Yellowknife's city streets and houses, the muffled roar of its engines diminished sharply. Several control surfaces whined open on the wing's trailing edge, providing more lift as its airspeed decreased. A nose gear and twin wing-mounted bogies swung smoothly down and locked in position.

By the time it was around a mile from the runway, the plane seemed to be almost gliding noiselessly— skimming along barely above bare granite outcroppings and scattered stands of pine and spruce. It came in very low over the white striped lines that marked the threshold . . . and touched down with just a puff of light gray smoke from its landing gear. Immediately, those big engines powered back up, howling shrilly as the pilot sharply reversed thrust and braked. Amazingly, it rolled to a complete stop in less than a thousand feet.

Beside Schofield, the RCAF warrant officer muttered, "Good Christ, that was—"

Schofield coughed meaningfully.

"Something I didn't see," the warrant officer finished.

"I do appreciate a fast learner," Schofield said with approval.

Together, they watched the black flying wing taxi farther down Runway 28, make a sharp left turn onto the airport's longer main runway, and keep rolling—obviously heading for the taxiway to the NORAD base. As it got closer, its true dimensions were more apparent. The aircraft was roughly the size of one of Scion's Gulfstream 600 business jets, though its overall configuration made it look more like a miniature B-2 Spirit stealth bomber.

Schofield turned to his guide. "I believe this is where you make yourself scarce, Warrant Officer McNeil."

"Yes, sir."

Schofield shook hands with the younger Canadian

and then handed him a business card. It was blank, except for a telephone number. "If you ever get bored with service in the regular armed forces, ring that number," he suggested. "We're always on the lookout for able and discreet people."

Five minutes later, he paced alongside the midsize jet aircraft as it slowly taxied into an empty hangar. Then he stood quietly off to the side, waiting while the hangar's big doors rolled closed, sealing them away from any curious, prying eyes. The low rumble from its engines died away, leaving only silence.

Moments later, a hatch opened below the cockpit and a short crew ladder unfolded. Wearing a black flight suit, Brad McLanahan slid down the ladder. He turned lithely at the bottom and helped Nadia through the hatch. With his arms still wrapped around her slender waist, he set her down gently on the hangar floor, where she stood perched on the tips of her carbon-fiber running blades. For a moment, the two of them just stood there, entwined.

Schofield cleared his throat loudly.

Brad swung toward him with a grin. "Hey, Ian." He took in the other man's neatly pressed battle dress. "I'm sorry that I had to pull you away from your training exercise."

"It was hard to leave all that lovely muck and mire behind," Schofield said complacently. "But sacrifices must sometimes be made."

They walked out from under the fuselage to join him. On the way, Brad proudly patted the aircraft's black radar-absorbent coating. "So, what do you think of her?" he asked. "A beaut, isn't she?"

"I *thought* this was my old friend, the Ranger stealth transport aircraft," Schofield said carefully. He, Brad, and Nadia had served together on three high-risk covert missions over the past several years—the first to attack Perun's Aerie, a cyberwar complex buried in the Ural Mountains, the second to hunt down and destroy Russia's war robots rampaging inside the United States itself, and the third, just last year, to pull Brad himself out of enemy territory. All three missions had been flown using a Sky Masters–designed stealthy, short takeoff and landing (STOL) tactical airlifter, the XCV-62 Ranger. "But up close, this particular aircraft seems . . . well, *bigger.* Especially those engines."

"Your grasp of the technical aspects of military aviation is, as always, eye-opening," Brad said with a laugh.

"He means that you are right, Ian," Nadia explained helpfully.

Brad nodded. "You're actually looking at the XCV-70 Rustler."

"Another of Sky Masters' experimental prototypes?" Schofield asked.

"Yep," Brad said. "Boomer set the design process in motion right after he read our classified after-action report on Perun's Aerie. He figured some improvements might be welcome."

Schofield nodded, remembering the risks they'd been forced to run, thanks to the older aircraft's inherent limitations. While it was a remarkable machine for its day, the Ranger's comparatively low subsonic speed, relative lack of maneuverability, and inability to carry any offensive weapons were serious disadvantages once things got hot. "I assume Dr. Noble and his design team succeeded?"

"Oh, hell yeah," Brad said with undisguised enthusiasm. "The Rustler's just as stealthy and STOL-capable . . . but she's got significantly more range and a hell of a lot more power. At least in short bursts." He pointed to the aircraft's four large wing-buried engines. "Each of those GE Affinity engines produces four thousand more pounds of thrust than the Rolls-Royce Tay 620-15 turbofans mounted on the XCV-62. Plus, they're supersonic-capable."

"But only at the cost of a considerable expenditure of fuel," Nadia reminded him.

Undaunted, Brad shrugged. "Sure, there's always a

trade-off. TANSTAAFL, right? 'There ain't no such thing as a free lunch,'" he quoted.

Schofield nodded his understanding. Aircraft design was always a blend of compromises between speed, maneuverability, sturdiness, range, and, in this age, stealth. Significantly improving one aspect of a plane's performance almost invariably entailed accepting somewhat weaker performance in other areas.

"The other good news is that we're not going in unarmed this time," Brad continued. He indicated two internal bays on the underside of the XCV-70's fuselage. "Besides the usual array of defenses—SPEAR, flares, and chaff—we can carry offensive weapons, a mix of heat-seeking air-to-air missiles and air-to-ground ordnance."

"Very nice, indeed," Schofield said with real feeling. In previous missions, he'd intensely disliked the sensation of being a helpless passenger strapped into the Ranger's troop compartment. Knowing that the Ranger itself was equally unable to fight back under enemy attack had made that feeling even worse. "So, when all's said and done, this XCV-70 Rustler of yours is faster, longer-ranged, and has teeth of its own." Brad nodded with a grin. "And the trade-off for all of that is?" Schofield asked.

"Significant reductions in the aircraft's cargo and

passenger capacity," Nadia informed him. "Where the XCV-62 could carry twelve of your troops or three of Iron Wolf's combat robots, the Rustler has room for only a small fire team, no more than four soldiers . . . or just a single Cybernetic Infantry Device."

Schofield raised an eyebrow. "Four passengers total?"

"Yep," Brad said.

"And we're flying in to extract a three-person Scion intelligence unit?"

Brad nodded again. "Uh-huh."

Elaborately, Schofield looked around the otherwise empty hangar as if noticing for the first time that he was alone. He turned back to the other man. "So if things go sour while the aircraft's on the ground inside Russia—?"

"You'd be our private, one-man field army," Brad acknowledged solemnly.

"You know, Brad," Schofield said carefully, "much as I relish a reputation for working miracles, there are limits."

"I'll bear that in mind," the younger man promised. "Look, I won't lie. The margin's pretty thin on every part of this mission. We'll be riding a razor's edge practically from the moment we take off. Given that, this is strictly a volunteer gig. If you want out, no harm, no foul."

"But the two of you are going anyway? With me, or without me?" Schofield asked, eyeing Nadia. "Despite the risks?"

She nodded. "Brad and I have worked through the mission plan to the best of our ability, Ian." She shrugged her shoulders slightly. "It will be dangerous. And very difficult. But I do not believe that it is necessarily impossible."

Schofield sighed. "Put like that, how can I refuse? Count me in."

SEVENTEEN

NATIONAL DEFENSE CONTROL CENTER, MOSCOW
A SHORT TIME LATER, MORNING (LOCAL TIME)

In the last years of his rule, Gennadiy Gryzlov had ordered the construction of a massive new military command center on the northern bank of the Moskva River, within a few kilometers of the Kremlin. Completed at enormous cost, the huge complex was supposed to demonstrate the growing power and sophistication of Russia's armed forces—both to bolster domestic public opinion and to frighten potential enemies. Nightly news programs had featured reports showing off vast, futuristic-looking control rooms, complete with IMAX-sized situation display screens and dozens of computer stations, all manned by dedicated young officers.

Now those rooms were empty, gathering dust.

For all their high-tech glamour, those overcrowded auditoriums had proved to be worse than useless during any real military crisis. Between the dizzying array of maps, status reports, and combat footage flashing across huge theater screens, and the hubbub created by a large audience of thoroughly useless subordinates, they were only breeding grounds for chaos and confusion.

Instead, Marshal Mikhail Leonov had established his own Defense Ministry command post far belowground. Surrounded by both human guards and automated defenses, it was much smaller—with just four workstations, one for him and three more for his chief deputies. Secure video links connected him to key military and intelligence service commands, including the FSB's headquarters and Q Directorate.

He glowered at the screens. The Scion spies they were hunting seemed to have disappeared into thin air. FSB officers had found the enemy agents' abandoned rental car behind a derelict garage on the road between Kansk and Krasnoyarsk. In all probability, that meant there was a third Scion operative in the region, a backup man or woman with another vehicle. He'd issued new orders to all the police checkpoints taking that into account. Beyond that, there was nothing more he could do but wait.

A secure phone beeped. One of Leonov's aides answered it and then swung toward him. "It's Minister of State Security Kazyanov, sir. He's requesting an immediate video connection."

"Put him through."

Kazyanov's broad face blinked into existence on one of his screens. He looked excited. "We've found something, Mikhail Ivanovich! Last night, the police stopped a van at a checkpoint outside Lesosibirsk. The driver claimed he was making deliveries to a number of businesses in the area. Since he appeared to be alone, they let him proceed after routine questioning. Fortunately, one of the local officers decided to check up on his story this morning—"

"Let me guess," Leonov interjected. "None of the customers the driver named received any packages."

"Correct."

"Has this fake delivery van passed through any of our other checkpoints north of Lesosibirsk?" he asked. Kazyanov shook his head. "So now we know where to concentrate our search," Leonov said with satisfaction. His eyes narrowed in thought. "I want the police and other local authorities to scour Lesosibirsk and the nearest villages. They know the ground better than anyone we can bring in from the outside."

"That's true," Kazyanov said. He hesitated only momentarily. "And the outlying areas? Who will search them? Between old logging huts and hunting cabins, there must be dozens of possible hiding places scattered through those woods."

Leonov nodded grimly. "I'm aware of that, Viktor." He opened another secure channel, this one to the headquarters of Russia's Central Military District in Yekaterinburg. "This is Defense Minister Leonov. Put me through to Lieutenant General Varshavsky. It's urgent."

He looked back at Kazyanov. "We'll let the army handle the job. Between them, Varshavsky's Third Guards Special Purpose Brigade and the National Guard's Nineteenth Special Purpose Detachment *Ermak* can deploy several hundred Spetsnaz troops and at least a dozen helicopters." He shrugged. "If the American spies are hiding in those forests, our soldiers will dig them out."

After he'd issued his orders to Varshavsky, Leonov broke the connection and sat back thinking hard. Was he missing something? His breath caught for a moment. What if Scion planned to fly its agents out? The same way the Americans had covertly retrieved their downed spaceplane pilot from Russia's Far East during the Mars One crisis?

Leonov shook his head in disbelief. It seemed impossible. The distances involved were much greater:

the Krasnoyarsk region was well over four thousand kilometers from any American or American-allied airfield. No known short takeoff and landing aircraft had that kind of range. Not even the stealthy transport plane the Iron Wolf mercenaries had used before in raids against the Motherland.

Still, he decided, it would be a grave mistake to dismiss this possibility altogether. Time and again the Americans had shown themselves willing to run almost insane risks. He opened another secure video link, this one to Colonel General Semyon Tikhomirov. Once his deputy, Tikhomirov had moved up to full command of the Aerospace Forces.

The connection went through in seconds.

"Yes, sir?" the other man asked.

"Contact the 712th Guards Fighter Aviation Regiment at Kansk-Dalniy. I want four MiG-31s on ready alert. And make sure the radar stations in our Arctic defense zone are fully operational. If they pick up even the faintest low-altitude blip on their scopes, I want to know about it immediately!"

EIGHTEEN

SCION SEVEN-ZERO, OVER THE ARCTIC OCEAN, NORTH OF NUNAVUT, CANADA
A FEW HOURS LATER

Twenty thousand feet above the Arctic Ocean, the XCV-70 Rustler stealth transport flew northeast in close formation with a much larger aircraft—a Sky Masters–owned 767 aerial tanker. The two planes were connected by the tanker's refueling boom. They were fifteen hundred nautical miles and a little more than three hours outward bound from Yellowknife. While the Rustler still had plenty of jet fuel remaining when it arrived at this midair refueling rendezvous, the immense distances they would have to fly to complete this mission ruled out turning toward Russia with anything but full tanks.

"*Scion Seven-Zero, this is Masters Two-Four, pressure disconnect,*" the boom operator aboard the 767 radioed. Brad knew that boom operator was several thousand miles away at a remote console, as were the pilots of that unmanned tanker. "*You're topped off and good to go.*"

"Copy that, Two-Four," Brad McLanahan replied from the Rustler's left-hand pilot's seat. He felt a quick *CL-CLUNK* as the boom nozzle slid back out of the slipway and retracted. "Thanks for the gas. Clearing away now."

Immediately, he tweaked his engine throttles back and pushed his stick forward a tad, lowering the aircraft's nose a couple of degrees. The roar from their big GE Affinity turbofans decreased as they descended a few hundred feet. At the same time, the bigger air tanker accelerated and climbed away from them, already banking as it made a gentle right turn back toward the distant Greenland coast.

Far below the two rapidly separating aircraft, Arctic ice floes stretched away in all directions. Lit by the midnight sun, they were rippling sheets of dazzling pure white broken only by narrow cracks of dark blue open water.

"Our promised Trojan horse is right where it is supposed to be," Nadia announced from the right-hand seat. She was flying as Brad's copilot and systems operator. Currently, one of her big multifunction displays was set to show all air contacts within several hundred miles. Most were civilian flights with active transponders and in communication with air traffic control centers in Canada, Greenland, Alaska, and northern Russia.

Thanks to a highly advanced data-link system comparable to those equipping F-35 Lightning II fifth-generation fighters, her computers could fuse information gathered from a wide range of friendly ground- and space-based sensors into a single coherent picture. As a result, freed from any immediate need to activate its own powerful radar, the Rustler could fly safely through even crowded airspace without giving its position away, cloaked in electromagnetic silence.

She tagged one of those air contacts on her display. Within milliseconds, the data-link system transferred its position, heading, and observed airspeed to the XCV-70's flight computer. A green line appeared, connecting them to the aircraft she'd selected. "Intercept course generated," she reported.

Instantly, a new steering cue blinked onto Brad's HUD. It was high up and sliding fast to the left across his field of vision.

"Turning to intercept," he said. He pushed his

throttles forward to full military power and pulled back and to the left on the stick. G-forces pushed them back against their seats as the Rustler rolled into a steep, climbing turn—chasing after the tagged air contact as it arrowed toward the north high above them.

Steadily, the steering cue moved back toward the center of Brad's HUD. Glowing green brackets appeared, highlighting a distant silvery dot against the pale blue sky. He rolled back out of his turn, but kept the XCV-70's nose up—soaring through thirty thousand feet and on past forty thousand feet before leveling off just above the altitude of the other aircraft. Their airspeed increased to 520 knots.

As they closed in, the tiny dot visible through the cockpit canopy grew bigger and took on more definition. Abruptly, it shifted to become the clearly recognizable shape of a very large, multi-engine aircraft painted in bright white and yellow stripes. "The contact is a Traveler Air Freight 747-8 cargo plane," he said.

"Copy that," Nadia confirmed.

Traveler Air Freight was another of Kevin Martindale's shell companies. Ordinarily he used its aircraft to discreetly ferry supplies, equipment, and personnel to various Scion teams operating covertly around the globe. But today's flight had a very different purpose.

Brad kept his left hand on the Rustler's throttles as they flew in behind the enormous wide-body cargo jet. Numbers appeared on his HUD, showing the distance between their two aircraft. Those numbers decreased rapidly at first and then slower as he reduced power, reducing the XCV-70's rate of closure. He was careful to stay slightly above the 747 to avoid running into any wake turbulence curling off its wings.

"Two hundred yards. Vertical separation one hundred feet," Nadia said quietly, counting down the remaining distance from her own station. "Our airspeed is now five hundred knots. Ten knots closure."

The Rustler shuddered slightly, buffeted by turbulence.

"One hundred yards. Vertical separation sixty feet."

Brad eased back even more on the throttles.

"Five knots closure." Nadia reported. She glanced across the cockpit. "Just how close are you planning to come?"

"Right . . . about . . . here," Brad said, scissoring a little from side to side to slow down and match the big 747's airspeed. Satisfied, he leveled out.

They were now hanging back only fifty to sixty feet behind and just slightly above the larger aircraft's tail assembly. That might not qualify as tight formation flying by the standards of a military aerobatics team like the Air Force's Thunderbirds or the Navy's Blue Angels, but it felt awfully close considering the size of both aircraft . . . and the fact that the 747's crew didn't have any real way to keep track of his position. Intellectually, he knew this wasn't much different from carrying out an air-to-air refueling, but tanking up from a Sky Masters KC-767 or KC-10 Extender was an operation that usually required only five to ten minutes . . . and there was always a boom operator ready to warn the tanker pilot if anything went wrong. To successfully pull off the stunt he had in mind, he'd need to stick like glue to the big Boeing-built jet for the next three and a half hours.

"You *said* you wanted to get close enough to count their rivets," Nadia said accusingly. She made a pretense of peering through the canopy. "Well, I cannot yet make out any rivets on that 747."

"That was mere poetic license, Mrs. Major Rozek-McLanahan," Brad said, with a smile concealed by his oxygen mask. "Trust me, this is more than close enough."

The truth was that the mammoth Traveler Air Freight 747-8 looming up ahead wasn't carrying any Scion weapons, explosives, or other gear in its cargo holds. Not on this trip anyway. Instead, its sole mission was to smuggle them into Russian airspace.

Like most military and espionage stratagems, Brad's plan was simple enough on paper—but very difficult to successfully pull off in practice. They were tucked up close enough to blend the Rustler's minimal radar signature with that of the much larger cargo jet. If everything worked right, Russia's probing air defense radars should see them only as a single, innocent commercial aircraft transiting the internationally recognized Polar Route 1 on its way to Mumbai in India.

After the collapse of the Soviet Union, the world's passenger and freight airlines were quick to recognize the enormous potential savings in time and fuel offered by routing aircraft over the Arctic and through previously off-limits Russian airspace. Within several years, a series of international agreements had opened specific, narrowly defined air corridors to declared civilian traffic.

Polar Route 1 was one of the busiest, with dozens of air transits every day. It opened north of Greenland and then ran almost due south across Russia—conveniently crossing high over Krasnoyarsk—before entering Chinese airspace on its way to India.

Mentally, Brad crossed his fingers. Either this gambit worked . . . or this would turn out to be one of the shortest and most futile rescue efforts in Scion's covert operations history. He glanced toward Nadia. "Time to the edge of the Murmansk flight information region?"

She checked her nav display. "At this speed, five minutes."

Brad buckled down to the job of keeping their aircraft slotted right behind the 747. Pockets of local turbulence affected the smaller, lighter XCV-70 more than they did the huge Boeing cargo jet. So it took constant adjustments to his flight controls to stay in formation.

Beside him, Nadia tuned to the radio frequency being used by the Traveler Air jet.

Not long afterward, they heard, *"Traveler Five-Five Three, Edmonton Center,"* through their headsets. *"Monitor VHF one-two-six point nine. At DEVID, contact Murmansk Oceanic Center, eight-nine-five-zero primary, one-one-three-nine-zero secondary. Have a good day."*

The Canadians were handing off the 747-8 cargo flight to their Russian air traffic control counterparts. DEVID was a fixed navigation point where all aircraft crossing the Arctic region were required to contact Murmansk.

Nadia changed frequencies. Moments later, they heard the Traveler Air Freight pilot radio. *"Murmansk Oceanic, Traveler Five-Five-Three, level four-zero-zero."*

The Russian-accented voice of a new controller replied immediately. *"Traveler Five-Five-Three, this is Murmansk, roger. Maintain flight level four-zero-zero."*

For now, the Rustler's threat-warning computer stayed silent. They were still well beyond the range of the air route surveillance radars posted to monitor Russia's northern regions.

They flew on, crossing high above the polar region. Below them, the ice cap was now a continuous sheet of white glare.

Forty-five minutes and 370 nautical miles after crossing through the DEVID intersection, the threat computer issued its first alert. *"Caution, S-band phased-array radar detected at twelve o'clock. Range approximately two hundred miles,"* a calm female voice reported. *"Evaluated as Russian Sopka-2 Arctic Air Surveillance Radar. Detection probability high."*

"Here we go," Brad murmured. That radar was sited on a small island at Sredny Ostrov, originally an ice airfield built as a staging base for Soviet Tu-95 Bear bombers tasked with attacking the United States if the Cold War had ever turned hot. It was located just off the much larger Severnaya Zemlya archipelago. Along with the new radar and at least one surface-to-air-missile battery, current intelligence indicated the Russians had upgraded Sredny's runway, enabling it to handle all-weather fighters like the MiG-31.

"Standing by on SPEAR," Nadia said. The instant it appeared that their ruse had failed, she planned to bring the system online and either seize control over that enemy radar . . . or blind it. With luck, she might be able to buy them enough time to reverse course, drop to low altitude, and scoot for friendly airspace at high speed.

Then they heard the same Russian controller's bored-sounding voice crackle through their headsets. *"Traveler Five-Five-Three, this is Murmansk. Radar contact. Proceed DIRIP to KUTET. Monitor VHF one-three-three point four. At NOTIS, contact Krasnoyarsk Control, six-six-seven-two primary, eight-eight-two-two secondary."*

"I'll be damned," Brad said in wonder. "This crazy-ass stunt is actually working. Those guys really don't know we're up here."

OVER CENTRAL SIBERIA
A COUPLE OF HOURS LATER

One of the icons on Nadia's navigation display turned red. "We are approaching the breakaway point. Thirty seconds out."

"Copy that," Brad said, nodding. Rapidly, he blinked away a stinging droplet of sweat. Although not quite as mentally taxing and physically exhausting as prolonged nap-of-the-earth flight, the effort required to keep their aircraft so close to the mammoth 747 for so long had been a serious strain. "Any status change on that Nebo-M radar?"

Nadia checked another of her displays, this one set to monitor hostile radars and other potential threats. Several minutes before, they'd picked up the emissions of a mobile VHF-band Russian air surveillance and tracking radar operating a couple of hundred miles to the west. She suspected it was assigned to an S-300 SAM regiment guarding the vital West Siberian oilfields. "No change," she reported. "The Nebo-M radar is still active."

"Too bad," Brad said. He shrugged. "Guess we'll just have to roll the dice."

This far out, that enemy radar shouldn't have any real chance to detect them—even when they broke away from the sheltering embrace of the Traveler Air Freight cargo jet. But there was always the possibility of some eagle-eyed Russian spotting something odd on his screen and raising an alarm. The Rustler's stealth design and radar-absorbent coating significantly reduced its radar cross section in some wavelengths and from certain aspects, especially from the front. But they couldn't render the Scion aircraft completely invisible.

"Ten seconds," Nadia said.

Brad breathed out. His hands settled firmly on the controls.

The nav icon on Nadia's MFD flashed green. "Execute breakaway!" she snapped.

Instantly, Brad throttled back to minimum power and rolled right, going almost inverted as he dove away from the bigger jet. As a last precaution, he'd turned west to keep his nose pointed toward that distant Russian air surveillance radar. He hoped that would keep XCV-70's radar cross section as small as possible during the critical few seconds before they fell below the Nebo-M's horizon.

Negative G's tugged him forward against his seat straps. The roar from the Rustler's engines faded away—replaced by the shrill shriek of the wind as it plummeted almost vertically toward the ground. The altitude indicator on his HUD decreased precipitously.

91ST RADIO TECHNICAL REGIMENT, NEAR THE EASTERN EDGE OF THE WEST SIBERIAN OIL BASIN THAT SAME TIME

Junior Sergeant Anatoly Yanayev frowned. Had he really seen what he'd just seen? He swiveled in his seat. "Captain Dyomin?" he said.

Frowning, his commander poked his head back into the operations van. He'd been enjoying a smoke outside in the early afternoon sunshine. "What is it, Sergeant?"

Yanayev indicated his console. "I think I've detected an unidentified air contact." He shrugged. "Well, at least for a second or two . . ." He let his voice trail off uncertainly.

With a sigh, Dyomin pitched his cigarette away and climbed back into the van. "Show me the recording," he demanded.

"I was tracking a big American air cargo jet transiting south about three hundred kilometers east of here," the young enlisted man explained. "As practice, you see."

Patiently, Dyomin nodded, deciding *not* to point out that Yanayev was only following the orders he personally had issued at the beginning of this training session. Tracking the passenger jets and air freighters using Polar Route 1 to cross Russian airspace wasn't exactly a challenging test of their equipment, even at such a long range, but at least it was a task he'd hoped might be within Yanayev's capabilities. The junior sergeant wasn't exactly one of the regiment's shining stars.

"Well, suddenly I saw this . . . er . . . second blip for a couple of seconds. It sort of looked like something maybe falling off that American 747." He pushed a couple of buttons beside his console's seventeen-inch LCD display, replaying the short sequence it had automatically recorded.

Dyomin sighed even harder, as he watched the tiny transitory radar blip flicker into existence slightly below the larger cargo jet and then vanish. "What you just saw, Junior Sergeant Yanayev," he said heavily, "was a perfect example of a minor systems glitch."

"But—"

"Unless you think FedEx is now dropping bombs on the Motherland?" Dyomin growled with biting sarcasm.

"No, sir," Yanayev admitted, chastened.

"Then wipe that useless recording," the captain ordered. "And get back to work." Shaking his head in disgust, he turned away, fumbling in his shirt pocket for another cigarette.

SCION SEVEN-ZERO, LOW OVER CENTRAL SIBERIA THAT SAME TIME

What had been a mostly featureless patchwork of green and brown earth cut by the winding blue trace of the Yenisei River grew sharper and sharper as the Rustler plunged downward at ever-increasing speed. Suddenly, an indistinct blur of green flashed into the needle-edged tops of pine trees stabbing upward.

Grinning wildly, Brad slammed his throttles forward. He leveled off only a few hundred feet above the treetops and banked hard left. Curving south, the Scion stealth aircraft streaked low across the forest canopy at nearly five hundred knots. "Engage DTF, two hundred, hard ride!" he ordered.

"DTF engaged," the Rustler's computer acknowledged.

He relaxed a bit. With their aircraft's digital terrain-following system engaged, they were reasonably safe flying this low, even at high speed. Using detailed maps stored in its computers and quick bursts from its radar altimeter, the DTF system enabled feats of low-altitude, long-distance flying beyond the ability of any unaided human pilot.

Beside him, Nadia leaned forward against her straps. Quickly, she toggled a sequence of virtual "keys" on her open navigation display, cueing up the precise coordinates of their preselected landing zone—a 1,600-foot-long clearing in the middle of the woods northwest of Lesosibirsk. They were currently a little over 150 nautical miles away, less than twenty minutes flying time. She selected it and tapped another icon. "LZ coordinates laid in."

The steering cue on Brad's head-up display shifted slightly as his computer accepted the updated information. He tweaked his stick left. The Rustler banked a touch, altering its heading by a fraction of a degree. "We'd better give Sam and her people the good news that we're getting close."

"I am on it," Nadia said. She opened a com window. Her fingers blurred across the display, entering a short message. As soon as she finished, their computer took over. It compressed and encrypted her signal into a millisecond-long burst and then transmitted it via satellite uplink. "Message sent."

NINETEEN

NORTHWEST OF LESOSIBIRSK
A FEW MINUTES LATER

Captain Oleg Panov peered forward through the Mi-8MTV-5 helicopter's windshield, looking for his next allotted target. He was flying low, practically skimming across the treetops at just one hundred kilometers per hour. In the left-hand seat, his copilot was eyes down, updating their mission plan on the center console computer. Since refueling at Krasnoyarsk's airport earlier in the day, they'd been sweeping these forests from the air—systematically overflying supposedly deserted hunting cabins and logging huts, looking for any signs of life. More than a dozen other Mi-8 helicopter troop carriers and Ka-52 gunships were engaged in this same task. So to avoid wasting time and fuel, it was important to check off each building they'd cleared and report the results to the Spetsnaz brigade staff back at headquarters.

Not more than a kilometer ahead and just off to his left, Panov caught the faint glint off a metal roof nestled among the trees. He swung the helicopter toward it. "Stand by on the sensors, Leonid," he ordered.

Obediently, his copilot looked up from their computer. "Standing by," he confirmed. "I am receiving good data from both pods."

The Mi-8MTV-5's upgraded cockpit had five modern multifunction displays set across its instrument panel—enabling its crew to rapidly and easily switch between different system readouts. Currently, the two leftmost displays were set to show imagery gathered by the sensor pods attached to their helicopter's pylons— one equipped with a forward-looking infrared camera and the other containing a ground surveillance radar.

Panov took them in right over the log cabin he'd spotted, coming in so low that his tricycle landing gear almost knocked over a thin metal stovepipe chimney rising above the roof. He only had time to see that it was two stories high and maybe big enough for a couple of separate rooms on each floor. A black plastic tarp covered what was probably a large woodpile. It fluttered wildly, hammered by their rotor wash.

Then they were past, clattering on across the top of the forest.

"Contact! Contact!" his copilot shouted. "I show heat emissions in that cabin. Human-sized. Multiple sources." He tapped a button, rewinding the thermal scanner images to show the moment of their pass. Green glowing shapes appeared briefly against the cooler background of the cabin's interior. Then he punched another control. "And look what our radar picked up at the same time!"

Panov whistled. Instead of a woodpile, that black tarp had been concealing a vehicle, some sort of van by its shape and size. Which meant that they'd found the American spies for sure. He keyed his radio mike. "Kingfisher Three to Kingfisher Base. Positive contact at Location Bravo Eight. Repeat, contact at Bravo Eight."

"*Base to Kingfisher,*" the Spetsnaz brigade commander's excited voice sounded in his earphones. "*I'm vectoring in additional helicopters and action teams. Deploy your troops to secure the perimeter. Remember, we want these foreigners alive, if at all possible.*"

"Understood, Base," Panov said. He pulled the helicopter into a tight turn back around. He'd spotted an opening in the woods not far from the hunting cabin.

Though comparatively small, it looked big enough to set down in. He switched to intercom. "Did you hear all of that, Captain Kuznetsky?"

From the aft passenger compartment, Spetsnaz Captain Vladimir Kuznetsky replied, "Loud and clear, Pilot." His clipped tones conveyed a clear impression of predatory eagerness. "My boys are ready."

"Right then," Panov said. "Stand by. We're going in now." Kuznetsky had two nine-man Spetsnaz teams under his direct command. Most of them were hardened veterans of combat in Ukraine, Chechnya, and Poland. Once they were on the ground, they shouldn't have any trouble keeping a handful of enemy agents from escaping into the surrounding woods.

At one of the second-floor windows of the cabin, Sam Kerr lowered a pair of compact binoculars. "Hell," she said coolly. "That tears it."

Beside her, Marcus Cartwright nodded. "They must know we're here." He looked up at the Russian helicopter as it circled back toward them. "They're headed for that clearing you found last night."

"Looks like it," Sam agreed. When they'd first arrived at this deserted building, she'd made a thorough reconnaissance of their immediate surroundings. It was standard Scion covert ops procedure to scout out possible enemy approaches to any safe house. That break in the trees—big enough for a helicopter, she'd judged—had been number one on her list, aside from the dirt road they'd driven in on.

She glanced at the big man. "Help Davey get that tarp off our van, Marcus." She pulled out her smartphone. "I'll handle this end." Cartwright nodded again and clattered down the stairs.

Sam typed in a short text message: KRAK ENG, but held her finger off the send button. She raised her binoculars again, watching the Russian helicopter as it slowed into a hover just over the clearing. Its fast-beating rotors churned up a swirling cloud of dust and dead grass.

The Mi-8 drifted carefully lower, gradually settling below the level of the treetops.

Deliberately, Sam pushed the send button on her smartphone.

During her reconnaissance, she'd decided to rig a welcoming present for any Russians who decided to crash their party, using some of the special equipment that had been hidden inside their van. Her "gift," a small, soda-can-sized plastic tube packed with C-4, was fixed to the trunk of a tall Siberian pine tree right at the edge of the clearing.

Now, triggered by her text message, the Krakatoa shaped-demolition charge exploded with enormous force. In a blinding flash, the detonation sent a colossal shock wave sleeting straight into a thin, inverted copper plate set at the plastic tube's open mouth, converting it instantly into a lethal jet of molten metal that speared outward at thousands of miles per hour. Hit squarely, the Russian helicopter blew up, killing every man aboard.

WHUMMP.

A huge ball of orange and red flame erupted above the treetops, momentarily outshining the late afternoon sun. Shards of torn and pulverized metal spiraled away from the center of the blast.

"Bet that hurt," Sam said under her breath. She turned away from the window and hurried downstairs. Outside, a thick pillar of oily, black smoke from the burning wreckage curled higher into the sky.

David Jones met her as she darted around the side of the log cabin. The young Welshman's face was tight. "Those Spetsnaz bastards weren't out on their own. There are more helicopters on the way . . . including gunships."

Off in the distance, the sound of clattering rotors could be heard growing steadily louder.

Marcus Cartwright looked up when they joined him

near the back of the battered delivery van. Discarded boxes and parcels were strewn across the ground behind its open rear doors. "This situation's just gone from bad to worse," he said grimly.

"It's definitely not ideal," she said, more lightly. "But at least our ride's on the way." She checked her watch. "McLanahan and Rozek can't be more than ten minutes out now."

"Unfortunately, we don't *have* ten minutes, Ms. Kerr," he pointed out. "Those Russian helicopters are going to be on top of us inside of five. Which means we need to buy some time."

Sam's eyes narrowed. "You're going all formal on me, Marcus. That's never a good sign."

Cartwright forced a wry smile. "True." He reached into the back of the van and dragged a small motorbike out from under the remaining boxes. Weighing just one hundred and eighty pounds, the Taurus was a Russian-built all-terrain vehicle with bulbous balloon tires. With a top speed of only twenty-two miles per hour, the motorcycle wasn't fast, but it was amazingly compact and agile. And it was even designed to fold up into a bag that would fit in a car trunk.

Sam glanced at Jones. He shrugged. "Mr. Cartwright asked me to put the machine together last night, while you were out scouting around. He thought it might come in handy, see?"

"And just how is this supposed to come in *handy*?" Sam asked, turning back to face Cartwright.

"You take the bike," he told her. "And then you head cross-country to the LZ as fast as you can."

"Leaving you and Davey behind, I suppose?" She shook her head stubbornly. "Not happening, Marcus."

Cartwright sighed. "Look, Sam, this is a Little Bighorn situation. And all the Indians in the world are about to charge over the hills. So Davey and I'll take the van and head to the LZ by road. Maybe we'll get lucky. And maybe we won't. But what really matters is that splitting up is the best chance for any of us to make it out alive."

"He's right, Ms. Kerr," Jones said softly. "So let us do our job, will you now?"

Wordlessly, Sam just stared at the two men for several seconds. Then, surrendering for the first time ever, she hugged them both tight, one after the other. She turned away with tears streaking her face, straddled the motorbike, and kick-started it. The Taurus's little Honda motor whirred to life.

Without looking back, she sped off into the woods. Behind her, the clattering roar of the approaching Russian helicopters grew louder still.

———

Three kilometers away but closing fast from the south, two Ka-52 Alligator helicopters darted low over the forest. Twin pairs of counterrotating, coaxial three-blade rotors blurred above each gunship. Each bristled with armament, including 30mm cannons, 122mm unguided rocket launchers, and laser-guided antitank missiles.

Aboard the trailing helicopter, Major Yuri Drachev scowled, seeing the thick black column of smoke from the downed Mi-8 rising above the forest. *Twenty-one Russian soldiers and airmen dead, including a detachment of elite special forces troops,* he thought bitterly. All because the higher-ups had foolishly believed these Western spies would meekly throw up their hands and surrender at the first sight of superior force.

But despite those appalling and unexpected casualties, their orders were unchanged.

"*Listen carefully, Kingfisher Six,*" he heard the Spetsnaz brigade commander snap over the radio. "*You will not engage the enemy with lethal force! Moscow still wants the enemy agents alive. Is that clear to you?*"

"Yes, that is completely fucking clear, Kingfisher Base," Drachev growled. "Six out." He glanced across the cockpit at his gunner, Senior Sergeant Pekhtin. "You know this is total bullshit."

Pekhtin nodded carefully, not daring to express his own opinion out loud. There was no percentage in getting caught in the middle of a shit storm between two senior officers.

"Six, this is Five," the lead helicopter suddenly radioed. *"I have a visual contact at my ten o'clock—a vehicle moving fast along a dirt track, heading northwest."*

Drachev craned his head, peering through the Ka-52's cockpit canopy. There, beyond and slightly to the left of the other gunship, he saw a plume of dust rising above the trees, drifting slowly away on the wind. "Five, this is Kingfisher Six. Stop that vehicle. But don't scratch its paint if you can help it, understand? Command wouldn't like that. We'll hang back half a klick and cover your ass."

"Acknowledged, Six," the other pilot replied. *"Moving to engage."*

Drachev watched the lead helicopter's long nose swing a few degrees left and banked his own Ka-52 to follow. They were flying along the trace of a narrow dirt logging road as it wound back and forth. Through the trees ahead, he caught a flicker of pale blue in that drifting cloud of dust. They were chasing the enemy agents' fake delivery van, he suddenly realized.

Abruptly, Kingfisher Five veered left and then cut back sharply to the right in order to cross ahead of the speeding vehicle. Flashes lit the helicopter's starboard side as it fired its 30mm cannon. A stream of high-explosive shells hammered the ground scarcely a hundred meters ahead of the van—smashing trees to splinters and blowing craters in the dirt road.

Coming in behind the lead gunship, which was now turning to make another pass, Drachev saw the blue van suddenly slew broadside across the logging track. Spraying more dust and dirt from under its spinning tires, it slid frantically to a dead stop. He bared his teeth in a fiercely satisfied grin. Now they had these bastards.

Through the haze, he saw someone scramble out of the passenger side of the vehicle. That was one big son of a bitch, he thought. The man reached back into the van's cab and came back out holding a long green tube over his shoulder. He pivoted toward Kingfisher Five just as the gunship finished its turn and straightened out.

Drachev's eyes widened in shock. That was a handheld SAM. "Five, look out!" he radioed frantically. "You're under missile attack—"

In a puff of white exhaust and dazzling flame, the surface-to-air missile slashed across the sky with incredible speed. It exploded just above the other helicopter's rotor assembly. Spewing smoke and shattered rotor fragments, the stricken Ka-52 spiraled down and crashed among the trees.

Beside Drachev, Senior Sergeant Pekhtin reflexively triggered a full salvo of 122mm S-13 rockets. In less than a second, five unguided rockets streaked down-range and slammed straight into the blue van. It vanished amid a rippling series of powerful explosions as the rockets' armor-piercing fragmentation warheads detonated.

When the smoke cleared away, there was nothing left of the vehicle or its occupants but a few smoldering pieces of blackened and twisted metal.

Pekhtin swallowed. "Oh, shit," he muttered.

Drachev nodded grimly. "Nice work, Sergeant," he bit out through gritted teeth. "Now we're totally fucked."

TWENTY

SCION SEVEN-ZERO, NORTHWEST OF LESOSIBIRSK THAT SAME TIME

"We are four minutes out from the LZ," Nadia announced. She glanced up from the computer-generated map showing their projected course. "Still no further signals from Ms. Kerr or anyone else in the covert ops team."

Despite her deliberately unruffled tone, Brad could sense her growing tension. He shared it. Apart from a brief acknowledgment of their first message, they'd heard nothing more from Scion's intelligence agents. But by now Sam and the others should have reached the edge of their planned landing zone and reported whether or not it was clear. Their continued radio silence was increasingly worrying.

He looked ahead through his HUD. They were flying south at four hundred knots, skirting along the western edge of the Yenisei valley. Low, forested hills rose off to the right. Higher, more rugged elevations were visible across the river on the left. At this altitude, the clearing they'd selected was still just over his visual horizon.

Brad banked a couple of degrees, starting a wide, curving turn that would bring them in from the northwest, along the LZ's long axis. He frowned. "We're getting really close to a 'go' or 'no go' decision on landing."

If he waited much longer to start configuring the Rustler for a rough field landing, they'd be coming in too hot and have to go around again—wasting precious time and fuel . . . which was definitely *not* a good idea this deep in hostile territory. To buy a little more time, he throttled back and climbed slightly, reducing their airspeed to three hundred knots. He pushed a button on his stick, shutting off their terrain-following system to take full control over the aircraft. "DTF disengaged."

A cursor flashed onto Brad's HUD, marking a lighter-colored patch among the otherwise almost unrelieved green of the pine forest. "Okay, I have the LZ in sight." He glanced across the cockpit. "See if you can get a better read on this situation. I really don't want to land blind."

"Copy that," Nadia said. Her fingers flew across one of her MFDs, ordering their computer to scan through multiple radio frequencies for any indication of trouble. Abruptly, she stiffened as a slew of frantic Russian voice transmissions sounded in her ears. "Brad! Something very bad is happening!"

She switched the active channel to his headset.

"Zimodorok Piyat' ne rabotayet! Sem' po marshrutu!" he heard through hissing static. *"Baza, nam nuzhno bol'she voysk zdes'! Seychas!"*

Suddenly Brad spotted columns of smoke curling up out of the woods ahead of them. Simultaneously, the Rustler's threat-warning system went active— bracketing three distant green-brown specks. It identified them as a Russian Ka-52 helicopter gunship and two Mi-8 troop transports. They were clattering just over the treetops, circling low above the rising smoke. More threat icons blazed across the horizon, high-lighting another wave of enemy helicopters much far-ther out, but definitely coming this way. He shook his head in disbelief. "Christ, it looks like we're headed straight into a pitched battle. So much for the subtle approach."

Reacting fast, Nadia brought the XCV-70's forward-looking passive thermal sensors online. In fractions of a second, the aircraft's computer analyzed the data it was receiving and transferred the resulting images to one of her MFDs. "I count two downed helicopters and the wreckage of one ground vehicle." She hesitated. "It could be the team's van."

"Hell," Brad said, feeling sick. "We're too late."

"Maybe not," Nadia said quickly. She leaned forward, zooming in on another faint thermal image their sensors had just picked up. Whatever it was, it was headed toward the LZ, weaving back and forth at high speed between the trees. Was that some kind of motorcycle?

A com icon flashed urgently in the corner of her left-hand display. She stabbed at it. "Scion aircraft, this is Sam Kerr," a familiar voice gasped through their headsets. "I'm coming as fast as I can . . . But Marcus and Davey aren't with me. . . . I don't know if they're alive or dead."

Brad made an instant decision. "We're go for landing," he snapped. He clicked the intercom. "Ian, you'd better get set. We're coming in hard and fast. And the LZ is about to turn hot."

"So I guessed," Major Schofield replied crisply from the troop compartment. The Canadian special forces expert sounded cool—almost as though he'd just heard they were arriving at a vacation resort. "I'll be ready to move the second you drop the ramp."

Nadia swore under her breath. "*Gówno.* Shit."

"More trouble?" Brad asked, entering a short command on one of his own displays. He'd just instructed his flight computer to configure the aircraft for a short-field rough landing.

"New Russian radio transmissions," she told him. "That gunship pilot is claiming they killed at least two enemy agents. He says they were trying to escape in a vehicle his gunner destroyed with rocket fire."

Brad grimaced. That made Sam Kerr the only survivor of the Scion covert ops unit.

Another quick control press on his stick selected a touchdown point at the western edge of the clearing. Obediently, his computer drew a glowing line across his HUD—giving him a visual cue. They were about three nautical miles out.

He throttled back more. Losing speed fast, the Rustler slid lower. Hydraulics whirred as computer-directed control surfaces opened. The muted roar from their four turbofan engines diminished. "Sixty seconds."

"*Vrazheskiy samolet v pole zreniya!*" he heard a Russian pilot yell over the radio circuit. "Enemy aircraft in sight!"

Nadia looked out her side of the cockpit, seeing the Ka-52 swinging toward them. "Hostile inbound!"

Focused entirely on the clearing rushing up toward them at nearly two hundred knots, Brad could only spare a single glance at his threat display. "That guy's not carrying air-to-air missiles."

Nadia shook her head decisively. "He has antitank missiles and a 30mm cannon. And we will be a sitting duck once we are on the ground." Her fingers flashed across her displays. "Weapons control transferred to my station."

"Make it fast," he warned. "I'm getting ready to lower the gear."

Nadia nodded. The moment that happened the Rustler's computer would automatically lock out all their offensive weapons. No sane aircraft crew wanted to risk firing a missile right through their own landing gear.

An image of the Russian gunship, now approximately five miles off their starboard wing tip, appeared on one of her MFDs. The glowing brackets highlighting the Ka-52 flashed red and a shrill, warbling tone sounded in her headset. "Target locked on." She tapped a missile-shaped icon. "Fox Two!"

Bay doors whined open. Instantly, an AIM-9X Sidewinder heat-seeking missile dropped out into the open air. The Sidewinder's solid rocket motor ignited before it had fallen more than a few feet . . . and it streaked out from under the Rustler—already curving hard to the right as it homed in on the Ka-52 at nearly two thousand miles per hour.

Alerted to the missile launch by his own sensors, the Russian pilot did his best to evade. The Ka-52's long nose dipped as it banked into a tight turn. Flares tumbled away from under the wildly maneuvering enemy helicopter, each a miniature sunburst against the bright blue afternoon sky.

The Sidewinder ignored them—slashing in to explode just a few feet from the gunship. Thousands of razor-edged titanium shards sleeted through its cockpit and fuselage with enormous destructive force. Caught partway through its evasive turn, the Russian helicopter tumbled out of control, plunged into the forest, and blew up.

"Good kill," Nadia confirmed. She saw the two surviving Mi-8 troop carriers in range suddenly veer away. Staying low, they fled southeast. The phalanx of other approaching Russian helicopters farther off altered course at the same time, also turning away. She smiled fiercely. Like all scavengers, they were afraid of any prey that bared its own teeth and claws.

With muffled bumps and thumps below the cockpit,

the Rustler's landing gear came down and locked in position. The clearing they were aiming for grew steadily larger through the forward canopy.

They came in low and slow, practically brushing against the treetops. Suddenly the green line marking Brad's preselected touchdown position flared brighter.

"Hang on!" he warned, chopping his throttles almost all the way back.

Robbed of the last few knots of airspeed that kept it aloft, the Scion aircraft dropped out of the sky and touched down with a tooth-rattling jolt. Brad swiftly reversed thrust to brake even faster, slamming them forward against their straps. Decelerating hard, the batwing-shaped Rustler bounced across the ground in a whirling storm cloud of dust and torn grass. They rolled to a stop not far from the tall trees lining the eastern edge of the clearing.

Grinning with relief, Brad pushed his throttles forward just a notch, feeding their engines just enough power to let him swing the Rustler through a 180-degree turn. Once he was lined up and ready for an immediate takeoff, he throttled back again and hit the ramp release.

Cameras set to cover the XCV-70's rear arc caught Ian Schofield darting out into the clearing. Bulky in his body armor, the Canadian dropped prone, covering the southern edge of the clearing through the sights of a long-barreled HK416 carbine. He had a man-portable antitank missile launcher slung across his back. Evidently, he'd taken his assignment as their one-man army quite seriously.

And then Sam Kerr burst out of the forest. Leaning far over, she slewed her small motorbike almost sideways through a sharp turn—straightening out only when she was headed right at the Rustler. She skidded to a stop just yards short of the ramp.

Wearily, she climbed off the motorcycle. But then, both physically and emotionally spent, she slumped to her hands and knees. In a flash, Ian Schofield was on his own feet. Slinging his carbine, he threw one arm across her shoulders and helped her up. Together, they staggered across the clearing and up the ramp into the waiting aircraft.

"Go! Go! Go!" Schofield yelled. "I have Ms. Kerr! We're inside!"

"On it," Brad replied. He tapped a control on his display. A high-pitched hydraulic whine penetrated the cockpit as the ramp closed and sealed. He advanced the throttles. Outside the cockpit, the Rustler's four large turbofans spooled up. He glanced at Nadia with a crooked grin. "Okay, now comes the hard part."

She nodded silently. They'd lost the element of surprise. The Russians knew they were here. And now their only way home meant crossing almost two thousand miles of heavily defended hostile airspace . . . in broad daylight.

Inside the Rustler's cramped passenger compartment, Ian Schofield finished strapping himself in. He studied Samantha Kerr for a few moments. The slender Scion agent looked exhausted and deeply sad. He unclipped a hydration pouch from his combat webbing, unscrewed the top, and offered it to her.

She took a small sip. Her eyes widened slightly. "That's not water."

"Indeed not," Schofield agreed. He took out another pouch and raised it in a toast. "To absent friends and comrades."

Blinking back tears, Sam imitated him. "To Marcus and Davey. They were the best," she said quietly.

Schofield nodded. "That they were."

With a sigh, she closed her eyes and leaned back against the bulkhead as the aircraft lifted off and banked sharply back to the north.

TWENTY-ONE

NATIONAL DEFENSE CONTROL CENTER, MOSCOW
THAT SAME TIME

Marshal Mikhail Leonov listened to Lieutenant General Varshavsky's bad news in silence. His face showed no discernible emotion. At last, the commander of Russia's Central Military District finished his dreary litany of disaster—two advanced Ka-52 helicopters shot down, one Mi-8 transport ambushed and blown up while landing, and nearly thirty Russian soldiers and airmen dead . . . along with at least two of the Scion agents they'd hoped to capture alive.

"So what is the situation now?" he asked calmly when Varshavsky fell silent.

"I've ordered my helicopter units to fall back and regroup at Lesosibirsk," the other man admitted.

Leonov nodded. That was a sensible move. Without support from the two downed helicopter gunships, the Spetsnaz force's surviving troop carriers were easy prey for the Americans' missile-armed stealth aircraft. He looked at the blurry picture hastily snapped by a combat cameraman aboard one of the retreating Mi-8s. It showed a distinctive black flying-wing-shaped airplane, one that bore a striking resemblance to the much-larger U.S. Air Force B-2 Spirit stealth bomber. When the photograph was taken, it was flying at very low altitude with its landing gear deployed.

He looked back at Varshavsky. "And you're sure the Scion aircraft made a rough field landing after your helicopters retreated?"

"Yes, sir," the general said. "But it took off again within minutes."

"Then at least one of the enemy agents is still alive," Leonov commented. "And on board that aircraft."

Varshavsky nodded. No other conclusion made sense. He looked stricken, like a man told he had an incurable disease. "My resignation will be on your desk this evening, Marshal," he said wearily. "I take full responsibility for this fiasco."

"Resignation?" Leonov snorted. "Don't be ridiculous, Nikolai. This wasn't your fault. We sent your troops out on a rabbit hunt . . . only to learn that we were chasing a bear instead." He shrugged. "What is it the Americans themselves say? Sometimes you get the bear—"

"And sometimes the bear gets you," Varshavsky finished grimly.

"Then let's have no more of this defeatist talk about resigning," Leonvov told him. "Send your Spetsnaz detachments back in, on the ground this time. I want that cabin and its surroundings searched from top to bottom for any equipment or documents those Scion spies may have been forced to leave behind. But make sure your troops are careful. We've just paid a high price to learn our enemies have a nasty habit of planting booby traps."

Vashavsky nodded. "Yes, sir."

Leonov swiped an icon on the screen, closing his secure video connection with Yekaterinburg. He swiveled toward another LED display, this one currently linked to the headquarters of Russia's Aerospace Forces. Colonel General Semyon Tikhomirov's worried face looked back at him. "Comments, Semyon?"

Tikhomirov frowned. "How could this enemy aircraft have penetrated so far into the Motherland?"

"We underestimated Sky Masters technology," Leonov said bluntly. "And not for the first time." He shrugged his shoulders. "Perhaps the Americans have successfully developed a stealth air refueling tanker after all."

"That would be . . . unfortunate," Tikhomirov agreed slowly. Several years before there had been reports indicating the U.S. Air Force was interested in applying stealth technology to a new class of tanker aircraft—with the idea of greatly extending the effective combat range of its F-35 Lightning II and F-22 Raptor stealth fighters.

"So it would," Leonov agreed. "But what matters most right now is that we intercept that Scion plane before it escapes."

Tikhomirov nodded. "Per your earlier orders, the 712th Guards Regiment has four MiG-31 fighters at Kansk-Dalniy armed, fueled, and ready for takeoff."

"Then get them in the air," Leonov told him. Those long-range supersonic interceptors should be over Lesosibirsk in less than fourteen minutes. Based on radar data and visual observations made during earlier encounters, the Scion stealth aircraft was subsonic only, with a top speed around 900 kph. Even with its current head start, the enemy plane shouldn't be able to escape its MiG-31 pursuers.

"What instructions should I give my pilots?" Tikhomirov asked. "Do you want them to try to force the Americans down?"

Regretfully, Leonov shook his head. Much as he'd hoped to take at least one of the enemy intelligence operatives alive, the risks were now too great. Learning that the stealth aircraft had air-to-air missiles of its own had changed the whole calculus. "Tell them to shoot that plane out of the sky, Semyon," he ordered. "The time for clever spy games is over."

OVER CENTRAL SIBERIA
A FEW MINUTES LATER

Eighty nautical miles and ten minutes after taking off again, the XCV-70 Rustler zoomed north over the rugged chain of thickly wooded hills paralleling the Yenisei River valley's eastern rim. Flying at 450 knots, with its terrain-following system active, the Scion stealth aircraft automatically pitched up to clear the ridges and hills in its path. And then it just as quickly dove back down into the sheltering embrace of the valleys beyond.

Brad clenched his teeth in concentration and banked right—steering into a tree-lined notch between two steeper hills that were each more than a thousand feet high. Even with the Rustler's DTF system holding them only two hundred feet above the ground, he wanted to take advantage of every piece of radar-masking cover he could find.

"Caution, multiple airborne L-band and X-band passive phased-array radars detected at five o'clock," their computer reported suddenly. *"Estimated range is one hundred and eighty miles. Detection probability at this altitude is currently nil."*

Nadia leaned forward in her right-hand seat. She pulled up a menu on her threat-warning display, watching while the computer compared the signatures of those radar emissions against its database. "The radar signatures match the Zaslon-M system," she told him.

Brad nodded tightly. Zaslon-Ms were the powerful radars carried by Russia's upgraded MiG-31BM interceptors. And their pre-mission intelligence brief had identified the Foxhound regiment stationed at Kansk-Dalniy as the most serious potential threat in this area. "Those guys are hellishly quick off the mark."

"Too quick," Nadia said quietly.

Normally it took more time to prep modern fighter aircraft for a combat sortie. Which meant the Russians had those planes armed up and ready to fly long before they'd tangled with those helicopters near the LZ. Brad grimaced. "You ever get the uncomfortable feeling that the bad guys are reading our minds?"

"Marshal Leonov is not a fool," Nadia agreed. She checked her threat-warning display again. By tracking small changes in the enemy radars' observed bearing and signal strength, her computer could estimate the heading and speed of those still-distant MiG-31 fighters. "I count four MiGs coming our way," she reported. "Probable speed is eight hundred knots. They're supersonic."

"Okay, that is definitely not good," Brad admitted. He rolled back left to steady up heading due north again. If nothing changed, those Russian fighter jets were going to be right on top of them in thirty minutes or less. Staying low in all this ground clutter would significantly decrease the range at which the enemy's phased-array radars could detect and track their stealthy Rustler—maybe even down to ten or fifteen miles. But it wouldn't make them completely invisible, not on radar, not against infrared search and track systems, and certainly not against the Mark I eyeball. The XCV-70's black radar-absorbent coating made excellent camouflage at night. In daylight it would stand out like a sore thumb.

"Then what can we do?" Nadia asked after he ran through his reasoning with her.

"Well, when I was a kid, the first rule of hide-and-seek was never to be where the other guy figured you'd be," Brad said with a quick, slashing grin. He toggled a control on his stick. "DTF disengaged."

He pulled back slightly and to the left. They climbed

to a thousand feet and rolled into a turn to the north-west, then leveled off. Ahead through the canopy, the broad blue curve of the Yenisei River stretched across the horizon. "I figure it's high time we shook the dust off those big new engines of ours," he said, advancing his throttles all the way forward. "Let's take this baby supersonic."

The roar of their turbofan engines deepened and grew louder. Their airspeed rose, climbing steadily past 500 knots, beyond Mach 1, and up to 750 knots. As they accelerated, forested hills and valleys seemed to leap toward them, rushing past and below on either side of the cockpit. Only a couple of minutes later, they streaked back over the Yenisei—crossing the mile-wide river in less than five seconds.

"We are burning a lot of fuel," Nadia warned, study-ing her system readouts.

Brad nodded. Running their low-bypass Affinity engines at supersonic speeds increased the XCV-70's fuel consumption by around 50 percent. That was a hell of a lot more efficient than older jet engines that had to go to afterburner to hit supersonic speeds . . . but it was still a heavy drain on their reserves.

Based on the mission flight plan he'd worked out before they took off from Yellowknife, he could only kick the Rustler above Mach 1 for twenty-five to thirty minutes, tops. Since their fuel consumption on the high-altitude flight into Russia had been lower than predicted, he thought he could eke out another couple of minutes of supersonic flight if necessary. But pushing much beyond those limits increased the chances that their fuel tanks would run dry somewhere over the Arctic. And since a crash landing out on the polar ice was practically the textbook definition of a "nonsurvivable aviation event," that seemed like a really bad idea.

"We'll stay supersonic just long enough to put us out pretty far ahead and off to the west of our predicted track," Brad promised. "With luck, that'll fox those MiG-31 pilots. For a while, anyway."

Watching their flight path as it arrowed northwest across her navigation display, Nadia saw what he intended. The enemy fighters hunting them were still headed due north, now flying along a steadily diverging course. The MiG pilots were obviously acting on the logical assumption that their quarry would take the shortest, most fuel-efficient route out of Russian airspace. And since they didn't know the Rustler could go supersonic for short sprints, their calculations of when they should intercept the Scion aircraft were going to come up short . . . off by dozens of miles.

NATIONAL DEFENSE CONTROL CENTER
  ## THIRTY MINUTES LATER

Leonov sat at his workstation, listening intently to the radio chatter between Tikhomirov's MiG-31 crews. Arrow-shaped icons moving northward across a large digital map showed them flying at five thousand meters over the jagged highlands of the Central Siberian Plateau, well to the east of the Yenisei River. The four supersonic interceptors were deployed across a two-hundred-kilometer-wide front—using their APD-518 digital air-to-air data links to share sensor information.

"Phantom Lead, this is Three," one of the pilots reported, sounding frustrated even through the hissing static. *"I still do not have any radar, thermal, or visual contacts. Repeat, no contacts. The sky's totally empty."*

"Same here, Three," the senior MiG pilot radioed back. *"But stay sharp. That American stealth plane can't be too far ahead of us."*

Leonov frowned. Something had gone wrong with this planned intercept. Based on relative airspeeds and predicted courses, he'd expected at least one of the MiG-31s to spot that fleeing Scion aircraft by now. Their powerful radars were optimized to pick out low-flying targets. So either the enemy plane's stealth technology was considerably more effective than seemed possible and the MiGs had somehow already flown right past it . . . or . . . *We're looking in the wrong place,* he realized suddenly. The Americans hadn't followed a straight-line course to escape. They must have veered away to the east or to the west, dodging Tikhomirov's fighters as they raced north.

"Mother of God," the other man muttered when he contacted him with his suspicions. "I think you're right, Mikhail. It's the only explanation that makes any sense."

"Order the MiGs to spread their search pattern wider," Leonov snapped. "Send two of them northwest and the other two northeast. That Scion plane hasn't disappeared off the face of the earth. It's out there, somewhere."

Tikhomirov nodded rapidly. "I also have Beriev-100 AWACS aircraft and more fighters taking off from bases near Moscow and Murmansk."

Leonov shook his head. "They'll be too late and too slow. Our MiG-31s are the only aircraft with any realistic hope of intercepting the enemy before they cross our Arctic coast."

"Those fighters have been supersonic for a long time," Tikhomirov warned. "Even with drop tanks, they'll be running up against the edge of their combat radius pretty soon."

"Screw their combat radius," Leonov growled, feeling his temper finally snap under the accumulated frustrations of the day. "If necessary, they can divert to Norilsk or Novy Urengoye." Both far northern airports had runways that could handle MiG-31s. He glared at the screen. "Tell your pilots to find that damned stealth plane and kill it—at all costs."

TWENTY-TWO

SCION SEVEN-ZERO,
OVER THE WEST SIBERIAN PLAIN
A SHORT TIME LATER

A seemingly endless marshland cut by innumerable small, stagnant streams unrolled ahead of the XCV-70 Rustler as it streaked north. Red-tinged late afternoon sunlight sparkled off the surface of hundreds of ponds and small lakes. There were no signs of human habitation, no roads or villages anywhere in sight. This vast stretch of flat, featureless country was almost wholly untouched and unspoiled by modern man.

Strapped into his seat in the Rustler's cramped cockpit, Brad McLanahan rolled his tight shoulders, trying to loosen them up a little. His muscles ached with the strain of flying so fast and so low for so long. Knowing that they were being hunted by an implacable enemy bent on revenge only added to his growing tension.

One side of his mouth twisted in a wry smile. The good news about flying over this vast, trackless swamp was that he didn't have to worry about slamming into trees or sharp-edged ridges or electric power pylons. The bad news was the reverse of the same coin. If they ran into a roving Russian fighter patrol or a surface-to-air missile battery out here, there was no cover at all—no higher ground to mask them from enemy radar and let them slip safely past.

"We are down to thirty-six percent of our fuel," Nadia reported from her right-hand seat. She had several status menus open on her MFDs. To make it possible for Brad to focus wholly on flying, she was monitoring their engines, avionics, and combat systems.

"Copy that," he replied. He forced a cheerful tone. "Kinda makes me wish I'd stashed a few more cans of jet fuel in the back."

The twenty-minute supersonic sprint he'd made earlier had enabled them to evade the first Russian attempt at interception. But the cost had been high. They were still more than fifteen hundred miles from the nearest possible point where they could safely rendezvous with a Sky Masters air tanker. Added to that was the inescapable fact that low-altitude flying drank fuel at an alarming rate. Taking the Rustler up into the thinner air at thirty or forty thousand feet would be a heck of a lot more fuel-efficient . . . except for the fact that it would also get them blown out of the sky by Russian SAMs or air-to-air missiles.

"How bad is this?" Nadia asked seriously.

"Remember that animated movie?" Brad said. "The one where the drunken sea captain climbs out onto the nose of a plane and belches alcoholic fumes into its tank to keep them flying just a few seconds longer?"

"Yes?" she said warily.

He grinned. "Well, it's not quite *that* bad."

"I would slug you if you were not flying this airplane," she growled.

Brad laughed. "And here people told me being a covert ops pilot was a dangerous job."

A sharp tone abruptly sounded in their headsets. "*Warning, warning, Zaslon-M radar emissions detected at four o'clock,*" the Rustler's computer announced.

"Evaluated as two MiG-31 interceptors. Estimated range eighty miles and closing. Moderate strength signal."

"Ah, crap," Brad muttered. "Okay, I take it back. This *is* a dangerous job."

His mind ran through their tactical situation with lightning speed. Put simply, it sucked.

Those enemy fighters were headed right toward them and fast. Within minutes at most, they'd be close enough for their radars and IRST sensors to pick out the Rustler against this billiard table terrain. And even if his crappy fuel state allowed another prolonged supersonic sprint, he couldn't outrun the MiGs. At high altitude, a MiG-31 could exceed Mach 2.8—twice the XCV-70's maximum speed. Worse still, the Russian interceptors were probably armed with R-37M long-range, hypersonic air-to-air missiles capable of reaching out and swatting them out of the air at up to two hundred miles.

All of which really only left them with one option.

Beside him, Nadia had obviously come to the same conclusion. "We cannot hide. And we cannot run," she said matter-of-factly. "So we fight?"

Brad nodded with equal coolness. "Definitely." He rolled into a tight right turn, coming around hard to head straight at the oncoming MiGs. The Rustler's radar cross section was smallest from the front.

"Twelve hundred and fifty knots closure," their computer reported. *"Range now seventy miles and closing fast. Time to radar detection estimated at two minutes thirty seconds."*

"Well, boys, I reckon this is it—" Brad started to joke.

Nadia forestalled him. "Do *not* say anything about 'toe-to-toe nuclear combat with the Russkies,' or I swear to God I *will* punch you and die happy," she warned.

Brad surrendered. "No, ma'am," he said devoutly.

Beside him, Nadia's fingers danced across her MFDs, prepping their defensive systems. "SPEAR is online and ready to engage. Chaff is configured for R-37 radar-guided missiles. Flares ready."

"Range now forty-five miles. Enemy radar strength climbing. Time to detection now one minute," the Rustler's computer interjected.

She glanced across the cockpit. "Do you have a plan? Or are we simply going straight for the enemy's throat?"

"I've got a plan," Brad assured her. Speaking fast, he outlined the tactics he had in mind.

A wolfish grin lit her face. "Oh, very sneaky! I *like* this plan!"

PHANTOM THREE, SEVENTY KILOMETERS SOUTHEAST THAT SAME TIME

Major Stepan Grigoryev glanced out his MiG-31's cockpit canopy. Phantom Four was visible only as a distant gray dot roughly ten kilometers off his right wing. Although their data links would have allowed a much wider separation, he wanted his wingman in close support range if they found the Scion stealth aircraft they were hunting. Intelligence briefings had stressed that the private American company's mercenary pilots were cunning and aggressive. So Grigoryev saw no point in giving one of them the chance to jump a lone aircraft. If this turned into a fight, he wanted the odds on his side.

"Radar detection!" Alexey Balandin, his weapon systems officer, yelled from the rear cockpit. "Small contact, probably a stealth aircraft, bearing three o'clock moving to four o'clock at very low altitude. Indeterminate range!"

Christ, Grigoryev thought coldly. Somehow the

Scion aircraft had sneaked around his flank . . . and now it was trying to slide in behind him.

"We show the same contact," Rudensky, Phantom Four's pilot, radioed excitedly. *"Turning to engage."*

Grigoryev yanked his stick right, rolling the big, twin-tailed MiG into a hard 4-G right turn as he followed his wingman around. A green diamond blinked into existence on his HUD. The enemy stealth aircraft was now somewhere out ahead of them, off to the northeast. He banked back left to keep the target centered and thumbed a switch on his stick. Two missile symbols appeared in the corner of his HUD. Two of his four R-37M radar-guided missiles were armed and set for a salvo launch as soon as they got a solid lock on this target. "Weapons hot!"

And then just as suddenly as it had first appeared, the green diamond vanished from his HUD.

"Contact lost!" Balandin said over the intercom. "I'm attempting to regain a lock."

"We've lost it, too," Rudensky admitted a second later. *"But the enemy aircraft was definitely headed northeast. And it was moving at around nine hundred kph."*

"Did anyone get a range?" Grigoryev demanded.

Balandin sounded hesitant. "It wasn't close, sir. Probably more than a hundred kilometers out."

Grigoryev nodded to himself. Having failed in its bid to slip past them undetected, the Scion aircraft must now be running hard—hoping to open the range further and evade their search again. "We'll chase along this heading for a while," he decided. "But stay on your toes. This bastard's a slippery customer. He may try that trick again."

Acknowledgments flooded through his headset as he trimmed the MiG-31 for level flight and headed northeast at high speed.

SCION SEVEN-ZERO
THAT SAME TIME

"SPEAR disengaged," Nadia reported. She looked across the cockpit with a slight smile on her face. "Both MiGs have turned northeast. They are pursuing my now-invisible ghost."

"Nice work," Brad told her. She'd used their ALQ-293 Self-Protection Electronically Agile Reaction system to spoof the enemy radars—creating a brief false contact for them to chase. To avoid triggering the anti-manipulation software protections built into Russian avionics, she'd deactivated SPEAR after a few seconds. Russian radars and other electronic systems now conducted periodic self-tests, looking for anomalies showing that their security was being penetrated. Although it was a crude measure, it did hamper Scion's ability to use SPEAR unchecked.

Much as he'd like to believe those enemy pilots would go on hunting along the wrong heading while the Rustler bolted for home, he knew that was a fool's dream. All too soon the Russians would figure out that they'd been tricked. He needed to finish this fight before that happened.

Brad pushed his throttles all the way forward and turned northeast after the MiGs. The XCV-70 accelerated smoothly, breaking past the sound barrier and going to 800 knots in seconds. Burning more fuel now would hurt them later . . . but going supersonic was the only way he could pull within Sidewinder range of those enemy fighters.

"Tease 'em again," he requested. "Only this time, plant the lure to make it look like we've dodged north of them, okay?"

Again, Nadia's fingers flashed across her displays, issuing orders to the SPEAR system. And again, the MiG-31s took the bait, swerving north to follow the flickering false image she'd planted in their radars.

Brad banked again, this time turning to come in behind and to the left of the Russian interceptors. Two target brackets popped onto his HUD. Each outlined a twin-tailed MiG-31, still invisible to the naked eye at this distance.

"Range now twenty-five miles," the Rustler's computer said.

He clicked a button on his stick. Three missile icons popped onto his HUD. They had three AIM-9X Sidewinders left in their internal weapons bays. Quickly, he assigned two of the heat-seekers to the lead MiG, saving the last missile for its trailing companion.

"Assigned targets are beyond effective missile range," the computer cautioned.

"Not for long," Brad murmured. "Just hold your horses."

"Command not understood," the Rustler responded primly.

Nadia snorted in amusement. Sky Masters–designed computer systems were high-tech marvels, but they had definite limitations, especially where English-language idioms were concerned.

PHANTOM THREE
THAT SAME TIME

"Contact lost again," Balandin reported over the intercom.

Beneath his oxygen mask, Grigoryev scowled. This

was getting ridiculous. Every time their radars seemed to get a grip on the enemy, the elusive American stealth aircraft somehow shook loose and vanished off their screens. "Keep on it, Alexey," he ordered.

In response to his radioed reports, Moscow was vectoring the other two MiG-31s in to join the pursuit—but they were still hundreds of kilometers away. For all the help they could offer in this deadly aerial game of hide-and-seek, they might as well be sitting back on the runway at Kansk-Dalniy.

His two fighters should try to catch the Scion plane in a pincer move, he decided—separating and then closing in on any new radar contact from different directions. Stealth technology wasn't a cloak of invisibility after all. So as the American pilot dodged away from one incoming MiG, the other Russian interceptor might find itself in a position to see it, lock on, and fire missiles.

Grigoryev clicked his mike. "Phantom Four, this is Three. Steer northeast for a minute and then come back in to the west. Let's see if we can—"

"New contact at two o'clock!" Balandin's startled call from the rear cockpit cut in.

Again a targeting diamond flashed onto Grigoryev's HUD, this time in the upper right-hand corner. The

Scion stealth aircraft had come up off the deck and was now a couple of thousand meters above them, he realized in surprise. Why? Climbing higher like this only made it easier for their radars to detect it and lock on. Unless—

BEEP-BEEP-BEEP.

The sudden shrill warning from their threat-warning sensors overrode conscious thought. Red threat icons speckled the upper right quadrant of his HUD.

"Missile attack!" Balandin yelled. "Multiple small bogies!" And then, "We're being jammed! The radar display's nothing but fucking green static!"

Reacting fast on trained instinct, Grigoryev yanked his stick hard left, hurling the big fighter into a high-G turn to the west. "Rudensky! Break left! Break left!"

Behind him, Balandin frantically jabbed at his multifunction displays to activate their countermeasures systems. Automated chaff dispensers fired, tossing cartridges into the air behind their MiG-31. They exploded, spewing thousands of Mylar strips across the sky to create false radar blooms that might lure away radar-guided missiles. A rippling curtain of decoy flares streamed out from under their fuselage, each momentarily brighter than the sun.

Straining against five times the force of gravity, Grigoryev suddenly saw two small gray blurs streak over his cockpit canopy. More enemy missiles! But these were coming from the wrong direction! From the southwest, not the northeast. Somehow the Americans had tricked them into turning directly into their real missile attack!

Desperately, he craned his head around—just in time to see Rudensky's MiG-31 vanish in a blinding explosion. Trailing pieces of debris and wreathed in smoke and flames, the shattered aircraft tumbled toward the earth.

BEEP-BEEP-BEEP.

"Christ!" Grigoryev yanked his stick back to the right . . . and a massive fireball exploded off their left wing.

The shock wave slammed the MiG-31 sideways. Red caution and warning lights lit up across the cockpit. *His left engine was on fire!* Desperately he punched controls—ordering the engine to shut down, cutting off the fuel flowing toward the flames, and triggering fire extinguishers.

Several of the red lights dimmed. The fire warning alarms went out.

Slowly, Grigoryev regained control over his tumbling fighter, sluggishly pulling it all the way through a complete 360-degree turn. With just one engine left, the huge, twin-tailed MiG wallowed through the air like a pig in deep mud.

"Our radar is back online," Balandin said suddenly over the intercom. "New radar contact! Twelve o'clock low! At thirty kilometers! I have a lock!"

This time Grigoryev saw the enemy aircraft with his own eyes. Outlined against the vast green marshland below them, its black batwing shape was plainly visible. Without hesitation, he squeezed the trigger on his control stick—commanding his computer to fire the two-missile salvo he'd readied earlier.

One of the two R-37M radar-guided missiles dropped from under the MiG's right wing and ignited. Riding a plume of fire and smoke, the huge four-meter-long missile slashed across the sky at six times the speed of sound. The second R-37 had been riddled by pieces of shrapnel when the American Sidewinder heat-seeker blew up. It detached, but its damaged rocket motor failed to light and it fell harmlessly toward the ground.

Without waiting to see the results of his attack, Grigoryev banked right again, urging his damaged fighter through a slow, shuddering turn to the northeast. More caution and warning lights came on as additional systems failed. Black smoke curled away from his wrecked turbofan engine. He just hoped he could hold this slowly dying machine in the air long enough to reach the emergency field outside Norilsk, two hundred kilometers away.

SCION SEVEN-ZERO
THAT SAME TIME

"*Warning, warning, radar missile launch at twelve o'clock,*" the Rustler's computer announced. "*One missile inbound at Mach six.*"

"Time to impact, fifteen seconds," Nadia said. Her eyes were locked on her displays. "Countermeasures ready."

Brad saw a streak of fire racing toward them from dead ahead. *Jesus,* he thought, *this is going to be close.* Jamming the MiG-31's radar wouldn't help them now. That R-37 was on inertial guidance, ready to switch to its own active radar seeker in the last moments of its attack.

The missile came straight at them.

"*R-37 seeker head is active,*" the computer reported. *Three. Two. One. Now!* He slammed the Rustler into a hard left turn, breaking across the Russian missile's flight path. G-forces shoved him hard back against his seat. His vision grayed out. "Countermeasures!" he snapped.

Nadia jabbed her defensive systems display. Chaff cartridges rippled out behind them and detonated. Unconvinced by the false radar images they created, the R-37 ripped on through the drifting clouds of Mylar strips and then began curving around to come back at them.

"Time to impact six seconds."

Brad rolled back right, turning in the opposite direction.

Gritting her teeth, Nadia leaned forward, fighting the G-forces pinning her in her seat. Her fingers flashed across her display, entering a new command. "Engaging that missile with SPEAR."

Streams of carefully tailored radio waves caressed the Russian missile's active seeker head. Seduced by false data, its simple-minded computer concluded that the enemy aircraft it was trying to kill was . . . right *here*. Relays closed.

And the R-37's sixty-kilogram fragmentation warhead detonated. A huge ball of fire lit the sky—well behind the XCV-70 Rustler.

Breathing hard, Brad rolled the aircraft out of its second high-G turn and swung back onto a heading that would take them across Russia's Arctic coast . . . and then home.

OVER THE ARCTIC OCEAN
SEVENTY MINUTES LATER

The Rustler sped onward, flying low over a wilderness of unbroken ice. Hundreds of miles farther south, night was at last beginning to fall across Siberia. But this far north, not far from the top of the world, the sun would never set during these summer months.

Nadia checked her engine and fuel status monitors again. Her mouth turned down. "Our fuel reserves are down to ten percent."

"That falls into the category of really bad news," Brad admitted. Between his earlier supersonic evasive maneuver and their tangle with that pair of MiG-31s, he'd blown through his safety margin. They should still be able to reach the Sky Masters air refueling tanker waiting for them north of Greenland—but it would be a very near-run thing. Pilots could bullshit all they wanted about "flying on fumes" when telling tall tales in the O-club. The truth was that the XCV-70 needed honest-to-God jet fuel to keep its big Affinity turbofans spinning. And right now, they were basically riding the knife edge between speed and fuel consumption.

"*Zaslon-M radar emissions increasing in strength,*" their computer said. "*Bearing now six o'clock and holding steady. Range sixty miles and closing.*"

"Swell," Brad muttered. They'd been picking up the radar emissions from two more MiG-31 fighters for the past several minutes—and it was clear that the Russians had a pretty good idea of where they were and where they were headed. Now those supersonic interceptors were closing in, getting set to launch their long-range missiles the moment they secured a solid radar lock. And that wouldn't be long now, no more than a few minutes. A combination of chaff and SPEAR might enable the Rustler to fend off one or two of the Mach 6–capable missiles. But there was no way they could stop a full salvo of eight R-37s.

Unfortunately, there wasn't anything more he and Nadia could do to break out of their increasingly grim tactical situation. They couldn't evade, because the Rustler was too short on fuel to maneuver effectively. And they couldn't fight, because they'd already expended all of its air-to-air missiles.

"You know what really pisses me off?" Brad said pensively.

"Slow drivers in the fast lane? Over-officious bu-reaucrats? The infield fly rule?" Nadia guessed.

Almost unwillingly, he smiled. "Well, yeah, them, too." He shook his head. "Right now, though, it's the possibility that Martindale was right about this being a suicide mission."

Brad felt her hand squeeze his shoulder.

"We are not dead yet, *drogie serce,* dear heart," she said gently.

"Two large unidentified airborne thermal contacts detected at twelve o'clock," the Rustler's computer broke in. *"Range indefinite, but closing at three-thousand-plus knots."*

"Scion Seven-Zero, this is Shadow Bravo One," Dusty Miller radioed from one of the fast-approaching S-29B spaceplanes. *"Hope you don't mind us crowding you a little."*

Brad felt a huge weight lift off his shoulders. "Not a bit, Bravo One," he replied. "Welcome to the party."

Beside him, Nadia saw a new com icon flashing on her left-hand display, indicating an urgent high-priority signal. She opened it.

Immediately, they heard a familiar voice come over their headsets. *"Mr. Martindale may have talked about leaving y'all hanging out to dry if you ran into trouble,"*

President John Dalton Farrell drawled. *"But I sure as hell never said any such thing."*

NATIONAL DEFENSE CONTROL CENTER
THAT SAME TIME

"Our air defense radars at Rogachevo, Nagurskoye, Sredny Ostrov, and Zvozdnyy all confirm the same thing. Two American Space Force S-29Bs have just dropped out of polar orbit and are moving to intercept our MiG-31s," Tikhomirov said grimly.

Marshal Leonov only nodded. "Recall your pilots, Semyon." He shrugged. "There's no point in tangling with those spaceplanes. Or in provoking an open military confrontation with the United States." He smiled dryly. "Not yet, anyway."

Tikhomirov looked relieved. "Yes, sir."

Leonov cut the secure connection. He sat back, deep in thought. While the escape of one of the Scion spies was exasperating, Russia would still profit from these events. If nothing else, the rapid, aggressive response of his Spetsnaz troops and MiG-31 fighters should convince the Americans that his fake Firebird Project spaceplane program was genuine. Equally important, thanks to the trap he'd sprung at Kansk-Dalniy, he'd successfully crippled Scion's espionage network inside Russia.

The Americans were now completely blind. He nodded in satisfaction. The timing was perfect. The first elements of Heaven's Thunder—the true focus of his secret alliance with the People's Republic of China—were only months away from launch. And by the time the United States and its allies realized what was really happening, it would be far too late.

TWENTY-THREE

U.S. SPACE COMMAND MISSILE AND SPACE LAUNCH WARNING CENTER, CHEYENNE MOUNTAIN COMPLEX, COLORADO
SEVERAL MONTHS LATER, IN EARLY 2023

Space Force Lieutenant General Daniel Mulvaney surveyed his new domain with quiet pride. Just a few weeks ago, a Pentagon directive had finally transferred control over the launch warning center to his new outfit, the U.S. Space Command. Making that move was one of the last pieces of the intricate organizational puzzle involved in bringing the Space Force to full operational readiness. Now America's newest armed forces branch had a clear chain of command from the earliest detection of possible hostile space action all the way up to the active-duty forces—Eagle Station and the S-29B spaceplanes—that would fight any battles in Earth orbit.

Sited two thousand feet beneath Cheyenne Mountain, the Missile and Space Launch Warning Center consisted of three stepped tiers facing several large screens—each currently showing digital maps of various parts of the world. Consoles with computers, displays, and secure communications links lined each level. Before the switchover to Space Command control, those consoles had been manned around the clock by officers and enlisted personnel from the Air Force, Army, Navy, and Marine Corps. Many of those same men and women were still here, performing the same duties. Only their uniforms, rank insignias, and unit patches were different, reflecting their lateral transfers to the Space Force.

Mulvaney ambled over to the desk belonging to the senior officer on watch, Major General Pete Hernandez. Hernandez, a former Marine Corps aviation wing commander, started to clamber to his feet in order to salute him.

"No need to make a fuss, Pete," Mulvaney said, waving the other man back down. "I'm just prowling, not inspecting." He took a seat. "How are things looking?"

"Pretty quiet so far today," Hernandez said with a shrug. "SpaceX has a launch slated from its Boca Chica site down near Brownsville, Texas, in a couple of hours."

"Anything interesting aboard?" Mulvaney asked.

"They're carrying out some kind of orbital rendezvous test," Hernandez replied. "As part of the president's lunar mining initiative."

Mulvaney nodded. A lot of private space companies in the United States, Canada, Europe, and Asia were ramping up their activity—hoping to snag some of the juicy contracts NASA was dangling. Based on what he was hearing, the tempo of space exploration and exploitation was set to increase exponentially. The historical analogy wrote itself. The Space Force was in much the same position as the old U.S. Army circa 1836, manning a few scattered frontier outposts just as the first wagon trains headed out on the Oregon Trail.

As he thought about the bandits and raiding parties who had preyed on those early settler caravans, Mulvaney's gaze slid to the large central display. It showed a map of Russia, its Central Asian neighbors, and the People's Republic of China.

Suddenly, a blinking red icon flashed onto the screen, centered about five hundred miles north of Moscow.

"Sir! SBIRS has detected an undeclared launch from the Russian Federation!" one of the junior watch officers reported.

With Mulvaney looking over his shoulder, Hernandez pulled up a data download from the Space-Based Infrared System's satellites. "Looks like a rocket launch from the Plesetsk Cosmodrome," he commented.

"Some kind of missile test?" Mulvaney asked. Plesetsk was often used to test new Russian ballistic missile designs.

Hernandez shook his head. "No, sir. The heat signature's enormous, much larger than that of any likely Russian ICBM." More information scrolled across his computer display. He whistled softly. "That's got to be one of their big heavy-lift rockets, one of the Energia-5VRs. And based on its current trajectory, it's heading into orbit."

Mulvaney frowned. He checked the boards, looking for Eagle Station's current position. It was high over the Western Pacific, just approaching the coast of Mexico. This suggested the Russians had deliberately timed their launch so that the U.S. space station was too far around the curve of the earth to see or engage the Energia's payload as it reached orbit.

What was Moscow up to?

Only minutes later, another red icon blinked into existence, this time over an island off the southern coast of the People's Republic of China.

"New launch! This one's lifting off from the PRC's Wenchang complex on Hainan Island," another watch officer reported.

Quickly, Hernandez studied the tracking data supplied by their satellites. "From the thermal signature, that's a Long March 5. And it's going into orbit, too."

Mulvaney's frown deepened. The Long March 5 was a large two-stage rocket, roughly in the same class as the American Delta IV Heavy. Though not as powerful as SpaceX's Falcon Heavy or Russia's Energia-5VR, it could still boost a serious amount of payload mass into low Earth orbit—somewhere around twenty-seven tons.

And then a third icon flashed onto the map. This one was in southwest China, near the southern tip of the PRC's Sichuan Province. "SBIRS confirms another Chinese Long March 5 launch," Hernandez said. "This time from the Xichang Space Center."

"From Xichang? That's supposed to be an *inactive* launch complex, isn't it, at least according to our goddamned intelligence reports?" Mulvaney growled.

"Yes, sir," Hernandez agreed. "The Chinese claimed they were shifting most of their civilian space operations to Wenchang, because launches from Xichang were too dangerous." He smiled wryly. "Apparently, the possibility that spent rocket stages might come crashing down on inhabited areas was seen as bad public relations, even in a communist dictatorship."

Mulvaney snorted. "Well, so much for that bullshit about bad PR." He stared at the screen, watching as the projected tracks for all three newly launched rockets curved across the large digital map. One undeclared Russian rocket launch was potential trouble. But three undeclared launches within a matter of minutes? One of them from a Chinese space complex U.S. intelligence had said was mothballed? There was no way what they were seeing was just coincidence, he decided. This was coordinated enemy action.

He donned a spare headset and plugged in. Then he reached for Hernandez's keyboard and entered a series of codes, activating a secure link to the White House. "This is Lieutenant General Mulvaney at USSPACE-COM. We are observing multiple non-ICBM launch events in both Russia and the People's Republic of China. I need to speak to the president."

SCION SECURE VIDEOCONFERENCE
SEVERAL HOURS LATER

"You guys ready?" Brad McLanahan asked quietly, with a glance at Nadia and Hunter Noble. They were in one of Sky Masters' Battle Mountain conference rooms, waiting for their satellite connection to the White House and Scion's Utah headquarters to go live. They nodded seriously, just as the wall-sized LED display lit up.

On-screen, President Farrell seemed as vigorous and full of life as Brad McLanahan remembered from earlier meetings. That made him an exception to the rule that most men and women who occupied the White House aged faster than ordinary people. If anything, the tall, broad-shouldered Texan seemed energized by the burdens of the Oval Office.

"I'd surely like to know just how we got caught with our drawers down . . . again," Farrell remarked dryly. "How in the hell did we miss the Russians and the Chinese prepping those rockets for launch?"

From Utah, Kevin Martindale shrugged. "It's the old story: too much ground to cover and not enough people, or, in this case, not enough space-based sensors, to do the job."

Beside him, Patrick McLanahan nodded. "We still only have a handful of reconnaissance satellites operational, Mr. President," he explained. "And they've been primarily tasked with tracking Russia's Firebird spaceplane program."

Though with slim results, Brad knew. In the months since the destruction of Scion's Russia-based intelligence network, America's spy satellites and Eagle Station's Space Force crew had captured a few images of what appeared to be spaceplane prototypes at airfields around Moscow and other sites. But so far none of those prototypes had been observed in flight—either inside the atmosphere or in orbit. So it was still impossible to get a handle on how much progress the Russian Firebird program had made since its first test flight at Kansk-Dalniy.

But even if Eagle Station's high-powered telescopes had been available to carry out other intelligence missions, they could not have spotted Russia's massive Energia-5VR rocket moving out to the pad. The Plesetsk Cosmodrome was too far north of the space station's orbital track—which probably explained why the Russians had chosen to launch from there, rather than the newer, more modern, and better-sited Vostochny space complex.

Reluctantly, Farrell nodded his understanding. Russia and China were still closed authoritarian societies, with their most vital secrets guarded by legions of secret police. Over the past several decades, American presidents and their national security teams had grown used to relying on satellite-driven intelligence. Robbed of the easy ability to peer down from orbit, and without the invaluable material provided so often by Scion's human agents, they were all wandering in the dark.

"All right, then," the president said grimly. "Let's cut to the chase. Now that we've found out the hard way that Beijing and Moscow are in cahoots: What's their plan? Are these surprise rocket launches aimed at building another armed space station?"

Brad understood his concern. A new Mars One circling Earth wouldn't give Russia or China unchecked dominance in space, not as long as Eagle Station was still intact—but it would restore a balance of terror in orbit . . . and greatly complicate America's ambitious plans to reach out to the moon and beyond.

He glanced sideways at Nadia and Boomer. They nodded encouragement. Bracing himself, Brad spoke up. "No, Mr. President," he said firmly. "Whatever the Russians and the Chinese are doing, they are *not* building a station in Earth orbit."

"You seem mighty confident about that, Major," Farrell commented.

"Yes, sir, I am." Brad shook his head. "For one thing, their spacecraft are not maneuvering for an Earth-orbit rendezvous. In fact, it would be completely impossible for them to dock now." He opened a file on his laptop. It was synched to their video link. Instantly, several 3-D visuals were mirrored for the president, his father, and Martindale. "For example, here's the current orbit of the Energia's third-stage booster and its payload." An image of the earth appeared, with a red line depicting the Russian spacecraft's path around the planet. It was a wildly elongated oval—almost seeming to brush against the earth on one side, while curving far out into space on the other. "As you can see, it's in a highly elliptical orbit, with an apogee nearly twenty-two thousand miles above the surface."

"And what's the perigee?" his father asked from Utah. "The lowest point of its orbit?"

"Just one hundred and twenty miles," Brad told him. He looked back at Farrell. "There's no way a severely elliptical orbit like that works for any kind of permanent manned military space station, sir. Apart from purely tactical considerations, any spacecraft in that orbit is yo-yoing up and down through both the inner and outer Van Allen radiation belts. No human crew could escape unharmed very long in those conditions, not without a hell of a lot more radiation shielding than would be practical."

"What about the two Chinese rockets?" the president pressed.

"They've also entered elliptical orbits," Brad answered. "Both Long March 5s carried Yuanzheng-2 upper stages with additional payloads. But given their present positions, neither Yuanzheng-2 booster has the delta-V necessary to achieve a rendezvous with the Russian spacecraft. At least not in any useful Earth orbit."

Martindale nodded his agreement. "Major McLanahan is right about all of that." He smiled thinly. "Nevertheless, as a precaution, Colonel Miller's S-29B is fully fueled and on standby at Eagle Station—ready to enter a fast-burn transfer orbit that will bring it within attack range if *any* of these spacecraft—Russian or Chinese—demonstrate hostile intent."

"Glad to hear that," Farrell said bluntly. "Now, I'd just as soon not start a new war in space. But if war comes, we're going to be the ones to finish it. Clear?"

"As crystal," Martindale said, speaking for all of them.

Brad's computer buzzed loudly, signaling an urgent message from the team of combined Scion–Sky Masters analysts assigned to keep tabs on those space vehicles. He heard Boomer's laptop making the same noise. His finger swiped across the screen. Instantly, a solid block of text and numbers popped open, accompanied by several blurry photos captured by ground- and space-based telescopes. He leaned closer, reading fast. His eyes widened in surprise.

"Holy shit," Boomer muttered out loud.

Farrell frowned. "Is there a problem, Dr. Noble?"

"We've just received new tracking data, Mr. President," Boomer answered. "Both of those Chinese Yuanzheng-2 boosters have restarted. And based on preliminary analysis, it looks like they're making translunar injection burns. If so, they're going to the moon."

"Carrying what?" Patrick asked.

Boomer shrugged. "We can't tell yet. Both payloads are still concealed by their fairings." Seeing their surprise, he nodded. "Yeah, that's pretty fucking weird right there."

Payload fairings, sometimes called shrouds, were thin metal shells intended to protect delicate satellites and other spacecraft from aerodynamic pressures and high temperatures during launch. They were ordinarily jettisoned once a rocket safely climbed out of the atmosphere and reached orbit. Usually, if those fairings failed to separate, the entire mission was doomed. But in this case it seemed likely that the Chinese were purposely retaining their payload fairings as a crude form of camouflage.

"The Russians are on the move, too," Brad reported. "The Energia third stage has just separated from its payload." He tagged one of the telescopic images and put it up on their screens. It showed a roughly fifty-foot-long spacecraft assembled from three different components—a blunt-nosed, cone-shaped capsule at the front, a larger cylinder in the middle, and what looked like nothing more than an egg-shaped fuel tank and rocket engine tied together by struts at the back. Solar panels extended off the central vehicle. "We're looking at a Federation command module mated to its service module, with a Block DM-03 space tug attached aft. And the engine on that space tug just finished a six-minute burn."

"Aimed where?" his father asked.

"Right where the moon will be in a little under three days," Brad said quietly.

"Son of a bitch," Farrell said in surprise. "So both the Russians and the Chinese are heading to the moon?"

Brad nodded. "Yes, sir. That's about the size of it."

"What the hell are they up to?"

Silence dragged on for several long moments. Without more information, no one felt able to provide a firm answer for Farrell's question. At last, Nadia leaned forward. "Whatever our enemies have planned, Mr. President, I do not think it will be good news for the United States." Her eyes darkened. "Or for Poland and the rest of the free world."

TWENTY-FOUR

MINISTRY OF FOREIGN AFFAIRS, BEIJING, PEOPLE'S REPUBLIC OF CHINA
A SHORT TIME LATER

China's Ministry of Foreign Affairs occupied a large gray modern building right in the center of Beijing, about three kilometers east of the Forbidden City. Its curving, convex front and adjoining wings surrounded a large central courtyard, whose most prominent feature was a garden where carefully manicured bushes and flower beds formed the outline of a dove of peace.

An amusing piece of visual propaganda, Russian foreign minister Daria Titeneva thought cynically. In her experience, the leaders of both her country and the People's Republic of China correctly saw diplomacy as a form of war waged through other means. In any negotiation between hostile powers, there would inevitably be winners . . . and losers. Those who proclaimed the virtues of mutually beneficial compromise were idealistic dreamers and fools. It was fortunate for Moscow and Beijing that so many of them held positions of influence in the West.

In her view, today's briefing for the international media was simply a somewhat more modern version of an age-old ruse. Time and again throughout history, emperors, kings, and generals had dispatched heralds of peace to their enemies, buying time with meaningless talk while secretly massing their armies for war.

Putting on a warm and gracious smile, Titeneva followed her older, male Chinese counterpart, Peng Xia, out into the Foreign Ministry's press briefing room. The two other human props in this little piece of diplomatic theater trailed behind her. Bearlike, with a shock of thick white hair, Anatoly Polikarpov was the head of Russia's state-owned civilian space corporation, Roscosmos. He dwarfed Shan Min, the director of China's National Space Administration.

Peng led them all to a lectern facing the assembled journalists and TV news crews. They lined up together, flanked by the red-, blue-, and white-striped Russian flag and China's gold-starred red banner. Huge projector screens covered the wall behind them. Titeneva and the others stood quietly for a few moments, giving the assembled journalists and camera crews time to take in this unexpected exhibition of high-level Sino-Russian diplomatic and scientific unity.

Murmurs and whispers tinged with sudden interest rippled through the crowded room. What had originally been billed as a relatively routine press conference after a meeting between the two foreign ministers now seemed more likely to produce real news.

With exquisite timing, Foreign Minister Peng moved forward to the lectern. "Honored comrades of the international press corps, thank for your presence here this afternoon." He offered them a slight smile. "I promise you that your diligence will be rewarded with more than the usual dull diplomatic platitudes." That earned him laughs from some of the Western journalists present. "As you may have guessed, this is no ordinary briefing," Peng continued.

To her amusement, Titeneva saw the array of reporters suddenly sit up even straighter. They reminded her of a pack of hungry dogs slavering at the sight and smell of a treat in their master's hand.

Peng paused briefly, allowing their anticipation to build. Then he went on, speaking calmly and precisely. "Earlier today, three rockets were launched into outer space—one from the territory of the Russian Federation and two from the People's Republic of China. The timing of these launches was not an accident. It was deliberate, the result of careful planning and many months of closely coordinated effort between our two countries." If anything, the assembled journalists grew even more eagerly attentive, straining at the leash, as they waited for more details.

Still smiling, Peng half turned and beckoned Titeneva to join him at the lectern. "I now invite my esteemed colleague, Foreign Minister Titeneva, to provide you with more details of this historic and unprecedented event."

She stepped forward, squaring her shoulders to present an image of resolute confidence. "Thank you for your gracious invitation, Minister Peng," she said with a quick nod. Then she turned back to the waiting journalists. "Ladies and gentlemen, I am honored to inform you that the People's Republic of China and the Russian Federation have today embarked on the first of a new series of peaceful voyages of discovery to the moon. Our first unmanned mission together is called Pilgrim 1—Cháoshèng in the language of our hosts or Palomnik in my own native tongue. This symbolizes the sense of awe and wonder with which we approach the moon, Earth's closest neighbor."

Left unspoken but perfectly clear, Titeneva knew,

was the vivid contrast between this seemingly peaceful Sino-Russian scientific mission and the greed and crass commercialism at the heart of America's own revived lunar program. Behind her, the briefing room's two large projector screens lit up.

Each showed full-color video imagery from the Yuanzheng-2 boosters heading toward the moon. Bright sparks flared on both screens as the boosters separated from their payloads and drifted off into the infinite blackness of space. There were more flashes as new explosive bolts detonated. Slowly, fairing panels detached and spun away, tumbling end over end—revealing the payloads flying toward Earth's moon for the first time.

Titeneva waited for a few seconds, allowing the first, sudden buzz of excitement and curiosity to fade a little. "What you see are the two halves of China's most advanced lunar lander, Chang'e-Ten," she explained. "One is its descent stage. The other is its ascent stage. If all goes well, these two spacecraft, controlled by their own onboard computers, will rendezvous in lunar orbit and dock. The goal of this first test of circumlunar vehicle assembly is to produce a single, mated lander . . . a spacecraft capable of carrying taikonauts and cosmonauts safely to the surface of the moon and then returning them to orbit."

She glanced toward the Chinese technicians control-

ling the video feeds. Obediently, they switched both
screens to a new view, this one showing the joined Federation command module, support module, and space
tug sliding away from the spent Energia third stage.
"And here is Russia's own Federation 2 spacecraft, also
on its way to lunar orbit. Once the Chang'e lander has
assembled itself and appears stable, ground controllers
on Earth will signal the Federation to match orbits and
dock." She shrugged. "If this were a manned mission,
that is when our cosmonauts and their Chinese taikonaut
comrades would transfer to the lander . . . and begin
their preparations to descend to the moon."

Titeneva saw a young woman, a reporter for one of
the American cable news networks, shoot to her feet—
evidently unable or unwilling to wait any longer to ask
a question. "Yes, Ms. Meadows?"

"But there aren't any cosmonauts or taikonauts
aboard that spacecraft?"

"No, there are not, Ms. Meadows," Titeneva said
firmly.

"Well, why not?" the young journalist demanded.
"I mean, if you're committing so many resources to
send these spaceships all the way to the moon . . . why
not just go ahead and land?"

Titeneva's polite smile broadened. "Because we are

not in a race, Ms. Meadows. Space flight is inherently dangerous, and our top priority is the safe return of any crews we do eventually send to the lunar surface." She adopted a more serious tone. "Pilgrim 1 is first and foremost a test flight—both of these brand-new spacecraft and of their ability to autonomously rendezvous and dock. As it stands, this multi-vehicle mission is already one of the most complicated space flights ever attempted. But I can tell you this: whatever happens, the experience we gain over these next several days *will* pave the way for future manned Sino-Russian expeditions to the moon."

With that, she signaled the men still waiting behind her to come forward. She turned back to the increasingly restless gaggle of journalists. "I'm certain that you all have many questions." She indicated her Chinese counterpart. "However, I'm equally sure that neither Minister Peng nor I is qualified to answer those questions. Now, if you're really more interested in the finer details of our most recent agricultural commerce talks, both of us would be glad to address those issues . . ." She let her voice trail off as the whole room broke into laughter.

With a chuckle of her own, Titeneva shrugged. "*No?* Then we will gladly yield the floor to Administrator Shan of China's National Space Administration and Director Polikarpov of Roscosmos. After all, this space mission is, as the Americans say, their baby."

Together, she and Peng left the room to a smattering of applause. Behind them, the two civilian space chiefs were already answering the first shouted questions. Inwardly, Daria Titeneva relaxed. She had carried out Marshal Leonov's instructions with consummate skill. Now the task of deception fell on other shoulders.

She knew that Polikarpov and Shan had been painstakingly briefed on what to say. No one listening to them would ever suspect that neither of their civilian agencies had any real role in the so-called Pilgrim 1 mission. For the time being, the knowledge that all three spacecraft now speeding to the moon were entirely controlled by Leonov and General Chen Haifeng, the commander of China's military space operations, would remain a tightly held secret.

TWENTY-FIVE

SKY MASTERS AEROSPACE INC., BATTLE MOUNTAIN, NEVADA SEVENTY-TWO HOURS LATER

Brad McLanahan glanced over his shoulder when his father and Kevin Martindale entered the secure conference room he'd commandeered for his special analysis team—which he realized was sort of a grandiose term for a group that really only consisted of him, Nadia, and Hunter Noble. Still, it was better than adopting Boomer's tongue-in-cheek suggestion that they call themselves the Triad of Genius Analysts, or TOGA for short. "Hey, Dad! Hey, Mr. Martindale. It's nice to see you guys in person for a change, instead of just on camera."

By air, Scion's Utah headquarters was only three

hundred miles from Battle Mountain—less than an hour's flight time for one of Scion's Gulfstream executive jets. He'd been hoping his father would take advantage of that. They hadn't seen much of each other lately. Between the joy of actually being married to Nadia and the day-in and day-out hard work needed to train new Space Force crews to fly and fight Sky Masters–built spaceplanes, whole weeks and months seemed to have slid past in a blur.

"Glad to be here, too, son," Patrick McLanahan said warmly. "With things heating up, we thought it was best to—"

"Is that situation board up-to-date?" Martindale interrupted, waving a hand at the conference room's large LED screen as he took a chair. The screen showed a 3-D image of the moon, with the orbital paths of different spacecraft depicted as green lines circling it. Red triangles indicated the current reported positions of each vehicle.

Nadia swung round angrily. Her eyes narrowed. She'd never had much patience with the former president's flashes of arrogance and condescension. There were moments when Martindale—highly intelligent though he was—completely misjudged the temper and tolerance of those around him.

Sensing the imminence of a full-on Rozek-McLanahan

explosion, Brad quickly interceded. "Yes, sir, it is." He helped his father to a seat, noting sadly how much more awkwardly the older man moved, even with the most recent software tweaks for his LEAF exoskeleton. "We're getting continuous updates from NASA tracking stations, from DOD's space surveillance satellites, and from its ground-based telescopes in New Mexico, Hawaii, and Diego Garcia."

Taking his cue, Boomer nodded. "Brad's right. We've got a pretty good handle on everything going on in lunar orbit," he told Martindale and Patrick. He shrugged. "Well, everything happening on the near side of the moon, anyway."

There was the rub. The United States didn't have satellites or telescopes in position to see anything happening on the far side of the moon—the side permanently hidden from anyone on Earth. Unfortunately, the same restriction did not apply to the Chinese or their Russian partners.

Five years before, China had put a communications relay satellite, called Queqiao, or Magpie Bridge, in a halo orbit around the Earth-Moon system's Lagrange-2 point, L2. Lagrange points were places where the gravitational forces of larger bodies, like the earth and the sun, combined to produce points of relative stability. Smaller spacecraft and satellites could hold station at these Lagrange points without having to expend large amounts of fuel. From L2, about forty thousand miles from the moon, the Magpie Bridge communications relay allowed Beijing and Moscow to continuously monitor space operations on the moon's far side.

Boomer pointed to a red triangle currently circling east to west across the moon's near side, about sixty miles above the Sea of Tranquility—the site of Apollo 11's historic landing way back in 1969. A tag identified it as the Chang'e-10. "So here's the deal. About five hours ago, both the ascent stage and the descent stage of that Chinese lunar lander successfully entered stable, circular lunar orbits. Right from the get-go, they were in close formation, maybe only five to ten miles apart." His mouth tightened. "That's pretty damned impressive flying, considering each machine covered more than two hundred and fifty thousand miles to get there."

Patrick McLanahan and Martindale nodded somberly.

Calmer now, Nadia took up the thread. "Two hours ago, during their second consecutive orbit, the Chinese vehicles conducted a successful docking maneuver. They are now mated together, apparently joined as a single spacecraft."

Martindale frowned. "Without any signs of trouble?"

"None," Brad answered. "From what we can see, everything about that lander appears nominal."

Patrick raised an eyebrow. "That's a pretty neat trick."

Brad nodded. "Yep." He pulled up a graphic of China's Long March 5 rocket. "But it explains how they blindsided us. The maximum payload a Long March 5 can send to the moon is around nine tons. Since any decent-sized crewed lander, like the Apollo Lunar Modules, weighs in around eighteen tons, we figured the Chinese would have to design, flight-test, and build a new type of heavy-lift rocket first. Before they could kick their plans to send taikonauts to the moon into gear, I mean. What we didn't figure on was the idea of sending a lander's ascent stage and descent stage to the moon separately . . . and then assembling them in lunar orbit."

"Which brings us to the next piece of this complex enemy space mission," Nadia said bluntly. Using a keyboard, she zoomed in on the 3-D image of the moon—revealing another red triangle so close to the Chang'e-10 that it had been invisible at the larger scale. Its alphanumeric tag identified it as the Federation 2. "The unmanned Russian spacecraft has conducted its own successful lunar insertion burn. And it now trails the Chinese lunar lander by just a few miles."

Martindale grimaced. "Good God," he muttered. "You're telling us they're actually going to make this work."

"Barring some unforeseen accident while docking, that's the way to bet," Brad agreed. He hesitated, just for a second or two, and then went on. "Which raises an ugly possibility . . ."

His father nodded. "That Beijing and Moscow are lying through their teeth. What if that supposedly *un-manned* Federation command module actually has cosmonauts and taikonauts aboard?"

"You think they might be planning a manned landing on the moon after all?" Nadia said slowly.

This time, Brad and his father nodded in unison.

"Whoa there, fellas," Boomer interrupted. "Now, I know thinking outside the box is kind of a McLanahan specialty, but that's pushing way beyond the envelope and out into wacko land." He shook his head. "Particularly when everything we know about Leonov and the Chinese leader, this Li Jun character, suggests they're both a hell of a lot more careful and cautious than the guys they took over from."

"Cautious and careful doesn't mean cowardly," Brad pointed out.

"No, but at a minimum it means these guys aren't stupid," Boomer retorted. He shook his head. "Okay, look, I get the drift. A surprise return to the lunar surface would be a huge propaganda win for Russia and China. But the risks involved in using a wholly untested spacecraft for a stunt like that are huge. One serious hardware malfunction or one software glitch at just the wrong time and five gets you ten, you end up with a bunch of dead guys drifting in orbit or smashed to pieces in some crater."

Nadia frowned at him. "You should not assume that Marshal Leonov and President Li Jun share our views on the value of human life."

"Oh, I'm pretty sure they don't," Boomer allowed. He gave her a wry smile. "But I do bet they know how to figure out the right side of a cost-benefit ratio."

Martindale looked pained, Brad noticed. He was probably remembering the argument he'd lost over rescuing Sam Kerr.

Boomer pressed his argument. "Look, guys, the Russians and the Chinese don't need to take any more risks than they already have to rub dirt in our faces. As things stand, even this one unmanned flight to the moon leapfrogs all of our half-assed plans to send astronauts back there."

"President Farrell's helium-3 lunar mining operation is a pretty big deal," Brad commented dryly.

Boomer waved that away. "One, it's still all on

paper. And two, even if that mine ever gets built, it's gonna be automated." He folded his arms. "Robots just aren't sexy," he said straightforwardly. "Not compared to real spaceman boots on the ground."

A chime interrupted them. On the screen, the icon representing the Russian spacecraft turned orange. Numbers appeared beside the orange triangle. They were decreasing.

"That's updated tracking data from NASA," Brad explained to his father and Martindale. He looked closer and frowned. "It looks like the Federation 2 is conducting its final maneuvers to close with that Chang'e lander." He turned back to them. "Based on those closure numbers, they'll be in position to dock somewhere around the far side of the moon."

"Well, there you go," Boomer said. "If those ships *are* manned and they're going for a real honest-to-God landing, we'll know soon enough. Just as soon as that Russian command module comes back around the edge of the moon on some orbit without the lander anywhere in sight."

TWENTY-SIX

ABOARD FEDERATION 2, IN LUNAR ORBIT
THAT SAME TIME

Colonel Tian Fan, China's senior military taikonaut, floated next to his co-commander, Russian cosmonaut Colonel Kirill Lavrentyev. He kept his arms and legs carefully tucked in. While the clean, spare, off-white interior of the Federation capsule was significantly less cramped than the old Soyuz and Shenzou capsules they were used to, it was still not spacious—especially with a full long-duration crew of four aboard. Its total usable volume was only about nine cubic meters, though that was about 50 percent bigger than America's Apollo-era command modules. Below their feet, Federation 2's other crewmen, Major Liu

Zhen and Captain Dmitry Yanin, were strapped into their couches, staying out of the way of their senior officers during this maneuver.

Lavrentyev was a little taller and heavier-set than the wiry Tian. One of his hands rested lightly on the Federation's flight control joystick. He studied the glowing readouts on their three multifunction liquid-crystal displays and grunted in satisfaction. "Everything looks good. We are go for docking with the Chang'e lander on this orbit."

Tian nodded. "And our communications links to Moscow and Beijing?" he asked. "No problems?"

In answer, Lavrentyev opened a new menu. A row of solid green bars showed the status of their data links. Through a network of data-relay satellites, a steerable antenna mounted in the service module's tail section kept them in constant touch with ground controllers in Russia and the People's Republic. To maintain the fiction that this was an unmanned test flight, there would be no radio voice transmissions for the duration of the mission. Instead, all messages between the spacecraft and its controllers were passed in encrypted data packets, hidden in the stream of routine telemetry.

"Very good," Tian said. He cocked his head, listening. Apart from the background hum of their air-recirculation fans and water pumps, there was very little noise. The contrast with earlier space flights— with their never-ending torrent of radio static and chatter with mission control teams—was striking.

He glanced at Lavrentyev. "This silence is . . . different."

The Russian cosmonaut's teeth flashed white. "It's so quiet, I can scarcely hear myself think."

Tian grinned back. "Perhaps that is just as well, Kirill. You know that thinking only gets you in trouble."

"*Eto tochno.*" Lavrentyev laughed. "So true." During their long months of training together, differences in their approaches to problem-solving had become both obvious and a source of some humor. The Russian favored quick action, figuring it was better to act decisively than to dither in a crisis. In contrast, Tian was more analytical, though his reaction times were also almost inhumanly fast. Intensive preparation, instruction, and hundreds of hours of practice in simulators had welded them into a smoothly functioning command team. They were perfectly matched to the challenges of this arduous and fiendishly complex space mission . . . the first necessary step toward making Heaven's Thunder an operational reality.

ABOARD THE CHANG'E-10 LANDER, IN LUNAR ORBIT
SEVERAL HOURS LATER

For three full orbits after docking with the unmanned Chinese-built lunar lander, the four-man Federation 2 crew worked hard to make sure Chang'e-10's ascent stage and descent stage were correctly assembled and in perfect working order. No one had ever tried having two separate spacecraft autonomously connect themselves into a single functioning ship before. The technique probably wouldn't have worked for a vehicle intended to fly in Earth's atmosphere and gravitational field. Fortunately, operations around the airless moon, with just one-sixth gravity compared to that of the mother planet, would place considerably less stress on the lander's structure.

Now, Colonel Tian Fan and Kirill Lavrentyev left Federation 2 and transferred to Chang'e-10. With everything checked out, it was time to find out if the lander could perform the mission for which it had been designed.

Tian tucked his feet under a bar to hold himself in place, connected his restraining straps, and looked ahead through his command pilot's triangular window. The gray surface of the moon curved across his horizon. Without any atmospheric distortion, the edges of every crater rim and rise appeared razor-sharp, perfectly distinct even from nearly one hundred kilometers up. Pitch-black shadows stretched out ahead of them.

He glanced at one of the large multifunction displays fixed between his station and his copilot's position. Rows of status icons glowed green. The Chang'e's main engine, attitude control thrusters, life-support system, lidar and star tracker navigation systems, and communications relays were all functioning perfectly. Compared to the dizzying array of dials, switches, and readouts crammed into the Apollo Lunar Modules, the Chang'e's control systems were a model of efficient simplicity.

Kirill Lavrentyev drifted down from the docking hatch over their heads and hooked in on his right. "We are closed up and sealed," he reported.

Tian nodded. With one gloved hand, he tapped a com icon on his display. For now, while they were crossing the moon's Earth-facing side, communications between the two linked spacecraft used a hardwired intercom. "Federation, this is Chang'e-Ten; our hatch is closed. What is your status?"

Through his headset, he heard Major Liu Zhen reply from the larger spacecraft. *"Copy that, Chang'e. We confirm both hatches are closed and sealed. Venting the tunnel now."*

Pumps cycled, depressurizing the short tunnel connecting the Federation command module and their lander. Both spacecraft shuddered slightly. Thrusters fired, automatically counteracting the tiny motion imparted by the gases venting into space.

Lavrentyev cycled through menus on his own screen. "Pulsing the lidar now," he said. Their flash lidar system fired low-powered lasers at the lunar surface and used the reflected pulses to create three-dimensional images of the terrain they were flying over. By comparing those images to maps stored in its memory, the computer could determine precisely where they were, relative to the surface, at any given moment. Seconds later, the Russian cosmonaut announced, "Navigation fix confirmed. We are crossing the Ocean of Storms and approaching the Hevelius crater. Ten minutes to LOS."

"Understood," Tian said. LOS meant loss of signal. It marked the point at which their spacecraft's orbit would carry it around the curve of the moon—cutting off radio transmissions and observations from Earth or near-Earth satellites. Since their communications were routed through China's Magpie Bridge relay at the L2 point, they would be completely unaffected by this transition. But the Americans, blind and deaf to anything happening on the moon's far side, would no longer be able to see what they were doing. He entered a code on his screen. A new menu lit up. "Initiating final pre-separation checklists."

Row after row of separate spacecraft systems flashed yellow and then cycled to green as the computer tested them and made sure they were properly configured. To ease the workload on their two-man crews, the engineers who designed China's Chang'e landers had built in a high degree of automation.

Nevertheless, Tian and Lavrentyev followed along at every step. No sane pilot put his whole trust in automated systems, especially not on an incredibly complex brand-new space vehicle making its first real flight. "Lander life support is good. Thrusters are go. Docking latches are ready to release. Descent engine is on standby."

Through their headsets, they could hear Liu and the other Russian cosmonaut, Captain Yanin, going through their own checklists aboard Federation 2. A tone sounded. Moments later, a computer-decrypted message scrolled across the top of their displays: AT YOUR DISCRETION, YOU ARE GO FOR UNDOCKING AND DESCENT BURN AS PLANNED. GOOD FORTUNE. LEONOV. LI JUN. MESSAGE ENDS.

The two men exchanged wry smiles. Did Marshal Leonov and President Li Jun honestly believe their explicit permission was necessary to men who were so far from their home planet? But since all crew conversations were automatically recorded and periodically downloaded to Moscow and Beijing, neither thought it especially wise to comment out loud.

"Checklist complete. All systems are nominal. Ready for separation at LOS plus sixty seconds," Tian announced calmly, as the computer finished its work. He reached up and slid the visor of his helmet down. It clicked into place. He heard the comforting hiss of air flowing through his space suit's umbilical hose. Next to him, Lavrentyev closed and sealed his own helmet.

Ahead through his window, Tian saw the moonscape change character. In contrast to the near side's vast dark basalt plains, the moon's far side was a rugged expanse of thousands of craters—some small, others hundreds of kilometers wide. A radio-antenna-shaped icon on his MFD turned red. "Loss of signal."

He tapped another icon on the display, setting an automated undocking sequence in motion. A digital readout appeared on-screen, counting down the remaining seconds. The Chang'e's sophisticated flight computer was now in complete control.

As a precaution, Tian put his hands on the two controllers mounted beneath his display. If the automated program glitched, he was ready to shut it down and take manual control.

"Ten seconds," Lavrentyev said quietly, following the computer-driven countdown.

Tian tensed, waiting as the seconds ticked by. Then, with a muted *clang-clang-clang,* the latches holding the Chang'e and Federation released. The lander jolted as its thrusters fired, pulling it away from the larger Russian command module. A com icon changed shape, signaling the transition from hardwired intercom to low-powered, short-range radio.

"Good separation," they heard Liu say. *"Chang'e-Ten, this is Federation, you are clear. Fifty meters separation and increasing at five meters per second. We are commencing our own thruster maneuver to open the range faster."*

"Copy that," Tian acknowledged. Looking ahead through his window, he saw a long chain of smaller impact craters curving roughly north to south across their flight path. He cued their nav system, and it confirmed his visual impression. They were approaching the Leuschner Catena. It was one of the aim points for their planned descent to the lunar surface. "All right, Kirill, let's deploy the landing gear."

Lavrentyev nodded. He opened another menu on his display and stabbed at it with a gloved finger. "Master Arm on."

Tian saw the confirming light. "Go on that."

"Landing gear deploy." The Russian tapped his display again. "Firing."

WHAANG. Another small vibration rattled through the Chang'e lander as tiny explosive bolts detonated. Released from the clamps holding them close against the spacecraft's hull, their landing struts swung down and locked in position.

"Chang'e-Ten, this is Federation," Liu radioed. *"Your gear is down. We see all four struts."*

Tian checked their flight path again. They were still right in the groove, orbiting westward around the moon at sixteen hundred meters per second. He glanced at Lavrentyev. "Go for landing?"

The Russian nodded decisively. *"Da.* We are go for landing."

"Initiating landing sequence . . . now," Tian said, entering the necessary command code. New menus opened on his display. "Automated sequence activated. The computer is in control."

In milliseconds, the Chang'e's flight programs assessed their position, heading, and speed, made the necessary calculations, and sent commands to different spacecraft systems. "Three . . . two . . . one," Lavrentyev counted down. Indicators flashed green. "Pitch over."

Thrusters popped, rotating the lander through 180

degrees so that its engine was aligned against their direction of travel. Inside the cabin, Tian and Lavrentyev were now looking "up" at the moonscape through their windows.

With a muted *whummp,* their descent rocket motor lit. Instantly the two men were jolted forward against their restraints. As the engine fired, the spacecraft's forward velocity decreased. Too slow now to resist the pull of the moon's gravity, the lander slanted downward.

Ninety seconds later, the engine cut out.

"Good burn," Lavrentyev announced. Numbers and graphics scrolled across his display. "No residuals. Our rate of descent looks good." He activated their lidar again, double-checking the computer. "Altitude now seventy kilometers. We are descending at one hundred meters per second. Speed over the ground eleven hundred meters per second."

More thrusters fired, pitching the Chang'e back around so that they could see where they were headed. The lander was sliding downward across the Hertzsprung crater. It was enormous, several hundred kilometers in diameter. Nearly a dozen smaller craters pockmarked its gray surface. Beyond Hertzsprung's west rim—torn and gouged by other aeons-old impacts—they could see more large craters, Kibal'chich, Vavilov, and Tsander.

Tian took another navigational fix, again checking to make sure the flight control computer was still hitting its marks. "Range to target area now eight hundred and thirty kilometers. Everything looks good. We are still go for landing."

Fifty kilometers downrange and thirty kilometers higher than the Chang'e-10 lander, the Federation 2 spacecraft spun end over end. Thrusters pulsed, stopping its rotation with the command module facing aft. Inside the Federation's cabin, Major Liu Zhen tracked Chang'e-10 through remote-controlled television cameras. Even at high magnification, the lander was more a blur of reflected sunlight from its gold- and orange-colored insulating foil than a distinct shape as it sloped downward. "Well, they're committed now," Liu commented to the Russian cosmonaut hovering close by.

Captain Dmitry Yanin nodded. Even if Lavrentyev and Tian aborted their landing at the last minute, firing their engine again to climb back into orbit, it was too late for their spacecraft to dock with Federation 2 again before both machines circled back around the moon's near side—and into view of America's spy satellites and ground-based telescopes.

In truth, neither Yanin nor Liu expected their fellow crewmen to abort. During the long months of training and preparation, both Tian and Lavrentyev had made it pretty clear that they'd prefer to die trying to land, rather than experience the humiliation of a failed attempt and a long trip back to Earth under the mocking gaze of their American enemies.

Holding on to the edge of the Federation 2's control console to avoid drifting off across the cabin, Liu spun slightly to look at Yanin. He indicated the descending lander, now little more than a pinpoint of light against the rocky, crater-strewn surface below. "Do you wish you were aboard? That we were the ones making this first landing?"

"My God, no," the Russian lied. "My parents raised me to be a spaceman . . . not a lunonaut." He shrugged. "Now, ask me again on our next trip . . . and you'll certainly get a different answer."

Liu nodded with a smile. If all went well, he and Yanin were slated to crew the next Chang'e lander.

An icon on one of the console displays pinged sharply, calling for their attention. It had been triggered by a coded ground controller message relayed through the Magpie Bridge comsat. Liu tapped at it. The icon opened into a menu headed DECEPTION OPERATIONS. Frowning, he checked their position. They were still thirty-odd minutes from AOS, or acquisition of signal, the point at which Earth-based sensors could see them.

"Moscow is impatient," he told the other man. "They want us to go ahead and deploy the decoy early."

"I guess now's as good a time as any," the Russian said offhandedly. "Not that we can do anything if there's a fuckup at this point."

"True. On both counts," Liu agreed. He scrolled to the first necessary command button and pushed it. "Decoy deployment arming switch enabled."

Floating close enough to read the display, Yanin followed along. "The switch is active," he confirmed.

"Deploying the decoy," Liu said. He tapped the button once. And then a second time, confirming for the computer that his first motion had not been an accidental swipe across the display screen.

POP-POP-POP-POP.

The Federation vibrated rhythmically for several seconds. Beyond the hatch, a cylindrical bag fixed around the upper outer hull burst open. Within seconds, a structure made of layers of interwoven Kevlar-like fabrics and vinyl polymer foam ballooned into being. Tightly tethered around the command module's hatch, it was the same size and shape as the now-departed Chang'e lander. Carefully placed radar reflectors studded the decoy's outer surface.

Readouts on Liu's console turned solid green. The decoy was secure, fully inflated, and holding its shape.

Both men smiled at each other with relief. To American surveillance satellites and telescopes, it would appear as if the Chang'e lander and the Federation 2 were still docked.

Aboard Chang'e-10, Lavrentyev set their lidar system to continuous pulse—providing the computer with the steady flow of data it needed to track their altitude, rate of descent, ground speed, and position. "Altitude now twenty thousand meters. Rate of descent still one hundred meters per second."

Through his window, Tian saw the battered outer rim of the Tsander crater growing larger as they slanted down. Tsander was ancient beyond measure. Over hundreds of millions of years, it had been pounded by debris raining down from space. In places, these impacts had almost obliterated Tsander's once-distinct edges—turning it into a jumble of secondary craters, slopes, and folds.

Another large crater was just coming into view, far away across a plain pockmarked and pitted by much smaller hollows. Its slopes rose gradually, steadily climbing until they were several thousand meters above the lower ground. They were relatively unmarked, splotched and scarred only in places by lighter-colored ejecta—masses of once-molten debris—hurled outward from the asteroid impact that had created this large crater. "I have Engel'gardt in sight," Tian announced. "Stand by for descent engine nozzle gimbal and re-light."

He flexed his hands on the two controllers. He was prepared to shut down their landing program and come in manually at the first sign of trouble.

From his position, Lavrentyev watched the indicators for their descent engine change color. Numbers scrolled across his display. "Gimbal complete. The angle looks good. Engine Arm light is on. Good fuel flow. Three . . . two . . . one—"

WHUMMP.

Once again, the two men swayed against their harnesses, jostled by the sudden deceleration. "Ignition. Throttling up to ten percent power," Lavrentyev reported. He switched to his nav readouts. "Rate of descent slowing to fifty meters per second. Forward speed dropping, too. Down to three hundred meters per second. Altitude now fifteen thousand meters. Coming down steadily."

This time, the lander's rocket motor kept firing. They could see the east rim of the Engel'gardt crater growing larger and larger in their windows. Seconds from landing, it was all they could see. They were coming in on top of a flattened peak rising higher than any other point along the rim wall. Only a few kilometers beyond this high point, the ground fell away, plunging steeply more than four thousand meters to the crater floor.

"Altitude one hundred meters. Down at ten meters per second. Twelve meters forward. Fuel at fifteen percent," Lavrentyev intoned, keeping up a running commentary as the computer brought them in.

Tian kept his eyes fixed out the window, watching the ground coming up at them with what felt like astonishing speed. There were only a few small boulders visible, widely scattered across the rim plateau. Part of him desperately wanted to shut down the computer and bring the lander in under his own control. Self-discipline instilled by years of training enabled him to resist the temptation.

Outside, a cloud of moondust billowed up, obscuring his view.

"We're at five meters. Zero relative forward velocity. Down to three meters. Two. One. Engine cutoff!" Lavrentyev snapped excitedly.

The rocket motor shut down and Chang'e-10 dropped the last few centimeters. The spacecraft rocked slightly and then came to rest on its four landing struts.

Tian breathed out. After sharing an exultant grin with the Russian, he opened a radio channel to the Magpie Bridge communications relay. "Beijing Flight Control, Moscow Control, Korolev Base here. Chang'e-Ten has landed."

TWENTY-SEVEN

KOROLEV BASE, HIGH UP ON THE EASTERN RIM
OF ENGEL'GARDT CRATER, THE MOON
THE NEXT DAY

The long shadow cast by the Chang'e-10 lunar lander stretched across a gray moonscape of compacted, fine-grained dust, rocks, and pebbles. There were no other shadows. This was the highest point on the lunar surface, rising nearly two thousand meters higher than Earth's Mount Everest. Of course, since the approach slopes were so much more gradual, the vistas were not as dramatic.

Bulky in his space suit, Colonel Tian Fan leaned over the wheeled lunar rover he had just successfully extracted from a storage bay in the lander's lower descent stage. He pulled open a small control box located on the rover's side and flipped a switch.

Inside the rover's chassis, a small rod of radioactive plutonium-238 slid out of its protective graphite container and into a radioisotope thermoelectric generator, or RTG. Now active, the RTG converted the heat produced by radioactive decay into electricity. An indicator light glowed green, showing that power was being produced. Unlike batteries or solar panels, the RTG would produce electricity continuously—even during the coming two-week-long lunar night, when temperatures would plunge three hundred degrees Celsius.

Tian waited a few more seconds for the system to stabilize and then flipped a second switch. This one activated the rover's computer. More lights glowed. Satisfied, he closed the control box and stepped back.

Moments later, the rover started up and moved off slowly across the lunar surface. Guided by its programming, it drove a couple of hundred meters away from Chang'e-10 and parked. Although it was approximately the same size as the rovers carried by America's long-ago Apollo missions, this machine had a very different purpose.

Equipped with a raised blade at the front and a hopper in place of seats, the rover was designed to scrape up regolith—loose dirt, dust, and rocks—and then feed it into an automated furnace and chemical reaction unit built into the base of the lander. Over the next several weeks, remotely controlled by technicians back on Earth, the system would accumulate stores of hydrogen, oxygen, and water separated out of the regolith. Those vital life-support and fuel supplies would significantly reduce the amount of payload mass needed by future manned missions to this site.

Tian turned and moved off toward where Kirill Lavrentyev was working, gliding and hopping across the loose gray surface at a rapid clip. Their EVA suits, though still awkward to move in, were more flexible than those worn by America's Apollo astronauts. "How's it going?" he asked.

"The last beacon is set and operating," the Russian cosmonaut reported, looking up. He backed away from the small radio antenna and transmitter he'd just finished anchoring in place.

"Excellent work," Tian said. Setting up a network of six radio beacons across a stretch of the crater rim had been one of their primary tasks for this landing. Signals from those beacons would help guide China's Mǎ Luó automated cargo landers to precise touchdowns during planned follow-on missions. "Then it's time for us to prep for takeoff."

"*Twenty-four hours seems a very short time to spend here after so many months of training,*" Lavrentyev said somberly. "*Especially after so many decades.*"

Tian knew what he meant. Both men were aware of the bittersweet irony involved in this mission. It had been more than half a century since anyone had walked on the moon. And while he and the Russian cosmonaut were only the thirteenth and fourteenth men in all of human history to do so, their achievement must remain a closely guarded secret for the time being. He laid a gloved hand on the other man's shoulder. "Remember, Kirill, we'll be back. And soon."

Lavrentyev nodded.

Together, they turned and headed back to the waiting Chang'e lander.

Two hours later, Chang'e-10's ascent engine fired. The upper half of the lander, separating from its descent stage, soared into space. It climbed fast along a rising arc that would intercept the Federation 2 spacecraft as it swung back around the moon's far side. From his command pilot's station, Tian monitored their progress. He glanced across the tiny cabin at Lavrentyev. "I show a good burn. Our trajectory looks perfect."

The Russian studied his own readouts and nodded. "I concur."

Quickly, Tian entered a series of orders on his display. "Ascent engine command override is off. Engine Arm is off." Now that they were off the surface and on course to rendezvous with Federation 2, they no longer needed their powerful rocket motor. From now on, Chang'e's smaller reaction control system thrusters would handle any necessary last-minute maneuvers.

Beside him, Lavrentyev moved on to his next task. "Standing by to deploy our camouflage stage." He entered a command on his own MFD. "Deploying now."

His order triggered another inflatable decoy. This one was shaped to mimic the visual and radar signature of Chang'e-10's discarded descent stage, still sitting far below them on the rim of Engel'gardt crater.

Aboard Federation 2, Major Liu Zhen saw the approaching lander's ascent stage change shape, seeming to double in size as what looked like Chang'e-10's missing lower half suddenly ballooned from its aft section. He swung toward Yanin. "They're coming in fast, Dmitry. We need to clear our docking hatch."

The cosmonaut nodded. His fingers danced across the control console. "I'm setting our decoy lander loose."

Federation 2 shuddered. Cut loose by tiny explosive charges, their own full-sized Chang'e-10-shaped decoy slowly drifted away. Seconds later, small, one-use thrusters that were attached to the decoy's Kevlar-like outer layer fired. The decoy veered away under lateral thrust, and when it was several kilometers off their orbital track, self-destruct charges detonated—shredding it into several thousand tiny fragments of torn fabric and bits of polymer foam in one blinding flash.

Liu triggered their lidar. Laser pulses confirmed Chang'e-10's ascent stage was still on track for its rendezvous. Like so much else on this mission, the sheer speed required for this maneuver was unprecedented. To keep the Americans from realizing they'd succeeded in landing on the moon, Chang'e-10 and Federation 2 had only a few minutes remaining to dock. There was almost no margin for error.

With breathtaking swiftness, the two spacecraft seemed to rush together. Tiny flashes of light briefly lit the lander's flanks and upper hull. It rotated slightly and decelerated. More numbers flowed across Liu's display.

"Chang'e, this is Federation," he radioed. "Range now two hundred meters. Closure rate is down to five meters per second." A red-tagged alert popped up on his display. "Time to AOS is now just ninety seconds," he warned.

"Understood, Federation," Tian replied coolly over the circuit. *"Stand by for docking."*

The lander closed in, growing larger and larger on-screen. Its thrusters fired again, distinct now as puffs of glowing gas. "Closure rate now two meters per second," Liu intoned. "Range forty meters. Time to AOS forty seconds."

Abruptly, Chang'e-10's upper hull thrusters fired longer than expected—decreasing its relative velocity to zero while the two spacecraft were still twenty meters apart. *"Automated docking program failure,"* Tian reported. Astoundingly, his voice sounded completely calm. He might have been announcing the weather on a clear, sunny day. *"I'm taking manual control. Stand by, Federation 2 . . . there might be a bit of a bang."*

"Shit," Yanin muttered in disbelief. "The fucking computer just crashed? Now?"

Liu felt his teeth clench. In less than thirty seconds, they would come back around the edge of the moon. On-screen, more thrusters pulsed and Chang'e-10 seemed to jump toward them.

"Range five meters," he said, swallowing hard as

the other spacecraft loomed up fast, completely filling their camera view. "Four . . . two . . ."

Anticipating an impact, Liu and Yanin gripped the edges of their control console.

SCREECH.

Chang'e-10's docking probe scraped noisily along the inside of the Federation command module's cone-shaped port and then came to rest. Latches closed around the probe and retracted, pulling the two spacecraft tightly together.

"*Capture,*" Tian declared, still sounding cool and collected. "*Docking complete.*"

Seconds later, the two mated spacecraft swung back around the curve of the moon and into full view of America's watching satellites and telescopes. To all appearances, this was just another routine orbit, one of nearly twenty since the Sino-Russian mission first reached the moon.

Four hours and two orbits later, Tian, Lavrentyev, Liu, and Yanin separated their Federation command module from the now-empty Chang'e-10 lander. Back under control of its onboard flight computer, the smaller Chinese-built spacecraft's thrusters fired again. It slowed and descended, curving downward under the pull of the moon's gravity. Eventually, the abandoned lander and its own attached decoy would crash close to the Reinhold crater on the moon's near side—disappearing in a brief burst of exploding fuel and debris.

Higher in lunar orbit, the DM-03 space tug's rocket motor relit. Boosted out of the moon's gravitational clutches, the Federation command module and its four-man crew began their three-day voyage back to Earth.

The first essential phase of Operation Heaven's Thunder was complete.

EISENHOWER EXECUTIVE OFFICE BUILDING, WASHINGTON, D.C.
SEVERAL DAYS LATER

Originally built in the late nineteenth century to house the Departments of State, War, and the Navy, the seven-story Eisenhower Executive Office Building had long since outgrown its original tenants. Since it was located immediately adjacent to the White House, its offices were now occupied primarily by the Office of Management and Budget, the National Security Council, and other aides working directly for the president and his senior staff. The building's ornate French Second Empire–style façade and its green slate and copper roof stood in stark contrast to the rest of Washington, D.C.'s federal buildings, which were either elegant neoclassical structures or ugly concrete monstrosities.

Apart from the vice president's ceremonial office and other elegantly appointed chambers used for formal occasions—like the Indian Treaty Room, where the United Nations charter had been signed in 1945—most of the building's more than five hundred rooms were assigned as ordinary office space. There were, however, a handful of larger conference rooms reserved for occasional interagency meetings.

Inside one of those rooms, Brad McLanahan and Nadia Rozek-McLanahan now sat side by side at a large oval table. Around them were more than two dozen men and women—all of them middle-ranked executives from NASA, the CIA, the Defense Intelligence Agency, and an alphabet soup of other federal agencies. Officially known as the Sino-Russian Space Alliance Analysis Working Group, these people had been meeting daily to coordinate the federal government's assessment of recent events in lunar orbit. At President Farrell's insistence, Brad and Nadia, as representatives of Sky Masters and Scion, had been allowed to participate in this afternoon's session.

But two hours into the meeting, Brad was beginning to think this would be more accurately labeled a "nonworking group." Most of the officials crowding this room seemed to have been picked for their ability to speak eruditely and at length, without actually committing their agencies to any firm position. And while none of them were openly impolite, it was obvious that they saw him and Nadia as unwelcome outsiders shoehorned in by a president who didn't fully appreciate how the permanent government was supposed to function.

Noting Nadia's tight-lipped mouth, Brad knew she'd already given up on these people. She was probably right. This group of bureaucrats seemed determined to remain undecided. Still, he decided to try again to shake some kind of action plan loose. He leaned forward, wishing for the hundredth time that he could get up and pace around the room to burn off some energy. Sitting on his ass while other people droned on and on for hours had never been on his list of "things Brad McLanahan is good at."

He held up his hand, interrupting someone from the CIA who was assuring everyone that her agency would keep them in the loop if any new intelligence materialized. That was a promise Brad was pretty sure he'd already heard the same woman make at least twice in the past two hours. "Excuse me?"

"Yes, Mr. McLanahan?" the Working Group's chairman said, raising a finely sculpted eyebrow. Adrian Yates was an executive in NASA's Office of International and Interagency Relations.

"Between Sky Masters and Scion and all of your organizations, we've already checked and rechecked every piece of data gathered since the first two Chinese Yuanzheng boosters headed for the moon," Brad pointed out. "Going over and over what's already known isn't going to get us any further. It might be smarter to focus on aspects of this supposedly unmanned lunar mission that don't make any real sense."

Yates frowned. "Such as?"

"Well, for starters, why did the Russians and Chinese keep that Federation 2 command module in Earth orbit for more than twenty-four hours after its return from the moon?" Brad suggested.

The NASA executive shrugged. "I fail to see that as some sort of deep dark mystery, Mr. McLanahan," he said. "I assume Moscow and Beijing were conducting additional systems tests on a brand-new spacecraft that had just completed a prolonged circumlunar flight. That would be sensible policy, after all."

"Maybe so," Brad agreed, not hiding his own skepticism. "But that delay also meant we didn't have any satellites in position to observe the command module's reentry. Or its landing on Russian territory. What if that was deliberate?"

Yates sighed. "Are you still suggesting the Sino-Russian Pilgrim 1 mission might have been manned?"

Brad nodded. "It's a possibility."

"Based on your personal involvement in regrettable past armed conflicts, I understand your ingrained habit of assuming the worst, Mr. McLanahan," Yates said with a wry smile. "But you should remember that neither the Russians nor the Chinese are really ten-feet-tall supermen. Besides, even if there were cosmonauts and taikonauts aboard Federation 2, what does it matter? When you boil the Pilgrim 1 mission down to its essentials, all Moscow and Beijing have accomplished is a test of lunar orbit rendezvous and spacecraft systems. That's nothing more than our Apollo 10 mission demonstrated, almost fifty-four years ago."

Fed up, Nadia snorted. "And could your agency repeat that Apollo 10 flight today, Mr. Yates?" she asked acidly.

Somewhat disconcerted, the other man admitted, "Well, no. Until our new heavy-lift SLS rocket is certified ready for flight, we can't—"

"Exactly," Nadia said. "So, at a minimum, Russia and China have just shown that they can reach the moon and return safely—a capability *we* no longer possess. Nor should we assume that is all they have planned. Because Brad is right: there are anomalies we must explore further." She used her tablet computer to pull up a sequence of images and then sent them to the conference room's larger screen for everyone else to see. "For example, this odd cloud of debris observed during Pilgrim 1's seventeenth orbit. What could it be?"

The pictures showed a swiftly dissipating cloud of radar reflective particles near the docked Federation 2 command module and Chang'e-10 lander as they circled back around from behind the moon. Obtaining those images had not been easy. The glare of reflected sunlight from the moon's surface made it impossible for ordinary optical telescopes to see small objects in close lunar orbits. These pictures had been taken by shooting a powerful beam of microwaves toward the moon from NASA's Goldstone Deep Space Communications Complex in California. Tiny radar echoes bouncing back from lunar orbit were then detected by the world's largest steerable radio telescope in Green Bank, West Virginia.

For a moment there was silence in the room. Then Yates chuckled. "Oh, come now, Mrs. McLanahan. You're not seriously asking us to waste our people's time by asking them to study a cloud of crystals from what was probably just a test of a waste dump system, are you?" His smile grew wider. "I don't think anyone here really needs an in-depth intelligence analysis of simulated Russian or Chinese urine, do you?"

During the wave of laughter that followed the NASA bureaucrat's quip, Nadia leaned close to Brad and muttered, "*Ci ludzie są głupcami.* These people are fools."

Grimly, he nodded. "Yeah, they are." He sighed. "Which is going to make figuring out what Leonov and Li Jun are really doing a hell of a lot harder."

TWENTY-EIGHT

PENGLAI PAVILION, ZHONGNANHAI, BEIJING, PEOPLE'S REPUBLIC OF CHINA
SOME DAYS LATER

Once a walled imperial garden, the Zhongnanhai compound's palaces, halls, pavilions, and other buildings were now the sole province of the higher echelons of the Communist Party's leadership cadre. In his capacity as general secretary of the Party, President Li Jun conducted most of his day-to-day administrative work inside the compound. Its spacious grounds and buildings were also used for meetings—both public and private—with important foreign dignitaries.

Penglai Pavilion occupied the southern end of an artificial island built six centuries ago for an emperor of the Ming Dynasty. Connected to the rest of Zhongnanhai only by a stone bridge, it was an ideal location for a top secret honors ceremony. Details of soldiers and stern-faced plainclothes security guards now blocked the bridge at both ends. No one without the highest possible clearance could get anywhere close to the island, let alone to the two-story pavilion.

Deftly, Marshal Mikhail Leonov finished pinning Russia's highest decoration, Hero of the Russian Federation, on Captain Dmitry Yanin's chest. The five-pointed gold star with its white, blue, and red ribbon dangled next to China's Aerospace Meritorious Service medal, awarded moments before by Li Jun. He shook the younger cosmonaut's hand warmly and stepped back.

Each country had, appropriately in Leonov's view, reserved its highest decoration for its own members of the Federation 2 crew. That was why cosmonauts Lavrentyev and Yanin were now Heroes of the Federation, while taikonauts Tian and Liu had just received China's Order of August the First from their own leader.

Beaming with pride, the four men stiffened to attention and saluted.

Gravely, Li Jun and Leonov acknowledged the salute. They watched in silence while security guards escorted Tian, Lavrentyev, and the others away. All four crewmen had an enormous amount of hard work and rigorous training ahead as they prepared for further military space missions.

When the two leaders were effectively alone, with their nearest aides well out of earshot, Li Jun turned to Leonov with a pleased smile. "I congratulate you, Comrade Marshal. You argued that many in the West would swallow our deception plan whole. And you were right."

"Does that include the American government?" Leonov asked.

Li nodded. "I've received a report from my Ministry of State Security. Our sources in Washington confirm what we hoped. The prevailing view among official circles is that the Pilgrim 1 mission was exactly what we said it was—an unmanned test flight." He shrugged. "Naturally, a tiny handful of people remain suspicious. But they are seen by most of those in the American government as either paranoid or wildly unrealistic."

"Even by President Farrell?" Leonov asked skeptically.

"Perhaps not," Li admitted. He smiled again. "But the American president is not an absolute ruler. Whatever his personal beliefs might be, he is still constrained, to a degree, by the views of Washington's bureaucracy.

And those officials are both risk-averse and unimaginative by nature and experience."

Leonov nodded. That much of what the Chinese leader said was true. After all, the former American president Martindale had created Scion, his private military and intelligence organization, largely because he'd so often been frustrated by bureaucratic inertia and caution while in office. But in this case, even if Farrell turned to Scion again, there should be little its paid mercenaries and spies could do. They were trained and equipped for covert operations on Earth or in low Earth orbit—not for missions in deep space or on the moon.

He looked at the other man. "Then you agree that we should press on with Heaven's Thunder?"

"Of course," Li said. His pleasant expression changed character, becoming infinitely colder and crueler. Plainly, the humiliating defeat the Americans had inflicted on him in the Paracel Islands still rankled. "And as rapidly as possible. For the moment, the Americans are still blind and deaf, totally ignorant of our true plans and capabilities. But even they will not slumber on in ignorance forever. By the time they do wake up, it must be entirely too late."

TWENTY-NINE

**THE WHITE HOUSE SITUATION ROOM,
WASHINGTON, D.C.
SEVERAL WEEKS LATER**

President John Dalton Farrell watched the damning sequence of high-resolution satellite photos play out across the Situation Room's wall-sized screen. His broad, square-jawed face settled into a thoughtful frown.

After the success of the Sino-Russian lunar mission, he'd urged U.S. intelligence agencies to track Russia and China's conventional space programs more closely. Despite being caught by surprise by the Pilgrim 1 rocket launches, the CIA, National Reconnaissance Office, and Defense Intelligence Agency had all pushed back hard against his requests. They viewed Russia's top secret Firebird spaceplane program as a more immediate threat to U.S. space operations. And none of them wanted to risk missing vital intelligence on Firebird just because a satellite was out of position—busy snapping useless pictures over ordinary civilian and military space launch centers.

Two years of experience as the nation's chief executive had taught Farrell several hard-earned lessons. First among them was the painful truth that no president could just snap his fingers and expect his orders to be obeyed. The career officials who managed the federal government's departments and agencies had long ago mastered the art of nodding agreeably whenever a president made demands—and then going right back to doing things the way they wanted as soon as the Oval Office heat was off.

So it had taken unremitting pressure to make sure that any of the handful of operational U.S. spy satellites were retasked to do the snooping he wanted. Pressure that included a number of personal presidential visits to the National Reconnaissance Office's headquarters out in Virginia, south of Washington Dulles International Airport. It was comparatively easy to "file" a White House request sent by email or on paper. Not many could manage the same trick with a stern-faced J. D. Farrell himself staring them squarely in the eyes.

His efforts had paid off.

During the past week, repeated satellite passes over Russia's Plesetsk and Vostochny launch complexes had spotted several heavy-lift Energia-5VR rockets and smaller, medium-lift Angara-A5 cargo rockets either ready for launch or in the final stages of preparation. And similar passes over China's Wenchang and Xichang rocket facilities showed another four Long March 5 boosters out on the launchpads, with additional rockets under assembly.

With the last of those satellite photos still up on the screen, Farrell swung back around to his assembled national security team. Worried faces looked back at him. "So there you have it," he said bluntly. "Those multiple Russian and Chinese launches for their Pilgrim 1 moon mission were just the start of whatever's going on. Right now, those sons of bitches in Moscow and Beijing have a shitload of space vehicles just about prepped and ready to go . . . and we're still stumbling around in the goddamned dark."

"Which is exactly where Marshal Leonov and President Li Jun want us," Kevin Martindale said. While it was unusual for any former president to participate in a national security meeting, no one around the table had been prepared to argue against his inclusion. Every member of the administration knew how much Farrell valued Scion's military and intelligence capabilities . . . and besides, it was a treat to have the popular, dynamic, swashbuckling former president here in person. "I don't think that's an accident."

"Meaning what?" the CIA director demanded. Unlike her predecessor, Elizabeth Hildebrand was a thoroughgoing intelligence service professional. She'd been working hard to repair the damage done to the agency's operations and analysis directorates during the previous administration, but it was an uphill battle.

Martindale grimaced. "That it seems increasingly likely that the Firebird spaceplane program we've all been fixated on was nothing more than a ruse. Right from the beginning, Firebird was intended to distract us from their real plan." He sounded disgusted. "We've been played for suckers, all of us—starting with me."

Farrell waved that off. "Save the blame games for later, Kevin. We all chased that same rabbit off into Leonov's briar patch. But right now, we need to square up and figure this situation out."

His White House science adviser, Dr. Lawrence Dawson, leaned forward from his place farther down the crowded Situation Room table. "On that score, Mr.

President, my guess would be that Moscow and Beijing are both still looking toward the moon."

"Is your assessment based on that new satellite the Russians just launched toward the Earth-Moon L2 point?" Martindale asked.

The rail-thin astrophysicist nodded. "Correct." Two days ago, one of Russia's Angara-A5 rockets had lifted off from Vostochny Cosmodrome. The satellite it had carried was currently on course for the same Lagrange point halo orbit currently occupied by China's Magpie Bridge communications relay. Dawson continued, "Naturally, I've asked Director Polikarpov for details of this mission."

Heads nodded around the table. Polikarpov was the head of Roscosmos, the government megacorporation running Russia's civilian space program.

"And?" Farrell prompted.

"He assures me their new satellite is merely a backup for China's Magpie Bridge communications relay." The dry expression on Dawson's thin, ascetic face plainly revealed his skepticism.

Patrick McLanahan nodded. "Yeah, that's definitely grade-A pure, unadulterated bullshit." He turned toward Farrell with a soft whine of servos from his LEAF exoskeleton. "Our best estimate puts the mass of this

Russian satellite at considerably more than a metric ton. That's at least twice the size of the Chinese com relay."

The president frowned. "And that's too heavy?"

"For a basic communications satellite? Absolutely," Patrick said. "No one wastes mass on any space mission. It's already incredibly expensive to put anything useful in orbit, let alone deadweight."

"So what's the real purpose of this Russian spacecraft?" Farrell wondered.

"I strongly suspect it's a sophisticated radar and infrared surveillance satellite, something in their *Kondor* class," Patrick said. "And if I'm right, pretty soon the Russians and Chinese will be able to track all space operations in lunar orbit, especially on the far side of the moon."

Farrell scowled. "Where we're totally blind." Patrick nodded again.

"Which brings us back to the central question," the president commented. "What can Moscow and Beijing hope to gain here? If you add up the costs of all those rockets they've got stacked up and ready to launch, you're looking at billions of dollars on the hoof."

"Maybe they're trying to beat us back to the moon," his secretary of state, Andrew Taliaferro, suggested. The former congressman's North Carolina drawl was even more pronounced than usual. "Considering how much political capital we've already invested in our helium-3 mining plan, seeing a couple of cosmonauts or taikonauts strolling around up there way ahead of us would be one hell of a kick in the teeth."

Grimly, Patrick shook his head. "I'm pretty confident the Russians and the Chinese have already won that particular race," he said flatly. "So whatever they have planned, it's got to be something considerably more dangerous to us than just sending a couple of men out onto the lunar surface for a few hours."

His blunt assertion drew startled looks from everyone else in the room.

"That's a mighty bold claim, General McLanahan," Farrell said calmly.

"Yes, sir, it is," Patrick agreed, with equal coolness. "But since just about everything Moscow and Beijing told us about their so-called Pilgrim 1 mission was a lie, I don't think it's really much of a stretch."

"Go on."

In answer, Patrick pulled up a set of images from his personal files and transferred them to the computer-controlled wall screen. As a security precaution, White House rules prohibited smartphones and personal laptops in the Situation Room. But those rules weren't designed to cover someone with his peculiar abilities and equipment. His LEAF exoskeleton contained wireless links, a neural interface, and its own powerful computer—enabling him to access information from a vast array of databases around the globe anywhere and anytime.

Farrell and his top national security advisers stared at the same expanding cloud of radar reflective particles Brad and Nadia had spotted near the docked Federation 2 spacecraft and Chang'e-10 lunar lander. Patrick zoomed in on the computer-enhanced image. Seen close up, the cloud looked like a swirling, glittering mass of sharp-edged crystals.

"What you're looking at was originally written off as evidence of a simulated waste or atmosphere dump . . . as just another test of normal spacecraft systems," Patrick said quietly.

Farrell raised an eyebrow. "And that was wrong?"

"Dead wrong." Patrick zoomed in even farther, isolating several of the brighter fragments. "Neither ice crystals nor frozen atmospheric gases reflect microwave energy efficiently—especially not radar pulses that have to travel 250,000 miles out and 250,000 miles back." He pointed at the screen. "Whatever those fragments are, they sure as hell aren't ice or clumps of frozen oxygen."

"Then what are they?" the president asked.

"Well, sir, that took some serious figuring," Patrick said with a hard-edged smile. "And a fair amount of supercomputer time." He zoomed back out to show the whole cloud as it expanded. "Boiling it down, what I did was take the observed motion of every identifiable component of this debris field. Then I had the computer extrapolate backward through time, taking into account possible collisions between fragments and the effects of the moon's gravitational field."

Lawrence Dawson looked suddenly very interested and clearly impressed. "And you found an origin point?" he guessed.

"I did." Patrick nodded. "Or, more accurately, multiple origin points . . . forming a distinct structure." He sent the result of the supercomputer's hellishly complex calculations to the screen.

For a few moments, everyone in the room just stared at the oddly irregular, almost amorphous, blob seeming to hover in space, not far from the docked Sino-Russian spaceships. "What in God's name is that thing?" Taliaferro asked, breaking the uncomfortable silence.

"You'll see, once the image is suitably enhanced," Patrick said coolly. As he spoke, the blob sharpened up, taking on added structure and definition, until it bore a striking resemblance to China's Chang'e-10 spacecraft.

"A second lunar lander?" Taliaferro said in surprise. "Where did that spacecraft come from? And why did it blow up?"

Patrick shook his head. "That wasn't a real spacecraft, Mr. Secretary. It was a decoy, a mock-up of the real Chang'e-Ten. One the Russians and Chinese used to make us believe their moon lander stayed in orbit . . . while it was really down on the lunar surface." Through the visor of his LEAF helmet, he looked grave. "One thing's clear: Moscow and Beijing have beaten us back to the moon."

Elizabeth Hildebrand frowned. "If that's true, why would Leonov and Li Jun keep it secret?" the CIA director wondered. "After all, the first successful manned moon landing in more than fifty years would be a huge propaganda coup. Why wouldn't they jump on the chance to rub that in our faces?"

"Right now, I don't know the answer to that question," Patrick admitted. His tone was somber. "But when we do find out what's happening up on the moon, I'm damned sure we aren't going to like it. Which means we can't afford to screw around anymore. We need eyes on the situation, especially around the far side of the moon."

Farrell nodded sharply. "You've got that right, General." He looked around the table. "I'm going to direct NASA to drastically accelerate its plans for a manned mission to orbit the moon."

"They'll squawk," Martindale cautioned. "Their SLS super heavy-lift rockets are still behind schedule and over budget."

"NASA can squawk all it wants," the president snapped. "But I'm going to give them a choice. They either figure out how to go and go soon using their own spacecraft . . . or they buy a ride on one of the private-sector rockets out there."

"A manned mission is fine," Patrick said slowly, thinking through the problem confronting them. "But continuous surveillance of everything going on in lunar orbit and on the surface would be even better. We need a satellite up there, along with our own communications relay."

Farrell nodded. "Good point." He looked down the table at Admiral Scott Firestone, the chairman of the Joint Chiefs. "Any ideas on how we can make that happen . . . and pronto, Admiral?"

Firestone's forehead wrinkled. "It's possible that we could repurpose a couple of satellites slated for launch into Earth orbit over the next several months." The short, stocky man spread his hands. "But equipping them to handle deep space won't be easy. Or cheap, Mr. President."

"I don't expect it will be, Admiral," Farrell told him bluntly. "But don't let that stop you. Reconfigure those birds and get them on their way—and the sooner, the better."

THIRTY

NATIONAL DEFENSE CONTROL CENTER, MOSCOW
SEVERAL WEEKS LATER

For once, Marshal Leonov was forced to admit that the theater-sized control rooms Gennadiy Gryzlov had built as a propaganda stunt served a useful purpose. During this status briefing on the progress of Operation Heaven's Thunder, their enormous, wraparound projection screens made the televised images streaming from the moon even more impressive.

Right now, he and General Chen Haifeng were watching a recording of one of China's large Mǎ Luó cargo landers as it touched down at Korolev Base, high up on the rim of Engel'gardt crater. Its rocket engine flared brightly in the last few seconds and then winked out. When the haze of dust cleared, they saw the spacecraft silhouetted against an infinitely black sky. Beyond it, they could see the shape of another cargo ship and the abandoned descent stages of three manned landers. One belonged to the first spacecraft to reach this site, Chang'e-10. The other two were more recent arrivals.

Slowly, the remote-controlled camera panned across the desolate moonscape. It zoomed in on what looked like an inflated, whitish-gray cloth cylinder anchored solidly to the surface. This was the first of the base's planned habitation modules. Based on concepts originally developed by a pioneering American space technology company, Bigelow Aerospace, Korolev One was twelve meters long and six meters in diameter. The inflatable habitat gave the four cosmonauts and taikonauts currently stationed on the moon close to three hundred cubic meters of living and working space. Multiple layers of insulation, foam, Kevlar, and Nomex cloth produced half-meter-thick walls—offering excellent protection against micrometeorites, radiation, and the moon's harsh temperatures.

Thick orange power cables snaked across the gray moonscape. They connected the habitation module to a much smaller, metal-walled upright cylinder deployed at the base of one of the Chinese cargo landers.

Chen peered intently at the three-meter-tall cylinder. "That is the fusion reactor?" Leonov nodded proudly. "So small," the Chinese general said slowly. He shook his head in amazement. "And yet it produces two megawatts of power."

"More than enough for all of Korolev's needs," Leonov agreed. The fusion power breakthrough Russia had achieved was what made the establishment of this manned lunar base possible in the first place. Without that reactor, its crew would have been dependent on solar panels—which were useless during the moon's fourteen-day-long nights—and on backup batteries, which were comparatively heavy and inefficient. Limited-duration visits would have been possible, but not any sort of permanent presence.

One of the Russian officers assigned to monitor communications with the base turned toward Leonov. "We have a live feed from Korolev Base, sir."

"Put it on-screen," he ordered.

Briefly, static flared across the huge displays. When it cleared, Leonov and Chen could see Colonel Tian Fan and his Russian counterpart, Kirill Lavrentyev, looking back at them. They had arrived on the lunar surface forty-eight hours ago, as part of the Pilgrim 3 mission—joining Liu and Yanin, who'd already been on the moon for nearly two weeks. The video signal, routed through the Magpie Bridge relay to Russia's network of military communications satellites, was remarkably clear, with only minimal distortion. Wearing green flight suits, the two officers sat next to each other at a console. Racks of electronic hardware and storage compartments lined the curving habitat wall behind them.

"Korolev Base here," Tian said without preamble. "All of the payload aboard that just-landed Mǎ Luó appears to be in good condition. Liu and Yanin are outside now, off-loading the consumables. Once we have those stored safely, we'll begin assembling the rest of the equipment."

"Excellent work, Colonel. And you, too, Lavrentyev," Leonov said warmly. While the automated furnace and chemical reaction unit built into Chang'e-10's descent stage could supply the base with precious oxygen and water separated out from regolith, food and other necessary stores still had to come all the way from Earth.

A little under two seconds later, he saw the two men nod as his words finally reached them. Every signal from Earth to the moon's far side had to travel 450,000 kilometers to the Magpie Bridge relay satellite and another 60,000 kilometers from there before it reached Korolev's antennas. The communications lag wasn't crippling, but it was just long enough to render conversations somewhat more stilted and less spontaneous.

"Thank you, Comrade Marshal," Tian replied.

Chen leaned in beside Leonov. "When do you believe your base will be fully operational?"

This time Lavrentyev answered. "We still have considerable EVA work left to excavate the necessary sites for our sensors and other hardware. But we expect to be finished by the time the next cargo lander arrives. After that, it should only take us a few days to install, camouflage, and test all our systems."

Leonov nodded. Teams at Vostochny Cosmodrome were preparing another heavy-lift Energia rocket for launch in the next week. Its payload was a third Chinese-built Mǎ Luó spacecraft destined for the moon. This robotic lander would carry the final components needed to make Korolev Base a full-fledged instrument of offensive Sino-Russian military power.

"Do the Americans realize we're here?" Tian asked seriously.

"Not yet," Leonov assured him. Chinese agents and cyberespionage had confirmed Washington's belated realization that Pilgrim 1 had been a manned mission . . . one that had successfully landed cosmonauts and taikonauts on the moon. In a way, that made the follow-on Pilgrim 2 and Pilgrim 3 missions easier, since they didn't need to carry and deploy decoy landers of their own. However, to hide the fact that crews were staying behind at a permanent base, Pilgrim 2 and 3's empty Chang'e ascent stages were flown back into lunar orbit under remote control. Once there, they docked with waiting Federation command modules, which then returned to Earth . . . supposedly carrying full four-man crews. To all outward appearances, Russia and China were simply carrying out a series of short-duration exploration landings—with the aid of rovers and other scientific equipment delivered by separate cargo spacecraft.

For now, Beijing and Moscow claimed they were keeping more details of their "purely scientific program" secret because they didn't want to provide data that could aid the United States in its greedy quest to "rape the virgin lunar soil for riches." Feeble though that excuse was, a number of Western environmental groups and left-wing political parties seemed willing to believe it.

President Farrell and his advisers were deeply suspicious, Leonov knew. All available intelligence indicated they were scrambling to mount their own missions to lunar orbit. But they were starting too far behind. The months they'd wasted trying to uncover the secrets of his fictitious Firebird spaceplane program simply could not be made up.

IN EARTH ORBIT
SEVERAL DAYS LATER

Two hours and forty minutes after liftoff from Cape Canaveral Air Force Station's Space Launch Complex 37B, the Delta IV Heavy rocket's powerful second-stage engine relit. Within seconds, as the booster accelerated, its attached payload began moving into a much higher, far more elliptical orbit.

Several minutes later, the RL-10B engine shut down on schedule. Bolts fired and slowly the Delta Heavy's second stage fell away from the satellite it had just launched toward the Earth-Moon Lagrange-2 point. This Advanced Extremely High Frequency (AEHF) U.S. military communications satellite, the seventh in its series, had originally been intended as a replacement for the aging AEHF-1 in geostationary orbit high over the Galápagos Islands. Now it had been given a new purpose. As the satellite moved away from the earth at more than twenty thousand miles per hour, its twin solar panels unfurled in response to commands from ground controllers.

It had taken weeks of frantic work by Space Force civilian contractors to make the hardware and software alterations needed to fit AEHF-7 for service in deep space. Once it reached stable orbit around the distant Lagrange point, the satellite would act as a jam-resistant radio and data-link relay for any U.S. or allied spacecraft operating in lunar orbit. Routing signals through its powerful antennas would give both human crews and robotic spacecraft the ability to communicate with Earth in real time while swinging around the moon's far side.

THIRTY-ONE

HANGAR TWO, MCLANAHAN INDUSTRIAL AIRPORT, BATTLE MOUNTAIN, NEVADA
A SHORT TIME LATER

Brad McLanahan watched the solid black Scion executive jet touch down. Slowing quickly, the Gulfstream G600 came to the end of the runway, turned, and taxied on toward Hangar Two. High overhead, its two Texas Air National Guard F-16C Falcon fighter escorts peeled away, rolling south as they flew off toward Nellis Air Force Base near Las Vegas. Late afternoon sunlight glinted off their clear bubble canopies.

For a moment, Brad stayed outside, watching the agile F-16s dart across the sky. At one point in his life, and not so long ago, either, flying high-performance aircraft like those Falcons for the U.S. Air Force would have been his dream job. He shook his head. Things sure had changed over the past few years. Silently, he turned and walked back inside the hangar to join the little group waiting there. He slipped into place between his father and Nadia.

Kevin Martindale checked his watch. "Well, at least they're right on time." He looked tense. "And a good thing, too. The turnaround on this visit is tight. Which is why I told that Gulfstream's flight crew not to screw around."

Next to him, Hunter Noble half turned with a quizzical look. "So what would have happened to your guys if they had run late? This time of year, that's not so unlikely, you know—between normal bad weather and air traffic control delays, I mean."

Martindale gave him a thin smile. "Bad things, Dr. Noble. Very bad things."

"Oh," Boomer said. He mimed a pistol pointed at his head. "As in *bang.*"

The former president snorted. "Of course not. I can't just have people killed on a whim."

"Well, that's a relief," Boomer said, winking quickly at Brad and Nadia, who were trying hard not to laugh out loud.

"Not legally, anyway," Martindale continued darkly.

Perhaps fortunately, the shrill, earsplitting whine

of the executive jet's twin turbofans made any further conversation impossible. Slowly, the Gulfstream rolled in through the hangar's big open doors. With its engines spooling down, the midnight-black aircraft swung toward them and then braked to a stop just a few yards away.

Its forward cabin door opened. Several serious-looking men and women in dark suits hurried down the Gulfstream's cabin steps and spread out into a semicircle. Slight bulges marked the holstered weapons concealed under their jackets. After a few moments, during which they carefully scrutinized their surroundings, one of them turned back toward the jet and nodded.

Brad and the others straightened to attention as a tall, broad-shouldered man emerged. Buttoning up his own suit coat against the cold, he trotted down the steps and came toward them with a friendly grin on his face. His security detail closed in around him, parting only when Martindale stepped forward with an outstretched hand.

"Welcome to Battle Mountain, Mr. President," the head of Scion said quietly.

A few minutes later, they gathered in a small, windowless room at the far end of the hangar. Ordinarily, Sky

Masters used it to brief pilots before test flights aboard new experimental aircraft. Now the president's Secret Service detail was stationed outside the briefing room's closed door. Corporate security personnel, all former military, held a discreet perimeter around the hangar itself.

"I wish we had time to give you a real tour," Brad told Farrell as they sat down. "From the air, Sky Masters is just a bunch of industrial-looking buildings. The really cool stuff goes on inside."

Farrell nodded regretfully. "I surely would have enjoyed that, Major. Maybe I'll get the chance someday when I'm not pretending to be somewhere else."

Right now, as far as the press, public, and, with luck, Russia and China were all concerned, J. D. Farrell was only on a quick working vacation at his private ranch in Texas's Hill Country—with no plans to go anywhere but back to Washington, D.C., in a couple of days. Arranging the logistics for this secret visit to Battle Mountain had taken a lot of doing. Overruling the Secret Service's objections to the president going anywhere without the usual army of White House staff, bodyguards, medical teams, helicopters, and armored limousines had finally required direct intervention by Farrell himself.

It would have been much simpler, Brad knew, to

hold this meeting by secure video link. But the president had made it clear he was tired of "dealing with y'all mostly through some damned television screen. Maybe it's old-fashioned, but I sort of appreciate seeing the folks working for me in person every so often."

Meaningfully, Martindale laid his smartphone faceup on the table. He'd set it to display the time remaining before they needed to hustle Farrell back aboard his plane for its return flight to Texas. "The clock's ticking here," he reminded them all.

"That's for sure," Farrell agreed. His mouth tightened. "So I'll get right down to it. Right now, we're getting our asses kicked by the Chinese and the Russians in deep space and on the moon . . . and all I hear from NASA are a lot of high-sounding explanations about why we can't do anything to change that. At least not in time for it to matter a damn."

Patrick McLanahan looked him in the eye. "That's a self-inflicted problem, Mr. President. This country's manned space efforts have focused almost entirely on operations in low Earth orbit for decades—ever since the end of the Apollo program."

Martindale nodded. "There were various plans for longer-ranged manned missions, but every administration's priorities kept shifting. So no one ever succeeded in setting clear, achievable goals for NASA." He looked dour. "Not even me."

"And now a lot of the best people have left the agency," Boomer volunteered from his end of the table. "Eventually, just about anyone who's seriously interested in doing real things in space ends up signing on with SpaceX, or Blue Origin, or one of the other innovative private aerospace companies."

"Like Sky Masters?" Farrell said with a wry smile.

"Yes, sir," Boomer acknowledged, matching the other man's lopsided smile. "There are still talented engineers and astronauts and technical people at NASA, but they're always fighting an uphill battle against the suits at headquarters to get anything done. And if there's any serious risk involved?" He shook his head in disgust. "Shit. Calling NASA HQ risk-averse is like saying Ebenezer Scrooge was a little tight with his money." He saw the suppressed grin on Brad's face and spread his hands. "Okay, yeah, I've had my share of new engine designs blow up, so maybe I lean a little too far the other way. But, hell, rockets are inherently dangerous machines. Sure, you can make 'em *safer* . . . but there's no way you can guarantee perfect safety, especially not with a new spacecraft. Well, not unless you don't ever to plan to actually fly it."

"Which just about sums up where we stand," Farrell said with a frown. He sighed. "I keep looking at that fancy NASA logo during their presentations, and all I can hear is what my old grandad always used to tell me. 'J.D., just because a chicken has wings don't mean it can fly.'"

He looked around the table. "Which is why I'm here. I need better answers than I've been getting in D.C. Boiling all their bullshit down, NASA can't send Americans back to the moon, not even on a flyby. Not anytime in the next twelve to eighteen months."

"By which time, our enemies may well be in a position of tremendous advantage," Nadia said grimly.

Farrell nodded. His frown deepened. "Let's just say this is a comedy of errors, except without the laughs. NASA's already built several of its brand-new Orion crew vehicles. And the European Space Agency's done the same with the service module it's building for the Orion program. Hell, everybody I talk to claims both of those spacecraft are flight-ready. So you'd think everything would be set to go for a manned lunar flyby—"

"Except we don't have any rocket capable of lifting an Orion crew vehicle and its service module off the launchpad and boosting them into a translunar injection orbit," Brad said quietly. "Because NASA's heavy-lift SLS isn't ready yet."

"Yep," Farrell agreed. "And none of the other private commercial rockets out there, not even a Falcon Heavy, can do the job."

Brad took a deep breath. "Well, sir . . . we may have a fix for that. See, Boomer, Nadia, and I have been working the problem pretty hard ever since my dad figured out the Russians and Chinese had already landed on the moon."

"No need to apologize, Major," Farrell said with a hint of amusement. "I'd kind of bet on that being the case." He looked at them more seriously. "Is this fix of yours something NASA's going to approve of?"

"Not in a million years," Boomer admitted.

"And why not?" Martindale wanted to know.

Brad shrugged. "Because we're proposing to steal a page out of the Chinese and Russian playbook."

"It's our new definition of genius," Boomer added smugly. "One percent perspiration. Ninety-nine percent sheer larceny."

Patrick smiled as he saw what they were driving at. "You want to assemble that Orion crew vehicle, service module, and booster in space."

"In Earth orbit," Brad confirmed.

Farrell looked surprised. "I asked NASA about the idea of doing something similar and they told me it was flat-out impossible."

"It is impossible . . . for NASA," Brad said bluntly. The space agency's reaction was perfectly understandable. Mating an Orion crew vehicle to the ESA-designed service module in orbit would be an intricate and complicated task. First, it meant checking, and if necessary, fixing the hundreds of bolts, power cables, and fuel and water pipes and conduits that tied the service module to its adapter ring. Then it required maneuvering the gumdrop-shaped crew vehicle into precise alignment with the adapter ring, all before carefully connecting an umbilical boom containing fluid, gas, electrical, and data lines. On Earth, at the Kennedy Space Center, the process took weeks of work by skilled technicians.

He saw the president eyeing him and walked through his reasoning. "So there's no way astronauts wearing standard EVA suits could handle the job," he finished.

"But you think Sky Masters can?" Farrell pressed.

"Yes, sir. We have the advanced equipment and we have the know-how," Brad said firmly. "The plan's not that complicated, although the execution's definitely tricky. Basically what we have in mind is this: NASA launches the unmanned Orion crew vehicle aboard a Falcon 9 or some other rocket in that class and has it dock with Eagle Station. Then we send the ESA-built service module up aboard a Falcon Heavy. Once everything's in orbit, a Sky Masters team will assemble the crew vehicle and service module—and then slot them onto the Falcon Heavy's second-stage booster."

He allowed his enthusiasm a little more free rein. "Then NASA's astronauts come aboard, maneuver away from Eagle Station, and light off that Falcon's Merlin-1D engine. And, zoom, our guys are on their way to lunar orbit."

"Do you have the facts and figures to prove this space-based assembly concept of yours is workable?" Farrell asked seriously.

"Yes, sir," Brad assured him.

"All right, then," Farrell said in approval. "If your numbers pan out, I'll get buy-in from the National Security Council and we'll wrestle NASA into submission. The agency can bitch all it wants, but if necessary, I'll damn well override them in the national interest."

He stood up, a move followed by everyone else in the room. "Let's get going, people. It's high time we kicked this country's manned lunar program into high gear."

THIRTY-TWO

MORRELL OPERATIONS CENTER, SPACE LAUNCH COMPLEX 37B, CAPE CANAVERAL SPACE FORCE STATION, FLORIDA
A FEW WEEKS LATER

From her command station, Space Force Colonel Kathleen Locke peered intently at her monitor. Floodlights showed a large orange-and-white rocket connected to a tall mobile gantry out at the launchpad, close to seven miles away. The 236-foot-tall Delta IV Heavy, with its core booster and two equal-sized side boosters, weighed more than eight hundred tons. Clouds of vapor curled away from the rocket, bright white in the lights.

Around her, the operations center's officers and senior enlisted personnel were equally intent on their own tasks. If anything went haywire with the Delta IV Heavy on its way into orbit, they would trigger its self-destruct systems. Locke mentally crossed her fingers. Her senior commanders had made sure she knew the classified payload aboard that rocket was critically important to America's national security. If this launch failed, it would take months to prepare a replacement.

Through her headset, she heard a steady stream of reports and announcements from the launch controllers.

"Minus fifteen."

"Go for ignition."

On-screen, showers of orange and white sparks started flaring out from under all three boosters.

"Ten . . . nine . . . eight . . . seven . . . six—"

"Booster start."

Jets of orange flame curled out from under the massive rocket, growing rapidly in size and intensity as all three huge engines throttled up to full power—producing more than two million pounds of thrust. Through the operation center's speakers, a deep, crackling roar echoed across Cape Canaveral's marshlands. Flocks of birds, stirred out of sleep by the sudden glare of light and thunderous noise, fluttered uneasily up into the air.

"Liftoff!"

Three steel gantry bridges pivoted away. Slowly at first, and then faster, the Delta IV climbed into the Florida night sky, borne aloft on three pillars of blinding fire. Within seconds, the rocket was visible only as a flickering column of flame powering higher and higher as it curved eastward across the Atlantic.

"Core booster going to partial thrust mode. Strap-on boosters look good in full thrust mode," a controller reported calmly. "Vehicle trajectory looks good. Right down the middle of the range track." Locke breathed out. Throttling down the center rocket motor was a normal measure to conserve fuel in the main engine. It was also another possible failure point, if the Delta's automated systems had glitched.

Long-range cameras tracked the rocket as it soared higher into the atmosphere. Nearly four minutes into flight, the same controller said, "Port and starboard boosters are throttling down."

For a brief second, a haze of pale, orange-tinted light surrounded the distant pinpoint of fire. It vanished as both side booster rockets shut down. Suddenly, two tiny lights sheered away from the speeding Delta IV. Each speck of light was a large 57,000-pound rocket engine and fuel tank now tumbling toward the ocean dozens of miles below. "We have jettison of both strap-on boosters. Core booster is throttling back up to full power."

Locke heard herself muttering, "Go, baby, go," under her breath. Embarrassed, she shot a quick glance at her second in command. His lips were moving too, in the same fervent prayer.

Five and a half minutes after launch, she heard, "MECO! Booster engine cutoff. Standing by stage separation."

Seconds later, they got the confirmation. "We have a good indication of booster separation." The Delta IV's second stage and payload were now ninety miles high and nearly five hundred miles downrange from the launchpad. They were traveling at nearly fifteen thousand miles per hour. "Good ignition on the RL-10 engine!" a launch controller crowed. "Payload fairing jettison."

A few minutes later, Locke and her team were able to confirm that the second-stage booster and its payload were in a stable orbit. While the civilian contractors and younger Space Force personnel exchanged jubilant high fives, she sat quietly, still feeling the tension in her shoulders. Her direct responsibility for the success of this mission might be over, but she knew there were more hurdles left to clear.

The next one came two orbits later.

She was listening in over the circuit to the Space Force Operations Center out at Peterson Air Force Base in Colorado. Terse reports flowed through her headset as the Delta's second-stage RL-10 engine began its next scheduled burn. Minutes ticked by while controllers evaluated their tracking telemetry. Finally, she heard them report: "That was a good burn, Command. And we show booster stage separation. Our Topaz radar reconnaissance satellite is on its way to the moon."

Now Colonel Locke allowed herself to relax. Once that radar satellite was in lunar orbit, the United States would finally be able to learn just what the Russians and Chinese were doing.

COMMAND CENTER, CENTRAL MILITARY COMMISSION OF THE PEOPLE'S REPUBLIC OF CHINA, BEIJING
THAT SAME TIME

President Li Jun waited impatiently for his secure connection to Moscow to stabilize. Routing an encrypted video signal through multiple satellites belonging to their two countries was a complicated task. They could have used a direct fiber-optic cable link, part of the

ERMC network running from Hong Kong to London. But neither he nor Marshal Leonov was willing to trust their most prized secrets to a line that could be tapped anywhere along the six thousand kilometers between their two capitals.

At last, he saw Leonov's image appear on his monitor. "You know about this most recent American rocket launch?" he asked.

The Russian nodded. "We've tracked it continuously from the moment it left the pad." He frowned, reading a new report just flashed from his own Space Force. He looked up. "Apparently, it has just completed a successful translunar injection burn."

"Do you know yet what its payload is?" Li asked pointedly.

"Not yet," Leonov admitted. "And unfortunately, we won't be able to acquire any imagery from either of our Okno space surveillance sites before the American spacecraft passes out of range."

Russia's two Okno (Window) complexes were networks of powerful telescopes and high-definition, low-light TV cameras. One was located high up in Tajikistan's Sanglok Mountains. The other, Okno-S, was located on a mountain just north of Vladivostok in Russia's Far East. At night, but only at night, their

instruments were capable of detecting and photograph-
ing satellites and other spacecraft up to fifty thousand
kilometers above the earth.

Li nodded. "That was undoubtedly deliberate, a
major factor in Washington's decision to conduct this
launch from Cape Canaveral well past midnight, local
time." Tajikistan was nine hours ahead of Florida, so
it was already daylight there by the time the American
spacecraft's initial orbit took it over the Russian surveillance site. The same applied to Okno-S, which was
fourteen hours ahead. A thin, humorless smile crossed
his narrow face. "Fortunately, we are not entirely dependent on technology for answers in this case."

"You mean your spies penetrated U.S. security
around this launch," Leonov said bluntly.

"Correct," Li agreed. "Which is how I know that
the Americans just sent a modified Topaz radar satellite toward the moon."

Leonov's eyes narrowed. "Modified in what way?"

"Apparently, they've increased the power and fuel
supply of its thrusters and engine, enabling them to
place that satellite in lunar orbit."

The Russian scowled. "How long have you known
what the Americans were planning?"

Li shrugged. "For several days."

"And you said nothing to us?"

The Chinese leader smiled dryly again. "Not all space launches succeed. There was a possibility the Delta IV rocket would either explode on liftoff or fail to place its payload in a stable orbit. So it seemed . . . unnecessary . . . to pass this information to you before now." Left unspoken was his natural aversion to revealing anything that might compromise the Ministry of State Security's espionage networks inside the United States. Or elsewhere, for that matter. China's current alliance with Russia was based on shared strategic goals. But it did not necessarily reflect a permanent alignment with Moscow. From the sour look on Leonov's face, he knew the other man clearly understood both his reasoning and his motivations.

After a moment of uncomfortable silence, the Russian evidently decided to let the issue drop. They now faced a more immediate threat. If there were any silver lining to this black cloud, it was the fact that Korolev Base's primary weapon was already operational. "Based on its current trajectory, this American spy satellite will reach orbit around the moon in just fifty-six hours."

"Yes, that matches General Chen's assessment of the data," Li said.

"And once that happens, the Americans will learn that we've established a permanent lunar base. More important still, they will know exactly *what* we are doing there." Leonov's gaze hardened. "Now we know why Washington was in such a hurry to deploy its own secure communications relay to the L2 point. Unless we act to prevent it, every radar image obtained by that Topaz satellite's sensors could be in President Farrell's hands within minutes."

Li looked back at him. "That would be unfortunate." His own eyes were cold. "I suggest that you send the necessary orders to your own satellite at the Lagrange point. And to Colonels Tian and Lavrentyev at Korolev Base."

Leonov nodded. He lifted a secure phone and then paused. "You understand that our actions will inevitably escalate the situation? No matter how the Americans first interpret the results?"

"Do you fear an uncontrollable escalation?" the Chinese leader asked calmly. For his part, he doubted the Americans would overreact. They were squeamish about suffering large-scale casualties.

After more thought, Leonov shook his head. "No, I don't think so." He pondered the possibilities for another moment. "However, we do have two more space missions scheduled to launch shortly."

Li frowned. One of those missions was another combined Federation-Chang'e flight intended to land two more crewmen at Korolev Base. The other would send a fourth Mǎ Luó automated cargo lander to the moon with additional supplies and equipment. "Are you afraid the Americans will attack them?"

"Not really," Leonov assured him. "In the short term, President Farrell's retaliatory options are extremely limited." He spread his hands. "Over time, though, it becomes somewhat more difficult to anticipate how he might react, either using his own forces or those of his mercenaries."

"Scion and Sky Masters," Li said tightly.

"Just so," Leonov agreed. "Even now, the Americans appear to be trying to assemble a manned lunar mission in orbit, using one of their Orion crew vehicles. In the circumstances, we should not assume this will be a peaceful, unarmed flight."

Li nodded. China's own ground-based telescopes and satellites were closely monitoring the recent surge of space activity around America's Eagle Station. At first, Chen Haifeng's Strategic Support Force analysts had pegged the arrival of an Orion crew vehicle at the space station as a routine test flight. Now, with a European-built support module and Falcon second-stage booster also circling the earth near Eagle, the intended American plan was clearer.

"That's why I think it would be wise to modify the payload planned for our next cargo lander mission.

Merely as a precaution, of course," Leonov continued.

Li stared at him in confusion. "Modify the payload? In what way?"

"My best scientists and engineers have been working very hard to adapt some of our most advanced weapons systems for use on the lunar surface," Leonov said coolly. "They have succeeded. And just in time to reinforce Korolev's defenses—against any possible attack."

As the Russian explained more fully what he meant, Li felt his eyes widen. He'd surprised the other man earlier by suddenly revealing the intelligence about America's Topaz radar satellite. Now it was Leonov's turn to remind him that Russia could play the same game.

THIRTY-THREE

KONDOR-L SATELLITE, IN HALO ORBIT AROUND THE EARTH-MOON LAGRANGE POINT 2
A SHORT TIME LATER

Four hundred and fifty thousand kilometers from Earth, Russia's Kondor-L satellite slid silently through space along its orbit around the invisible Lagrange point—held in its course by the combined gravitational forces of the earth, moon, and sun all interacting with each other. Its hexagonal radar dish was angled toward the moon. A thin metal strut connected the radar dish to the core satellite, which was a rectangular box studded with antennas, infrared sensors, small thrusters, and the nozzle of a somewhat larger orbit-correction motor. Two solar panels extended off the main body, providing electricity to power its S-band radar and other systems. From time to time, the Kondor's tiny attitude control thrusters fired in sequence, rotating the satellite to keep the dish properly aligned.

Now, obeying instructions radioed from Moscow, a tiny spacecraft—less than a meter long and only centimeters in diameter—detached from the larger radar reconnaissance satellite and drifted away. Coated in jet-black radar-absorbent materials, this small stealth vehicle, called the *Chenaya Osa* or Black Wasp by its creators, was effectively undetectable by any U.S. ground- or space-based sensors.

Aboard the tiny craft, relays closed. Its battery-powered ion thrusters lit up. They glowed a faint blue as the positively charged ions stripped out of a xenon gas plasma were hurled outward into space. Compared to chemical rockets, the thrust provided by this form of electric propulsion was minute . . . but the speed it imparted built steadily over time.

Gradually, minute by minute and hour by hour, the Black Wasp accelerated. It curved away from the Kondor-L along a transfer orbit. In time, its track would intersect that of the much larger American AEHF-7 communications satellite as it looped around the same Lagrange point.

U.S. SPACE FORCE OPERATIONS CENTER,
PETERSON AIR FORCE BASE,
COLORADO SPRINGS, COLORADO
FIFTY-PLUS HOURS LATER

Subdued, blue-tinged overhead lighting gave the Space Force Operations Center a deceptively calm and peaceful atmosphere. Stepped tiers of computer stations were manned by officers and enlisted personnel wearing flight suits and communications headsets. Along the forward wall, displays showed the current positions of Eagle Station and two S-29B Shadow spaceplanes in Earth orbit. A large center screen showed the current status of the Space Force's first lunar reconnaissance mission.

From an open observation platform looking down into the dimly lit room, Patrick McLanahan watched the icon representing the Topaz-M radar surveillance satellite move steadily along the curving path it had been following for more than two days—ever since the Delta IV sent it winging toward the moon's predicted position at more than twenty-four thousand miles per hour. All through that time, it had slowed steadily as the earth's gravity exerted its pull.

Now, more than fifty-five hours into its flight, the

Topaz-M's speed was down to just a little over two thousand miles per hour. But its velocity was already starting to increase again, because the satellite had crossed into the influence of the moon's own gravitational field. As planned, it was falling toward the lunar surface. A circle not far ahead along its projected track was marked LOI, for Lunar Orbit Insertion—indicating the position at which the Topaz-M would fire its own engine for the first time, making a short burn intended to put the reconnaissance satellite into a stable orbit around the moon.

Patrick glanced at the three men standing next to him at the railing. Eager to get their first real look at what the Chinese and Russians were doing around the other side of the moon, both President Farrell and Kevin Martindale had come out to Colorado Springs in person. The third man, General Richard Kelleher, was the Space Force's recently appointed chief of staff. As far as the media knew, the president was simply here to inspect the new Space Force field headquarters and other facilities. The Topaz-M mission was still a closely held secret.

Kelleher was short and fit, with close-cropped, salt-and-pepper hair. Before taking charge of the Space Force, he'd already held most of the U.S. Air Force's space-related commands. Although Patrick didn't know him personally, mutual friends had assured him that he was a good pick—"smart and tough enough to handle the job, and ornery enough to kick Pentagon bureaucratic ass when necessary."

Right now, Kelleher was on a phone, getting a status report from Brigadier General Rosenthal, the senior officer on duty in the ops center itself. "Thanks, Jill," he said. "I'll pass the word on." He hung up and turned to Patrick and the others. "So far, all the telemetry looks good. The Topaz's com antennas are already slaved to our L2 AEHF relay, so we'll be in constant touch with that satellite even when it swings around the far side of the moon."

Farrell nodded. "Any indication that the Russians or Chinese are getting antsy?" he asked.

Kelleher shook his head. "No, sir." He leaned forward over the railing a little, taking a quick look at the smaller displays that showed satellite views of various parts of the globe. "Naturally, we're keeping a close eye on all of their launch complexes right now. But apart from the Energia and Long March boosters assigned to their next announced Pilgrim mission and another of those robotic cargo landers, we haven't seen any new rockets moving out to the pad. Plus, we're not picking up any new activity in lunar orbit."

For the moment, Patrick held his own counsel. On the large central screen, he saw the radar satellite's icon slide forward into the circle marked LOI. It began blinking rapidly, signaling that the spacecraft's rocket motor had begun its Lunar Orbit Insertion burn on schedule.

He gripped the railing. Maybe Moscow and Beijing had been caught off guard by the Topaz launch. And maybe not. One way or another, they were about to find out.

NATIONAL DEFENSE CONTROL CENTER, MOSCOW
THAT SAME TIME

"The American radar satellite is entering lunar orbit, sir," Major General Panarin, one of Leonov's staff officers, announced from his station. "Our tracking data shows this was a good burn."

Leonov nodded impassively. "What is the status of our Black Wasp?"

Panarin checked his screen. "On station." He looked back at his superior, obviously eager to proceed. "Your orders, sir?"

"Patience, Sergei," Leonov said calmly. On his own monitor, he pulled up the latest live feed from their

Kondor-L orbiting around the Lagrange point. Even from sixty thousand kilometers away, its radar and infrared sensors were powerful enough to pick out the American Topaz spy satellite as it swung above the moon at an altitude of one hundred kilometers. A digital readout at the top of his screen showed the time remaining before the enemy spacecraft crossed behind the moon. When it reached "0," he nodded to Panarin. "Activate the Black Wasp."

The younger officer's fingers rattled across his keyboard. With a quick flourish, he entered the last command and looked up. "Our signal is on its way."

Far out in space, hovering invisibly just a few meters from the American AEHF communications relay, the tiny Black Wasp hunter-killer satellite received Moscow's encrypted command. Even traveling at the speed of light, the signal had taken one and a half seconds to reach its destination. It required considerably less time for the little spacecraft's computer to carry out its orders.

Obeying the directives hardwired into it, the Black Wasp pulsed its ion thrusters for milliseconds—closing the gap with the American satellite. A wire-thin probe extending from its forward section brushed against

AEHF-7's box-shaped core, signaling contact between the two spacecraft.

Instantly, the shaped explosive charge that made up most of the Black Wasp's mass detonated. A lance of molten metal tore into the American satellite with tremendous force. Knocked out of its stable orbit, the gutted communications relay spun off into space— trailed by a widening cloud of mangled antennas, bits of broken solar panels, and other pieces of debris.

From several thousand kilometers distance, Russia's Kondor-L surveillance satellite witnessed the American spacecraft's death and reported the news to Moscow. Leonov allowed himself only a moment's satisfaction before opening a secure video link, this one to Korolev Base, on the far side of the moon.

Through a slight haze of electromagnetic interference, Colonel Kirill Lavrentyev's face looked back at him. "Sir?"

"The Americans are deaf again, Colonel. We've destroyed their radio and data relay." Leonov kept his tone level. "Accordingly, you are authorized to conduct immediate direct action against their Topaz radar reconnaissance satellite." He tapped a key, opening a new window on his computer to check the necessary codes.

"My authentication for this order is Omega Seven Nine."

Two seconds later, he saw the cosmonaut colonel nod sharply and then look down at his own computer. "I confirm that authentication code," Lavrentyev said. His chin lifted. "As directed, I must check this order with Colonel Tian."

"Very well," Leonov said calmly. "I will stand by." The military agreement between Russia and China required approval from the highest levels of both governments before Korolev Base could undertake any offensive operations against the United States or its allies. Neither Moscow nor Beijing wanted to risk being dragged into a conflict not of their own choosing.

Lavrentyev came back on-screen. "Beijing has just transmitted the same action order," he reported. Even across a communications gap of several hundred thousand kilometers, his sudden eagerness was obvious. Weeks of hard and dangerous work and months of elaborate planning were about to come to fruition.

"Then good hunting," Leonov told him. "Hit that spy satellite on its first pass, Kirill. It's vital that we deny the Americans any useful information for as long as possible. Is that clear?"

"Perfectly clear," Lavrentyev replied stoutly. "It will be done."

U.S. SPACE FORCE OPERATIONS CENTER, COLORADO
THAT SAME TIME

"Shit," one of the Topaz mission controllers suddenly blurted out loud. The lines of data streaming across his computer screen had stopped dead in mid-byte. He swiveled toward the senior officer on duty in the ops center. "I just lost contact with the AEHF relay, ma'am!"

"Same thing here," another officer reported from his station. "One second, we were receiving good data from the comsat itself and from the Topaz-M . . . and now, nothing."

More voices rose from around the room: "No connection to SHF Downlink Array One or Two. They're both gone."

"Satellite Crosslinks One and Two are out, too. Everything just dropped off-line in mid-signal."

"No joy with any of the dish antennas, ma'am. I can't route a connection request through any of them."

Brigadier General Jill Rosenthal kept her cool as the noise level increased. The petite, dark-haired officer stayed seated. "Settle down, people," she ordered. "Let's work this problem by the numbers. Start running diagnostic programs on your hardware and software."

She rocked back to talk more privately to her deputy. "Get on the horn to the backup operations group over at Shriever AFB, Phil. See if they're still in contact with AEHF-7. Let's make sure this isn't just a systems or computer malfunction on our end before we freak out."

The colonel nodded and picked up a phone. "Shriever Ops Center, this is McMahon at Peterson. We need you to—" Interrupted, he listened for a few moments. His expression darkened. "Okay," he said at last. "Keep trying. Call us back pronto if you get anything."

Rosenthal glanced at him. "No dice?"

He shook his head. "They've lost contact with the satellite, too."

"Well . . . that sucks," she said meditatively. Then she straightened back up. "Okay, let's see what we can do about this." She began snapping out orders to the various sections of her mission control team—setting in motion different methods of regaining touch with the distant communications satellite, and through it, the Topaz-M radar satellite, which was currently out of sight somewhere on the other side of the moon.

For the next several minutes, the once-calm space operations room was a hive of focused activity. But one by one, their attempts to recontact the AEHF com relay orbiting L2 failed.

Stone-faced now, Rosenthal came up to the rear observation platform to report to the president, General Kelleher, and the other VIPs. Briefly, she recounted the efforts her team had made so far to restore their links to the communications satellite.

"Without any result?" Kelleher pressed.

"No, sir," she admitted.

Martindale frowned. "Have you found anything that could explain what's gone wrong with that spacecraft?"

"Nothing definitive," Rosenthal said. "Although we have spotted one weird anomaly in the last megabytes of data we received from the satellite."

Patrick's jaw tightened. "What kind of anomaly?"

"The AEHF's tracking and stabilization subsystems show what appears to be strong, unexplained motion perpendicular to its orbit . . . just prior to the loss of signal."

"You're saying it looks like something hit it?" President Farrell realized.

"Yes, sir," Rosenthal said quietly.

"Some kind of space debris?" Kelleher asked. Comets streaking through the inner solar system sloughed off long trails of dust and tiny rocks. They were a known hazard for craft on deep-space missions. On its way back from Mars in 1967, NASA's Mariner 4 probe had run headlong into one of those drifting dust clouds—taking repeated impacts that tore away insulation and even knocked the spacecraft itself askew.

"Possibly," she said, sounding unconvinced. "But if so, it was a hell of a lot bigger chunk of rock than we've ever detected around that Lagrange point."

Patrick turned to look at the operations center's central display. It showed that they had a little over twenty minutes left before the Topaz-M surveillance satellite was expected to emerge from around the moon. Once that happened, they could expect to reacquire its signals and download the results of its first radar sweep across the far side.

But only if everything went according to plan. *Which isn't the way to bet,* he thought bitterly. He swung back to Rosenthal. "You might want to alert Goldstone and Greenbank, General. Just as a precaution."

She nodded her understanding. If they couldn't regain contact with the Topaz-M as scheduled, radar images obtained by using those large antennas should give them a look at the satellite itself. "I'll get on that right away."

An hour later, a tight-lipped Brigadier General Rosenthal showed them the first images picked up close to where the Topaz-M should have reemerged around the curve of the moon. They revealed a small field of debris drifting in a slowly decaying orbit. Quick calculations showed that those scraps of torn and twisted metal would impact the lunar surface sometime over the next several days.

"Those floating bits and pieces are all that's left of our radar satellite?" Martindale asked pointedly.

"Yes, sir," she answered, nodding. "The orbit's slightly off. But that's no surprise, given the force evidently used to destroy it."

"What in holy hell just happened up there?" President Farrell demanded.

Patrick answered him. His tone was tight and ice-cold. "Our spacecraft were attacked, sir. One satellite going dark could be an accident. But two dying over just a few minutes?" He shook his head grimly. "That's enemy action, Mr. President. Somehow, the Russians and the Chinese have deployed weapons on the moon and in cislunar space."

EAGLE STATION, OVER THE PACIFIC OCEAN
THAT SAME TIME

Four hundred miles above the cloud-covered ocean, three small, odd-looking spacecraft maneuvered between the aft section of the Orion crew module docked at Eagle Station and its thirteen-ton service module, a stubby cylinder topped by an adapter ring. The service module hung separately in space a few yards away. A much larger and more massive Falcon Heavy second-stage booster rocket was in a parking orbit somewhat farther off. Both the service module and booster were motionless relative to the space station, even though they were all circling Earth at nearly seventeen thousand miles per hour.

These one-person spacecraft were egg-shaped spheroids about nine feet high and a little under eight feet in diameter at their widest. Each was equipped with several mechanical limbs that ended in flexible appendages that resembled large, articulated metal fingers. Dozens of tiny thruster nozzles studded outer surfaces covered in advanced composite armor.

Called Cybernetic Orbital Maneuvering Systems, or COMS for short, they were yet another variant of Jason Richter's first war robots. But unlike the CIDs, these human-piloted space robots were intended primarily for zero-G operations and orbital construction tasks. Experiments had shown that a single machine was more efficient than ten astronauts wearing conventional EVA space suits. Although they'd been used as improvised weapons platforms during Scion's commando raid to seize Mars One, now Eagle Station, from the Russians, today the COMS were finally getting a chance to do the work for which they'd originally been designed.

Cocooned inside the cockpit of his COMS robot, Brad McLanahan, triggered a short burst from his thrusters. They popped in a computer-controlled sequence that moved him closer to the service module's open adapter ring.

He peered inside. Through his neural link with the robot's computer, the visual and other sensors set around its outer shell gave him an unobstructed view of his surroundings. It was eerily like floating in space without a helmet. Green indicators blinked into existence, highlighting several of the bolt assemblies securing the adapter ring to the rest of the spacecraft. "Okay, bolts twenty-seven through thirty-three look solid."

"*Copy that,*" Nadia radioed. Her COMS was over on the other side of the ring. "*I show a problem with seventy-eight.*" One of her robot's manipulator arms swung down holding a power tool and began tightening the loose bolt she'd identified. As she worked, multiple thrusters fired around the COMS hull, holding her securely in position despite the fact they were in zero-G.

Over near the docked Orion crew module, Peter Vasey's COMS hovered near the umbilical connection interface. Spotlights glowed bright, illuminating the dark interior of the open port.

"*Both the CM bracket assembly and line support check out,*" the Englishman commented. Like Brad and Nadia, he was one of Sky Masters and Scion's most experienced COMS pilots.

Brad smiled. This was their second full EVA and they were already ahead of schedule. If they could keep this pace up, it should be possible to finish mating the Orion crew module to its service module in three or four more days. Once that was done, they could begin the delicate task of maneuvering the fully assembled Orion spacecraft into position with the Falcon Heavy second stage.

"*Priority override,*" his COMS computer suddenly told him. "*Encrypted radio transmission from Peterson Space Force Operations Center.*"

"Put it through," Brad ordered. What was so urgent that it couldn't wait until they were all back aboard Eagle Station in a couple of hours?

"*Stand by for General McLanahan,*" a crisp woman's voice said through his headset. A second later, his father's familiar tones came over the link. "*Brad, we need the three of you to stop what you're doing and get back inside Eagle Station. The Russians and Chinese just blew the shit out of our two satellites near the moon. The president's put a hold on that Orion flight you're prepping.*"

"A hold?" Brad asked, stunned by the news. "For how long?"

"Damned if I know, son," his father replied. "But I can tell you one thing for sure, there's no way in hell we're sending an unarmed manned spacecraft to the moon. Not now. The next astronauts who head that way had better be ready for a fight."

THIRTY-FOUR

THE WHITE HOUSE SITUATION ROOM,
WASHINGTON, D.C.
A FEW DAYS LATER

Long before he took the oath of office, President John Dalton Farrell had known there would be days and maybe even weeks and months that would make him want to tear his hair out, set it on fire, and then go looking for a fight—just to ease some of the tension. It was the nature of the job, where all of the nation's troubles seemed to land on one man or woman's shoulders, and too many people outside the government expected whoever sat in the Oval Office to work miracles. Put that together with too many people inside the government who spent their time explaining why nothing could ever be done to solve any problem, and you had a recipe for sheer gut-busting, artery-popping frustration.

Being president would try the patience of a saint, and saints were in short supply in politics. *And you sure as hell ain't one of them, J.D.,* he admitted to himself. Which left him wrestling right now with the urge to haul off and slug someone—Russia's marshal Mikhail Leonov or China's president Li Jun, for choice.

With that in mind, Farrell looked down the long table to a relative newcomer, General Richard Kelleher. Given the nature of this sudden crisis, it had been an easy call to include the Space Force chief of staff in this White House meeting with his national security advisers. "Let me get this straight, General. Right now, the Russians and Chinese have four separate payloads intended for the moon in Earth orbit."

Kelleher nodded. "That's correct, Mr. President. All of them launched within the past hour."

"Li Jun and Leonov are busy sons of bitches, I'll grant 'em that," Farrell growled. "Okay, what are my options here? Can we use Eagle Station's plasma rail gun or our armed spaceplanes to turn any of those rockets into floating scrap? Because I'd surely like to send Beijing and Moscow the only kind of cease-and-desist message they'll understand before this day gets much older."

At that, Secretary of State Andrew Taliaferro and several others exchanged worried looks.

"You have a problem with that, Andy?" Farrell asked.

To his credit, Taliaferro didn't waffle. "Yes, sir," he said firmly. "Without clear evidence that our satellites were actually destroyed by the Russians and the Chinese, most of the rest of the world would see U.S. military action against their spacecraft as unprovoked aggression." He turned to Kelleher. "And as I understand it, General, we don't have that kind of evidence. Nor are we likely to get it."

The Space Force chief of staff nodded reluctantly. "That's true. Short of somehow retrieving pieces of wreckage from AEHF-7 and the Topaz-M for forensic examination—which is essentially impossible—we can't prove what killed them. Space is a dangerous place . . . and accidents do happen, especially to complex spacecraft. And plenty of countries out there will be looking for reasons to avoid confronting Beijing and Moscow over this issue."

Looking out at them from one of the wall screens, Nadia Rozek-McLanahan spoke up. She and Brad were participating in this emergency national security meeting via a secure link to Eagle Station, currently orbiting high over the Indian Ocean. "The physics of this situation already make any attack impossible. By the time we come around the curve of the earth into view of those Russian and Chinese spacecraft, they'll have begun their translunar injection burns and be well outside our plasma rail gun's effective range. The same thing goes for the S-29s, which have a much shorter-ranged laser weapon."

Farrell allowed himself a wry smile. "Y'all are starting to piss me off with these inconvenient facts." He sighed. "Trouble is, I can't afford to replace you with a bunch of sycophants, even if I wanted to. Look where that got poor old Stacy Anne in the end: up shit creek without even a canoe, let alone a paddle."

His predecessor, President Barbeau, had been infamous for packing the ranks of her senior advisers and cabinet officials with nonentities, tame "yes-men" and "yes-women" who never bucked her decisions or challenged her assumptions. In the end, left entirely to her own whims and preconceived ideas, she'd run the United States into grave danger, damaged its standing in the world, and, ultimately, wrecked her own hopes of winning a second term in office.

"Speaking truth to power is our duty," Nadia said

seriously. Her chin lifted slightly to emphasize the point. Even this tiny motion, in zero-G, caused a lock of her thick, dark hair to float across her face. Impatiently, she brushed it aside. Then she smiled. "Admittedly, doing so is much safer from here. The rest of your advisers trapped down there on Earth with you will just have to take their chances."

That sparked a soft ripple of laughter from around the table.

"Well, all right, then," Farrell said after a short pause. "Is there some way we can stop them from sending any new spacecraft to the moon?"

"By imposing an orbital blockade over their launch sites?" Kelleher asked.

Farrell nodded. "Something along those lines, General. Whatever Moscow and Beijing are doing on the lunar surface, shutting down their ability to reinforce and resupply from Earth could be crucial."

"You're right about that," Patrick McLanahan agreed. "But—"

"Ah, hell," Farrell grumbled. "It's impossible, right?"

Patrick shot him a rueful smile. "I'm afraid so. One of our S-29 spaceplanes would only be in effective range of any of those Russian and Chinese launch complexes for about two minutes out of every ninety-eight-minute orbit. Between life-support limitations and the need to cover different orbital tracks, seriously blockading their launch sites would take a force of dozens of armed spacecraft. Building that many spaceplanes would take years."

"Years we don't have."

"That's about the size of it," Patrick admitted.

Farrell scowled. "Are y'all telling me we're just going have to sit tight and do nothing? Because I will be damned if I intend to let those bastards Leonov and Li lock us out of the moon and all its resources."

"Whatever weapons Moscow and Beijing have deployed to the moon are around on the far side," Taliaferro pointed out. "So they're only a threat to spacecraft going into lunar orbit. What if we just skipped that part of any moon mission and sent our rockets straight to the near side—where everything suggests the highest concentrations of helium-3 are anyway?"

Kelleher shook his head. "Direct descent to the lunar surface might work for some unmanned missions, but it's awfully risky. One small engine misfire or bad burn and you end up with bits and pieces of expensive hardware scattered across several hundred square miles of the moon. And you sure can't take those kinds of risks with live astronauts. Shooting for lunar orbit first at least gives you the option of a free-return trajectory, where the moon's gravity slings your ship back toward Earth if anything major goes wrong."

"Like Apollo 13," Farrell realized. Kelleher nodded.

"Even if we were willing to take those risks, we'd only wind up being too late," Patrick said. "All along the way, the Russians and the Chinese have been ahead of us. Once they learn we're planning to send landers and mining equipment straight to the lunar surface— which isn't something we can keep secret—there'll be nothing stopping them from deploying additional weapons to the near side of the moon."

Farrell grimaced. "What you're saying is that we either win this fight now, somehow . . . or we kiss the moon, its resources, and everything they can do for our economy, our technology, and our future, good-bye."

"Yes, sir," Patrick agreed solemnly. "That's the way it lays out."

A grim silence fell across the Situation Room.

"Excuse me, Mr. President," Brad said quietly over the link from orbit.

Farrell looked up. "Yes, Major McLanahan?"

"On that score, Nadia and I have been working through some alternatives," the younger man told him. "And we've come up with what we think could be a workable mission plan for an armed reconnaissance of the moon's far side."

With a skeptical look on his face, General Kelleher leaned forward. "Using what hardware, exactly?" He snorted. "Reconfiguring that Orion crew vehicle and our other deep-space-capable craft to carry weapons would take years of engineering and flight testing."

"The Orion's not going to cut it," Brad agreed evenly.

Kelleher frowned. "If you're not going to fly the Orion, what have you got in mind? There's no other piece of human-rated space hardware in our inventory that's designed to go beyond Earth orbit, never mind all the way out to the moon and back."

Brad looked stubborn. "I'd rather not get into specifics just yet, sir." He focused his gaze on Farrell. "Nadia and I are reasonably confident we can use existing, off-the-shelf hardware and technology for this lunar recon mission, Mr. President. But we'd really like to consult more closely with Sky Masters and Scion weapons and astronautical engineering experts before we get everybody's hopes up. And we definitely want to run some in-depth computer simulations to test out our rough concept."

Without hesitating, Farrell nodded. "Then I want

your behinds back down here ASAP . . . so you can start refining this plan of yours." He looked serious. "Because I know you two well enough to bet big on whatever wild-eyed scheme you're cooking up."

"Yes, Mr. President," Nadia said solemnly.

VNUKOVO INTERNATIONAL AIRPORT, OUTSIDE MOSCOW
THE NEXT DAY

While a smartly uniformed Honor Guard Battalion military band played China's national anthem, "March of the Volunteers," President Li Jun descended the stairs from his official aircraft, a Boeing 747-8 wide-body passenger jet. Though he wore a heavy overcoat and scarf against a freezing wind sweeping across the tarmac, he was bareheaded—in part to demonstrate the youthful vigor that helped keep potential political rivals at bay.

At the foot of the stairs, Marshal Mikhail Ivanovich Leonov snapped a quick salute and shook hands with him. "Welcome to the Russian Federation, Comrade President," he said in a booming voice. He smiled broadly.

Cameras clicked rapidly all around them. Moscow's

entire international press corps had been invited out to witness this beginning of Li's state visit to the Russian Federation. Officially, he was here to celebrate the ongoing success of their joint "peaceful and scientific" Pilgrim missions to the moon. Unofficially, both leaders wanted the American president and his close advisers to know they were confronted by a solid Sino-Russian military alliance, both on Earth and in space.

Li donned his own answering smile. "Thank you, Comrade Marshal, for your kind greeting. I look forward to our upcoming talks. We have much to congratulate each other on, and a shared fraternal future to discuss."

As he had expected, that last somewhat vague and even innocuous phrase created a stir among the assembled journalists. Within minutes, he knew, the internet and the world's airwaves would be full of breathless and uninformed speculation about just what China's leader might have meant.

A few minutes later, after a rapid inspection of the Russian honor guard—presenting arms at rigid attention in their gray fur caps, overcoats, and polished jackboots—Li followed his Russian host into the back of a long black limousine. Gratefully, he settled back against its heated leather seats. "A useful show," he commented dryly.

Leonov nodded. "I hope it will make Washington think very carefully about its next moves."

Both men intended this open demonstration of Russian and Chinese solidarity to help restrain the American president's otherwise aggressive instincts. The longer Farrell hesitated, the better for Moscow and Beijing. After all, delay worked in their favor—buying time for more supplies and military hardware to reach the moon. And for the cosmonauts and taikonauts at Korolev to further refine their defenses.

"For the moment, I do not think we need worry excessively," Li said with a shrug. "Our telescopes and space-based sensors all show that the Americans have stopped work on their Orion spacecraft docked at Eagle Station."

"Ours, too," Leonov agreed. A trace of a frown crossed his broad Slavic face. "Although we did observe one of their S-19 Midnight passenger spaceplanes departing the station several hours ago—apparently bound for the Sky Masters facility in Nevada."

"It was probably just returning their space construction crew to Earth," Li suggested without much concern.

"Perhaps."

Li glanced sidelong at his Russian counterpart. "You do not agree?"

"I only hesitate to assume the Americans will surrender control over the moon so meekly," Leonov told him.

"Meekly? Perhaps not," Li said with a humorless smile. "But for the moment, I see no signs of any imminent American reaction to the destruction of their two satellites. In fact, I consider it especially significant that Washington hasn't made those losses public. Nor has it even accused us, either openly, or privately through diplomatic back channels, of being responsible."

"That is . . . odd," Leonov said.

Li shook his head. "On the contrary, President Farrell may be wiser than I first believed. Perhaps he is simply unwilling to risk enraging his countrymen by revealing a defeat—especially one he cannot avenge?"

"Let us hope so," Leonov said somberly. "Though I admit that I can't see what the Americans can hope to do against us, at least on the moon."

Now the Chinese leader laughed. "Come, Comrade Marshal, relax. Your strategy is working as planned. That's a cause for celebration, not sudden misgivings."

Leonov forced himself to smile in response. In all probability, Li's confidence was justified. Careful study of America's space capabilities—even those of its mercenary corporations like Sky Masters and Scion—showed nothing that could threaten the Sino-Russian alliance's military hold on Earth's moon. *Then why do you feel so uncertain suddenly, Mikhail?* he asked himself privately. Was this merely a case of nerves? Or was it something more serious, a premonition of real trouble headed their way?

THIRTY-FIVE

**KOROLEV BASE, ON THE RIM OF
ENGEL'GARDT CRATER, THE MOON
   TWO DAYS LATER**

Captain Shan Jinai carefully closed the Chang'e-13 lander's outer hatch and sealed it. Now that the Americans knew China and Russia had established a presence on the far side of the moon, there was no further need for any subterfuge. Instead of waiting for a deceptive rendezvous with the Chang'e's unmanned ascent stage, the Federation spacecraft that had ferried Shan and Major Andrei Bezrukov here from Earth was already several hours into its long journey home. And so Chang'e-13's unused ascent stage could wait here empty, high up on the crater rim, until the day it was needed to carry humans back into lunar orbit.

Moving awkwardly in his bulky EVA suit, the taikonaut slowly climbed down the Chang'e's ladder and
stepped off onto the powdery surface of the moon. He
turned around and saw Bezrukov waiting near one of
the landing struts.

Shan went over to him—practicing the half-gliding,
half-hopping gait that experience had shown was the
most efficient in this strange, low-gravity environment.
From here, all of Korolev Base stretched out before
them.

Parts of seven other spacecraft dotted the desolate plain. Four were large Mǎ Luó cargo ships. The
rest were the spent descent stages of earlier crewed
Chang'e landers. Brightly colored insulated inflatable
tanks ringed some of the space vehicles. Each contained stores of oxygen, water, or hydrogen reclaimed
from the lunar soil. Low, mounded heaps of loose dirt
and rock showed where buried hoses and conduits
connected these tanks to the base's cylindrical habitat
module.

Farther away, beyond the array of landed spacecraft and other infrastructure, Shan spotted several
automated rovers moving. They were sharply outlined against the pitch-black sky. Rooster tails of fine-
grained dust sprayed out from behind their wheels
and scraper blades. Each rover was collecting the

regolith needed to feed Korolev's furnaces and chemical reactors.

Out near the very edge of the crater rim, the taikonaut could see three larger mounds of soil and rock rising several meters above the surrounding plain. Each was topped by what appeared to be a matte-black dome. Power conduits stretched across the moonscape, linking each mound to the small metal cylinder containing Korolev Base's two-megawatt fusion reactor. For a few moments, he studied them more closely. In the end, the powerful weapon and sensors hidden beneath those domes were the whole reason for this difficult and expensive undertaking so far from Earth.

"An incredible sight, isn't it?" the Russian cosmonaut said, sounding awed.

Silently, Shan agreed. Together, their two countries had built mankind's first permanent fortified settlement off its home planet. Effectively, Korolev Base gave them complete control over everything in lunar orbit. As a result, once they developed their own affordable, reusable rocket technology to match that of the Americans, Moscow and Beijing would be the ones to unlock the awesome potential of the moon's helium-3 resources. Russia and China would control the world's future, not the United States.

HANGAR THREE, MCLANAHAN INDUSTRIAL AIRPORT, SKY MASTERS AEROSPACE INC., BATTLE MOUNTAIN, NEVADA
SEVERAL DAYS LATER

Scion's big, black S-29B Shadow spaceplane sat parked in the middle of the large hangar. Not far away, several rows of folding chairs faced several video display screens and a podium.

Dry-mouthed, Brad McLanahan watched President J. D. Farrell and his closest national security advisers, including his father and Kevin Martindale, file in and take their seats. They were followed by General Kelleher, his top staff officers, and the cadre of Space Force pilots and crewmen that he, Nadia, and Hunter Noble had helped train.

"Man, that is one hell of a lot of brass," Boomer muttered. Grinning wickedly, he leaned closer to Brad. "You know, this looks like a tough crowd. Want me to go out first and tell a few dirty jokes to loosen 'em up a little for you?"

Before Brad could reply, the other man suddenly grunted. Rubbing his side, Boomer glanced warily at Nadia. "Hey, that *hurt*."

Wearing an innocent expression, she shrugged. "With pain comes wisdom, Dr. Noble."

Despite his growing tension, Brad felt himself smile. "Settle down, kids. Don't make me stop this car and come back there."

Geez, we all sound kinda punch-drunk, he realized. Ever since he and Nadia returned from orbit, the team they'd put together had been working almost around the clock to refine and validate their mission plan for an armed reconnaissance flight around the moon and back. Whatever sleep they'd gotten had come in the form of grudgingly snatched catnaps on cots in empty offices between simulator runs. Meals had been equally sporadic, more often than not sandwiches, chips, and candy bars from vending machines instead of real food.

In fact, up to this moment, Brad would have been willing to bet that every ounce of adrenaline in his body had long since been burned up—replaced by caffeine from the dozens of cups of coffee he vaguely remembered drinking. But now, looking out over an audience full of the most senior officials in the U.S. government, he was all too aware that his nerves were starting to twitch.

Given a choice, he'd much rather fly in combat than make any kind of a speech. But that was the trouble. He didn't really have a free choice in the here and now. Because no one was flying anywhere unless he could sell this idea to the president and his national security team. So even though he wasn't really cut out by training or inclination for this particular job, that didn't matter.

"Well, I guess I'd better get this dog and pony show started," Brad said reluctantly, knowing that he sounded like a kid about to hand his parents a really crappy report card.

Nadia pulled him down for a quick, passionate kiss. "You will be fine," she told him after their lips parted. "Do not worry."

Somewhat dazed, he nodded. He didn't know exactly how she did it, but she had the ability to take his emotions, stir them around, and somehow leave him feeling a hundred times better.

Squaring his shoulders, Brad moved to the lectern. "Mr. President, ladies and gentlemen," he said. He supposed strict etiquette would have required separately identifying every cabinet-level secretary and general officer, but that would have taken forever. Plus, he'd probably only have ended up pissing off someone important by leaving them off the list. "Thanks for coming. I'll try to make this as quick and to the point as I can."

Farrell and his father both gave him encouraging smiles.

"A few days ago, I mentioned that we were working

on a possible plan for an armed reconnaissance of the moon's far side," Brad went on. "The good news is that after crunching all the numbers and running detailed simulations, we're now confident our proposed mission plan is feasible."

General Kelleher spoke up from his place. "And I'm going to repeat my earlier question, Mr. McLanahan: Where's the actual honest-to-God spacecraft that's going to fly this hypothetical armed recon you're talking about?"

Brad ignored the other man's somewhat insulting refusal to address him by the major's rank he'd earned with the Iron Wolf Squadron. Like many officers in the U.S. armed forces, Kelleher probably wasn't exactly comfortable with the idea of private military units. Besides, this wasn't the time to get into a pissing contest over nonessentials. With a slight shrug, he mentally pulled the pin on the rhetorical grenade he was about to toss into everyone's laps. Then he turned and nodded to the large S-29B Shadow spaceplane parked nearby. "You're looking right at it, General."

Kelleher stared hard at him. "If that's your idea of a joke, I'd advise you to drop it fast and get serious."

"I'm not joking," Brad said quietly. "We can send that S-29 to the moon."

Now he heard a muttered storm of protest from

around the room. Even President Farrell looked uncertain. Only his father nodded thoughtfully. *Figures,* he thought. His dad was usually about ten steps ahead of everyone else when it came to adapting military hardware to new and never-imagined uses.

Martindale, however, was clearly somewhat less flexible—at least in this case. He shook his head in disbelief. "Cut the crap, Major," he snapped. "The S-29s and their sister spaceplanes are designed solely for limited-duration missions in low Earth orbit and in the atmosphere. It's sheer fantasy to propose flying something that's half airplane, half spaceship out into deep space, around the moon, and then all the way back to Earth."

To his own surprise, Brad stayed calm. If anything, he suddenly realized, he was actually enjoying this chance to play the contrarian. Maybe he was more like his father than he'd ever imagined. "It's not fantasy at all, Mr. Martindale," he said bluntly. "Like I said earlier, my team and I have run this concept through detailed analysis and simulation." He signaled the Sky Masters computer techs controlling their audiovisual equipment. "And with the necessary modifications, there's no reason that an S-29B can't handle this reconnaissance mission."

The display screens behind him lit up, showing

computer-generated visuals to accompany his presentation.

"First, we're going to cut the S-29's crew from the normal complement of five to just two—a pilot and a weapons and systems specialist," Brad said. On-screen, the S-29B schematic showed the whole aft cabin emptied of its crew workstations, acceleration couches, and other equipment and stripped down to bare metal. "In addition, we'll need to remove all four defensive microwave emitters." Again, the schematic changed—now visually deleting the two wingtip microwave pods, the third pod mounted on top of the forward fuselage, and the last emitter set below the S-29's aft fuselage.

"What does that gain you?" one of the Space Force staff officers asked curiously.

Brad could feel the atmosphere in the hangar start to shift. He could tell that many of those who'd at first thought the idea of using a spaceplane for this mission was crazy were beginning to wonder if they might have been wrong. "Cutting the crew size and stripping out the microwave pods gets us just enough mass and cubic capacity for the additional life-support and stellar navigation gear we need to make a long-range, deep-space mission feasible."

He continued. "Running through all the numbers, the Shadow's five LPDRS engines, firing in pure rocket mode, are powerful enough to make a translunar injection burn from Earth orbit possible—as long as the spaceplane is fully fueled before departure."

Another of Kelleher's staff officers raised a hand. "But that'll pretty much leave the S-29 with dry fuel tanks," she pointed out. "So you get only one pass across the far side before using the moon's gravity to slingshot you back toward Earth on a free-return trajectory. That's a serious limitation for any reconnaissance mission, especially if the situation turns hot and the enemy starts shooting."

"No doubt about it," Brad agreed. He smiled. "Pretty early on in our sims, we identified the fuel constraint as a serious operational problem. Fortunately, we've come up with a solution for that. Granted, the maneuvers required are a little tricky, but they're not beyond the capabilities of a good pilot."

Speaking carefully, he outlined this revolutionary element of their mission plan. Behind him, the screens depicted the necessary spacecraft modifications, timing, and anticipated maneuvers in intricate detail. When he finished, you could practically hear a pin drop across the hangar.

From near the back row, Colonel Miller broke the silence. "You know, Brad, that's really fucking clever."

"Thanks, Dusty," Brad acknowledged with a grin.

"It's also the kind of cockeyed scheme that only someone who's basically batshit crazy would even think of in the first place," the S-29B pilot went on.

"Maybe so," Brad allowed. He shrugged stubbornly. "But it will work."

Miller nodded. "Oh, no doubt about that." He grinned back at the younger man. "I just wanted to go on record with my assessment of your fundamental mental health."

Smiling broadly himself, Brad waited for the subsequent laughter to die down before picking up the threads of his briefing. Miller's quip had broken a lot of the remaining tension.

Another Space Force staffer asked a question: "Without its defensive microwave emitters, won't the Shadow be more vulnerable to enemy attack?"

Nadia stepped up to the lectern to answer this one. While Brad, Boomer, and Jason Richter worked through orbital mechanics and life-support problems, she'd put in a lot of time analyzing the military aspects of their proposed mission. "That is true only if the Russians and Chinese are using modified air-to-air or surface-to-air missiles as their weapons against targets in lunar orbit. We consider that highly unlikely."

"Why is that?" President Farrell asked.

"Because, given the costs involved in ferrying

payload mass from the earth to the moon, it would be remarkably inefficient to rely on relatively bulky, single-use missiles," she explained.

The president's eyes narrowed. "Then what do you think we're facing?"

"Quite probably a version of the same Russian-designed plasma rail gun we captured on Mars One," Nadia told him.

And just that quickly, Brad sensed the tension in the room return to its previous high pitch.

"Jesus," Farrell muttered. "Powered by what? Some kind of solar array? With battery backups?"

Now it was Jason Richter's turn to answer a question. "No, sir. My guess is they've also developed a smaller version of their helium-3 fusion reactor. My engineering teams don't see any technical hurdles that would prevent the Russians from scaling down that ten-megawatt reactor they built for Mars One." He shrugged. "A smaller reactor, somewhere on the order of one or two megawatts, would only weigh one or two tons. That's well within the payload capacity of one of those Chinese cargo landers. And having that much power available would be very useful for any lunar base."

Farrell grimaced. "It's sure starting to sound like y'all are proposing a suicide mission. Just getting to the moon's hard enough. Going up against a fully powered plasma gun at the end of the trip seems liable to be one step too far."

Brad shook his head. "No one up here's interested in turning kamikaze, Mr. President. For one thing, that enemy weapon, whatever it is, has to be based on the lunar surface. If the Russians and Chinese had a weapons platform orbiting the moon, we'd already have spotted it."

"Which means their weapon's effective range will be significantly restricted," Kelleher realized.

"Yes, sir," Brad agreed. "Plasma guns and combat-grade lasers are strictly line-of-sight weapons. They can't shoot through mountains or crater rims, or at anything beyond their visual horizon. Worst case, a surface-deployed plasma gun will only have a range of around five hundred miles against a target in orbit."

"So it can still shoot a lot farther than the laser on our spaceplane," Martindale pointed out dryly. "That doesn't sound too promising to me."

To Brad's surprise, Kelleher cut in to respond to this, sounding far more positive than he had at the beginning of the briefing. "Our S-29s have conducted a large number of practice engagements against Eagle Station's plasma gun, Mr. Martindale. The evasive maneuvers my pilots have pioneered should give the crew of that spaceplane a fighting chance—even if they are outranged."

"Yes, sir," Brad said. "Which is why we're confident this mission is doable, especially with an experienced crew at the controls."

"So who do you have in mind for this little jaunt?" Farrell asked quietly.

"Boomer and I have the most actual flight and simulator time," Brad replied. "So we should go."

Beside him, Nadia muttered something angry-sounding under her breath in Polish. This was an argument she still wasn't ready to admit she'd lost.

Abruptly, Kelleher stood up. "No, sir," the Space Force general said flatly. "This isn't a job for civilians." Seeing their faces tighten, he held up his hand. "Lord knows, I respect the skill and courage you folks have shown in the past several years. But this mission rightly belongs to my pilots and mission specialists. Thanks to our training maneuvers, they have more practical experience than anyone else when it comes to flying against the kinds of Russian and Chinese weapons you're talking about."

Behind him, the uniformed Space Force pilots and crewmen nodded their agreement.

Kelleher turned to Farrell. "The United States has invested a lot of money and other resources to stand up the Space Force, Mr. President. And with respect, it's time you committed us to active service against our nation's enemies."

Slowly, Farrell nodded. "I think you're right about that, General." He looked over at Brad and the others. "Y'all have put your lives on the line for the U.S. and our allies again and again. Usually when there wasn't anyone else with the guts or brains needed to take on the fight. But that's not the case here. It's time for the regular armed forces to step into the breach."

Brad's jaw tightened. "Sir, I—"

Farrell shook his head. "My mind's made up, Major McLanahan." He shrugged. "Besides, it's just barely possible that the Chinese and Russians might hesitate to fire on a Space Force S-29 and risk a wider conflict with this country. They'd have no such hesitation in firing on a spacecraft flown by folks they've called mercenaries and space pirates."

Nadia frowned. "That is a very thin reed to cling to, Mr. President," she warned.

"I know it," Farrell said evenly. His face was somber. "But given all the other risks involved in this lunar recon mission, I figure we should play every last card we can."

THIRTY-SIX

COMMAND CENTER, CENTRAL MILITARY COMMISSION OF THE PEOPLE'S REPUBLIC OF CHINA, BEIJING
SEVERAL DAYS LATER

President Li Jun looked up from a sheaf of reports when General Chen Haifeng came in. Silently, he motioned for his aides to withdraw and then politely gestured to a place across the table. "Be seated, General."

Chen did as he was told. The general looked thinner, worn down by the months of unremitting work involved in managing China's part of Operation Heaven's Thunder. In any given week, he was either out at the Xichang and Wenchang space complexes to supervise launch preparations, or he was in Russia, coordinating with Leonov and his staff. Today he had just returned from Moscow.

"You have news from our ally?" Li asked.

Chen nodded. "Leonov shared his country's most recent intelligence with me."

"And?"

"It confirms our own reports from the Ministry of State Security," Chen told him. "The Americans have pulled one of their armed spaceplanes off active duty. From what we can tell, it landed at the Sky Masters facility in Nevada. One of the Sky Masters–owned unarmed S-29s has also dropped out of sight."

Li frowned. "For what purpose? Routine maintenance? Or something more?"

"We don't know, Comrade President," Chen admitted. "The entire Sky Masters complex is under strict security measures—with a reinforced guard detail that apparently includes three CID combat robots. Neither our agents nor those of the Russian GRU have been able to get anywhere near the perimeter."

Li pondered that. From all reports, the piloted war machines were terrifyingly effective. But they were also extremely expensive, with only a handful in existence. He doubted the Americans would have committed so many CIDs to a passive security role without good cause. Whatever was going on in Nevada, they were determined to keep it secret. "Anything else?"

"A commercial SpaceX Falcon Heavy launch slated for two weeks from now has just been scrubbed," Chen said.

Li raised an eyebrow. "And why is that significant?"

"Because it was scrubbed by direct order from the White House, on national security grounds," Chen told him. "Instead, the Americans want the rocket on standby to lift another payload into orbit."

"What kind of payload?" Li demanded.

Apologetically, Chen shrugged his shoulders. "Neither the Russians nor our own people have been able to find out. All we know is that, whatever this secret payload is, it was flown to the Kennedy Space Center in Florida aboard a Sky Masters–owned cargo aircraft—with another Scion combat robot along as an escort."

"Sky Masters and Scion again," Li said with a scowl.

"Yes, Comrade President."

"Do you or Marshal Leonov have any theories about what the Americans are planning?"

Somewhat hesitantly, Chen nodded. "It's possible that they are readying a retaliatory strike against one or more of our space launch complexes, using a combination of their spaceplanes and some type of new orbital weapons. Without any real ability to act offensively on or around the moon, the Americans may see this as their only real option. Serious damage to Plesetsk, Vostochny, Wenchang, or Xichang would make it difficult to keep Korolev Base operational."

Li nodded his understanding. Periodic shipments of food, spare parts, and other consumables were necessary to sustain the cosmonauts and taikonauts stationed at the lunar base—and to keep their sophisticated sensors and other hardware running in an airless environment marked by wild temperature swings and high radiation. He pinned Chen with a cold-eyed gaze. "In your military judgment, could such an attack succeed?" he snapped.

"Our defenses around each site are very strong," Chen replied. But his uncertain tone belied those confident words.

Again, Li nodded. All four space complexes were ringed by networks of powerful phased-array radars and regiments of advanced S-500 surface-to-air missiles. S-500s were very long-ranged and they were designed to engage and destroy ballistic missiles and even spacecraft attacking at hypersonic speeds. On paper, any enemy S-29 raid should be doomed to failure. Unfortunately, both he and Chen were only too aware of previous American victories achieved in the face of what seemed like overwhelming odds.

He reached out and picked up a phone. "This is the president. Arrange a secure satellite link to Moscow at once." While waiting, he looked across the table at Chen. "I have no intention of waiting for the Americans to unleash their planned counterstroke. Before they move, Marshal Leonov and I will make it very clear to President Farrell that an attack on any Chinese or Russian space launch complex will be treated as an existential strategic threat by both our governments."

Chen's eyes widened. "One that would trigger an immediate nuclear response?"

Li nodded gravely. "Exactly so. Somehow I do not believe that even this Texas cowboy will risk the destruction of San Francisco or Dallas or New York for so small a prospective gain."

THE WHITE HOUSE, WASHINGTON, D.C.
A SHORT TIME LATER

Tight-lipped with anger, President Farrell took the printout of the "joint communiqué" sent by Moscow and Beijing and fed it unceremoniously into the classified materials shredder next to his desk. As it whirred into oblivion, he turned to Kevin Martindale and Patrick McLanahan. "I guess it's nice to know those bastards are starting to feel a little nervous."

Martindale smiled. "And that they're looking in completely the wrong direction." From the beginning, their own tactical analysis had shown that any spaceplane attack on Sino-Russian launch sites would be a pointless disaster. Learning that their enemies feared the possibility enough to threaten nuclear war offered a useful window into their mind-set.

"That won't last long," Patrick cautioned. "As soon as we launch our S-29s and other mission components into orbit, the Chinese and Russians will start putting the pieces together. And there's no way we can hide any translunar injection burns. So any cosmonauts and taikonauts stationed on the moon's far side will have days of warning about what's headed their way."

Farrell nodded grimly. Thanks to their Magpie Bridge com relay and *Kondor*-class radar surveillance satellite stationed out around the Earth-Moon Lagrange-2 point, Moscow and Beijing had complete situational awareness of everything in cislunar space and lunar orbit. Tactically speaking, any spacecraft the United States launched toward the moon was in essentially the same situation as a group of soldiers forced to attack uphill across a barren slope against an entrenched enemy.

Every move they made could be observed. There was no real way to achieve surprise.

He wished, for the hundredth time, that there was some way to knock those satellites out. Unfortunately, given the enormous distance to the L2 point from Earth, that was effectively impossible. Even if the United States had hunter-killer satellites of its own, any launch toward the Lagrange point could be detected and monitored throughout its flight—giving the Chinese and Russian satellites ample time to evade an attack . . . or to eliminate it, with their own defenses.

No, he realized, subtlety was out the window here. The Space Force crew about to head for the moon on his orders would just have to bull ahead and hope luck broke their way.

THIRTY-SEVEN

Two hundred and fifty miles above the cloud-dappled peaks and snow-choked mountain valleys of the Rockies, two large black spaceplanes flew in tandem—circling the world together at more than seventeen thousand miles per hour. One was a Space Force S-29B Shadow now configured for a voyage to the moon. It was piloted by Colonel Scott "Dusty" Miller and Major Hannah "Rocky" Craig. The second was an unarmed civilian S-29A refueling tanker with two Scion pilots, Peter "Constable" Vasey and Liz Gallagher, at its controls.

Aboard Shadow Bravo One, Hannah Craig peered up through the forward cockpit windows. The other spaceplane hung just a few yards above the top of their fuselage—sharply outlined against a deep black sky strewn with the hard, bright pinpoints of uncounted thousands of stars. Relative to them, the S-29A was flying upside down and backward. A long, flexible boom extended from one of the two silver-colored fuel tanks inside its open cargo bay. The end of the boom was now seated firmly inside the S-29B's refueling receptacle.

"How's it look from your angle?" Miller asked from the left-hand pilot's seat.

"Real solid," she replied. She radioed the other spaceplane, "I confirm contact, Shadow Alpha Three."

"Roger that," Gallagher replied. *"Commencing JP transfer now."*

Aboard the tanker, pumps whirred. Inert helium gas was used to "push" JP-8 jet fuel into the S-29B Shadow's tanks in zero-G conditions—replenishing the stores consumed during its rocket-powered climb into orbit. Earlier in this evolution, the S-29A tanker had refilled their separate oxidizer reserves with highly explosive borohydrogen metaoxide, or BOHM. BOHM was essentially refined hydrogen peroxide and, when mixed with ordinary jet fuel, it enabled combustion inside their five LRDRS engines outside the atmosphere.

Minutes passed as the two spacecraft swung southeastward high over the lush Mississippi River valley, the cloud-covered Appalachians, and then out across the Atlantic. Ahead through their cockpit windows, Miller and Craig saw a patch of lighter-colored green-blue shallows appear, surrounded on all sides by the dark ultramarine waters of the deeper ocean. They were coming up on Bermuda.

"JP-8 transfer complete," Liz Gallagher reported from the tanker. *"Detaching the boom now."*

With a gentle *CL-CLUNK,* the boom's nozzle slid back out of their fuel port slipway. Tiny thrusters attached to the end puffed in microsecond bursts as the long boom slowly retracted back into the S-29A tanker's cargo bay and latched along one end.

Miller flipped a switch to close the slipway doors above and behind their cockpit. His hands settled on the controls for spaceplane's hydrazine reaction thrusters. "Separating now, Shadow Alpha Three," he radioed.

Peter Vasey's English-accented voice replied through his headset. *"Copy that, Bravo One. We're on the move, too. Good luck. And give my regards to those bastards on the far side of the moon, will you?"*

"Thanks, Constable. We'll do our best," Miller promised with a quick grin. He activated the controls. His hands made small, precise movements to fire thrusters positioned at different points along the spaceplane's nose, fuselage, wings, and tail. Brief flashes of light against the darkness of space showed that Vasey was using his own thrusters. Slowly, carefully, their two spacecraft edged away from each other, separating both vertically and horizontally.

Now several miles away, and with its job done, the S-29A tanker lit its main engines. Decelerating fast, the other spaceplane dropped out of orbit—heading for the atmosphere as Vasey and Gallagher began the powered reentry maneuver that would eventually bring them back to Battle Mountain.

Miller keyed his mike. "Peterson Mission Control, this is Shadow Bravo One. We're gassed up and ready to go. What's the status on that Falcon Heavy?"

"*The Falcon Heavy is go for launch, Dusty,*" Major Tony Kim radioed. Kim was one of the Space Force pilots tapped to act as CAPCOM, their intermediary with the mission controllers working this lunar flight from the ground. "*T-minus thirty seconds and counting.*"

Miller glanced across the spaceplane's crowded cockpit. "Wanna see this?"

"Oh, yeah," Hannah Craig said simply. She checked one of her flight control menus. "You came in way under our thruster-use budget while refueling, so we've got plenty of hydrazine to spare."

More quick bursts from their thrusters spun the S-29

end-over-end so that they were facing back toward the distant east coast of the United States. The SpaceX launch site at Cape Canaveral was already invisible over the curve of the earth. Through their headsets, they heard Kim echoing the countdown. *"T-minus six. Side booster ignition. Four . . . three . . . two . . . ignition . . . and lift off!"*

Seconds later, they saw a wavering spark of light rising steadily through the lower atmosphere. Even from nearly fifteen hundred miles away, it was the brightest object in sight, outshining even the stars above them. Their own rapid flight carried them too far around the earth to spot the Falcon Heavy's self-landing side boosters when they detached, but they did see the trail of fire from its main engine reappear above the horizon as the rocket climbed higher—accelerating toward orbital speed. Moments later, that bright light winked out.

"MECO. And first-stage separation!" Kim reported. Almost immediately, a new, dimmer point of light appeared, now just above the sharp blue band that marked the division between the earth's atmosphere and space. *"Second-stage start-up. Payload fairing separation confirmed. Everything's looking good. The Falcon's on its way, Dusty."*

"Copy that," Miller replied. Quick tweaks on his thruster controls flipped the S-29 back around so that its nose was pointed along their current orbital path. Satisfied that they were back in the groove, he turned to his copilot. "Looks like this mission is a go!"

Jubilantly, Craig nodded. Her fingers danced across her multifunction displays, pulling up navigation and flight control displays. She set a series of automated checklists in motion. If necessary, they could have completed several more orbits before conducting the next maneuver. But with the definite success of that Falcon Heavy launch there was no further reason to delay. "Translunar injection insertion burn in five minutes."

Those minutes passed in a blur of activity as they double-checked the S-29B's computers at every step.

"Stellar navigation systems are go," Craig announced. That was vital. Once they left Earth orbit, there would be no GPS to guide them. Like the earlier Apollo astronauts, they would have to rely entirely on triangulation using the relative bearings of prominent stars to determine their current position. "Position cross-checks complete. TLI trajectory confirmed."

"Communication and encryption systems look good."

"Our targeting laser radar system is operational. All indicators from the weapons laser itself are green."

"Life support systems are go."

"LPDRS engine readouts are nominal. Ready for relight."

At last, Miller sat back. "Peterson Mission Control, this is Shadow Bravo One. We are go for TLI. Repeat, we are go for TLI."

"*Roger that, Bravo One,*" Tony Kim replied. "*Stand by for a final go/no go on that translunar injection burn.*"

Impatiently, Miller and Craig waited while the mission controllers along with General Kelleher back on Earth conducted a last-minute poll to decide whether or not to approve their planned flight to the moon. For both of them, the seconds seemed to tick by with agonizing slowness. At last, Kim came back on the circuit. "*Shadow Bravo One, this is Peterson Mission Control. We confirm that you are go for translunar injection.*"

"Understood, Peterson," Miller acknowledged. He glanced at his head-up display, checking their computer-driven countdown clock. "Thirty seconds to TLI." He tapped their thrusters again, pitching the S-29's nose up to align the spaceplane for its upcoming burn.

His eyes flicked toward Hannah Craig. "You ready for this, Major?"

In answer, she laughed. "I suppose it's too late to hit the john?"

Miller grinned back. "Afraid so. You'll just have to hold it—" The indicators on his HUD flashed green. Cued by the flight computer, he shoved their engine throttles all the way forward.

With a muffled *whummp*, the S-29's five big rocket motors fired.

Immediately, G-forces slammed Miller and Craig back against their seats. "For . . . just . . . a few . . . more minutes," he grunted, forcing the words out against the sudden intense acceleration.

Those minutes dragged on and on. Steadily, the spaceplane's speed increased. "Nineteen thousand miles per hour," Miller said tersely. They were now pulling around five-G's. He nudged the sidestick controller slightly to follow the steering directions sent to his head-up display. In response, all five LPDRS engine nozzles swiveled a degree, minutely changing their direction of thrust. "Nineteen thousand five hundred . . . miles per hour. Still accelerating."

Beside him, Hannah Craig strained to read the engine status readings on one of her MFDs. They were starting to blur out as the blood drained out of her brain and pooled in her lower body. "Temperatures and pressures . . . still look good," she reported.

Nearly ten minutes after their TLI burn started, Miller saw the readouts on his HUD shift. "Ten seconds to engine cutoff . . . four . . . three . . . two . . . one." He pulled all the way back on the throttles. "Shutdown."

The engines cut out. And as quickly as it had come, the powerful acceleration that had slammed them back against their seats disappeared. Now back in zero-G, they floated forward against the safety harnesses holding them in place. Through the cockpit canopy, stars blazed across the black depths of space. The earth was somewhere out of sight behind them, receding fast. The moon, still far, far away, hung out in space off to the side of their spacecraft.

Miller let go of the throttles and controller and locked them out. He tapped at his own displays, checking their numbers. "That was a good burn. We're outward bound at a scooch over twenty-one thousand miles per hour," he said in satisfaction.

"Well, nuts. I guess we're not gonna break the record," his copilot said with a wry smile. On their way back from the moon in May 1969, the crew of Apollo 10 had captured the all-time speed record for any manned flight, hitting 24,791 miles per hour.

"Afraid not," Miller agreed. He turned more serious. "How're we doing on fuel?"

Craig pulled up the readings from sensors inside their tanks. "Our JP-8 and BOHM are down to eight percent, a little better than we'd hoped. Thruster hydrazine looks very good, with ninety-five percent remaining."

"Outstanding," Miller told her. He keyed his mike. "Peterson Mission Control, this is Shadow Bravo One. Our TLI was good. Our fuel status is nominal. We've got enough gas to make our rendezvous burn when needed."

"*Copy that, Bravo One,*" Kim responded from Earth. "*We confirm your good burn. You should intercept that Falcon fuel load in approximately ten hours.*"

Several hundred miles ahead of the S-29B Shadow, the Falcon Heavy's spent second stage detached from its payload—two connected BOHM and JP-8 fuel tanks coupled to a pair of remote-controlled booms identical to those developed for the S-29A tanker spaceplane. Thrusters studded around the Falcon booster fired. Slowly, it drifted away, deflected onto a trajectory that would impact the moon's near side in several days. The twin JP-8 and BOHM fuel tanks flew onward, gradually being overtaken by the slightly faster spaceplane coming up from behind.

Three hours later, aboard the Space Force Shadow, Dusty Miller and Hannah Craig finished an array of final post-TLI navigation, life support, and other systems checks. Then, obeying their mission plan, they dimmed the spaceplane's cockpit lights and settled back to try to sleep while still strapped into their seats. The next several hours were set aside as a mandatory crew rest period. Both of them knew they would need to be fully alert when the time came to make the first-ever deep-space refueling attempt.

THIRTY-EIGHT

SKY MASTERS AEROSPACE INC.,
BATTLE MOUNTAIN, NEVADA
THAT SAME TIME

Sky Masters technicians had converted one of the company's conference rooms into a miniature replica of the Space Force mission control room at Peterson Air Force Base. Computer displays echoed the telemetry and video received from the spacecraft on its way to the moon. And secure communications gear allowed those present to monitor all transmissions between the crew and ground controllers. For the duration of the S-29B's lunar reconnaissance mission, this room would be manned around the clock by Sky Masters and Scion personnel—ready to offer technical assistance or tactical expertise as needed.

From his station, Brad McLanahan listened to Dusty

Miller and Hannah Craig sign off from their S-29 Shadow out in cislunar space. With a frustrated sigh, he slipped off his headset. Then he frowned. "Man, I hate this."

"Hate what?" Nadia asked quietly.

"Just sitting here doing nothing, and watching other people take all the risks."

Patrick McLanahan nodded sympathetically. "Welcome to the higher echelons of command, son," he said. "The ones where other men and women put their lives on the line carrying out your plans or following your orders."

"Does it ever get any easier?" Brad asked.

"No, it really doesn't," his father said simply. He shrugged. "Which is why I did everything I could to make sure I still flew combat missions myself." Then, with a twisted smile, he tapped the metal LEAF exoskeleton that helped keep him alive. "Given how I ended up in this semi-robotic hunk of junk, that was probably for a lot longer than I should have."

Brad nodded grimly, remembering the horrifying moment when a Chinese fighter jet's 30mm cannon shells riddled the bomber he and his father were flying. But as bad as that had been, at least they'd been together, sharing the same risks. Sitting safely on the ground like this, hundreds of thousands of miles from the action, still felt deeply wrong somehow.

"Colonel Miller and Major Craig are very competent," Nadia said softly, offering what comfort she could.

"Yeah, I know," Brad said. "And if it comes down to it, General Kelleher was right when he pushed to make this a Space Force mission. They've got way more hours of advanced combat training in those spaceplanes than we do." His gaze shifted back to one of the displays. It depicted the S-29B's projected path as it curved away from Earth—heading toward the point in space where the moon would be in roughly seventy hours. His jaw tightened. "But I also wish we weren't in a position where we have to bet everything on one roll of the dice."

"It's always good to have a backup plan," his father said. "That's why I've had a team going through everything in the Sky Masters inventory—including prototypes, whether they've ever been flown or not—looking for any other space hardware that could give us another way to get to the moon . . . if we need one."

Brad looked hard at him. Ever since he was old enough to notice, he'd realized that his father had a habit of playing his cards close to his chest—keeping everyone else at a distance while he worked out his own plans. "You sure kept that pretty quiet, Dad."

His father shrugged again. "It seemed like a long shot. Plus, I didn't want to distract anyone from the mission prep for Miller and Craig's recon flight. In most ways, that's still our best option."

"So did your team find something?" Nadia asked sharply.

"Possibly," Patrick said cautiously. "Originally, it was a piece of civilian space technology we thought might come in handy for a Sky Masters bid on part of the president's lunar helium-3 mining operation."

"And now?" Nadia demanded.

Patrick smiled at her. "Now we think this equipment could be just what we need. Well, after some serious, and seriously expensive, modifications, anyway."

Brad pushed back his chair and stood up. Beside him, Nadia did the same. "Okay, Dad," he told his father. "Let's go see this rabbit you think your guys just pulled out of the hat."

KOROLEV BASE, ON THE FAR SIDE OF THE MOON THAT SAME TIME

Colonel Kirill Lavrentyev stared at the split-screen images of Marshal Leonov and President Li Jun in disbelief. "The Americans are doing *what*?"

"One of their armed spaceplanes is now headed toward lunar orbit," Leonov repeated patiently. "Based on its current speed and trajectory, it will reach the moon in something under three Earth days."

Colonel Tian Fan leaned in beside his Russian counterpart. "Do we know yet what combat capabilities they have sacrificed to make this long-range mission possible?"

"An excellent question, Tian," Li said in satisfaction. He nodded to someone offscreen and his image disappeared, replaced by a grainy picture of the winged American spacecraft. "Our ground-based telescopes were able to take several photographs before the American S-29 moved out of range."

Lavrentyev and Tian studied the fuzzy image of the American space vehicle with great care. One alteration was immediately obvious. The wing and fuselage pods Russian and Chinese intelligence had tentatively identified as microwave emitters were gone. Both men nodded in sudden understanding. Removing those microwave pods and their associated electronics had allowed the Americans to add additional life-support and navigation equipment to the spaceplane.

"Which leaves a turret-mounted laser as its chief weapon," Tian commented.

"In combat against our own less-capable Elektron spaceplanes, this laser scored kills at nearly five hundred kilometers," Lavrentyev said slowly. He frowned. "It represents a serious threat to our base."

"But your plasma rail gun has a significantly longer effective range," President Li argued, reappearing on their monitor. "Correct?"

"*Da*, Comrade President." Lavrentyev nodded.

Li shrugged. "Then I fail to see what you have to fear. Yes, the Americans have surprised us with this unexpected gambit, but you will still have the upper hand in any combat."

Tian held his face carefully immobile, hoping that Lavrentyev would have the good sense to do the same. It was easy enough for Li, safe on Earth and surrounded by the whole might of the People's Republic, to dismiss the threat posed by the approaching enemy spaceplane. Those stationed here at Korolev Base, however, understood how vulnerable they were to an enemy attack from orbit. Right now, their lives depended on a single inflated habitat module. Its half-meter-thick Kevlar, foam insulation, and Nomex cloth walls were ample protection against the moon's airless environment, wild temperature swings, and radiation. But a two-megawatt weapons-grade laser would slice through them like butter.

"With respect, Comrade President," he said evenly. "Our choice of tactics depends on whether we believe the Americans will opt to fire on us first. Before they obtain hard evidence that we destroyed their two satellites."

Leonov spoke up from Moscow. "I do not believe the Americans will come in shooting, Colonel Tian." He shrugged. "Farrell may be far more aggressive than some other recent American presidents, but even he will be reluctant to order what could be painted as an unprovoked act of war against what the world has been told is a peaceful Sino-Russian science outpost."

"Especially since the Americans know our own Lagrange point satellites give us a complete picture of everything happening on the moon's far side," Li agreed. "Besides being futile, any surprise attack against your base would destroy their whole international reputation and shred the military and economic alliances they've built up against us."

Which would be small consolation to those of us who were killed, Tian thought acidly.

Leonov nodded when China's leader finished speaking. "In the circumstances, I'm confident this spaceplane is making a reconnaissance first—undoubtedly intended to gather intelligence that will let the Americans make a more determined and effective attack during a later orbit . . . or on a later mission, if the S-29 only swings around the moon once and then heads back to Earth on a free-return trajectory."

"Your reasoning is persuasive, Marshal," Lavrentyev acknowledged. "However, although we have camouflaged our more warlike installations to some extent, our *maskirovka* is unlikely to deceive that American spaceplane's powerful radar and thermal sensors for long. By the time it finishes its first pass over Korolev Base, its crew will know all our secrets."

"Quite so," Leonov said with a cold smile. "And that is why, regardless of whether or not the Americans open fire on you, you will destroy that spaceplane before it can report back to Earth."

Tian saw Li nod his approval. A chill ran down his spine. Their undeclared war against the United States was about to turn hot.

THIRTY-NINE

SPACE VEHICLE ASSEMBLY CLEAN ROOM, SKY MASTERS AEROSPACE INC., BATTLE MOUNTAIN
A SHORT TIME LATER

Followed by his father and Nadia, Brad McLanahan entered the large space vehicle assembly room wearing a hooded sterile coverall, surgical mask, safety goggles, and slip-on booties over his shoes. Nobody wanted bacteria, dust, or other contaminants damaging sensitive electronics. The room itself was close to the size of a football field, with a hundred-foot-high ceiling. At the far end, a floor-to-ceiling door led out to a loading dock. From there, the Sky Masters satellites and other space vehicles assembled here could be ferried off to different launch sites by cargo aircraft, tractor trailer, or rail.

A long, hanging screen cut off their view of half of the clean room. Jason Richter and Hunter Noble waited for them near the end of the screen. Richter was Sky Masters' CEO and chief inventor. Besides being a brilliant cybernetic engineer in his own right, he was also a remarkably gifted high-technology project manager. Over the past few years, the steady stream of innovative aircraft, space construction robots, satellites, and other hardware pouring out of labs and factories under his guidance had made Sky Masters hugely profitable.

"Ready to see what we dug up for you from Hangar Five?" Boomer asked eagerly. Hangar Five was used to store Sky Masters' experimental aircraft, space vehicles, and other pieces of advanced hardware that had never made it into large-scale production. Helen Kaddiri, the company's president and chairman, sometimes cynically referred to the hangar as "Never-Never Land" or "the Warehouse of Expensive Dreams." Boomer and Richter, on the other hand, saw it as a place of as-yet-unrealized potential. Maybe the prototypes stored in Hangar Five hadn't found a market yet—but they all represented revolutionary design concepts and technologies that might someday prove invaluable.

Brad smiled at his friend's obvious enthusiasm. This level of excitement was almost always reserved for machines that had the potential to explode in new and interesting ways. "Sure, Boomer. Go ahead and spring your big reveal."

"As you wish." Boomer turned toward a Sky Masters technician waiting by a set of wall panel controls. "Hey, Sarah, you can pull the curtain now."

The tech flipped a switch. Overhead, an electric motor kicked in. Slowly, the screen rolled back—revealing a forty-foot-long white cylinder resting horizontally on what looked like glorified helicopter landing skids. It was ten feet in diameter. At one end of the cylinder, a truncated cone cap ended in a docking port and hatch. A large rocket nozzle surrounded by gold-colored spherical fuel tanks was fitted to the other end. Four smaller thruster motor assemblies, two on each flank, were mounted along the cylinder's longitudinal axis. On one side, below the thrusters, a wide, curved hatch opened into the interior.

They stared at it in silence for a few moments. "Okay, what the hell is that?" Brad asked at last. "A giant beer can for really out-of-control office parties?"

"Not a bad thought, but no," Boomer said, clearly amused. He gestured grandly. "Behold the next big thing in lunar lander designs . . . the XEUS, pronounced like 'Zeus' with an 'X.'"

Nadia frowned. "It looks more like a rocket's upper stage turned on its side," she said critically.

"Well spotted, Major," Jason Richter said. "Xeus stands for eXperimental Enhanced Upper Stage. It is basically a Centaur stage from the Atlas V rocket converted into a revolutionary lander. That big motor at the back is an Aerojet Rocketdyne RL-10 cryogenic main engine burning liquid hydrogen and liquid oxygen. And those Katana side thrusters you see give it a vertical landing and vertical takeoff capability. Overall, we think it should be able to ferry around five tons of payload, either personnel or cargo or a combination of the two, down to the lunar surface and back up into orbit."

Brad moved closer to the cylindrical spacecraft. He glanced back at Richter. "Is this one of your designs?"

The other man shook his head. "I wish I could claim the credit, because it's a really cool concept . . . but no, this isn't one of mine. Xeus was originally developed by one of our competitors, another innovative private aerospace company called Masten Space Systems—working in tandem with Lockheed Martin and Boeing's United Launch Alliance." He shrugged. "But they shelved the program about five years ago. And since Sky Masters is always on the prowl for nifty technology, we moved in and picked up both this prototype and the rights for a song."

"It sure doesn't look like any other lunar lander prototype or mock-up I've ever seen," Brad mused.

Richter nodded. "That's because engineers are fundamentally conservative," he said. "Nobody messes with success. So, since the Apollo LM worked beautifully, the holy writ has been that all future lunar landers should be scaled-up or scaled-down versions of that same machine."

That certainly applied to China's Chang'e landers, Brad realized. From the outside, they appeared to be almost exact replicas of the four-legged spacecraft that had carried Neil Armstrong, Buzz Aldrin, and the other Apollo crews to the surface of the moon in 1969.

"But the Apollo LM was designed for a very specific purpose and for very specific missions," Richter went on. "There are no real laws of physics or spacecraft design that say something like the Xeus here can't handle the job of landing on a low-gravity, airless moon. In fact, my bet is this design will turn out to be significantly more cost-effective and efficient."

Slowly, Brad nodded. He could feel the broad outlines of a possible alternate attack plan coming together somewhere in the back of his mind. Admittedly, it was kind of wild and probably risky as hell, but at least it gave him a place to start. He made a mental note to reach out to Richter privately once they were finished here. He looked away from the beer-can-shaped prototype spacecraft. "So how do we get this thing to the moon in the first place?"

"Adding in propellant and payload, the total mass comes to around twenty-three tons," Boomer told him. "That's right in line with what that Falcon Heavy second stage we've already got parked near Eagle Station can put into lunar orbit."

Nadia raised an eyebrow. "And you truly believe people can voyage to the moon in this . . ." She struggled to find the right words. "In this glorified fuel tank?"

"Yep," Boomer said confidently.

Richter added more detail. "There's no technical barrier to equipping the Xeus lander with life support for up to three astronauts. My team has already worked out most of the details. In fact, even with all the necessary hardware—crew seats, a lavatory, oxygen and water supply and recycling systems, carbon dioxide scrubbers, and the rest—this vehicle's still going to be less cramped than the Apollo command module or the new Orion crew module."

"What about power?" Brad asked. "I don't see any solar panels on this thing. Or any places you could safely put them, for that matter."

"We don't need them," Boomer replied. "Xeus can

meet all of its electrical power requirements using a small onboard hydrogen- and oxygen-burning motor."

"Sweet," Brad said. Not having to rely on sunlight to generate electricity opened up a lot of potential landing sites and times, including during the two-week-long lunar nights or perpetually shadowed deep craters near the moon's north and south poles.

Nadia studied the spacecraft in silence for a few more moments. Then she turned back to Boomer and Richter. "Very well, you claim this Xeus lander can take three astronauts to lunar orbit and then down to the surface, along with their equipment. Correct?"

They nodded.

She frowned. "But how do the astronauts return to Earth once they've completed their mission?"

"Well, see . . . there's the problem," Boomer admitted. He shrugged. "That's one of the kinks we still need to work out. . . ."

SPACE EXPLORATION RESEARCH & DEVELOPMENT (SERD) LABORATORY, SKY MASTERS AEROSPACE INC.
SEVERAL HOURS LATER

Under a cloudless, blue sky, the sharp-edged mountain peaks and ridges surrounding the sprawling Sky Masters complex were a lifeless brown. Heat waves shimmered across the landscape. The company's newer hangars, office buildings, labs, and warehouses stretched eastward across what had been brush-covered wasteland, without even a hint of landscaping to add color. Flush with federal and private industry aviation and aerospace contracts, Sky Masters was expanding fast—so fast that construction crews were hard-pressed to keep pace. Amenities beyond paved roads and parking lots were pretty far down the priority list.

The Space Exploration Research and Development Laboratory, a massive structure with a rounded black roof, towered over all the other new buildings. It was more than a thousand feet long, two hundred feet high, and at least three hundred feet wide. There were some windows set in its curving, white-painted steel sides, but not many.

Richter himself was waiting for Brad and Nadia just inside the nearest entrance. "Hey, guys! Welcome to my newest slice of engineering heaven," the tall, athletic-looking older man said eagerly.

With a wave, he led them through a pair of double doors and into a wide, high-ceilinged corridor that seemed to stretch the whole length of the enormous building. Branching hallways intersected it at different intervals. There were dozens of doors and interior observation windows opening into labs, computer rooms, and other spaces packed with machinery and electronic hardware. Stairwells and elevator shafts led to higher floors. Rather than waste minutes walking, technicians and scientists traveled from place to place using golf carts.

"So . . . what do you think?" Richter asked.

"It's quite . . . large," Nadia said carefully.

"You should write our press releases," the older man said with a grin. Then he turned more serious. "What you're looking at is more than a million square feet of state-of-the-art science and engineering labs and our very own supercomputer. Plus, we have special chambers fitted out with pressure pumps, high-temperature heaters, freezer units, and radioactive sources. Those allow us to test new hardware in simulated environments ranging from the vacuum of outer space to the lunar surface to the bottom of the ocean."

Richter ushered them over to a golf cart marked "Chief Mad Scientist." "Hop in the back . . . and I'll give you a quick tour on our way."

"On our way to where?" Nadia asked pointedly, climbing in beside Brad.

"It's kind of a surprise," Brad told her.

She frowned. "The kind I like?"

"Maybe," he answered, sounding hopeful.

As they zoomed off, Nadia smiled and slipped her arm through his. "Be brave, *mój bohater.* My hero. If I do not like your surprise, I will give you a thirty-second head start."

"Sounds fair," Brad said with an answering smile of his own.

For the next several minutes, they listened with growing interest while Richter drove them down the central corridor—rattling off quick explanations of some of the projects going on in the labs they were whizzing past. Basically, under his leadership, teams of cybernetic engineers and scientists were developing many of the robotic components needed for America's planned lunar helium-3 mining operation.

It also quickly became clear that Richter could scarcely contain his enthusiasm for the president's plans. He was like a kid given an unlimited budget and turned loose in a candy store. "Mining helium-3 in usable quantities is just the first step," he told them. "Because once we can actually build and fuel serious fusion power plants and some of the direct fusion spaceship drives we're designing now, the whole solar system starts to open up. Mars, Jupiter, Saturn . . . the asteroids. Everything from here all the way out to the Oort Cloud, someday."

Nadia leaned forward over the golf cart's seat. "All

of which is incredibly exciting," she agreed. "But I still have one question."

"Only one?" Brad murmured.

She elbowed him and turned back to Richter. "Why are we here now? We're not engineers or fusion power experts."

"True," Richter said, glancing over his shoulder with a lightning-fast grin. "But you two also happen to be the world's most experienced surviving CID pilots."

"You have developed a new human-piloted robot design," Nadia realized.

"Got it in one, Major Rozek-McLanahan," Richter acknowledged. He pulled in beside a large metal door and hopped out. A sign over the door announced that this was the MANNED LUNAR ACTIVITY LAB. "Come on, I'll show you. I think you're gonna like this."

Cybernetic Infantry Devices, or CIDs, were combat robots. First developed by Richter years ago in a U.S. Army research lab, every piloted war machine carried far more firepower than a conventionally equipped infantry platoon. Protected by highly resistant composite armor, their powered exoskeletons were faster and stronger than any ten men combined. Haptic interfaces and direct neural links to a CID's computers and sensors allowed the robot to move with uncanny nimbleness and precision—while also giving its human pilot astonishing situational awareness. In the right hands . . . or in the wrong ones, now that the Russians had developed their own, slightly less capable designs . . . CIDs were, quite literally, killing machines.

Richter swiped his own ID card through an electronic reader next to the door. It slid open and Brad and Nadia followed him inside.

Across a large room filled with computer equipment and large 3-D parts printers, technicians were busy around a pair of almost twelve-foot-tall, humanlike machines. Each had two arms, two legs, a broadshouldered torso, and a six-sided head studded with sensor panels. At first glance, they appeared identical to combat-rated CIDs, but on closer inspection they seemed slightly shorter and squatter. They were also bright white.

Richter nodded toward the two large robots. "Well, there they are: the first prototype CLADs."

Nadia raised an eyebrow. "CLADs?"

Suddenly Richter looked slightly less sure of himself. Somehow, whenever he came up with names or acronyms for new pieces of equipment, something always went wrong. No matter how memorable or descriptive he thought his choices were, everyone else usually thought they were dorky—like the LEAF life-support exoskeleton he'd designed for Brad's father or the CIDs themselves. "CLAD, as in Cybernetic Lunar Activity Device?" he offered.

Now he waited uneasily while Nadia gave it some thought. "CLADs?" she muttered, sounding it out. "CLAD." Then she shrugged, and to his obvious relief, admitted, "You know, that is not actually a *completely* horrible name, Dr. Richter. And just what are these manned robots for?"

"Originally, I designed them for construction work on the lunar surface," Richter said. He led them across the lab, shooing the techs away so they could get a better look at the large robots. "I spent a lot of time studying the records and films of all the Apollo-era EVAs. And it was pretty obvious just how tough even ordinary physical labor was in those bulky conventional space suits—even in low gravity. Those guys were really sweating just to grab rock samples and set up a few experiments. And between exhaustion and limited battery power, the Apollo astronauts couldn't spend much time outside on the moon. Heck, the longest EVA back then was only something like seven and a half hours."

He patted one of the big machines affectionately. "But an astronaut riding inside one of these guys will have superhuman strength, dexterity, and speed. One Cybernetic Lunar Activity Device could handle tasks that would otherwise require a whole bunch of specially designed and extremely expensive construction robots. And with additional life support and backup batteries and fuel cells, you could operate for up to forty-eight hours outside a spacecraft or a lunar base shelter."

She nodded her understanding. Early on, it had become clear that CID pilots could go for long periods without needing sleep while neurally connected to their machines. Bad things happened to any human who pushed that too far—psychosis and other mental disorders, among them—but it gave them a useful edge in certain conditions. "You said you first designed these CLADs for construction work," she said slowly. "And now?"

Richter's expression turned somber. "Now, we're refitting them for war, Major."

FORTY

"*Radar contact at twelve o'clock. Range is eight miles and closing,*" the S-29B's computer reported. "*Contact is the combined JP-8/BOHM fuel tank stack.*"

Colonel Scott Miller peered ahead though the canopy. At this distance, the fuel tank stack was just a tiny sunlit dot. That would change pretty fast, though. He glanced at Major Hannah Craig. "What's our closure rate?"

She had her head down, intent at her various navigation displays. "A little over seventy feet per second, Dusty."

He nodded. Although they were each slowing down as Earth's gravitational pull continually tugged on them, both the fuel stack and their spaceplane were still headed toward the moon at relatively high speed. What mattered now was how much faster their spaceplane was moving than the object they were chasing. Running the math, their speed differential was just around fifty miles per hour, which meant they'd overtake the fuel stack in roughly ten minutes.

Slowly, they crept up on the fuel stack. As they drew closer, it took on added shape and definition. Through their zoomed-in forward cameras, it was clearly visible as a pair of cylindrical fuel tanks slotted together inside an open metal framework. The twin flexible refueling booms were plainly visible—latched alongside their corresponding tanks.

"Uh-oh," Craig muttered.

"Something wrong?"

"Take a closer look," she told him. "That fuel stack is rotating. Not very fast, but it's definitely spinning around its long axis."

Suddenly, Miller saw what she meant. They were close enough now to see that the whole assembly was rotating as it flew onward through space. That was a big problem. Even if they matched velocities with the fuel stack, refueling would be impossible unless they also matched its precise rotation. Otherwise, either of those twin refueling booms would only wind up ripping out of their spaceplane's slipway and fuel receptacle as the stack spun away from them. And if that happened while they were transferring highly combustible boro-hydrogen metaoxide, the whole damned thing could blow up. "Well . . . shit," he grumbled.

Craig nodded. "It must have happened when the Falcon Heavy second stage jettisoned. If one of the latches hung for just a millisecond too long, it'd impart that kind of rotation."

"I can probably match the spin by using our thrusters," Miller thought out loud. Doing so meant putting the S-29 into a very tight orbit around the slowly rotating fuel stack assembly. Accomplishing that without causing a collision between the two spacecraft would require multiple short thruster bursts, precise piloting, and some luck.

"Yeah, but establishing that kind of orbit and then holding it long enough to refuel will cost us a chunk of our hydrazine reserves," she warned, running a quick computer projection of the maneuver. "Looks like somewhere around ten or fifteen percent."

Miller frowned. Ten or fifteen percent thruster fuel consumption didn't sound like much . . . except that they would need practically every available drop of their hydrazine for evasive maneuvering during their planned reconnaissance passes over the Sino-Russian base. "Well, that tears it," he said quietly. He shook his head. "I guess we're going to have to abort this refueling rendezvous after all."

And without enough main engine fuel to make a lunar orbit insertion burn, they'd only get one fast pass across the far side of the moon before using its gravity to sling them back to Earth.

"Maybe not," Craig said abruptly. Her fingers flew across her multifunction displays. Radio signals crossed the steadily narrowing gap between their S-29 and the fuel stack. New menus blossomed on her screens. She now had remote control over the twin refueling booms.

"You have a plan?" Miller asked.

"Yep."

Trusting that his copilot knew what she was doing, he swung the spaceplane around so that its five main rocket motors were pointing back against their direction of travel. He inched the throttles forward slightly, igniting a quick, low-powered burn to shed fifty miles per hour of relative speed. Their thrusters could have done the same job, but, tactically speaking, right now hydrazine was more precious than JP-8 and BOHM.

"Contact now at nine o'clock. Zero relative velocity," the S-29's computer intoned. *"Range fifty yards."*

Looking out the left side of the cockpit, Miller saw the fuel stack's two refueling booms unlatch.

They unfolded, extending outward into space in opposite directions. Suddenly, puffs of gas showed that the tiny thrusters on each boom end were firing almost continuously . . . working to counteract the fuel stack's spin. Almost imperceptibly, the rate of rotation slowed . . . and then . . . stopped.

With a sigh of relief, Craig lifted her fingertips off her multifunction displays. She turned toward Miller with shining eyes. "Ready to proceed with refueling, Dusty."

He shook his head in admiration. "That was nice work, Major. And damned quick thinking."

Her cheeks dimpled slightly. "All in a day's work for an honest-to-God space fighter pilot, sir."

From that point on, their deep-space refueling operation was almost routine. A couple of quick thruster pulses brought the S-29 close enough for the two refueling booms to make contact with its receptacle. Then, one after the other, guided and controlled by Craig, the booms connected—transferring thousands of pounds of BOHM and jet fuel into their tanks.

When they were finished, another short main engine burn took them on out ahead of the now-empty fuel assembly. With their spaceplane's tanks topped up, Scott Miller and Hannah Craig now had plenty of gas left for a lunar orbit insertion burn . . . and their return trip to Earth.

KOROLEV BASE, ON THE FAR SIDE OF THE MOON
A SHORT TIME LATER

Colonel Tian Fan studied the most recent radar images transmitted from the Russian Kondor-L satellite. They showed the American S-29 spaceplane conducting a deep-space rendezvous with what Earth-based intelligence analysts believed was a collection of fuel tanks launched at almost the same time.

Beside him, Kirill Lavrentyev was looking at the same pictures. "An impressive demonstration," the Russian cosmonaut commented. His once-crisp flight suit was grimy, streaked with smudges of moondust. No matter how hard they tried to wipe down their space suits and boots in the habitat module's air locks, every EVA tracked in more and more of the clingy, finely ground dust—which had been repeatedly pulverized by billions of years of meteor and asteroid impacts. A faint, acrid smell like that of burnt gunpowder hung in the air. "I wouldn't have thought refueling a spacecraft so far from Earth was possible."

"Our adversaries seem determined to add to their list of firsts," Tian agreed sourly. "This one makes them even more dangerous. With extra fuel aboard, that spaceplane can go into orbit and conduct multiple passes over this base."

Lavrentyev shrugged. "It won't matter. Our plasma rail gun will destroy the S-29 in its first orbit." Tiredly, he wiped the back of his hand across his forehead. It came away covered in sweat and ground-in dirt. His nose wrinkled as he stood up. "*Gah.* I need a wash."

Tian nodded sympathetically. Although showers were theoretically possible in the moon's one-sixth gravity, the need to ration their scarce water meant washing involved either disposable wipes or barely moistened cloths. Neither was a particularly effective means of getting clean.

He watched the burly Russian pass through the curtain-draped door separating the small command center from the rest of the habitat. Then he turned back to the radar images on his computer screen with a thoughtful frown. The taikonaut understood his counterpart's need to express absolute confidence in Russia's advanced energy weapon. But it wasn't a confidence he shared. The evasive maneuvers developed by the Americans during their war games around Eagle Station might give that S-29 spaceplane a good chance to close within striking range before it was destroyed. With that in mind, it would be wise to take his own precautions.

Tian turned toward the command center's other occupant. Captain Shan Jinai was the officer on duty, tasked with monitoring their communications gear and sensor data from the Kondor radar satellite. "I have some work for you, Captain."

"Yes, sir?" the younger man said.

"When your shift is finished, I need you to make another EVA," Tian told him. "I want your Chang'e-Thirteen lander prepped for a possible rapid launch."

Shan's eyebrows rose in bewilderment. "But, Colonel, the next Pilgrim mission isn't scheduled to arrive for three months." Pilgrim 5 was set to bring two more crewmen to Korolev—replacing Major Liu and Captain Yanin, who would be returning to Earth aboard the Federation spacecraft after spending more than six months on the moon.

"I'm well aware of that, Shan," Tian said with a touch of iron in his voice. "I have another mission in mind for Chang'e-Thirteen."

"Yes, sir," the other man acknowledged hurriedly.

"In the meantime, put me in touch with Beijing Flight Control," Tian ordered. "I need to speak with General Chen Haifeng as soon as possible."

Twenty minutes later, he saw the commander of China's Strategic Support Force appear on his monitor. "What is it, Colonel?" Chen asked.

"I need our best computer experts to make certain

modifications to Chang'e-Thirteen's navigation, rendezvous, and docking programs."

Now it was Chen's turn to look puzzled. "What sort of modifications?"

Carefully, Tian explained what he needed and why. When he finished, the general let his breath out in a soft whistle. He nodded slowly. "Very well, I understand. I'll put our people to work on the coding at once." His expression was deadly serious. "But I hope you will never need to put your plan into action."

"So do I," Tian assured him earnestly.

FORTY-ONE

SHADOW BRAVO ONE, ENTERING LUNAR ORBIT
SIXTY-PLUS HOURS LATER

For most of their three-day voyage, the moon had been a presence off the S-29's right forward quarter—a sphere half-blazing with reflected sunlight and half-cloaked in utter darkness that grew larger with every passing hour. Now, instead of seeing it as an object that they were flying toward, Scott Miller and Hannah Craig's perspective of the moon had abruptly shifted. Its gray, cratered surface curved across the spaceplane's entire cockpit canopy . . . and it was very obviously *below* them.

They were coming in at just under three thousand miles per hour, too slow to break free of the moon's gravity and also too slow, for the moment, to enter a stable orbit that would stop them from ultimately slamming into the ground. Instead, the S-29 Shadow was steadily losing altitude as it flew westward across the moon—gliding along a descending arc that would bring them down to an altitude of around sixty miles as they swung around the far side and lost radio contact with Earth.

The Apollo missions had come in faster, heading around the moon at five thousand miles an hour before slowing down to enter orbit. With an armed enemy lunar base waiting somewhere on the far side, that wasn't an option open to them.

From her right-hand seat, Craig carefully studied the terrain visible through their cockpit windows. Quick glances down at the detailed topographic map shown on her navigation display enabled her to fix their position and course. "Okay, I've got the Helvius crater rim just sliding past our right side. Grimaldi's off the left wing. And that's Riccioli there up ahead, just a little off to the left of our track. We're headed right down the middle, Dusty."

Miller saw the ancient crater she meant. It was huge—more than ninety miles across. Shallow ridges of debris thrown outward from more recent impacts streaked the floor. A layer of darker lava spilled across its northern half.

They were flying a course closely aligned with the moon's equator. That would allow the S-29's radar and thermal sensors to "see" more of the sites Space Force planners had picked out as possible locations for the Sino-Russian lunar base.

"Copy that," he said. "How are we fixed for our LOI?"

Craig smoothly shifted her attention to their main engine readouts. "Temperatures and pressures all look good. Fuel status is good. No red lights. We are still go for our planned lunar orbit insertion burn in eight minutes, thirty seconds."

"Okay, let's seal up now, while we've got time." Miller's gloved hands slid the visor of his helmet closed and locked it in position. Beside him, Hannah Craig followed suit. Fresh air hissed through the umbilical hoses connecting their suits to the S-29's life-support system.

Several minutes later, they heard Tony Kim's voice through a faint hiss of static. Their fellow S-29 pilot was back on CAPCOM duty for this critical part of the mission. *Shadow Bravo One, this is Peterson Mission Control. Stand by for loss of signal in sixty seconds. We estimate reacquisition of signal in forty-six minutes.*

"Understood, Peterson. LOS in sixty seconds," Miller radioed. "Talk to you on the other side."

General Kelleher's gruff voice came on the circuit. *"Peterson Mission Control to Bravo One. Fly safe. Stay cool. But if those sons of bitches open fire on you, give 'em hell!"*

Miller nodded vigorously. "You can count on it, sir," he promised. "We'll—"

Suddenly, a loud roar and crackle of static washed through their headsets. *"Loss of signal,"* the S-29's computer confirmed. Now they were on their own, entirely cut off from communication with Earth. And up ahead, hidden somewhere in this torn and tattered moonscape pockmarked by thousands of craters, was a hostile enemy base—a base whose Sino-Russian crew knew exactly where they were at any given moment, thanks to their own satellites stationed high overhead at the L2 point. *"Lunar orbit insertion burn in twenty seconds."*

Miller tweaked his thruster controls, aligning the spaceplane as directed by the steering cues that had just popped onto his head-up display. Then his hand settled on their main engine throttles. "Stand by for burn," he warned. "Ten seconds."

"We're still good to go," Craig told him, checking over her readouts. "All lights are green."

Indicators blinked on Miller's HUD. "Throttling up," he snapped. "Going to thirty percent thrust."

WHUMMP. The Shadow's five big LPDRS engines ignited in rocket mode.

Inside the cockpit, Miller and Craig were pushed back against their seats by the renewed acceleration. Although they were only pulling a little over one and a half G's this time, the three days they'd spent weightless made it seem like more. This same phenomenon had been experienced by some of the Apollo astronauts during their own lunar missions. Steadily, their velocity increased.

Ninety seconds later, Miller yanked the throttles all the way back. The muted roar from the back bulkhead stopped instantly. "Engine cutoff."

Craig checked their navigation systems. "That was a good burn," she reported. "We've entered a stable, circular orbit sixty miles above the surface."

There were risks involved in coming in this high, since it automatically increased the distance at which the enemy's plasma rail gun could hit them. But orbiting lower would have significantly reduced the ranges at which the S-29's sensors could detect any unusual activity on the rugged, lunar surface. And since this was chiefly a reconnaissance mission, their first and most important objective was to pinpoint the Sino-Russian base and strip away its secrets.

Besides, they both knew, coming in much lower carried its own dangers. Maintaining a stable orbit grew more difficult the closer you got to the surface of the moon. At certain points, there were "mascons"—mass concentrations, or gravitational anomalies—buried below the lunar crust. They had been created by huge asteroids slamming into the still-cooling moon billions of years before. Like hidden tides and jagged shoals, these gravitational anomalies could tug low-flying spacecraft out of orbit or push them disastrously off course.

With their burn complete, Miller rolled the S-29 upside down. This maneuver gave them an uninterrupted view of the heavily cratered moonscape they were flying over. More important, it gave their two-megawatt gas dynamic laser, mounted in a retractable turret on top of the spaceplane's fuselage, a clear field of fire.

A low whine permeated the cockpit as actuators raised the laser turret into its combat position and locked. "Our laser is online," Craig reported. "Targeting lidar on standby." She touched more controls. "Our search radar is active. Thermal sensors are live."

Miller tapped an icon on one of his MFDs, turning on the spaceplane's voice command system. "Initiate evasion program," he ordered. "Synchronize the laser's fire control system."

"*Evasive flight program initiated,*" the S-29's computer confirmed. "*Laser fire control synchronized.*"

Immediately, several of the spaceplane's fuselage-mounted thrusters fired. It jolted sideways and then pitched nose-down. A second or two later, other thrusters fired, bouncing the spacecraft a few yards higher along its flight path. From now on, the computer would randomly activate different thrusters at short, unpredictable intervals—yawing, pitching, and rolling the S-29 through all three dimensions as it hurtled onward above the moon.

Thrown against their harnesses and then tossed wildly from side to side, the two Space Force pilots gritted their teeth and settled down to endure the wild ride. Simulator training and multiple practice attack runs against Eagle Station over the past several months had taught them how to handle the stomach-churning nausea induced by these random evasive maneuvers. But no amount of practice could teach them to enjoy it.

COMMAND CENTER, KOROLEV BASE
THAT SAME TIME

"The American spaceplane is maneuvering evasively," Major Liu Zhen announced. He was monitoring the tracking data passed to them from the Kondor-L radar satellite, stationed nearly forty thousand miles away at the Lagrange-2 point. Like everyone else in the base except for Colonel Tian, he was wearing a bulky pressure suit as protection against explosive decompression if the habitat module was breached during the battle they all expected.

Tian himself had donned a full EVA-rated space suit, leaving only his helmet off for the moment. He held it cradled under one arm.

"What is the range to the enemy S-29?" Lavrentyev asked.

"Sixteen hundred kilometers, and closing at one point six-one kilometers per second," Liu told him. "We will have a clear plasma rail gun shot in just over eight minutes."

Captain Dmitry Yanin looked over from his own station. "Should I bring our fire control radars online now?" For the next several minutes, the tracking information provided by the Kondor would give them a reasonably accurate picture of the developing tactical situation. But when the time came for action, only Korolev's own ground-based radars could provide the fire control data the plasma gun needed in battle. Even at the speed of light, it took nearly a half second for a radar return to reach the Russian satellite and then be repeated back to Korolev Base. And by that time, the enemy spaceplane would already be more than six hundred meters away from its reported position. Relying on the Kondor satellite's radar data in combat would be like expecting a rifleman to hit a moving target after he'd closed his eyes a half second before pulling the trigger.

"Not yet," Lavrentyev decided after a quick glance at Tian.

Tian nodded. "There is no point in alerting the Americans now, Dmitry. We'll let them come farther into the kill zone." For a few seconds, he stared over Liu's shoulder, watching the blip representing the S-29 as it orbited toward them. The Americans were following the lunar equator, about five and a half degrees of latitude south of their position on the rim of the Engel'gardt crater. He turned back to Yanin. "At their current altitude and speed, how long will the Americans be in plasma gun range before their laser can hit us?"

"Nearly three minutes," the younger cosmonaut replied.

"And how many times can you fire the rail gun in that time?"

"Eight times," Yanin said. "It takes roughly twenty seconds for our fusion reactor to recharge the weapon."

Tian frowned. "Only eight shots."

"Yes, Colonel."

"Can you guarantee a hit with one of those first eight shots, Captain Yanin?" Tian asked quietly. "Against an unpredictably maneuvering target?"

For a moment, Yanin hesitated. "My computer is analyzing the S-29's evasive maneuvers now, sir— using the radar data we're collecting. If it can crack the random-number generator the Americans are using in the next few minutes . . ." His voice trailed off. Then he shook his head. "No, Colonel. I can't guarantee a hit, not before that spaceplane gets much closer."

Tian nodded somberly. He looked across the tight, crowded command center at Kirill Lavrentyev. "You see the tactical problem?"

The larger man grimaced. "Unfortunately, yes. We are just as vulnerable to their attack as they are to ours."

"More so, I suggest," Tian pointed out. "The Americans can dodge. Stuck down here on the surface, we cannot. And as soon as we open fire, they will know the exact coordinates of our plasma rail gun—and our radars."

"But our orders—"

Tian shook his head dismissively. "Our orders do not require us to commit suicide, Kirill. Which is the likely outcome of going off half-cocked and opening fire at the first possible moment . . . in the faint hope of scoring a lucky kill. We need to fight this battle with our brains instead of our balls." Rapidly, he outlined the tactics he proposed.

When he finished, Lavrentyev nodded thoughtfully. "*Da, to, chto vy govorite, imeyet smysl.* Yes, what you say makes perfect sense." He forced a thin, humorless smile. "After all, why shouldn't we make these Americans take all the risks first?"

FORTY-TWO

SHADOW BRAVO ONE,
OVER THE FAR SIDE OF THE MOON
   SEVERAL MINUTES LATER

The S-29B Shadow jolted downward and then rolled onto its left side—leaving Major Hannah Craig able to see only a narrow slice of the lunar surface they were flying toward at more than thirty-six hundred miles per hour. She just had time to get a hazy impression of sharp-edged smaller craters strewn across the vast interior of a much older, far more eroded basin. And then the spaceplane's thrusters fired again, pitching its nose back up and to the right.

"Christ almighty," she muttered. "I hope the computer knows where we're headed, because I sure as hell don't."

"Me neither," Miller forced out through clenched teeth from his own seat. The pilot looked pale. Droplets of sweat that had shaken loose from his forehead during brief moments of acceleration fogged patches of his helmet visor. But his hands remained rock-steady on his flight controls. As the Shadow rocked hard in another computer-triggered evasive maneuver, he fought to focus his blurred vision on the navigation map open on one of his control panel displays. "Looks like we're about a hundred and fifty miles east of the Korolev crater . . . which is probably that big basin out there."

Craig nodded tightly. Right now, her stomach felt like it was ready to come crawling up her throat. "Yeah, that fits."

"Multiple radar and thermal surface contacts," the S-29's computer announced abruptly. *"At one o'clock low. Range two hundred and sixty-plus miles. On the east rim of the Engel'gardt crater."*

"Son of a bitch," Miller said, sounding almost surprised. "We actually found them."

"And sitting right on the moon's highest elevation," she noted. Her teeth flashed in a quick smile. "Looks like McLanahan won his bet."

Miller nodded. During their pre-mission planning sessions, Brad had told them he was almost certain the Russians and Chinese had sited their base someplace up high on the lunar surface. Wherever they were on the far side of the moon, they'd want the best possible field of fire for their plasma rail gun.

"Lock our long-range cameras on to those radar and thermal contacts and magnify," Craig ordered the computer. The feeling of nausea she'd been fighting had completely disappeared.

Right away, virtually crystal-clear images appeared on their multifunction displays, with only a faint hint of distortion. Like their weapons laser, their visual sensors were synchronized with the computer's evasion program—enabling them to adjust relatively smoothly to the spaceplane's split-second maneuvers . . . unlike its human crew.

"I count four of those big cargo landers," Miller said. "Plus another three Chang'e descent stages. And one intact lander, still with its ascent stage in place." His eyes narrowed. "Plus what looks like some kind of big tent or something, not far from all those parked spacecraft."

"That's probably a Bigelow-style inflatable habitat," Craig said absently. Then she stiffened. "Take a look at those domes right near the edge of the crater rim, Dusty."

He saw what she meant. There were three raised mounds of rocks and dirt out near where the slope fell away, gradually descending thousands of feet to the darker plains below. Each mound was topped with a black dome. Their radar was having a hard time locking on to any of them, which indicated the black coating might be some sort of radar-absorbent stealth material. "Gee, I wonder what our friends are hiding under those?" he murmured sarcastically. "A bunch of peaceful, innocent scientific instruments, no doubt."

"And here I was thinking it was more along the lines of 'Oh, my, Cosmonaut X, what a big plasma rail gun you have there.'" Hannah Craig's fingers hovered over her fire control menu. "Doggone it, I sure wish I could zap them, just in case. They're inside our weapons range."

Unfortunately, their orders were clear. They could fire on the Sino-Russian base only if they were fired on first—unless they were able to obtain clear and undeniable proof that the Russians and their allies had already positioned offensive weapons on the moon. But suspicion, however strong, was not proof, especially when you took into account the international community's ever-present desire to look the other way when it was asked to consider unpalatable truths about Russia and the People's Republic of China.

"Yeah, but we'll keep the cameras and other sensors running," Miller said. "And then we'll dump every picture and piece of data to Peterson Mission Control and Sky Masters as soon as we come back around to the near side. My bet is that either our Space Force intel guys or Brad and Nadia will put enough pieces together to get us the green light for an attack run during our second orbit."

"New radio transmission received," the S-29's computer reported. *"Origin point is the presumed enemy base."*

"Put it through," Miller directed.

Immediately, they heard a voice with a slight Russian accent crackle through their headsets. *"American spaceplane, this is the Friendship Lunar Science Station. Welcome to the far side of the moon. Please accept our congratulations on your historic flight."*

Miller snorted. "Science station, my ass."

"Are you going to reply?" Craig asked.

He shook his head. "Hell, no. We didn't come two hundred and fifty thousand miles out from Earth to swap polite lies with a bunch of Russian and Chinese assholes. Let 'em sweat."

COMMAND CENTER, KOROLEV BASE
THAT SAME TIME

"No response, sir," Captain Yanin said.

Tian shrugged. "Hardly surprising." He turned to

Lavrentyev. "But at least Marshal Leonov's analysis was correct. The Americans must have positive orders that prevent them from attacking us without provocation."

The Russian nodded silently. A nerve twitched at the corner of his right eye. The S-29 was now less than one hundred and fifty kilometers from Korolev Base—passing south of them as it orbited along the lunar equator. Even against the infinite darkness of space, the black-winged spaceplane was plainly visible to their own long-range infrared cameras. Although its wing- and fuselage-mounted thrusters still fired repeatedly—pushing the enemy spacecraft through a range of random evasive maneuvers—the American spacecraft continually rotated to keep its nose and laser weapons turret aimed in their direction. Their own radar warning receivers emitted a continuous warbling set of tones, indicating that the S-29 was still scanning them with its powerful radar.

"The range to the enemy spaceplane is beginning to increase," Major Liu reported, checking the tracking data supplied by the distant Kondor-L radar satellite. "Its orbit is now carrying it away from us."

Over the next minutes, as the distance between them widened inexorably, Tian kept his attention on Yanin.

As more and more data poured into his computer, the younger Russian cosmonaut was fully immersed in his study of the American spaceplane's evasive maneuvers. Since the S-29's crew initiated their automated program, the Kondor-L radar satellite had detected literally hundreds of different maneuvers. Each was cataloged, correlated, and analyzed to find some pattern . . . but so far without any effective result. Within certain broad parameters, the enemy's movements were foreseeable. For example, the spaceplane never left its larger orbital track or rolled or pitched or yawed in any way that would take its laser weapon off-target. But even within those known limits, there still seemed no way to calculate precisely where the Shadow would be at any given second.

The Russian plasma rail gun was astonishingly effective against spacecraft caught by surprise or locked into a predictable orbit or trajectory, Tian thought coolly. But it was not invincible. Against an alerted enemy, the weapon had weaknesses the Americans had clearly learned to exploit. Still, the enemy spaceplane faced its own constraints, including a hard cap on its thruster fuel reserves. If its ability to maneuver was restricted in any way, or the Russians scored a lucky hit, that S-29 was dead.

"Range to the American spaceplane is now four hundred and eighty-five kilometers," Liu said. "Still opening at one point six one kilometers per second."

Expectantly, Tian turned toward Lavrentyev. Based on their best available intelligence, the S-29's weapons laser was now beyond its effective range.

The Russian colonel nodded back with a set, hard face. He took one short breath and then snapped out a string of orders. "Bring our radars online, Dmitry! And activate the plasma gun!"

"Yes, sir!" Yanin punched controls at his station. "Radars powering up. Plasma gun elevating into firing position."

SHADOW BRAVO ONE
THAT SAME TIME

"We're three-hundred-plus miles downrange, Dusty," Hannah Craig said after a check of her own navigation display. "If those shit weasels are going to try anything on this orbit, it's gonna be soon." Miller nodded.

"*Warning, warning. X-band and L-band radars detected,*" the S-29's computer announced calmly. "*At ten o'clock low. Range three hundred ten miles.*"

Their zoomed-in cameras showed antennas rising smoothly out of two of the rock-and-dirt-covered domes. The center dome slid open, revealing a stubby cylinder surrounded by electronic components in a six-arm, starfish-shaped array.

"Plasma rail gun!" Craig said tersely.

"Confirmed," Miller grunted. His fingers flashed across one of his multifunction displays as he gave the flight control computer instructions to set up a new main engine burn.

Suddenly the Russian rail gun disappeared behind a dazzling pulse of light . . . just as the S-29 skidded sideways, shoved hard to the left by multiple maneuvering thrusters firing along its right side. A wave of deafening static roared through their headsets and then faded to silence. A toroid of highly ionized plasma had just slashed right past them at six thousand miles per second.

"They missed!" Craig said gleefully.

"Yeah, but not by much." Miller brought the controls for the spaceplane's five big LPDRS engines back online. Another random evasive maneuver rolled the Shadow ninety degrees back to the right. Through their forward cockpit windows, the rugged lunar surface seemed to tilt sideways. "So we're done with coasting along up here like one of those stupid ducks in a carnival shooting gallery."

Hundreds of miles away, a second blinding flash lit

the blackness. A new hissing roar of static signaled yet another near-miss.

Indicators turned green on Miller's head-up display. The flight control computer had finished its calculations. "Hold tight," he snapped. Then he shoved all five throttles forward to maximum power. The big engines relit instantly—flaring brightly as they burned hard against the S-29's direction of travel.

Jolted forward against their harnesses by enormous deceleration, the two Space Force pilots saw the cratered lunar surface coming up at them fast. Slowed far below the velocity needed to stay in orbit, they were again falling along a descending arc. A third dazzling flash erupted, this time right on the edge of the horizon. The static noise in their headsets was softer. This rail gun shot had missed them by a wider margin.

Straining to breathe under 5-G's of deceleration, Craig focused on her instrument readings. "Our altitude's down . . . to . . . forty miles." At this range, more than four hundred miles from the Sino-Russian base, they were now also below the plasma weapon's line of sight. "Rate of descent is . . . three hundred feet per second . . . and increasing."

"Copy that." Slowly, Miller pulled the throttles back all the way. "And . . . main engine cutoff." Blessed near-weightlessness returned. "Discontinue evasion program."

"*Order confirmed,*" the computer agreed. "*Evasive flight program discontinued.*"

Twenty miles above the jagged surface of the moon, Miller flipped the S-29 end-over-end so that its nose pointed forward again. Then he throttled back up—accelerating to arrest their descent. Another short, 5-G burn took them up to almost 3,700 miles per hour, the velocity needed to orbit this close to the moon.

Slowly, he floated back against his seat. "Well, that got ugly fast."

"Sure did," Hannah Craig agreed.

Miller glanced across at her. "You ready to tangle with those guys again, Major?"

"Yep." She nodded. She was already busy entering targeting data on one of her multifunction displays. "You have a plan, Colonel?"

"I sure do," he told her with a quick, fierce grin. "This time around, we'll come in low, say about sixty thousand feet off the deck . . . where they can't see us until our laser is in range. Then we pop up, and you nail that damned plasma gun first thing. After that, I figure we blow the shit out of the rest of that base. And then, we head on home."

Ahead of them, as they came back around the curve of the moon, they saw the half-lit blue-and-white earth as it rose—majestically outlined against the black backdrop of space.

"It's a great plan, Dusty," Hannah Craig said quietly, gazing up in wonder at their native planet in all its breathtaking beauty. "Especially that part about heading home."

FORTY-THREE

SKY MASTERS AEROSPACE INC.,
BATTLE MOUNTAIN, NEVADA
A SHORT TIME LATER

From his workstation in the improvised Sky Masters control center, Brad McLanahan listened closely to the radioed transmissions between Colonel Miller and Major Craig and Space Force headquarters out at Peterson Air Force Base in Colorado. Despite the two hundred and fifty thousand miles between them, there was remarkably little electromagnetic interference. Fortunately, the sun was in a quiet phase.

"Yes, sir, we are down to about forty-five percent of our hydrazine," he heard Miller tell General Kelleher. *"But since we're going to come in low this time, we won't need to run the evasion program until just before*

we pop up to make our attack run. So we should have a decent margin. The same goes for our main engine fuel reserves."

As the Space Force pilot continued outlining their attack plan, pictures of the Sino-Russian base taken by the S-29's sensors during its first pass scrolled across the control center's wall screens. Through its communications array, the spaceplane's powerful computers were automatically transferring vast amounts of data back to Earth.

"Very well, Colonel," Kelleher said. *"You and Major Craig have a green light to proceed."*

Brad smiled dryly. He understood the general's desire to put his seal of approval on the Shadow crew's upcoming attack. But that didn't alter the fact that Kelleher's permission was completely redundant. If Dusty Miller and Hannah Craig had planned to head home right after their first pass against the Sino-Russian base, they would have made a transearth injection burn to boost out of lunar orbit while they were still around on the far side of the moon. Since they hadn't done that, they were already committed to a second pass—no matter what anyone on back on Earth said or thought about the idea.

"Understood, sir," Miller radioed. *"We'll recontact you before loss of signal. Bravo One out."*

Slowly, Brad sat back. His eyes were hooded.

"What do you think?" Nadia asked carefully.

"It's a solid concept," Brad said. "In fact, it's exactly what I'd do if I were the one flying that bird . . ." His voice trailed off uncertainly.

"But?" she prompted.

He sighed. "It's just that, with those two satellites hovering overhead at the Lagrange point, the Russians and Chinese can see exactly what our guys are doing, along every part of their orbit."

"And the enemy always gets a vote," Nadia realized.

Brad nodded somberly. "Always."

COMMAND CENTER, KOROLEV BASE
A SHORT TIME LATER

In silence, Colonel Tian Fan studied the tracking information supplied by Russia's Kondor-L radar satellite. It confirmed that the American spaceplane had altered its orbit. The S-29 was coming around the moon much lower this time, less than twenty thousand meters above the surface. At that altitude, its weapons laser would already be in range by the time their own plasma rail gun could spot them and open fire.

Briefly, he closed his eyes. It didn't help. He couldn't

shake the image of that black-winged spacecraft as it streaked toward Korolev Base at close to six thousand kilometers per hour—coming on like the avenging angel of death so feared by some primitive believers. Resolutely, he forced himself to be calm. Death was simply an end, not a beginning.

Tian opened his eyes again and looked over at Kirill Lavrentyev. "These Americans are not fools," he said quietly. "Their next attack stands every chance of success."

Grimly, the Russian nodded. His broad face was pale beneath its gray-black streaks of moondust. The failure of his country's most advanced weapon in its first serious combat on the lunar surface was humiliating.

"Then we must adopt the tactics I have devised," Tian said flatly. Using both hands, he donned his EVA helmet and locked it into place on his space suit's neck ring. "We have no alternatives left."

In answer, Lavrentyev clasped Tian's gloved hand. "I wish it were not so, my friend." Then he stepped back and saluted briskly. Silently, Captain Yanin and Major Liu stood up from their own stations and saluted, too.

With a tight smile, Tian returned their salutes. Then

he closed his visor, turned awkwardly, and pushed through the curtain separating the command center from the rest of the habitat module. A narrow corridor led to the nearest air lock. He clambered inside and dogged the hatch shut. Then he activated a vacuum pump. It whirred silently, pulling all the oxygen out of the air lock.

Minutes later, he was out on the lunar surface. "Tian to Korolev Base," he radioed. "Status check."

"*Korolev here,*" Liu replied. "*No observed change in the S-29's altitude or orbital inclination. Estimated time to hostile engagement is now twenty minutes.*"

He had no more time to waste, Tian realized. Turning away from the habitat module that had been his home for weeks, he bounded fast toward the waiting Chang'e-13 lander. Even in his heavy EVA suit, ascending its short ladder was easy in the moon's one-sixth gravity.

Once inside the lander's tight confines, he closed the hatch. Quick key presses brought its control systems to life and started the flow of stored oxygen to pressurize the cabin. Lights flickered on across Chang'e-13's multifunction displays. Environmental system indicators turned green.

Satisfied, Tian unlatched his helmet visor and

stripped off his bulky gloves. For this task, he wanted to be able to feel the flight controls with his own hands. He strapped himself in position.

"Korolev Base, this is Chang'e-Thirteen," he radioed. "Ready to depart."

"*Fly well, Chang'e-Thirteen,*" Liu replied.

Swiftly, Tian checked the rows of status lights on his displays. Everything was ready. He entered a code into the flight program computer. An acknowledgment flashed onto his screen: MANUAL CONTROL ENABLED. AUTOMATED LAUNCH SEQUENCE ACTIVATED.

Tian put his hands back on the two controllers at his command pilot's station, waiting for the rocket motor's ignition. Seconds later, explosive bolts detonated and the engine lit. Cut free from its four-legged lower half, Chang'e-13's ascent stage climbed into the black, starlit sky.

Not far above the surface, he reduced the ascent engine's thrust and triggered a succession of attitude control thrusters. Obeying his command inputs, the lander pitched over ninety degrees. Soundlessly, Chang'e-13 flew out over the crater rim and down along Engel'gardt's long, eastern slope—slanting east-southeast at high speed across a desolate plain pockmarked by smaller hollows.

SHADOW BRAVO ONE,
OVER THE FAR SIDE OF THE MOON
A SHORT TIME LATER

"We're crossing the northwestern rim of Vavilov crater," Craig reported. "That puts us four hundred and fifteen miles out from the primary target. We'll be in range of the enemy's plasma rail gun in less than two minutes."

With the S-29 rolled upside down again, Miller looked "up" through the cockpit canopy at the relatively sharp edges of the crater they were flying over. It was new, by the standards of the moon—probably no more than a few hundred million years old. Much of the ring-walled, four-mile-deep depression overlaid the remains of an older, far more eroded crater dating back billions of years. Solid black, impenetrable shadows stretched westward across Vavilov's terraced floor. "Weapons status?" he asked.

"All systems are green," she assured him. "Our attack program is ready to run." Once they popped up into view of the Sino-Russian base, a single command would set their orchestrated attack in motion—with the S-29B's two-megawatt laser destroying targets according to a preselected sequence, starting with the plasma gun and its fire control radars and ending with the enemy's habitat module. The gas dynamic laser had enough fuel to fire up to twenty five-second bursts, more than enough to reduce the enemy base to ruins.

"Solid copy on that," Miller said in satisfaction. He kept his eyes riveted on his HUD. They were closing in on their chosen attack position at more than a mile per second. The moment they reached it, he planned to fire the spaceplane's thrusters and "pop" them up several thousand feet—just high enough to bring them over the visual horizon of the Russian plasma gun. "Stand by."

BELOW THE VAVILOV CRATER RIM
THAT SAME TIME

Deep within the dark shadows cast by the crater's steep west wall, a small spacecraft, Chang'e-13, hovered motionless. It was almost invisible to the naked eye. Tiny reaction control thrusters flared around its boxy fuselage—holding it aloft against the pull of the moon's gravity.

Inside the lunar lander's cramped cabin, Tian watched his thruster fuel readouts closely. The numbers were decreasing fast. His mouth tightened. The Chang'e's fuel reserves wouldn't last much longer. At most, he would be able to maintain this position only for another minute or so.

BEEP-BEEP-BEEP.

Drawn by the insistent alarm, his eyes flicked to Chang'e-13's lidar system display. He'd set its low-powered navigation lasers to continuous pulse—but instead of scanning the rough crater floor six thousand meters below, they were aimed at the sky above him. And now, those reflected laser pulses painted the blurred image of a winged vehicle, the American S-29B, as it flew past high overhead.

Tian reacted instantly. His right hand stabbed at a touch-screen display, activating the lander's hastily modified docking and rendezvous program. Using the control in his left hand, he rotated the spacecraft—tilting it to aim at the fast-moving enemy spaceplane. With a muted *whummp*, Chang'e-13's ascent rocket motor reignited at full power. Now guided by the navigation lasers locked on the S-29, the Chinese lunar lander streaked higher, accelerating rapidly.

"Warning, warning. *Low-power laser impacts on the aft fuselage,"* the spaceplane's computer said suddenly. *"New warning. Thermal detection at six o'clock low. Range close. Continuous low-power laser impacts."*

Miller's eyes widened in surprise. "What the hell—?"

Instinctively, he fired thrusters and spun the S-29 through a half circle, turning to face the oncoming threat. To his astonishment, he saw the gleaming white shape of another spacecraft climbing toward them out of the shadowed Vavilov crater. Brief, bright puffs of glowing gas appeared around the Chinese lander as it matched their maneuvers.

"Christ, Dusty, that guy's a kamikaze!" Craig exclaimed.

Gritting his teeth, Miller pitched the spaceplane's nose up and fired all five main engines, going for a hard, fast rolling climb in a desperate bid to evade their attacker. Only seconds later, the boxy Chang'e ascent stage flashed right past their cockpit, missing them by yards at most. "Zap that son of a bitch!" he ordered.

Face tight behind her helmet visor, Hannah Craig obeyed. Her fingers flew across her weapons control display. The S-29's laser pod slewed on target and fired—hitting the lightly built Chinese spacecraft just as it swung around to make another pass at them. In a fraction of a second, the powerful, two-megawatt laser slashed through its thin metal skin. Flames jetted into space as the oxygen in its cabin ignited. And then, as its propellant tanks ruptured, the tiny craft ripped apart. In a cloud of frozen nitrogen tetroxide, torn and tattered pieces of debris spiraled downward, caught in the moon's gravitational pull.

More than six hundred kilometers away, Captain Dmitry Yanin saw the American spaceplane appear on his radar screen. For one brief moment, as it evaded Tian's doomed Chang'e-13, the S-29's maneuvers were predictable. A bright red box blinked into existence onto his display. Korolev Base's X-band fire control radar had locked on. "Target locked!" he snapped. He punched a control. "Firing!"

Half a kilometer outside the habitat module, the Russian plasma rail gun pulsed again—hurling a glowing toroid of superheated dense plasma toward the distant American spaceplane at ten thousand kilometers a second.

Hit squarely, the S-29B Shadow was knocked end-over-end—briefly engulfed by an eerie blue globe of lightning. Dusty Miller and Hannah Craig were slammed against their harnesses by the enormous impact. Searing heat flashed through the cockpit. Control boards, instrument panels, and displays all erupted in dazzling showers of sparks as they short-circuited.

Three of their five main engines cut out. But the

other two, both under their right wing, kept burning as the spaceplane spun wildly through space. Lashed by uncontrolled electrical surges cascading through conduits and wiring, random thrusters triggered, sending it further out of control.

Blearily, Miller fought to lean forward against his straps. Hard, sharp jolts threw him from side to side. The cockpit was pitch dark. None of the emergency lights were working. *Aw, shit,* he thought.

He felt for the side of one of his dead multifunction displays and pushed the buttons set there. With their flight control computers knocked off-line or dead, their only chance was trying for a hard reset.

Nothing happened.

Through the cockpit canopy, he could see the jagged lunar surface coming up fast. Dragged downward by its two misfiring engines, the S-29 whirled around and around like an untethered kite caught in gale-force winds. Stubbornly, he tried resetting the computer again—aware that his copilot was trying the same procedure with her own control panels.

Ahead, Vavilov's stony rim wall climbed more than four miles from the crater floor. They were plunging straight toward it at high speed. *Damn,* Miller realized. They were out of time, maneuvering room, and ideas. He sat back, feeling strangely calm. They'd done their best. They'd fought the good fight. And in the last seconds before impact, he felt Hannah Craig's hand take his in the darkness and hold on tight.

Still flying at more than two thousand miles per hour, the S-29B Shadow slammed into the crater rim in a huge cloud of dust and shattered rock. And then it vanished in a brief, blinding flash of light as thousands of pounds of highly explosive fuel and oxidizer detonated.

FORTY-FOUR

SKY MASTERS AEROSPACE INC.
AN HOUR LATER

"Shadow Bravo One, this is Peterson Mission Control, do you read? Shadow Bravo One, this is Peterson Mission Control, do you read? . . . Shadow Bravo One—"

Slowly, Brad McLanahan removed his headset, cutting off the melancholy radio calls to a crew and spaceplane lost forever. The failure of the S-29B to come back around the edge of the distant moon signaled its fate all too clearly. He put the headset down and looked up at the subdued faces of Nadia, his father, Boomer, and Peter Vasey. "Well," he said quietly. "That's it. Looks like we're up."

Nadia, red-eyed with sorrow, nodded fiercely.

Beside her, Vasey offered him a wry smile. "I should

have listened to my old dad," the Englishman said, shaking his head. "'Never volunteer,' he told me a thousand times. 'You'd have to be daft to volunteer for anything.' Now I know what he was rattling on about."

"Which means you'll go?" Brad asked.

"Of course," Vasey said. "If you've all gone stark, raving mad, why should I pretend to be the only sane person left in the room?"

Reluctantly, Brad smiled. Then he turned to the Sky Masters technician in charge of their communications setup. "Patch me through to the president."

After several minutes, President Farrell's strained and somber image appeared on-screen. He had been following developments from the Oval Office. "Yes, Major McLanahan? What is it?"

"Sir, we've worked out another plan of attack," Brad told him. "My team and I believe that it's vital that we go again—and go as soon as possible. Right now, the Russians and Chinese are probably figuring out how to strengthen their lunar base defenses. If we give them too much time to prepare, they're likely to deploy lasers of their own, and maybe even long-range, guided missiles. And once that happens, no force we can possibly send to the moon will ever be able to take that base on with any hope of success."

"Hold on there, Major," the president said heavily.

"One thing's for damned sure: I will not authorize another spaceplane raid against the Sino-Russian moon base. God knows, I admire your guts . . . but I am most definitely *not* in the business of abetting suicide. Because from where I'm sitting, there's no way in hell a spacecraft in orbit can take on that Russian plasma gun in a straight-up fight and win."

Brad nodded. "Yes, sir, I agree," he said evenly. "That's why we plan to go in on the ground this time—"

KOROLEV BASE, ON THE FAR SIDE OF THE MOON
THREE WEEKS LATER

Even across four hundred thousand kilometers, Colonel Kirill Lavrentyev could tell that Marshal Leonov and President Li had more bad news to share with him. Discovering that the Americans could send armed spacecraft to lunar orbit had already shaken the strategic and operational assumptions on which all their plans were based. But even so, no one had imagined the spaceplane's attack might come so close to success. *No one except for Tian,* he reminded himself silently. From the beginning, his Chinese counterpart had foreseen the danger . . . and gone on steadfastly to prepare to meet it—knowing all the while that doing so might mean his own death.

Leonov pulled no punches this time. "Our space sensors and ground-based telescopes have detected a new American spacecraft on its way to the moon."

"Another one of their S-29s?" Lavrentyev asked, unable to hide his sudden concern.

"No, Colonel," Leonov assured him. He sketched out what they knew. Some hours before, another Falcon Heavy rocket had launched—this time from the SpaceX complex near Brownsville, Texas, on America's Gulf coast. Originally scheduled to carry commercial satellites for a number of different private companies, the rocket instead had carried a secret U.S. government payload into space. Neither Russia's GRU nor China's Ministry of State Security had been able to learn much more about this mysterious payload except that it had originally arrived in Texas aboard a Sky Masters–owned 747F cargo jet.

After entering a parking orbit—probably to check out its systems and flight readiness—the Falcon's second-stage Merlin-1D engine had boosted this payload outward, toward the moon. Still concealed by its fairings, it was on course to enter the moon's gravitational influence in approximately forty-eight hours.

"But nothing else is known about its nature?" Lavrentyev pressed. "This must be some kind of weapon, right?"

"That is undoubtedly so," Li said. For once, the Chinese president's tone conveyed his own sense of unease. "General Chen Haifeng and his Strategic Support Force experts have speculated this might be a maneuverable orbital bomb, perhaps even equipped with a nuclear weapon."

Lavrentyev nodded slowly. In the absence of an atmosphere, nuclear detonations in space or on the moon could not destroy their targets with blast or thermal effects . . . but their radiation effects were far greater—with a lethal radius ten to twelve times bigger than on Earth. True, Korolev's habitat module offered excellent protection against ordinary lunar and cosmic radiation. But while its half-meter-thick walls might shield his crewmen against a distant nuclear blast, the habitat could not save them from the radiation produced by a nuclear bomb going off at close range. And if anything, the base's plasma rail gun and radars were even more vulnerable.

"If Chen and his officers are correct, can you defeat such a weapon?" Li asked curtly.

Lavrentyev forced himself to put a brave face on the situation. "I believe so, Comrade President. Major Liu and Captain Yanin have thoroughly analyzed the different evasive maneuvers employed by the American

S-29 Shadow. Repeated computer simulations have helped them develop aiming protocols to enable our plasma rail gun to achieve kills against maneuvering targets—at least during prolonged battles fought out at long range."

"Let us hope your confidence is justified, Colonel," Li said dryly. "I would hate to see so many of my nation's precious resources wasted—especially after the sacrifice of China's bravest and most experienced taikonaut."

From the sour look on Marshal Leonov's face, Lavrentyev knew the Chinese leader's thinly veiled gibe had struck home. Both nations had already committed huge sums of money and precious equipment to their attempt to gain control over Earth's moon—and over the space-faring future it represented. Clearly, the near disaster three weeks ago had strained the alliance between Moscow and Beijing, at least to a degree. That was especially true now that Russia's boasts about its "invincible" weapon had proved somewhat . . . hollow.

"As it happens, the Americans also appear supremely confident in their new weapon, whatever it may be," Li continued. "Isn't that right, Marshal?"

Leonov shrugged. "It seems so." He turned his attention back to Lavrentyev. "We've observed a burst of renewed extravehicular activity near Eagle Station.

Sky Masters space construction robots have gone back to work on the Orion crew vehicle and service module docked there."

Li nodded coldly. "The conclusion seems obvious: the Americans expect to destroy your base and so they are again preparing for their own manned flight to the moon."

THE WHITE HOUSE, WASHINGTON, D.C.
THAT SAME TIME

President John Dalton Farrell stared down at the glossy printouts Patrick McLanahan had just placed on his Oval Office desk. Taken by the S-29B's long-range cameras during its first pass around the far side of the moon, the enlarged, computer-enhanced photographs showed the Sino-Russian base in amazing detail. Working together, Sky Masters, Scion, and Space Force technical intelligence analysts had spent weeks poring over the images—doing their best to identify every single structure and piece of equipment.

With a worried look on his face, Farrell pulled out one of the photographs. It showed three oddly human-like shapes standing motionless on the lunar surface near the enemy's habitat module. An inflated tunnel with three separate branches connected them to one of the habitat's air locks. He glanced up. "Are those god-damned things what I think they are?"

"Yes, sir," Patrick said quietly. "The Russians have deployed moon-rated versions of their own robotic war machines, their *Kiberneticheskiye Voyennyye Mashiny*, at that base."

"Do Brad and the others know about this?"

"They do," Patrick told him. "Our analysts spotted those KVMs several days ago. I briefed the crew myself during one of their final mission planning sessions."

Farrell frowned. "Several days ago? So why am I only finding out about this now, General McLanahan?" His face hardened. "When it's far too late for me to call this mission off—even if I wanted to?"

"Because the team asked me to keep this information tightly restricted, sir," Patrick replied. He didn't sound particularly apologetic. "They didn't want to risk an abort, even in these circumstances."

"Jesus Christ," Farrell muttered. "I think your son and daughter-in-law and that crazy Brit Vasey are gutsy enough to charge hell itself with a bucket of ice water."

"Probably so," the older McLanahan agreed somberly. For just a moment, the lines carved on his face by age, pain, and stress deepened, revealing his own fears for those he loved more dearly than life itself.

Farrell sighed. "Give it to me straight, Patrick. Do

our people have any realistic hope of pulling this off and coming home alive?"

"I honestly don't know," the other man admitted. "But I guess that's something we'll find out for sure in just a little under three days from now."

FORTY-FIVE

ABOARD LUNAR WOLF ONE, APPROACHING THE MOON
FORTY-EIGHT HOURS LATER

Brad McLanahan floated across the Xeus lander's small cabin and grabbed on to the back of his crew seat. Nadia looked up at him. She was already strapped in to the next seat over. Her dark hair billowed around her head like a halo.

"Is everything all right?" she asked.

"Seems to be," Brad allowed. "But I thought I heard a kind of funny noise coming from one of the atmospheric pressure control valves."

Peter Vasey leaned around from his position at the end of the row of three crew seats. "Like a metallic rattling sound?"

"Yeah," Brad said. "Why?"

Vasey shrugged tiredly. "Because that's the same bloody noise I heard about ten hours ago, while you and Nadia were catnapping." He smiled. "I just banged on the side a few times until it stopped."

"Ah, you know my methods, Watson," Brad said dryly.

Sky Masters engineers and technicians had worked miracles to fit out the Xeus lander prototype with a working life-support system, flight controls, and navigation sensors in less than three weeks. But not even their superb craftsmanship and attention to detail could overcome the fact that this was essentially a shakedown cruise for a brand-new spacecraft. Meshing so many complicated mechanical and electronic systems and expecting them to work together perfectly the first time out was just not realistic.

Brad, Nadia, and Vasey had been lucky so far. Nothing major had gone wrong. But they'd been kept busy over most of the past two days in space improvising fixes for minor electrical faults, computer control program software glitches, and other small mechanical problems. As a result, none of them had gotten much deep, restful sleep. They were either working on some piece of equipment to keep the Xeus's different, interconnected systems up and running . . . or worrying about what might crap out on them next. Brad had gotten to the point where he'd scrawled a notation on a page of their maintenance logbook: *Next time, bring more chewing gum and duct tape . . . plus several reels of baling wire.*

Maneuvering carefully in zero-G, Brad pulled himself over and down into his seat and buckled in. Then he reached out and tugged his control panel and its attached hand controllers away from their "at rest" position against the lander's curved forward bulkhead. A key press on one of the panel's three LCD touch screens brought it live.

Nadia pulled her own panel into place. "Approximately ten minutes to our planned correction burn," she announced after a quick check of their navigation program.

Brad nodded. Ever since the Falcon Heavy's second stage had boosted them toward the moon at more than twenty-four thousand miles per hour, the Xeus had been coasting "uphill" against Earth's constant pull. Now it was just about to glide over the top of that gravitational gradient and enter the moon's own influence. And as the lander sped up again, they needed to make a very precise, short burn with its main RL-10 rocket engine—one that would align the spacecraft to come in very low over the lunar surface as it raced around the far side. "Okay," he said. "I guess it's time to pop the top on this space-going beer can of ours."

"It has been getting a bit stuffy in here," Vasey said. He pulled up a command menu on his own display and quickly entered a key code to activate it. Then he tapped one of the menu bars. It glowed green. "Fairing jettison Master Arm is on." He glanced toward Brad with just a hint of devilish glee. "Permission to set off a number of explosive charges just outside our space-craft, Major McLanahan?"

"Be my guest, Constable," Brad said grandly.

Nadia rolled her eyes. "Boys and their toys."

"You're just upset because *I'm* the one who gets to push the button," Vasey noted.

"Well, yes," Nadia admitted with a smile of her own.

"Thought so," Vasey said. Triumphantly, he tapped the glowing menu bar.

WHAANG. Small explosive bolts detonated, shearing through the connections between the twin halves of the payload fairing and the Xeus itself. Fractions of a second later, powerful springs shoved both fairing panels away. Cameras rigged to various points outside of the lander showed them whirling off into space.

"This would be a lot cooler if we had windows," Brad said meditatively. Unfortunately, Jason Richter and Boomer had adamantly vetoed the idea of adding windows or viewing portals to the Xeus. Given the short time available to finish retrofitting the prototype for space flight, neither of them wanted to risk the structural integrity of what was basically just a converted fuel tank by slicing through its hull any more than was absolutely necessary.

From her station, Nadia set their stellar navigation program in motion, instructing her computer to find their position relative to three prominent stars. Comparing those results to the data provided by their inertial guidance system, which had been measuring every change in the spacecraft's velocity or direction since liftoff, yielded a remarkably precise fix—accurate to within a few hundred feet, despite the fact that they had already traveled more than two hundred thousand miles.

Using one of his hand controllers, Brad rotated the Xeus, swinging the spacecraft around so that its main engine was aimed correctly for the upcoming burn. He opened new windows on his LCDs. They showed information collected by the sensors set to monitor different parts of the RL-10 engine. "Fuel line temperatures look good," he said aloud. "Tank pressures are good, too. The engine looks ready to go." He glanced along the row of seats at his crewmates. "Fingers crossed, guys."

Nadia and Vasey both nodded seriously. This was a make-or-break moment for their mission. If the Xeus's big cryogenic rocket motor failed to ignite on its first-ever use, they would be condemned to swing around the moon on a free-return trajectory . . . a sitting duck for the Russian plasma rail gun deployed high up on the Engel'gardt crater rim.

"Coming up on the mark," Brad said, watching as their computer counted down the time remaining. The digital readout flashed to zero. In response, he tapped the engine ignition icon on his panel. "Firing now."

The Xeus start to vibrate slightly and they felt a sensation of weight return as acceleration pressed them back into their seats. On their screens, a camera set to monitor the RL-10's nozzle showed it glowing bright orange amid the darkness around it. Seventy seconds later, the orange glow faded and weightlessness returned. "Main engine shut down. Right on time," Brad reported.

Nadia ran her navigation program again. "That was a good burn," she said in satisfaction. "We are on our planned trajectory."

"Copy that," Brad said in relief. He opened a radio channel to the earth far behind them. While the Xeus had been concealed inside its payload fairing, they hadn't been able to communicate with ground control. Now the spacecraft's computers were making up for lost time, dumping a huge amount of accumulated telemetry to both Sky Masters in Nevada and Peterson Air Force Base in Colorado. To hide the fact that this flight carried a human crew, Scion communications protocols would encrypt and compress any of their voice transmissions before they were sent. He checked their flight computer's numbers and then keyed his mike. "Lunar Wolf One to Sky Masters Control, we are go for LOI. Repeat, we are go for lunar orbit insertion in fourteen hours and four minutes."

NATIONAL DEFENSE CONTROL CENTER
A SHORT TIME LATER

Leonov frowned in perplexity at the blurry radar images captured by the Kondor-L satellite. What sort of spacecraft was this? Even from what little detail could be made out, it didn't look like anything in the known inventories of America's private space companies or those of NASA itself. He turned to the younger staff officer who'd summoned him the moment the American craft jettisoned its payload fairing. "What do you make of that, Sergei?"

"I'm not sure, sir," Major General Sergei Panarin admitted. "Our top analysts haven't yet been able to positively identify it. Nor have the Chinese." He nodded toward Leonov's screen. "We may have better luck once those images are enhanced. Teams are working on that now."

"No one has any ideas?" Leonov said sharply. "None at all?"

Panarin looked uncomfortable. "One of my most junior people did suggest that it resembled an experimental prototype he read about some years ago on an American space technology website."

"Show me," Leonov snapped.

Chastened, the younger man leaned over his superior's desk and searched through the internet to find the appropriate site. "It was this one," he said quickly, pointing to an artist's rendition of a cylinder equipped with a rocket engine, an array of smaller thrusters, and helicopter-style landing skids.

Even more puzzled now, Leonov skimmed through the article on a long-shelved commercial lunar lander prototype called the Xeus. *An interesting concept,* he decided silently. And perhaps even better suited to its proposed task than China's giant, enormously expensive Mă Luó cargo landers. But the American machine had never been flown in space. Not even on a single short test flight in Earth orbit. So who could have resurrected it now?

The likely answer flashed into his mind a moment later: Sky Masters, in all probability. Or maybe Scion, at the orders of its troublesome leader, Martindale, and his crippled warrior-engineer, Patrick McLanahan.

But if this was a Xeus spacecraft, what was it carrying now? All available information suggested the craft had originally been intended as an automated lander, ferrying cargo between NASA's since-canceled lunar orbital station and the surface of the moon. If so, that seemed to confirm Chen Haifeng's theory that the Americans now planned to use it as a robotic bomb carrier.

Panarin's own computer chimed abruptly, signaling the arrival of an urgent message. The younger officer's eyes widened in surprise when he read it. "What the devil?" he muttered. "That's damned odd."

"Tell me," Leonov demanded.

"We've just received new information on the American spacecraft's trajectory," Panarin told him. "Unless it makes another correction burn sometime in the next several hours, it's going to cross around to the far side of the moon at an altitude of less than three thousand meters!"

Leonov felt his own eyes widen. Less than three thousand meters? That was dangerously low, even for a manned spacecraft. Could the Americans really have developed an automated flight program capable of navigating safely so close to the moon's rugged surface? And if so, were they planning to fly this Xeus toward Korolev Base as if it were an aircraft trying to avoid radar detection on Earth—weaving in and out of craters and behind mountains, until it was close enough to detonate the bomb it must be carrying?

He stared up at Panarin. "Put me through to Colonel Lavrentyev on a secure link, Sergei! Now!"

FORTY-SIX

ABOARD LUNAR WOLF ONE,
CROSSING TO THE FAR SIDE OF THE MOON
FOURTEEN HOURS LATER

The Xeus's crew was shoved forward against their harnesses as the spacecraft's main engine fired a second time. This time it was aligned directly against their direction of travel—burning at full power to slow them down as the lander streaked just above the moon at more than five thousand miles per hour.

"And . . . MECO, main engine cutoff," Brad McLanahan said three minutes later. Zero-G returned as the rocket motor shut down. He spun the lander back around.

"Good burn," Nadia reported from her seat. "No

residuals. We are in lunar orbit. *Very* low lunar orbit," she emphasized.

No shit, Brad thought edgily, watching the rounded peaks, escarpments, and craters of the moon's far side rushing toward him at more than a mile per second. At an altitude of roughly five thousand feet, they were practically skimming the surface—darting low across a battered landscape that might make Hell itself look like the Garden of Eden. They were coming in along an orbital track just a few degrees north of the lunar equator, circling west straight toward the Sino-Russian base that had killed Dusty Miller and Hannah Craig.

Seeing a chain of interconnected craters curving ahead across one of his displays, he fired thrusters—climbing just high enough to clear the steadily rising terrain. That was the Leuschner Catena, the result of a massive asteroid impact that had created the moon's vast, 560-mile diameter Mare Orientale more than three billion years before. Huge masses of molten rock, hurled outward from the center of that collision, had cascaded down across this part of the lunar surface, hammering out this series of linked craters.

Brad kept his attention riveted to his screens. Sweat was starting to puddle up under the communications cap that held his headset and mike in position. Orbiting this close to the rough moonscape required constant adjustments to his flight path with the lander's four vertical thruster arrays—both to clear steep-edged crater walls and scarred mountains, and to cope with sudden changes in lunar gravity caused by unseen anomalies buried deep below the battered surface.

Given several more months to prep the Xeus for this mission, Sky Masters engineers and computer techs could have equipped it with the equivalent of a digital terrain-following system to handle this low-level orbit. Without it, piloting the spacecraft through these hazards required a man in the seat . . . and Brad was that man. The fact that he had to rely on exterior cameras to see anything outside the spacecraft cabin was one more worry. One minor electrical fault could leave them flying blind, without anything except the computer's inertial navigation system to tell them where they were at any given moment.

"That's the Michelson crater dead ahead," Nadia told him. She was tracking their progress on the navigation computer's detailed maps. "And we're passing Kohlhörster now, off to our right."

Brad saw the feature she meant growing larger across his forward-looking screen. Michelson was heavily eroded, almost erased by dozens of newer, smaller craters. He fired more thrusters, shaving off some altitude to come over its slumped rim wall at no more than a few hundred feet. It was imperative that they stay well below the horizon of the Russian plasma gun all the way in on this run.

"Thruster fuel is at sixty-eight percent," Peter Vasey reported. While Nadia handled navigation, he was charged with monitoring their engines, fuel status, and other systems.

"Twenty seconds to the Hertzsprung crater," Nadia warned.

Brad nodded tightly. Hertzsprung was another huge-impact crater. Billions of years old, it was even larger than some of the dark volcanic plains that early astronomers had mistaken for seas. And like the moon's other big craters, Hertzsprung contained a significant gravitational anomaly buried at its core.

The anomaly made itself felt the moment they crossed the crater's outer western rim. Here, the moon's gravity was stronger, tugging them ahead faster and also dragging them downward toward Hertzsprung's center, which lay nearly fifteen thousand feet lower. If they'd been orbiting higher up, the effects wouldn't have been as pronounced and they would have had more time to react. As it was, Brad rotated the Xeus a few degrees and went for a prolonged thruster burn to offset the higher gravitational pull.

"Our thruster fuel reserves are down to fifty-five

percent," Vasey said coolly. That was a little lower than they'd predicted in their planning and simulator sessions back on Earth. The digitized maps created from hundreds of thousands of oblique images taken by earlier orbiting satellites hadn't fully revealed the ruggedness of some terrain features or the exact irregularity of the moon's gravitational field so close to its surface.

Brad eased up slightly on his burn, letting the Xeus drop a couple of hundred feet as they sped over the western curve of Hertzsprung's inner ring wall, a rugged massif made up of four-billion-year-old anorthosite rocks flung upward when the original asteroid slammed into the moon at more than thirty thousand miles per hour. Seconds later, the sheer escarpment that marked the vast crater's outer eastern rim appeared over the horizon. It was around forty miles off—less than a minute's flight time at their current orbital velocity.

Frowning in intense concentration, he took the lander right through a gap torn in the cliff by debris from a later asteroid strike. Their side-view cameras showed slopes rising almost vertically above them, studded with broken boulders that were easily a hundred feet high.

He breathed out a bit as they emerged from the gap and headed across a steadily rising plain. A couple of minutes later, he spotted what looked like a jumbled mess of secondary craters, torn cliffs, and rounded hills.

Nadia leaned forward, peering closely at her display and then comparing it with her maps. "That is the Tsander crater," she said confidently.

Brad nodded again. Tsander, large and heavily battered over hundreds of millions of years, was as far as they could safely go, even at this low altitude. Once past this ancient, eroded crater, they would come out onto a wide plain dotted with hundreds of much smaller craters. Across that steadily rising plain, the Russian plasma gun, mounted high up on the rim of Engel'gardt crater, would have a clear field of fire against anything flying more than a few dozen feet above the surface.

He twisted his hand controllers, spinning the Xeus around on its axis so that its main engine pointed ahead, against their direction of travel. Brad switched his display to the cameras rigged to the aft end of the lander. His eyes narrowed as he watched Tsander's scarred outer edges grow larger and more distinct.

"Almost there," he muttered, more to himself than to Nadia or Vasey. One side of his mouth twitched upward in a crooked grin. Could he really call this "flying by the seat of your pants" if the only thing holding him in his seat in zero-G was his safety harness? On his screens, he saw a tiny craterlet come into view.

Sited several miles east of Tsander's broken rim wall, it was more of an indentation in the lunar soil than a real crater. But it was definitely the aiming mark he'd picked out after spending hours studying maps and photos of their projected course. "Coming up on our retro burn . . . just . . . about . . . *now*." He punched the RL-10 engine icon on his touch-screen control panel. "Main engine ignition."

This was a hard, full-power burn to shed their orbital velocity. Slammed against his seat straps by deceleration, Brad fought to stay focused as his apparent weight tripled and then quadrupled in a fraction of a second. As the Xeus slowed rapidly, it began dropping toward the surface, now just a couple of thousand feet below.

Brad's eyes darted back and forth between the aft-mounted cameras and others set on the lander's underside, which showed the ground coming up with dismaying speed. As soon as the spacecraft's forward velocity dropped to nothing, he shut down the big rocket engine and then immediately triggered the lander's vertical thruster arrays to slow its rate of descent.

Less than a minute later, as their thrusters flared brightly, he brought the Xeus in for a landing. Dust billowed up, obscuring his view just before the skids touched down. He chopped the thrusters off, and they dropped the last few feet—hitting the ground with a *thump* that rattled the cabin.

Smiling in relief, he turned to the others. "Okay, maybe that wasn't exactly smooth. But at least it was definite. We've landed. So . . . welcome to the moon."

In answer, Nadia leaned over and gave him a lingering kiss through his open helmet visor. "You are a wonderful pilot, Brad McLanahan." He felt his face redden.

With a big grin of his own, Vasey reached around her and clapped him on the shoulder. "Not bad for a Yank, I guess." His smile faded as he unstrapped himself and stood up, moving carefully in the moon's low gravity. "If we had champagne, I'd offer a toast . . . but we're on the clock, so—"

Brad nodded and reached for his own safety harness release buckle. The other man was right. This successful landing only completed the first phase of their attack plan. But they were still more than two hundred miles from the Sino-Russian base. Since they had been under constant observation by the Kondor-L radar satellite as they orbited around the moon, they couldn't hope to achieve complete surprise. But there was at least a slim chance that moving fast now might throw the base's Chinese and Russian crew off-balance.

He stood up and helped Nadia get out of her own

seat. Then he turned to Vasey. "Okay, Constable, the ship is yours," he said quietly.

Solemnly, the Englishman nodded. He was tasked with waiting here to fly in and pick them up if they succeeded . . . or to die alone, if they failed.

Minutes later, Brad and Nadia stood outside on the surface of the moon. For now, the slim, silvery carbon-fiber space suits they wore kept them alive in this airless environment. Another Sky Masters innovation, the suits used electronically controlled fibers to compress the skin instead of pressurized oxygen. But EEAS suits were not designed for prolonged use under these supremely hostile conditions. Both of them were already starting to sweat as their suits' limited environmental systems struggled to handle temperatures that hit 260 degrees Fahrenheit in full sun.

"We're set," he radioed Vasey. "You can open the cargo hatch."

"*Roger that,*" the other man replied. "*I'm activating the hatch now. Stand clear.*"

There was no sound as the wide, curved hatch on the flank of the Xeus unlatched and swung open—revealing the lander's crowded cargo compartment. More machinery spun into gear. Silently, pulleys and gear systems extracted two large, humanlike machines from the compartment and deposited them onto the surface. Insulated packs containing weapons, explosives, and other gear followed them out.

The two combat-modified Cybernetic Lunar Activity Devices, or CLADs, were no longer bright white. Instead, their composite armor "skin" was covered by hundreds of small, gray, hexagonal tiles. Made of a special material, these tiles could change temperature with amazing rapidity. Using data collected by its sensors, a CLAD's computer could adjust the temperature of each tile to mimic that of its surroundings—rendering the robot virtually undetectable by infrared and other thermal sensors. Under combat conditions, that could be a lifesaver. But even on Earth, rapid movement with an active thermal camouflage system would drain batteries and fuel cells. Here, given the moon's wild temperature fluctuations, where it was possible to experience swings of five hundred degrees or more just by moving from sunlight into shadow, this thermal camouflage system could only be used for very brief moments.

Each CLAD carried a second camouflage system, this one even more advanced—but equally limited by power constraints. Paper-thin electrochromatic plates covered each thermal tile. Tiny voltage changes could change the mix of colors displayed by each plate, giving the robot a chameleon-like ability to blend in with its environment while motionless or moving cautiously.

Brad glided over to the nearest machine. He reached up and pushed a glowing green button on a hatch set in its back. It cycled open. "Let's mount up."

"*On my way,*" Nadia radioed. She hit the hatch button on her own Cybernetic Lunar Activity Device, pulled herself up a short ladder, and crawled inside the machine. The hatch sealed behind her.

Brad did the same thing. As usual, he felt a momentary touch of claustrophobia as he wriggled upward into the lower level of the robot's tiny cockpit. Green lights glowed on the right-sleeve control panel of his space suit. With its hatch closed and a human pilot on board, the CLAD's own life-support systems had pressurized the cockpit.

Carefully, he undogged his helmet and pulled it off. His nose wrinkled at the faint odor of machine oil. Yeah, there was air in here, all right. Squirming out of the rest of his snug carbon-fiber suit in these tight confines took some doing, but at last he managed it. Then he worked his way upward some more, squeezing deeper into the robot's haptic interface, a gray, gelatinous membrane. This was the material that took his body's central nervous system's signals, processed them, and turned them into robotic movement. At the same time, it acted as a direct neural link, meshing his mind with the machine's sensors and computer systems.

For a moment, the small cockpit blurred around him and then vanished. It was as though his vision had grayed out in a high-G turn. And then just as quickly, his sight returned—only now he was looking directly out across the moon's rugged surface and seeing it with crystal clarity, rather than through a helmet visor. The flood of information from the robot's active and passive sensors through his neural interface gave him an almost godlike view of his surroundings.

Systems status check, he thought.

Instantly information flooded into his consciousness: *All systems are fully operational. Power reserves at ninety-nine percent. Current life-support capability estimated at forty-four hours.* He knew the status of every subsystem, every byte of computer output, and the position of every limb down to the fraction of an inch, just by thinking of it.

Good enough, Brad thought. He opened a secure connection to Nadia's CLAD. "Wolf Two to Wolf Three, does your ride check out?"

"Wolf Three to Two," Nadia replied. "I am claws out and ready to run."

"Copy that, Three." Brad turned away from the grounded Xeus lander. He picked up one of the camouflaged weapons and equipment packs and slung it into position across his robot's back. Nadia took the other pack and did the same. "Then follow me."

Together, the two machines bounded off to the west, moving easily in the moon's low gravity.

FORTY-SEVEN

KOROLEV BASE, ON THE EASTERN RIM OF ENGEL'GARDT CRATER
A SHORT TIME LATER

"You've lost radar contact with the American spacecraft?" Marshal Leonov asked, evidently taken aback.

"It dropped off our feed from the Kondor-L satellite about thirty minutes ago and we haven't been able to regain contact since," Lavrentyev said. He glanced at Major Liu for confirmation and saw the taikonaut nod. The Chinese officer was monitoring Korolev's radar and thermal detection systems. "At the time, the enemy vehicle was still well below our own radar horizon."

Leonov's brow furrowed in thought. "Where exactly did the Kondor lose contact?"

"Just east of the Tsander crater," Lavrentyev told

him. "About three hundred and fifty kilometers away." He expressed his hope. "It's possible that it crashed. Naturally, our altitude estimates were imprecise, but that spacecraft had to be coming in very low. And it was moving so fast, nearly six thousand kilometers per hour—sixteen-hundred-plus meters per second!—that any tiny error in its computer flight program could easily have led to disaster."

Leonov shook his head. "That seems unlikely, Colonel. Highly unlikely." His mouth turned downward. "You've seen the American flight path. After so successfully navigating through a gravitational and terrain maze like the Hertzsprung crater, why should its systems fail just now?"

"But if that spacecraft didn't crash—"

"Then the Americans have landed," Leonov said bluntly. "And our analysis of the situation was completely wrong. That Xeus lander was not flown by a computer. It carried humans, military astronauts."

Lavrentyev suddenly saw what the other man meant. He felt like he'd been punched in the stomach. "You think the Americans intend a ground assault," he realized. "Using some of their own combat robots."

"What else?" Leonov said grimly. "Why should we believe we were the only ones who thought of modifying such weapons for use on the moon?" His mouth tightened. "You and the others had better don your KLVMs and look to your defenses. Hand over all responsibility for your sensors and the plasma rail gun to Major Liu and Captain Shan, in case we're wrong again . . . and the Americans have some other trick up their sleeves."

"I could send one of our machines out to find and destroy the American lander," Lavrentyev suggested uncertainly.

Leonov dismissed the idea with a curt wave of his hand. "Too dangerous, Kirill. Any KLVM you dispatched could be ambushed. And even if it succeeded in wrecking the enemy's spacecraft, weakening your own forces there might lead to disaster. We cannot afford to trade pawns with the Americans in this game. The security of your base is paramount. It *must* come before any other considerations."

Lavrentyev swallowed hard. "Yes, Marshal. I understand." Yes, he and the other Russian cosmonauts were trained to pilot the base's three *Kibernetischeskiye Lunnyye Voyennyye Mashiny*, its Cybernetic Lunar War Machines. But never in his worst nightmares had he ever imagined they would have to use them in actual combat. Up to now, their KLVMs had functioned primarily as heavy construction equipment— accomplishing tasks that would have been impossible for any cosmonaut in a conventional space suit. Even knowing that it was easier to defend than to attack, especially across the long, barren slopes below the crater rim, he found the prospect of actually going head-to-head with piloted American combat robots deeply unsettling.

NORTHEAST OF ENGEL'GARDT CRATER
SEVERAL HOURS LATER

Brad dug in to the loose scree piled just below the rim of a minor crater and cautiously pulled himself up the slope. Grains of soil and small rocks slid soundlessly downhill behind his CLAD. A hundred yards to his right, Nadia's robot toiled up the same steep hillside.

One of the eerier effects of piloting a robot through a neural link was that you soon lost all distracting awareness of self. Within a matter of moments, you were no longer cognizant that you were directing a machine from inside its cockpit. Instead, you essentially wore the large cybernetic device as if it were a second skin— controlling its limbs, systems, and sensors as easily and unconsciously as if they were your own from birth.

A few feet below the crest of the rise, Brad halted in place and crouched down. So did Nadia. For most of their long approach march from the Xeus, they had been able to cover ground quickly, gliding and bounding at speeds of up to forty miles an hour across stretches where the going was firm. But now that they were almost within striking distance of the Sino-Russian base, it was time to exercise considerably more caution.

While the oblique photos taken by the S-29B's cameras during its first orbit hadn't revealed the precise types of weapons the enemy's own war machines carried, it was a safe bet that they included 25mm or 30mm rifled autocannons with armor-piercing ammunition. Since the moon was airless, only its weak gravity would act on any projectile. In practical terms, that meant weapon ranges were effectively limited only by lines of sight. On the other hand, it also meant nobody on either side was likely to be blasting away on full automatic—spraying hundreds of rounds per minute downrange. Without an atmosphere, it was far more difficult to radiate away the heat generated by high rates of fire. Experiments at Sky Masters Space Exploration, Research, and Development Lab had shown that the best way to avoid a weapons jam in combat on the lunar surface was to revert to semiautomatic shooting, where a trigger pull would fire just one round at a time.

The enemy's robots might also be equipped with some kind of man-portable, guided missiles—but that was less likely. Without an atmosphere, aerodynamic control vanes or fins were useless, so only missiles with vanes to deflect their own rocket thrust would be able to track and hit moving targets. An even bigger problem was that the moon's extreme temperature swings would rapidly drain the batteries needed to power any missile's electronic components and cool its infrared seeker. After a few minutes outside on the lunar surface, any unprotected missile would probably be inoperable.

Kind of ironic, Brad thought. Come to the moon to fight a war and find yourself mostly facing weapons that were developed decades before. Then again, any large, armor-piercing round was a serious threat. In this brutal environment, a single significant hull breach could mean death.

He opened a very low-powered radio link to Nadia's robot. Passive sensors might alert the Russians to the fact that their enemies were communicating. But since their transmissions were automatically encrypted and compressed to millisecond bursts, the odds were against anyone getting an accurate fix on them. "I'm going to take a quick look," he said. "Hold your position."

"Copy that, Wolf Two," she answered. She swung the weapons and equipment pack off her back and pulled out her electromagnetic rail gun.

He felt a smile cross his face. Power constraints limited the Sky Masters–designed rail guns to just one shot each, but they were definitely the most lethal weapons in their arsenal—able to hurl small, superdense metal projectiles across enormous distances at Mach 5. Clearly, Nadia wanted to be able to reach out and kill someone if he drew enemy fire.

Which was something he planned to do his level best to avoid. The Sino-Russian lunar base was still miles away and several thousand feet above them. So if a patrolling Russian war robot spotted him now, he and Nadia would have no chance of getting in close enough to fight and win a decisive battle. A long-range sniping duel would only favor the enemy. To win, the Russians and Chinese simply had to hold their ground until Brad and Nadia's life-support systems ran out of power and failed. *Engage upper quadrant thermal adaptive and chameleon camouflage systems,* he thought.

Camouflage systems online, the CLAD's computer reported. *Power consumption levels spiking.* The six-sided head, shoulders, and upper arms of his robot shimmered into near invisibility, both in the visible and infrared spectrums.

Moving carefully to avoid dislodging any rocks, Brad raised up just high enough to see over the crest. Beyond the crater they were using as cover, the ground fell away for several hundred yards. But then it rose steadily across miles of open ground, climbing higher and higher until it merged into the towering rim wall of Engel'gardt crater. Apart from a few massive boulders and shallow heaps of aeons-old debris strewn at random, there was no cover at all.

Warning, his computer suddenly announced unemotionally. *Movement alert at twelve o'clock high. Crossing from right to left along the edge of the large crater. Range twenty thousand yards.*

Reacting instantly, Brad locked one of his long-range visual sensors onto the contact. Magnified hundreds of times, he saw the manlike shape of a Russian combat machine striding along the rim wall. Bristling with antennas and other sensors, its ovoid head swiveled from side to side. The robot carried a long, rifle-like weapon at the ready. Small, ring-shaped fins studded the barrel, probably intended to help shed heat in a vacuum.

The weapon appears to be a modified version of the Russian NR-30 30mm autocannon, the computer reported, picking up his sudden focus through their shared neural link.

That made sense, Brad realized. The NR-30 had already been tested in space in 1974 as part of an early Soviet military space program called Almaz, or Diamond. The weapon had been fired aboard Salyut 3, which was one of the Almaz platforms disguised as a civilian space station.

He dropped back below the edge of the crater rim. *Deactivate all camouflage systems,* he thought.

Thermal adaptive and electrochromatic systems are off, the CLAD confirmed. *Life-support capability reduced to thirty-six hours at current power consumption levels.*

Brad grimaced. That was seriously bad. Going to full stealth mode with just a fraction of his robot for a little over sixty seconds had just burned three full hours of life support. He'd known intellectually that running the robot's camouflage ate power at a prodigious rate. Experiencing it in the field brought that knowledge home with a vengeance. And it meant there was no way he and Nadia could hope to rely solely on their stealth systems to cross the deadly swath of open ground ahead of them. Their batteries and fuel cells would be drained before they covered even a third of the distance.

"Well, what did you see?" Nadia asked.

In answer, he focused mentally, ordering his computer to produce a complete compilation of all its sensor data. Then he flicked a finger, electronically transferring the files to her own robot as easily as a whisper.

"Interesting," she said quietly, comprehending the

accumulated data with lightning speed. "The Russians have deployed only a single sentry to cover this avenue of approach." She hefted the electromagnetic rail gun she carried. "I can eliminate him with a single shot."

Brad nodded. "Sure. And then all hell breaks loose." He sighed. "We might be able to nail a second enemy robot with our last rail gun shot . . . but then what? We'd still have to rush the last Russian war machine up that long, empty slope. One of us might make it. Maybe. With a lot of luck." He shook his head. "But that's a house edge I do *not* want to go up against."

"House edge?" Nadia said accusingly. "You have been spending far too much time around Boomer and his favorite casinos."

Almost unwillingly, he grinned. "You grow up in Nevada, you learn the lingo. It's a habit."

"Then what do you propose?" she asked.

"That we move around more to the right," Brad answered. He thought out his rough plan on a digital map file and sent it to her. "See, there's a spur extending off the main crater rim wall a few miles off in that direction, along with a chain of smaller, ejecta craters we can use as cover to get up onto the reverse slope of the spur. If we move fast, and use our camouflage systems sparingly, we ought to be able to make it all the way up onto the rim itself. That'll also put us northwest of the base itself, pretty much the opposite of where they should expect us. If we're lucky, they won't be keeping quite as close an eye on that area, figuring we'll have to move in quick from the east before our batteries run dry."

"And if the Russians *are* guarding it?" Nadia asked seriously.

He shrugged. "Then we slug it out at closer range—hoping our stealth tech and rail guns give us enough of an edge to win."

"And pray?"

"That, too," he agreed. One of the surprises of their married life had been learning that Nadia was more religious than he'd imagined. Faith had never been a big part of his own upbringing, so maybe it wasn't too astonishing that he'd been caught a little off guard by her quiet, unobtrusive belief. Now, two hundred and forty thousand miles from home and from everyone who loved them, he realized her rarely expressed convictions were a source of strength he both envied and admired.

FORTY-EIGHT

ON THE RIM OF ENGEL'GARDT CRATER
AN HOUR LATER

Inside the cockpit of his KLVM robot, Sentinel Two, Major Andrei Bezrukov scowled, deeply discontented by the hours they'd wasted patrolling around and around the outer perimeter of Korolev Base. Of the three cosmonauts stationed on the moon, he was the only one who'd completed the advanced cybernetic war machine combat course back on Earth. During the preparations for Operation Heaven's Thunder, Lavrentyev and Yanin had been given a few weeks of basic training, just enough to teach them how to pilot the robots and employ their weapons and sensors. But neither of them fully comprehended the best way to use these fearsome machines in real warfare.

By their nature, KLVMs were better suited to offensive operations—quick, slashing commando-style
raids using their incredible speed and agility. This kind
of static defense robbed them of most of their advantages. Worse yet, it risked yielding the initiative to the
Americans. Why give the enemy the luxury of choosing when and how to open this inevitable action?

The simulated battles Bezrukov had fought through
during his intensive training in Siberia's Kuznetskiy
Alatau mountains had shown the importance of constant movement. Data-linked war robots won by or-
chestrating swift surprise attacks from unexpected
directions. For a KLVM pilot, speed was life. Hunker-
ing down like this, tied to a fixed position, was asking
for trouble.

Continuing on his assigned circuit, he strode rapidly along the outer edge of the high crater wall—
using his infrared and other sensors to scan the
barren slopes below. *Nothing,* he realized. As usual.
His scowl deepened as he passed one of the big, four-
legged Chinese cargo landers off to his left. This was
pretty much the boundary of Korolev Base. A few
hundred meters beyond the grounded Mǎ Luó, this
relatively wide, plateau-like portion of Engel'gardt's
rim fell away and narrowed down to a knife-edged

ridge as it curved around to the north and west. Several kilometers away, a rugged spur of rock snaked upward a couple of thousand meters to join the main crater wall.

Bezrukov's eyes narrowed. Ripples and folds along the steep ridge between this high point and that spur created occasional patches of dead ground—areas that were impossible to observe from here because of undulations in the terrain. He'd spotted this potential covered approach to the base hours ago, on his first patrol. But Lavrentyev, afraid to weaken their perimeter defenses, had denied him permission to go beyond the plateau itself. Now, just looking out across this area of vulnerability every time he circled around the perimeter was a constant irritant.

Just then he felt a sharp jolt sizzle across his brain as the KLVM's computer sent an alert through his neural link. *Weak Ku-band radio transmissions detected,* it warned him. *Signatures consistent with U.S. multifunction advanced data link.*

Location? he snapped.

Impossible to triangulate, the computer admitted. *Insufficient data.*

Bezrukov grimaced. Those data links were built into America's F-35 Lightning II fighters and B-2

Spirit strategic bombers . . . and its own combat robots, the Cybernetic Infantry Devices. A cold chill ran down his spine. He suddenly felt as though someone out there was watching him.

True, speed was life. *But so was trained intuition,* he decided. Abruptly, he turned and strode away to the left, acting as though he were simply continuing his routine patrol around to the other side of Korolev Base. But this time, once he was far enough back on the plateau to be out of sight of anyone advancing along that narrow ridgeline, he darted behind the Chinese cargo lander. From there, staying low, he headed east to the very edge of the rim wall . . . and then out onto the steep slope beyond it.

Carefully, Bezrukov descended a couple hundred meters and then swung back to the north—moving across the slope instead of down it. Pebbles dislodged by his KLVM's feet rolled away downhill. For a moment, he considered reporting his suspicions to Lavrentyev and Yanin. Then he discarded the idea as too risky. The Americans were close enough now for him to pick up their data-link signals, so they would certainly be able to detect his own radio transmissions.

Instead, he raised his 30mm autocannon and kept going. If the Americans had already sneaked up onto the crater rim, they were about to learn a hard lesson in tactics: dead ground worked both ways.

Brad edged along the steep slope, one step at a time—cautiously testing his footing before allowing the robot's full weight to come down. Taking a spill here was not an option, not unless he wanted to tumble head-over-heels several thousand feet down to the base of the crater rim. A hundred yards farther on, the ridge he was traversing bulged outward in a fold that hid him from the higher ground ahead. Nadia was behind him, out of sight beyond another undulation in the slope. Once he took up a covering position, she would come forward to join him.

Warning. Hostile to the front, his CLAD's computer snapped.

A Russian war machine reared up from behind the same bulge that he'd planned to use as cover. Its 30mm cannon flashed once, eerily silent in the absence of any atmosphere. The round slammed into his robot's torso armor with bone-crushing force, knocking him sideways. Bits of shattered thermal tiles spun off into space.

Jesus, he thought in shock. Desperately, he dug his feet into the ground and powered up his electromagnetic rail gun.

Another 30mm shell hammered his right shoulder. *Right arm hydraulics damaged. Torso armor holding, but significantly degraded. Fuel Cells Three and Four down. Battery circuit one-bravo damaged. Torso and right arm thermal and chameleon camouflage partially compromised,* his computer warned. *Lifesupport capability down to less than eight hours.* Accompanying detailed damage reports flooded through his neural link, appearing as a display where whole sections of system schematics were lit with red and yellow caution and warning flags. Resolutely, Brad ignored them. A third round tore across one side of his robot's hexagonal-shaped head—ripping away sensor panels and shielded antennas. Darkness fell across part of his vision.

Rail gun ready.

He squeezed the trigger. In a burst of bright, white plasma, a tungsten-steel alloy slug smashed into the Russian war machine at more than thirty-eight hundred miles per hour and ripped it apart. Molten fragments sprayed outward from the point of impact. Its antenna-studded head spiraled off across the slope.

Deflected from its course as it slashed through the enemy robot, the glowing rail gun round arrowed across the black sky like a meteor in reverse. Christ, Brad wondered numbly, is the damned thing headed into orbit?

Negative, his computer assured him. *Its velocity has*

been reduced below orbital speeds. It should impact on the other side of the moon, somewhere near the Sea of Tranquility.

Which would make it the longest ricochet in human history, he realized—not sure whether to laugh or cry at his narrow escape. His robot was damaged, but, miraculously, its hull was still intact, despite being bushwhacked at point-blank range. He shook his head, trying to regain focus.

"Brad!" Nadia called.

He turned. Her robot came bounding along the slope toward him, moving with reckless speed. She skidded to a stop beside him. Rocks and dirt scattered through a wide arc. "You must fall back!" she said urgently. "Leave the rest to me!"

Brad set his jaw. "Not happening." He tossed his now-useless rail gun aside, and used the robot's un-damaged left arm to pull another weapon, a 25mm Bushmaster autocannon suitably modified for lunar combat, out of the pack slung across its back. "My ride's taken a beating, but it's operational." More red and yellow warnings cascaded through his neural link as additional systems dropped off line. "Okay, *mostly* operational," he corrected himself.

He checked his functioning sensors. There was still no sign of the other Russian war machines headed toward them, but this momentary lull wouldn't last long. Even if the two remaining enemy pilots didn't yet know their compatriot was dead, they'd figure it out soon enough. "The subtle approach just went to shit, so we're down to one option—"

"We go in quick and dirty," Nadia finished.

He nodded. "I'll head left along this side of the rim wall. You move to the right, along the other side of this ridge. Use your camouflage systems to sneak through any kill zones you run into."

"And you?"

"I'll do the same," Brad promised, mentally crossing his fingers behind his back. Even if he could still afford the power drain, a full third of his thermal tiles and chameleon plates were either damaged or destroyed. Both camouflage systems were basically reduced to just deadweight. When he charged toward the Sino-Russian base, he was going to be right out in the open—an easy mark for any enemy robot in position. That sucked, but right now their best chance to win this battle was to catch the enemy in a pincer move. If the Russians fixated on him and missed detecting Nadia, giving her a shot at them from behind, so much the better. *After all, it doesn't count as suicide if you've still got a chance to survive,* he told himself.

Instinctively, her robot's right hand came up and

gently caressed the battle-scarred side of his own machine's head. "Remember that I love you," she said softly. Then she turned and headed upslope at a run— already fading from view as she activated her stealth systems.

FORTY-NINE

"Sentinel Two, this is Sentinel Lead, do you copy?" Colonel Kirill Lavrentyev repeated. But there was still no reply over the secure channel he'd opened to Bezrukov. Only the faint hiss of static. His KLVM crouched lower, taking cover behind one of the abandoned Chang'e descent stages. Sweating inside the tight cockpit despite its cooling systems, he connected to Dmitry Yanin's Sentinel Three. "Do you see any sign of Bezrukov's robot?"

"*Negative,*" the younger officer reported from his own position near the southern edge of the base perimeter, more than a kilometer away. "*Do you think his com systems have gone down?*"

Lavrentyev bit down on a curse. "I think his whole damned robot is down, Captain. And that he's dead. Because the Americans are here. Somewhere." He shook his head in dismay. "Bezrukov was right. They must have circled around to hit us from behind."

"*Then what should we do now, Colonel?*" Yanin asked.

Lavrentyev forced himself to think. Before joining the Russian Space Force as a military cosmonaut, he'd flown Su-27 fighters. He was not a foot soldier by training or inclination. Well, modern combat aircraft flew in fighting pairs, with each wingman protecting the other. Perhaps the same principle applied here. "Close up on my position, Yanin," he directed. "I'll cover you."

"*On my way,*" the other man acknowledged.

Through his sensors, Lavrentyev saw the other KLVM sprinting toward him at high speed across the gray, powdery plateau. Yanin's robot dodged from side to side and then dropped into cover behind the south side of a large Chinese Mǎ Luó spacecraft about a hundred meters behind him. Their three-meter-tall fusion power reactor sat near one of its landing legs.

From where they each crouched now—roughly halfway between the base's habitat module and their chain of two radar emplacements and the plasma rail gun mount out near the edge of the rim wall—Lavrentyev and Yanin could cover most of the plateau. There were a few blind spots, mostly behind other landers, but their fields of fire covered most of Korolev's key installations. Best of all, anyone who wanted to take a shot at them would have to come out into the open.

"Now what?" Yanin asked quietly.

"Now we wait," Lavrentyev replied. "We'll let the Americans come to us."

"Sentinel Lead, this is Korolev Base," Liu's excited voice suddenly blared over the com circuit. *"Small radar contact! Along the eastern crater rim, north-northeast of your current position!"*

Startled, Lavrentyev looked in that direction . . . and swore. One of the other cargo landers blocked his view of that section of the rim wall. He shook his head in consternation. Another age-old military maxim had proved true. His "brilliant" plan to hold their ground and fight from cover hadn't survived first contact with the enemy. He jumped up, readying his autocannon. "Yanin! Come with me!"

Brad McLanahan clambered awkwardly up the last few yards of the slope and scrambled out onto the plateau. He dropped to one knee and scanned his surroundings.

Damaged sensors created patches of darkness across his field of vision. But he could still see well enough to make out a bleak landscape dotted with grounded spacecraft, a weird-looking, off-white cylindrical habitat module, and, most important of all, the three raised mounds of dirt and rock topped by the enemy's radars and plasma rail gun.

Microwaves suddenly lashed his CLAD. Through the neural link, the sensation translated into something like needles stabbing his chest. *Warning, X-band radar has locked on*, his computer reported.

"Ah, crap," Brad muttered to himself. He'd hoped to come in under that radar emplacement's horizon . . . but his navigation system had fritzed out a couple of minutes ago and he'd obviously misjudged his exact position. This robot was dying under him, as system after system shut down—either because of damage or because its power demands were too high for the juice left in his surviving batteries and fuel cells. On the other hand, he finally had a clear line of sight to their mission's primary target.

He raised his 25mm autocannon. His computer silhouetted the stubby cylinder and starfish-shaped supercapacitor array of the Russian plasma rail gun. Without waiting, he squeezed off a shot. And another.

And then, shifting his aim slightly, he fired a third time . . . all in fractions of a second. Three brief, blue-tinted flashes strobed across his vision.

Hit twice, the plasma gun's cylindrical firing tube shattered. Brad's third armor-piercing round tore through the weapon's supercapacitors. They blew up. A huge orange flash lit the plateau—temporarily over-loading his damaged visual sensors. When they cleared, Brad saw that the plasma gun had been turned into a heap of half-melted slag.

"Not exactly an earth-shattering ka-boom," he said with satisfaction. "But it'll do." He opened a secure channel to Nadia's robot. "Wolf Two to Three, the enemy's plasma gun is kaput."

Warning, movement alert, his computer blurted. *Two hostiles to the right front. Range close, two hundred yards.* The enemy combat machines had suddenly appeared out of one of his sensor blind spots.

"Damn it," Brad growled. He swung his autocannon toward the charging Russians. Too late. They were already firing their own weapons.

A series of hammer blows across his chest and arms smashed him backward. He toppled over the edge of the crater rim in a spray of torn armor. As the robot tumbled and rolled down the steep slope in a boiling avalanche of loose rock and dust, he was slammed against the sides of the cockpit—thrown around like a rag doll tossed into a blender. Red failure warnings shrieked through his dazed, pain-filled mind. *Total hydraulic system failure. Fire control system inoperative. Life-support systems failure. Neural link deteriorating. Multiple hull breaches.*

"Oh, Christ," Brad mumbled, barely conscious. Now he could hear the high-pitched whistle of his oxygen venting out into space. He fumbled desperately for the helmet he'd stowed somewhere in the cockpit . . . just as his neural link went dead . . . and everything went black.

Lavrentyev slewed to a halt next to the edge of the rim wall and peered over. The American combat robot lay motionless in a twisted heap several hundred meters down the slope, half-buried by the debris torn loose by its uncontrolled fall. Quickly, he queried his KLVM's sensors. *Power readings?*

None, the computer assured him.

"Did we kill it?" Yanin asked. The younger cosmonaut had his robot facing back the way they'd come, ready to open fire at the first sign of movement anywhere among the spacecraft and other installations dotting the plateau.

"We did," Lavrentyev answered. He breathed out in relief. "That one's just wreckage. It's no longer a threat."

"*So that's one down,*" Yanin said. "*Out of how many?*"

Lavrentyev shrugged, feeling more confident now. The American war machines were not invincible after all. "They couldn't have crammed very many of those robots inside their lander," he pointed out. "Maybe only two total."

As if to prove his point, Liu broke into their circuit again. "*Korolev Base to Sentinel Lead. We just picked up a new contact.*"

"Where?"

"*Somewhere inside the base,*" the taikonaut told him. "*Possibly over by Chang'e-Ten's descent stage in the southwest corner of the plateau. Unfortunately, we couldn't get a lock before it faded out.*"

Lavrentyev and Yanin both dropped prone. If there was another enemy combat machine on the loose, they wanted to present as small a target as possible. "We'll move in your direction, Major," he radioed. "Keep your eyes open."

"*Yes, sir,*" Liu agreed. But then he snarled, "*Tā mā de! Damn it! My radars just went down!*"

Lavrentyev swiveled toward the radar emplacements along the crater wall. Both arrays were collapsing in slow motion. They'd obviously been hit several times each by armor-piercing and high-explosive rounds. He jumped to his feet and waved Yanin upright. "Let's go, Captain," he snapped. "We need to hunt this marauder down and destroy it, before it wrecks the whole fucking base around us!"

Together, the two Russian war robots darted south— still being careful to use every available piece of cover.

Nadia glided back behind the Chinese lander descent stage. She slid her autocannon back into her weapons pack and then reactivated her camouflage systems. *Life-support capability down to twenty hours,* her computer warned. *At current settings, stealth systems will consume all available power in less than one hundred seconds.*

Be silent, she thought curtly, dismissing the alarms. All she needed was enough time to finish this mission. After that, nothing else really mattered. Not now. Not since she had seen the icon representing Brad's robot flare bright red and then vanish from her tactical display.

Inside the darkened cockpit, tears slid down Nadia's face. Impatiently, she brushed them away with her hand, a motion eerily imitated by the robot she piloted. *Grieve later,* she told herself angrily, *if there is a later.*

Her task now was to kill the men and machines who had just destroyed the man she loved.

Filled with renewed determination, she sprinted north across the plateau, heading for the rear of the enemy's habitat module. On her display, blips appeared and disappeared as her thermal sensors picked up heat sources weaving in and out among the landed spacecraft. *Very good*, she thought coldly. Lured by her destruction of their radars, the Russian war machines were coming this way.

Nadia reached the corner of the habitat module and crouched down in the deep, dark shadow it cast. Through her link with the computer, she deactivated the thermal tiles and chameleon camouflage across her robot's legs and lower torso. That would conserve at least some power while she lay in wait for those she'd marked as prey.

And then she saw the two Russian robots. Tall, with spindly arms and legs, and topped by eyeless spheres crowded with sensor antennas, they stalked into view—prowling across the dull gray lunar surface with menacing grace. They slowed and then stopped, their torsos and heads swiveling in different directions as they sought her out. They were approximately a hundred yards from her position, near one of the big Chinese cargo landers. They were very close to an upright three-meter-tall metal cylinder erected at the lander's base. Conduits snaked away from the cylinder to different installations across the base perimeter. It glowed brightly in her thermal sensors. *Data indicates that is probably the enemy fusion power plant,* her computer told her helpfully.

"*Tak, wiem,*" she said softly. "Yes, I know."

Slowly, Nadia eased her electromagnetic rail gun out of her pack. Powering it up would instantly reveal her position, so she needed to wait for precisely the right moment . . . aware all the while that her batteries and fuel cells were draining at a rapid pace.

The solution to the tactical problem she faced was simple on the surface, but remarkably complex in its execution. If the Russian robots hunting her had separated, she could have destroyed them one by one, from ambush. But these two were operating as a fighting pair, staying close to each other for mutual support. With any of the weapons available to her, she could destroy one of the two enemy machines . . . but that would give its partner ample time to kill her in turn. The question, then, was how to eliminate both of them with a single shot.

Nadia's eyes narrowed down to slits as she watched

the Russians trying to decide their next move. Quick staccato beeps pulsed through her headset, indicating that they were talking to each other. Like their American equivalents, the robots' radio transmissions were first encrypted and then compressed into millisecond-long bursts. Plainly they were reluctant to move away and expose the base's vital fusion reactor to her attack. Slowly, the enemy war machines converged, moving to within a couple of yards of each other.

Close enough, she decided tightly. She flicked on the power to her rail gun and sighted down its short barrel.

Alerted by the strong electromagnetic signature suddenly picked up by their sensors, both Russians spun in her direction. Their weapons lifted.

"Too late," Nadia snarled. "Far too late." She squeezed the trigger. A burst of sun-bright white light flared as the rail gun sent its projectile slashing across the intervening space at Mach 5. It streaked right between the two enemy robots and tore through the thick-walled fusion reactor.

She whirled away and threw herself prone.

When the reactor's magnetic containment field ruptured, plumes of helium-3/deuterium fusion plasma erupted—spewing outward for a brief microsecond before they cooled and dissipated. But in that almost infinitely short moment, the two Russian war machines were caught amid temperatures above one hundred million degrees Fahrenheit, hotter than those found at the core of the sun itself. When the enormous glare faded, there was nothing left for yards around where the reactor had been—only a cooling circle of glass and fused metal.

FIFTY

KOROLEV BASE
A SHORT TIME LATER

Weeping openly now, Nadia stalked through the remains of the Sino-Russian base. Periodically, she stopped to destroy pieces of enemy equipment—automated rovers and inflatable tanks containing oxygen, water, and hydrogen—with her autocannon. She'd already summoned Peter Vasey to fly here to this place of death and desolation. What she hadn't yet decided was whether she would board the Xeus when it arrived, or remain here, waiting to join Brad in death.

Despite the robot's sensors, sorrow had narrowed her world. She moved on, conscious only of targets yet to be destroyed and the wreckage she had already left behind. And so she was taken completely by surprise when an ever-more-urgent warning flashed across her neural link with the machine.

Hostile movement alert, the computer signaled, somehow sounding desperate despite its cool, emotionless tone. *Six o'clock low. Threat level extremely high.*

Startled, she reset her visual sensors to look directly behind her robot. And there she saw the two men in bulky EVA suits. One Chinese taikonaut was down on one knee, with a launch tube on his shoulder, ready to fire. The other stood at his side, with another of the tubes slung over his shoulder. *Weapon is a* Hóng Jiàn-12, *infrared-homing antitank guided missile,* the computer reported.

They must have been hiding inside the base's habitat module, Nadia realized, suddenly angry at her own stupidity. She had left the inflated habitat untouched in her rampage across the plateau, knowing that she would need to set explosives to breach its half-meter-thick walls. It was a mistake that was going to kill her. And it was also going to kill Peter Vasey, since the base's surviving crewmen had another antitank missile to use against the Xeus lander when it came within range.

Knowing she would be too slow, no matter how fast she moved, she started to spin toward the Chinese missile crew . . . and then stopped.

The kneeling taikonaut's space helmet exploded.

Already dead, he jerked forward, falling slowly in the moon's low gravity. The other Chinese crewman turned in surprise and then folded over. A huge fountain of blood, black in the weird half-light, erupted from the hole drilled through him.

Nadia's eyes widened in amazement as an astronaut wearing a silver carbon-fiber space suit limped slowly into view. With a gesture of disgust, he tossed away the pistol he'd just fired twice and headed in her direction. *Weapon is a Russian-made Vektor SR-1M 9mm pistol captured by Major McLanahan during the capture of Mars Station almost two years ago,* her computer announced.

"My God," she whispered. "Brad?"

"*Yeah, it's me,*" she heard a familiar, pain-filled voice say over the radio.

Unable to speak for the moment, she stumbled toward him, with her CLAD's large, armored arms held open.

"*Whoa there,*" Brad said, backing away a bit with a hand held up in caution. "*Please, please, please* . . . do not *hug me . . . at least not just yet.*" Through his helmet visor, she saw his familiar, crooked grin. "*Especially not while you're still wearing that big-ass robot. Because I think I cracked a few ribs falling halfway down that damn rim wall.*"

Now it was Nadia's turn to smile. "You have a bad habit of making me think you might be dead, Brad McLanahan."

"True," he admitted. *"But I promise it's a habit I'm going to try real hard to break from here on out."*

Over the radio, they both heard Peter Vasey's voice calling. *"Wolf Two and Wolf Three, this is Lunar Wolf One. I'm approximately two minutes out from your location. Since it looks as though you've made a bit of a mess of things, could one of you find me a safe place to set this beast down?"*

Turning toward the east, they saw a faint spark against the black sky—a spark that grew ever brighter as the Xeus drew nearer.

ABOARD LUNAR WOLF ONE, DEPARTING ENGEL'GARDT CRATER TWO HOURS LATER

Strapped awkwardly into the lander's rightmost seat, Brad listened to Vasey run through his pre-liftoff checklist. Not even counting his own injuries, both he and Nadia were physically exhausted and emotionally numbed by the battle they'd just fought and won—and only by the narrowest of margins. Neither of them was in any fit state to argue with the Englishman when he'd told them he'd be handling the out-bound flight on his own.

"Main engine on standby," Vasey announced. "Thrusters are go. Flight control and lunar navigation systems are go." He turned his head, checking over his passengers with a faint smile. "We are go for liftoff. Any unfinished business you two need to take care of before we spread our wings and fly?"

Brad shook his head tiredly. "Not me, brother."

"I, too, am ready to leave," Nadia confirmed. She reached out and took Brad's hand, holding on tight as if she never intended to let go.

With a satisfied nod, Vasey tapped his control panel. Seconds later, the Xeus lifted off from the plateau—riding thruster plumes that carried it higher in a swirling cloud of dust. Behind them, bright flashes flickered across the high crater rim as the demolition charges they'd rigged to destroy their CLADs and the Sino-Russian habitat detonated in sequence.

Several thousand feet above the surface, the Englishman lit their main rocket engine, throttling up slowly to spare Brad's cracked ribs for as long as possible. Steadily, the lander accelerated, climbing higher on its way into orbit around the moon.

Forty minutes later, they watched in awed silence as the beautiful, cloud-streaked blue orb of the earth rose over the barren, cratered landscape sixty miles below. Then Vasey cleared his throat and keyed his radio mike. "Sky Masters Control, this is Lunar Wolf One. Our mission is complete. I say again, our mission is complete. Requesting assistance, over."

For what seemed an eternity, they heard only static-filled silence. All of them were only too aware that the Xeus could not carry them home. Their only hope was a rescue here in lunar orbit before their oxygen and supplies ran out.

But then Hunter Noble's voice crackled over the radio. *"Copy that, Lunar Wolf One. This is the Sky Masters Orion. I've just completed a good translunar injection burn. I'll rendezvous with you in just a few days."*

EPILOGUE

ABOARD THE ORION, HOMEWARD BOUND
A FEW DAYS LATER

The cramped Orion crew vehicle's lights were dimmed. Except for the faint hum of air-recirculation fans and water pumps, everything was quiet. Wearing a clean flight suit sent out with the repurposed NASA spacecraft, Brad McLanahan lay back in his reclined crew couch, feeling pleasantly lazy. Nadia lay cozily entwined in his arms. Behind them, Boomer and Vasey were asleep in their own seats. This was a crew rest period, so even the radios were silent.

Through the windows above their heads, they could see the earth growing steadily ahead of them. The moon, now far behind, would be tiny in comparison. Neither felt sorry they could no longer see it.

"We will have to go back soon, you know," Nadia said softly, from inside the circle of his arms. "Us, or those like us. Those who are warriors at heart."

Brad looked down at her in surprise. "Back? To the moon?"

She nodded seriously. "We have destroyed one base built by our enemies. But they can build another . . . unless we stop them."

He ran a weary hand over his face. "You mean we'll need an armed outpost in orbit around the moon."

"Yes," Nadia agreed. "And more people, armed with combat robots, on the lunar surface—to protect the helium-3 mining operation your president wants to build against attack and sabotage."

Brad sighed. "That's going to jack up the costs one hell of a lot. For what was supposed to be a purely civilian enterprise, I mean."

She smiled sadly. "Yes, it will. But while preparing for war may be expensive, the cost pales in comparison with the price of defeat and dishonor. And *that* is a price I will never be willing pay."

He tightened his grip around her, looking down along her slender body to the place where her legs used to be, aware of the price she had already paid. He nodded somberly. "Me neither." Gently, he stroked her beautiful dark hair. "Which means we only have one road in front of us: *Zwycięstwo albo śmierć*. Victory or death."

With that, Brad and Nadia both fell quiet again, watching their home come closer in all its majesty.

QINSHAN NUCLEAR POWER PLANT, NEAR SHANGHAI, THE PEOPLE'S REPUBLIC OF CHINA THAT SAME TIME

Marshal Mikhail Leonov climbed down out of the Harbin Z-20 helicopter that had ferried him here from Shanghai's main international airport. Unhurriedly, he walked over to the lone figure waiting for him near the edge of a concrete embankment overlooking the brown, silt-laden waters of Hangzhou Bay. The massive containment domes of two of Qinshan's seven operating nuclear power plants dominated the southern skyline.

General Chen Haifeng greeted him with an impassive nod. "President Li regrets his inability to welcome you in person."

Inwardly, Leonov shrugged. Their defeat at Korolev Base had come as a terrible shock. In the circumstances, it wasn't surprising that China's leader had no interest in losing further face by associating himself directly with Leonov, the Russian architect of a failed strategy. The only small mercy was that knowledge of this catastrophe was still confined to a tight inner circle in their two countries. For the moment at least, no one in Washington, D.C., Moscow, or Beijing was admitting there had even been armed clashes on the lunar surface. Neither side saw any benefit yet in making their undeclared war outside Earth orbit public.

He decided on bluntness. "Does this mean our alliance is at an end?"

"On the contrary," Chen told him. "The president is determined to intensify our efforts. True, we have lost the opening round, but that was a mere skirmish. The fact remains that we cannot allow the Americans to dominate space." The Chinese general shrugged. "Our tactics were inadequate, not our strategic vision. Victory in this new kind of warfare goes to those with speed and hitting power, not to those crouched behind fixed fortifications."

Leonov kept a rein on his expression. Though it pained him to admit it, Chen's analysis was accurate. Twice now, his chosen means to establish superiority in space—the powerful Mars One orbital station and Korolev lunar base—had been overwhelmed by attacks carried out by small, highly mobile American units. "And you have a way to build spacecraft with the necessary speed and combat power?" he asked dryly.

Chen smiled thinly. "Both our nations have talented

scientists and engineers with the skills and knowledge for such a task," he replied. "So long as we provide them with the means to turn their visions into reality." He turned and nodded at the Qinshan nuclear power plant containment domes looming over them. "As a first step, we must dramatically increase our stockpiles of helium-3, the vital element in the fusion generators we will need."

Leonov raised an eyebrow at that. It was technically possible to generate helium-3 in both light-water and heavy-water nuclear power plants, but the process was both incredibly expensive and inefficient. "The costs alone . . ."

"Are immaterial," Chen said gravely. "President Li is very clear on this, Marshal. My country is willing to pay any price to defeat the United States . . . and to establish itself as a preeminent power in outer space." His gaze hardened. "Now, is Russia willing to do the same?"

Swallowing his misgivings, Leonov nodded. "*Da.* We will stand shoulder-to-shoulder with you in this battle."

Inside, though, he could not shake the sudden, unnerving feeling that the tiger he had planned to ride now had plans of its own. . . .

Glossary:
Weapons and Acronyms

1MC—U.S. Navy shipboard internal communications system

ALQ-293—SPEAR electronic combat system

Angara-A5—Russian medium-lift rocket

AN/SPY-1—phased-array radar system aboard guided missile vessels

BDU-33—practice bombs

Chenaya Osa—Black Wasp, a Russian anti-satellite weapon

CIC—Combat Information Center

CID—Cybernetic Infantry Device, a manned combat robot

Chang'e-10, -11, -12, and -13—manned lunar lander spacecraft built by the People's Republic of China, similar in basis design to the Apollo Lunar Module

CLAD—Cybernetic Lunar Activity Device, a variation of a CID used for construction work on the moon

COMS—Cybernetic Orbital Maneuvering Systems, a variation of a CID made for orbital construction work

DF-26—Dong Feng-26, a Chinese long-range anti-ship missile

DTF—Digital Terrain Following, a system for flying at very low altitudes and high airspeed without using radar

Eagle Station—a captured Russian military space station in Earth orbit

EEAS—Electronic Elastomeric Activity Suit, a space suit that uses compressible fabric instead of oxygen for pressurization

Energia-5VR—a Russian heavy rocket

EVA—Extra Vehicular Activity, a space walk

FONOP—Freedom of Navigation Operation

Harbin Z-20—PRC medium-lift helicopter

HJ-12—*Hóng Jiàn-12*, modern, man-portable Chinese anti-tank guided missile

HUD—Head-Up Display

ICBM—Intercontinental Ballistic Missile

IFF—Identification Friend or Foe, coded aircraft identification sysem

IRBM—Intermediate Range Ballistic Missile

JY-9—a Chinese missile guidance radar

Ka-52 Alligator—Russian helicopter gunship

KC-767—an American aerial refueling aircraft

KLVM—*Kiberneticheskaya Lunnaya Voyennaya Mashina*, Cybernetic Lunar War Machine, a manned Russian combat robot

LEAF—Life Enhancing Assistive Facility, a wearable life-support system

lidar—an imaging system using lasers

LM—Lunar Module

Long March-8, -9—Chinese heavy rockets

LPDRS—Laser Pulse Detonation Rocket System, a hybrid turbojet-scramjet-rocket propulsion engine

Mǎ Luó—a large automated cargo lander spacecraft built by the People's Republic of China, a derivative of Blue Origin's Blue Moon cargo lander

Mars One—a Russian combat space station

MFD—multifunction display

Mi-8MTV-5—Russian medium transport helicopter

MiG-31—Russian supersonic jet fighter

MQ-55 Coyote—combat unmanned aircraft

MQ-77 Ghost Wolf—advanced combat unmanned aircraft

Okno—Russian space surveillance system

Oort Cloud—a shell of trillions of ice comets surrounding the solar system

PRC—People's Republic of China

Queqiao—Magpie Bridge, Chinese communications sattelite

regolith—loose soil or debris covering bedrock

Roscosmos—Russian space agency

RTG—radioisotope thermoelectric generator, a small nuclear power generator

S-29 Shadow—American single-stage-to-orbit space-plane

SAM—surface-to-air missile

SBIRS—Space Based Infrared Surveillance, American missile launch detection satellite system

SH-60 Sea Hawk—American carrier-based helicopter

Shenyang J-15—advanced Chinese jet fighter

SM-2—American naval antiaircraft missile system

SPEAR—Self-Protection Electronic Agile Reaction, American advanced electronic warfare system

taikonaut—Chinese astronaut

toroids—a circular object with a hole in the center

Type 052C—Chinese guided missile destroyer

Type 366—Chinese surveillance radar

UAV—unmanned aerial vehicle, a drone

XCV-62 Ranger, XCV-70 Rustler—American stealthy short takeoff/vertical landing tactical transport aircraft

Xeus lander—a prototype lunar lander designed conceived by Masten Space Systems and the United Launch Alliance. Subsequently purchased and modified by Sky Masters Aerospace Inc.

YJ-62—Chinese anti-ship cruise missile